OPHELIA'S MUSE

OPHELIA'S MUSE

RITA CAMERON

KENSINGTON BOOKS
www.kensingtonbooks.com

KENSINGTON BOOKS are published by

Kensington Publishing Corp.
119 West 40th Street
New York, NY 10018

All Kensington titles, imprints, and distributed lines are available at special quantity discounts for bulk purchases for sales promotion, premiums, fund-raising, educational, or institutional use.

Special book excerpts or customized printings can also be created to fit specific needs. For details, write or phone the office of the Kensington Sales Manager: Kensington Publishing Corp., 119 West 40th Street, New York, NY 10018. Attn. Sales Department. Phone: 1-800-221-2647.

Kensington and the K logo Reg. U.S. Pat. & TM Off.

eISBN-13: 978-1-61773-857-9
eISBN-10: 1-61773-857-3
First Kensington Electronic Edition: October 2015

ISBN-13: 978-1-61773-856-2
ISBN-10: 1-61773-856-5
First Kensington Trade Paperback Printing: October 2015

10 9 8 7 6 5 4 3 2 1

Printed in the United States of America

To my parents, Al and Marlene, who taught me to love art and books. To my husband, Sean, for being my best friend and having faith in me. And to my children, Cal and Bea, who gave me lots of good excuses to shut my laptop and head outside to play.

ACKNOWLEDGMENTS

I want to thank my friend and agent, Jeff Ourvan, for his invaluable support, and my editor at Kensington, John Scognamiglio, for his help and guidance. I would also like to thank all of the coffee shops whose seats I hogged in Brooklyn and San Jose: Your caffeine and Wi-Fi made this all possible.

For Hamlet and the trifling of his favour,
Hold it a fashion and a toy in blood,
A violet in the youth of primy nature,
Forward, not permanent, sweet, not lasting,
The perfume and suppliance of a minute; No more . . .

Then weigh what loss your honour may sustain,
If with too credent ear you list his songs,
Or lose your heart, or your chaste treasure open
To his unmaster'd importunity.

—Laertes to Ophelia, *Hamlet*, Act I, Scene iii

$\mathscr{C}$HAPTER I

London, 1850

Lizzie Siddal pushed her needle through the stiff satin of a black bonnet, attached the last piece of rose trimming, and tied off the thread with an expert knot. Putting the bonnet aside, she slipped the thimble from her finger and shifted on the hard bench. She longed to stretch, but she sat shoulder to shoulder with a dozen other girls. The custom in London's millinery shops was that the girls must stay in place until their shift was finished, and Lizzie had no wish to risk the anger of the head milliner.

The workroom of the Cranbourne Alley shop was small and cramped, with a long table and a single window at the far end. The shelves that lined the walls held the materials of their trade: rolls of muslin, silk, and satin; lengths of wire and pasteboard; and baskets of feathers, spangles, and silk flowers. Behind a door was the front of the shop, where the bonnets were displayed on glass counters.

At this late hour the shop was closed, and the milliners worked by candlelight, rushing to finish the orders for the next day. Evening had come and gone, and the chatter that animated the girls at midday was now only a murmur. They stared at their work with tired eyes, trying their best to look industrious even as they grimaced at each movement of their swollen fingers.

Lizzie paused for a moment before taking up her next bonnet, thinking that there was no point in rushing if she was going to be there all night. She startled guiltily at the touch of a hand on her shoulder, and turned to see the commanding form of the head milliner, Mrs. Tozer, behind her.

But Mrs. Tozer didn't look angry. "Miss Siddal," she said, "you may go. And mind you go straight home. I expect the shop to be busy tomorrow, and I need you looking fresh. You'll be working in the front, behind the counter."

"Yes, ma'am," Lizzie said, relieved that she was being let out early and not reprimanded for idleness. She gathered up her tools— brightly colored spools of thread, a jumble of needles and pins— and placed them on her tray. As she tidied her space, a few girls gave her a nod and a smile, but there was no good-natured joking or gaily called goodnights, as there would have been for another girl.

Though she tried her best to be friendly, Lizzie wasn't close with the other milliners. Most were country girls who came up to London to find work. Lizzie, born and raised in the city, couldn't help but think them simple and occasionally crude. They, in turn, laughed at her careful manners, which they found pretentious, and whispered about her, asking why a girl with such a fine accent should have to work as they did. They didn't know that her elegant deportment was nothing more than a relic of her family's better days, and that she was now as dependent upon her wages as any of them.

Lizzie's looks also garnered undue and unwelcome notice from the other girls. She was tall for a woman, and at nineteen she stood as tall as many men. But though this might have made her awkward, she carried herself with a graceful gait, and she was often called striking, though rarely pretty. Her skin was pale, and she had large gray eyes with heavy lids. But her most remarkable feature was her thick red hair, which glinted gold in the light and tumbled down her back in loose curls when it wasn't tied up for work. The shopgirls, like many of their class, considered red hair bad luck—a sign of witchcraft and a bad omen for the shop.

Lizzie picked up her bonnet and cloak and slipped from the

room. Behind her, she heard someone do a decent imitation of Mrs. Tozer's high, fluttering voice: "Miss Siddal needs 'er beauty sleep! Make sure Miss Siddal 'as a cushion for her feet!" The other girls dissolved into giggles, but Lizzie pretended not to hear them.

She opened the shop door, and the empty street rang with the sound of their girlish laughter. Stepping under the street lamp, her hair glowed like copper for one moment before she placed her bonnet firmly on her head and extinguished its flame. She had no wish to attract attention. She wrapped her cloak around her shoulders and stepped out into the night, merging into its shadows.

The January air was cold and clear—a welcome change from the stuffiness of the workshop. The great bustle of commerce that daily descended upon Cranbourne Alley, pushing and hollering its way through the narrow passage, had long ago dispersed for more comfortable quarters, and a heavy rain had swept the street clean of its rubbish, leaving only puddles of yellow light beneath the gaslights. A single carriage raced down the street, and the clatter of horses' hooves echoed from the fronts of the closed-up shops. In the distance, the bells of St. Martin's began to ring. The sound of the chimes skipped across the rooftops, marking the hour as nine o'clock.

She was halfway down the street when she heard the door open again and a girl cry out, "Wait up, Lizzie!"

She turned to see Jeannie Evans hurrying to her side, her cloak half on and her blond curls bouncing. Like Lizzie, Jeannie was often picked for one of the coveted positions in the front of the shop.

Jeannie fell into step with Lizzie, and together they set off into the twisted web of alleys that made up the commercial quarter of Leicester Square. As they walked, the streets gradually widened and then spilled into the bustling stretch of the Strand. In Cranbourne Alley, the only signs of life at this hour were concealed behind the closed doors of the workshops. But the Strand was lively under the lights of cafés and theaters. Restaurants threw their windows open, beckoning the passersby with the savory scent of meat pies and the sweet aroma of fresh apple fritters. The shows were just letting out, and the sidewalks filled with people, the men in top hats and spats, and the women in crisp satins and furs. The well-to-do crowd attracted a swarm of beggars, flower-sellers, and buskers, and Lizzie and Jeannie were forced to step off the sidewalk and into the muck of the curb to get around them.

They hurried past the theater crowds and struck east toward Fleet Street. An icy wind blew in off the Thames, and Jeannie winced as she pulled her gloves onto her tender hands. "That shop *will* be the death of me," she said. "I never stopped sewing for ten minutes altogether, and I'm still behind on my orders. Eight bonnets done, frame to ribbons, and still Mrs. Tozer was fit to be tied. I thought the old devil might have me there all night! And it's bound to get worse—the Season ain't even started yet!"

"She was very cross today," Lizzie said. "But what choice does she have? We're behind on the orders and there's two girls fallen ill."

Jeannie giggled and looked at Lizzie with surprise. "Ill? You *are* an odd duck, aren't you? Didn't you hear the talk in the shop today?"

"Has anyone said anything worth hearing? Or worth repeating?"

Jeannie rolled her eyes. "Well, even you will want to hear this, I expect. Bess Bailey ain't ill at all. In fact she was in fine health when I saw her in the alley just last night. Someone had clapped a brand new silk gown on her back, and it was cut as low as you please." Jeannie made a clownish curtsy and flashed Lizzie a knowing smile, but Lizzie stared back at her blankly. Jeannie shook her head and said, as if she were explaining something to a child, "She was on the arm of a young swell, and he looked *very* satisfied with her indeed."

Lizzie drew in her breath. "Really, Jeannie, you shouldn't spread such rumors!"

"Well, I'm sorry if I've shocked you," Jeannie sniffed. "But really, you can't be surprised! You must've heard her father's been out of work, and with her brother passed away last spring, the family can't be too particular about where the money comes from. There's a quick profit to be made in the street, and God knows we work hard enough at Mrs. Tozer's for the pittance we bring home."

Lizzie slipped her hand into her pocket and felt the small weight of her week's wages. She would have to turn them over to her mother as soon as she got home. "Then I'm very sorry for her, that her family has sunk so low. She deserves our pity, Jeannie. What will become of her?"

"Aye, it's no easy thing," Jeannie agreed, her tone softer now. "I wouldn't trade places with Bess Bailey for ten new silk dresses, even with the long hours at Mrs. Tozer's. But really, d'you think we're any better off? There's no fortune to be made in Cranbourne Alley, not for the likes of us. Not in the shops or on the street."

Lizzie nodded, knowing that her own family was not immune from such misfortune, despite their tenuous pretensions to the middle class. One piece of ill luck, and the worn thread that kept them moored to the shores of decent society could snap, leaving her adrift in the dark London night with no hope for rescue. "But I would never let that happen to me," Lizzie cried, as if to banish the possibility. "She'll have no chance at marriage now. What man would have her?"

"Half the girls in the shop are married and it ain't saved them from hard work."

"Then they've made foolish matches," Lizzie said, knowing even as she said it that many of the girls had no real hope for anything better. "But I won't be working at Mrs. Tozer's forever."

"No? And what will you do, then?" Jeannie asked.

Lizzie glanced at Jeannie, wondering if she should speak freely with her. She usually kept her thoughts to herself, not wanting to give the shopgirls any more reason to laugh at her. But the news of Bess Bailey's hard luck made her bold. "Perhaps I'll marry well. And when I do, the only time that you'll see me at Mrs. Tozer's Millinery will be when I come in to order my new bonnets—once in the spring and once in the fall."

"And if you don't meet a fine gentleman?"

"Then I suppose I'll have to make my own way. I haven't got the proper education to be a governess, though I'm sure I've read more books than half the girls who pass for accomplished in the great houses. But I won't die an old maid hunched over Mrs. Tozer's worktable. It's too dreary to even think of."

Jeannie laughed. "You've pinned your hopes very high! But I

wish you luck. Anything to get out of that workroom. You can't feed a cat on the wages."

"And it's so tedious," Lizzie said. "To wait on all those fine ladies and never have anything nice for ourselves. But never mind, Jeannie, surely things can only get better."

Jeannie nodded, and they walked on in silence, each entertaining well-worn daydreams. But something Jeannie said tugged at Lizzie's memory. "Surely Louisa hasn't taken to the streets as well?" Lizzie asked, thinking of the other assistant who had been out.

"No, no, not Louisa," Jeannie said, serious now. "It's her eyes. The strain . . ." She trailed off. Every milliner and seamstress in the city knew that the detailed work, often done by candlelight, was hard on her sight. They had all heard the stories of girls who went blind from it.

"Might she recover?"

Jeannie shook her head. "I heard today that Mrs. Tozer sent a present of extra wages round to her family. That usually means that a girl ain't coming back." She turned to give Lizzie another quizzical look. "You must have your head in the clouds—the talk in the shop was of little else! What *do* you think of all day?"

Lizzie fought a rising wave of panic. She quickened her step, as if she could feel, lapping at her heels, the same ill tide of poverty that had dragged the other girls under. She turned to Jeannie, a fierce expression on her face. "What do I think of all day?" she asked, no longer caring if Jeannie thought her ridiculous. "Why, I think of poems and stories: the Knights of the Round Table and the ladies of the court; the moors of the countryside and the finest drawing rooms of the city. I dream myself among them, away from all this . . ."

She waved her hand to indicate the street around them, the many girls just like themselves who were trudging home from factories and shops to boardinghouses and tenements. Then she looked at Jeannie and saw on her face the beginnings of a grin, as if Lizzie had made some sort of joke.

Lizzie sighed. It wasn't fair to expect a girl like Jeannie, whose education had consisted of little more than her letters and numbers, to understand. The other shopgirls hadn't read the books that Lizzie had; they couldn't imagine a world beyond the crowded alleys of Leicester Square.

"Poems?" Jeannie finally asked. "Well, don't tell any of the other girls. They already think you're strange. You're lucky that you're a favorite with Mrs. Tozer, you know, so they leave you alone."

Lizzie bristled. "I don't think that I'm better than them, if that's what they think." But to herself she thought: not better, perhaps, but certainly different.

"Don't be prickly. They're just jealous that Mrs. Tozer lets you work in the front of the shop, while they're stuck in the back, filling the orders."

"I can't help it, you know that." The fact was that Mrs. Tozer liked the more elegant girls up front, and Lizzie, though lacking Jeannie's flaxen curls and pink cheeks, had a face that wasn't easily forgotten.

"It wouldn't hurt to join in more," Jeannie said. "They do think you're an awful snob. But of course if you're too busy thinking of *poetry* . . ."

Jeannie giggled at her joke, and Lizzie blushed. But before she could make a retort, they were nearly knocked into the curb by three little girls skipping by them in the street. The girls held bouquets of wheat and flowers, and they chanted a song in high voices as they headed toward the church of St. Clement:

"Agnes sweet, and Agnes fair, hither, hither, now repair; bonny Agnes, let me see, the lad who is to marry me."

"There you go, Lizzie!" Jeannie cried. "It's St. Agnes' Eve. The night for virgins to dream of their husbands." She smiled suggestively at Lizzie, and Lizzie blushed again. Together they watched the girls toss their flowers onto the white stone steps of the church, and then clasp their hands together in an earnest prayer.

"Why don't you make an offering?" Jeannie teased. "Maybe you'll have a vision of your husband tonight! Here," she said, stooping to pick up a flower that one of the little girls had dropped, then handing it to Lizzie. "Willing to try your luck for a glimpse of your white knight?"

Lizzie shook her head, but she put the flower into the pocket of her cloak. "I don't care what he looks like," she said lightly, embarrassed that she had confided in Jeannie, who would surely spread gossip around the shop. "So long as he appears! I'm dying of boredom at Mrs. Tozer's—I must have some new adventure."

"Just take care that you don't end up like Bess Bailey. She has adventure in spades now, to be sure." Jeannie grinned at Lizzie and then gestured to a little street on her right. "I'm just up this way. I hope that they kept some supper warm! Goodnight then, Lizzie, and hurry home."

She turned with a wave and darted up her street, leaving Lizzie, who had no intention of hurrying, alone in the midst of the crowded city.

Lizzie set off, determined to enjoy her solitude. No one would expect her at home for at least another hour, and it wasn't often that she had a few moments to herself. At home she shared a small room with her sister, Lydia, in a crowded house, where it always seemed that there was a baby crying or a teakettle screaming for attention. To be alone with her thoughts, or better yet, with a book of poetry, was a treat worth savoring.

Fleet Street was still crowded, even at this late hour. Newspapermen were stumbling back to work after a few at the pub, and messenger boys darted past them, running tips and copy between the offices. Wishing to escape the crush, she slipped down a side street and into the parklike oasis of the Inns of Court. A narrow path wound between the gracious limestone and brick chambers of the city's barristers, and through the windows Lizzie saw the glow of their lamps as they hunched over their writs and pleas. Passing under a stone arch, she entered a series of courtyards made pleasant by manicured hedges and whispering fountains. She was only steps from the noise of Fleet Street, but the Inns were so quiet that she could have been miles away. The tap of her boots hitting the flagstones was the only sound as she followed the path past an expanse of green lawn and down toward the Thames. Cutting right, she made for Blackfriars Bridge, which would lead her across the river and home to Southwark.

She paused on the bridge to lean against the stone rail and look out at the water below. The river shimmered darkly under the night sky, and a light fog rolled along its banks. The bridge was lively in the afternoons, but now it was quiet and shrouded in mist, and Lizzie was glad for the privacy that it offered.

She sighed and removed her gloves. It was a cool night, but she didn't hurry on. Instead, she placed her fingers against the cold stones of the bridge, using them to soothe her raw hands.

The sounds of the city washed over her: the lap of the water against the bank, sailors calling to each other from their ship decks, the hum of wheels and the crack of hooves as a carriage passed behind her. It was a pleasant change from the millinery, where the incessant gossip was punctuated only by the sharp voice of Mrs. Tozer, criticizing some poor girl's handiwork.

Lizzie had forgotten that it was St. Agnes' Eve. She thought of the girls throwing their flowers onto the church steps, and another, older memory of the night surfaced: Lizzie, at thirteen years old, slipping a dusty volume of Keats from the shelf in the parlor. She had carried the book to bed with her, and burned down one of her mother's precious candles reading a poem of romantic love fulfilled on the Eve of St. Agnes. She could still recite her favorite verse, and she now began to whisper the dreamy words to the night air:

> *They told her how, upon St. Agnes' Eve,*
> *Young virgins might have visions of delight,*
> *And soft adorings from their loves receive*
> *Upon the honey'd middle of the night,*
> *If ceremonies due they did aright;*
> *As, supperless to bed they must retire,*
> *And couch supine their beauties, lily white;*
> *Nor look behind, nor sideways, but require*
> *Of Heaven with upward eyes for all that they desire.*

Lizzie smiled and slipped her hand into her pocket. The flower was still there, wilted but intact. Glancing around to make sure that she was unobserved, she threw it into the river and began to mouth the words of the old chant: "Agnes sweet, and Agnes fair, hither, hither, now repair; bonny Agnes, let me see, the lad who is to marry me."

The flower landed on the water and quickly sank below the surface. Her prayer had begun as a game, a moment's folly as she stood daydreaming. But as she stared down into the water, she struggled to contain the hope that beat against her chest and rose into her throat. "Please, please," she whispered to the silent waters, "show me some sign that I will love, and be loved!"

But of course she saw nothing. The dark water offered no sign, and if she had allowed herself to indulge for a moment in childish hope, she now brushed it from her mind. It would take more than a whispered prayer to escape a life of drudgery in a millinery shop.

She was lost in her thoughts and plans when a footstep behind her brought her firmly back to the present. For one wild moment she imagined that this might be her vision, her future come to reveal itself. She had almost turned, a smile forming on her face, when she came to her senses. Whoever was behind her was no vision, but a living, breathing man.

The heavy footsteps drew nearer and she tensed, her skin growing clammy despite the cold. The empty bridge, so recently a haven, now felt desolate and foreboding.

The man was now close enough that she could hear the pant of his breath. With a chill, she caught the sour scent of alcohol on the air. It was a tramp, or worse. She pulled herself up to her full height before turning around, her most commanding expression on her face.

"Oh!" she said, letting out her breath. The man behind her was no tramp—he was an older gentleman, in evening clothes of obvious quality. There was nothing to fear from him. But as he came closer, too close, she saw that his cheeks were red with drink, and the broken vessels across his nose mapped a history of many such nights.

Lizzie began to edge away from him, but he stepped closer, blocking her way.

"Evening, pretty," he slurred. "May I join you?"

"Certainly not!" Hands shaking, she pulled her cloak tighter, as if it offered her some real protection.

He grabbed her arm. "You look like a good sort of girl. D'you work in the shops? Let me show you a nice time—I'll take you out on the town! A pretty girl like you shouldn't be all alone."

Lizzie looked across the bridge toward Southwark, wishing that she had just hurried home, as she ought to have done. If anyone she knew were to see her with this man, it could ruin her. She didn't dare to make a scene, but she had to get away.

"You must excuse me. My companion is waiting," she cried, hoping that the specter of a chaperone might scare him off. She gestured toward the other side of the bridge. "I really must go," she added, and then stopped, hating the pleading note in her voice.

"Your companion?" He squinted at the empty road. When he turned back to her, the thin veneer of drunken jollity had fallen from his face. "Now, don't be coy with me, or I'll teach you your place with the back of my hand." He looked her up and down, taking her measure with his eye. "Girls like you are ten to a penny."

Without warning, he tightened his hand around her arm and pulled her closer, his fat, ring-laden fingers holding her like a vise. She felt his hot breath against her cheek and shuddered.

"You're nothing so special as you think, missy," he hissed. "Girls like you always end up lifting your skirts for some bloke or other. You all think you're different, but I know better."

Their eyes met for a moment, and Lizzie recoiled at what she saw—neither pity nor desire, but only a terrible blankness. She tried desperately to pull away, but the man had her pinned firmly. She cried out, no longer caring what anyone might think, just wanting to get away. Her breath came fast and shallow, and her mouth felt dry. The man's face grew dim before her eyes, and her knees gave way with a sickening lurch.

The old drunk didn't hear the other man until he was nearly upon them. Lizzie saw him first, over the drunk's shoulder, a young man hurrying toward them, calling out and waving. As he drew nearer the drunk turned, surprised, and his hand went slack. Lizzie took her chance, twisting away from his grasp.

She ran without seeing, not wasting a moment or glancing behind her. She felt herself brush past the stranger, but she didn't stop.

"Wait! Miss! Are you all right?" he called. His voice, deep and calm, broke the spell that fear had cast upon her.

She took a few more steps, and then, feeling that she had gained a safe distance, she paused and looked over her shoulder. The drunk was leaning against the rail, and the other man had positioned himself between them. He looked at her curiously, and despite the fog, she thought she could see real kindness in his regard. Was it possible that his eyes were the same pale gray as her own? She watched as he looked at the drunk, his jaw setting with contempt. Could he guess what had happened?

The emotion of the last few minutes flooded through her, leaving her weak and shaking. She felt a mad impulse to go to this stranger, her rescuer; to lean on his arm and seek his protection. But the feeling diminished as quickly as it came, and instead she turned and ran on, anxious to get away.

The man called after her again, but she didn't stop and he didn't follow her. When she reached the street she gathered her courage and looked back, but she was alone. She turned and fled into the alleys of Southwark, grateful, for once, to be running toward the familiar outlines of its crumbling streets.

CHAPTER 2

In the main hall of the Royal Academy of Arts, Dante Gabriel Rossetti found himself in the awkward position of nodding off during a lecture. Try as he might, he could not force his eyes to stay open, and his head dropped forward over and over, only to snap back to attention with a jerk.

The professor droned on in that aloof and nasal monotone particular to academics and the nobility, of which he was both. But his dry tone didn't stop the other students from leaning forward in their seats as they transcribed his every word with a chorus of scratching pencils. Rossetti alone was indifferent to the professor's words.

He was beginning to think that he would have to find his future outside of the halls of the Royal Academy, where conformity and tradition were valued above all else. He'd been drawn to the Academy by its excellent reputation and delighted when he was accepted; graduates of the Academy were practically guaranteed a steady income from their art, and even a chance at making a great name for themselves, so long as they painted in the accepted style. But to Rossetti, such a path was beginning to seem impossibly dull. He was twenty-one, and he felt himself too old for lessons and too young to compromise his ideas about art for a steady income earned with stodgy paintings. He stifled a yawn and stared idly at the paintings that hung on the walls above him while the professor continued his lecture.

The Royal Academy occupied quarters in the new National Gallery on Trafalgar Square, and the lecture hall was lined with an impressive collection of paintings in heavy gold frames. The pictures formed a catalogue of the Academy's illustrious history: a pompous self-portrait of Sir Joshua Reynolds, the Academy's founder; Sir Edwin Landseer's paintings of well-fed dogs and preening deer, which were much loved by Queen Victoria; and the dramatic seascapes of J. M. W. Turner, which were the best of the lot, in Rossetti's opinion.

Rossetti turned his attention back to the professor, who was smacking his stick against the side of the lectern for emphasis and saying, for at least the tenth time: "You must look to Raphael, you see, and nowhere else, for your proportions of light to dark. The light is an accent to be sparingly used. Do not be tempted to stray from these classical proportions. Raphael attained the highest excellence in execution and form, and it is toward his example that you must strive."

Rossetti let out a snort, which was noted with raised eyebrows by a few students near him. Classical proportions were all well and good, Rossetti thought, but true art should celebrate vibrant color and the beauty of light, the romance of imagination and the truth of nature. It could hardly be denied that Raphael had attained near perfection when it came to the classical forms, but the Academy was now so slavishly dedicated to his example that they no longer cared, in Rossetti's opinion, whether a painting contained real truth or beauty.

The professor turned his attention to critiquing a bland painting that sat next to him on an easel, and Rossetti began to nod off again. The paintings above him swam and floated before his eyes: Landseer's dogs paddled through Turner's raging seas, while Sir Joshua Reynolds looked on from the deck of the ship, disapproving. "Sir Joshua, Sir Sloshua," he muttered sleepily.

He leaned back in his chair, content to wait out the end of the lecture with a nap. But as he gazed at the Turner seascape, the professor's words echoed through his mind like the dissonant tones of a cracked bell: "You must look to Raphael, you see, and nowhere else, for your proportions of light to dark. The light is an accent to be sparingly used." But here, right in front of him, was a painting that radiated light, as if it were illuminated from behind. He sat up straight and stared at the seascape as if he were seeing it for the first time. The golden sun bled into the water below and reflected off of every conceivable surface, gilding the edges of the clouds and the crests of the waves, and catching in the full sails of the ships. It captured the exact feeling of watching the sea, when the sun reflects so strongly off the water that you have to squint to look at it, and the clouds shift constantly overhead, bathing the shore in unreal washes of yellow and gray.

Rossetti let out a low laugh. So Turner had strayed from the rigid practices of the Academy, and yet they had hung his picture in a place of honor. Perhaps, he thought, the Academy's rules only applied to the mediocre. If you were truly great, a genius, they didn't give a damn if you followed the rules or not.

At last the class came to an end, and there was a general shuffling as the students stood up to leave. The student in the next chair noticed that Rossetti was still staring at Turner's seascape. "It's a fine painting," he said.

"It's more than fine," Rossetti declared. "It's genius."

"Well, yes, of course," the man said, taken back by Rossetti's zealous tone. "Turner is one of the Academy's most esteemed graduates."

"It's genius," Rossetti repeated, "but not for the reasons that you think. In fact, I suspect that if you've been listening to this travesty of a lecture, you're completely blind to the very things that make it great."

"Well, I say!" The student stared at Rossetti, as if he suspected that he'd been insulted, but wasn't entirely sure how.

"Oh, never mind," Rossetti muttered. There was no point in arguing over the merits of the Academy with its acolytes. He gathered up his portfolio and stalked off, leaving his fellow student staring in his wake.

Outside the lecture hall the other students were standing on the terrace overlooking Trafalgar Square and lighting pipes, popular among the more bohemian element at the Academy.

A tall, young man in a paint-spattered smock waved Rossetti over and slapped him on the back good-naturedly. "Dante! I can see that you got a lot out of that class. A lot of rest, that is. I saw you nodding off. Not too impressed with the learned old Academician?"

"Hardly," Rossetti sniffed, not caring if the other students thought him arrogant. "This place becomes less of a school and more of a shrine every day."

"Harsh words!"

"Perhaps. But what else am I to think when we are asked to worship dead masters as our gods, and make ourselves over in their images? There is nothing to be learned here. We would all be better off in a field, painting a flower and learning from nature."

He spoke loudly and his words drew a small crowd of students, as they always did. Rossetti might have been considered eccentric by many at the Academy, but he was the sort of person who always drew others toward him. They may have admired him or despised him, but he was rarely ignored—even his critics were secretly proud of a kind word from him about their work. When Rossetti turned his attention on you, it was as if the sun shone brighter, and when he left a gathering it often signaled the end of the evening. But his growing resentment of the Academy was a sore point among many of the other students, for whom winning a place at the Academy was their proudest achievement. One of these students was shaking his head as Rossetti spoke. "I, for one, am honored to study at the feet of such masters!" he exclaimed.

"Then you shall learn to paint on your knees. What satisfaction is there in churning out pale copies of another man's work?"

The man flushed with anger, but before he could reply, Rossetti added: "Of course, the lecturers would be very pleased with your attitude. The Academy has a habit of rewarding cleverness in execution, rather than talent or originality."

"And I suppose that you think yourself much possessed of the latter? Tell me, has all your talent and originality made you a rich man, or even gained you a single spot at the Exhibition?"

The other students laughed, and Rossetti colored. He had, as of yet, only sold a few small watercolors, and he'd finished no major works in oil that would be suitable for the Exhibition. But he had high hopes for his current picture, though its style, almost medieval, was so far from the current fashion for the picturesque that he had shown it to only a few close friends.

"If I'm not a rich man yet," he said, "it's only because the public buys what the Academy sanctions—mostly fruit bowls and brown cows dotting a muddy country lane, as far as I can tell. I have no wish to paint decorations for drawing rooms."

"And what do you want to paint, then?"

"Beauty and light! The style today has become so dark and dreary. We're taught to pay attention to form and perspective, at the cost of truth and beauty." He spoke carefully, trying out an idea that was bound to be unpopular with the other students, but in which he fervently believed. "There was more perfection in a single face or scrap of tapestry in a medieval painting than there is in a whole gallery of Landseer's insipid portraits. I want to paint with the rich color and the pure light of the old Italian masters, before we became so enamored of Raphael's exacting ratios. I've no wish to make proficient paintings, when there is true beauty in the world."

"But don't you find the earlier work quite primitive? All those saints with shining faces crowded in upon each other, with no perspective to speak of?"

"Hardly. Is beauty primitive? I want my art to celebrate beauty, as it is, as I see it. I don't want to bend it through the lens of what the Academy thinks is right, or proper, or appropriate." He spat out the last word, as though it pained him.

"But surely you admit that Raphael is the greatest of all the masters?" pressed the other student. "That can no more be argued with by any sane man than that Shakespeare is the greatest writer of the English language!"

"I admit nothing of the sort. In fact, I propose to you that the works of Raphael were the first step in the long decline of Italian painting."

A few students gasped at this sacrilege, but Rossetti continued unabashed. "They're not so bad in and of themselves, of course." He paused as the men laughed at his casual tone. "But they had the unfortunate effect of setting a precedent, and a very static one at that, for every work that followed. They've made art so mannered, and so elegant, that it no longer shows anything of life. I want to break free from all that. I want to recapture the romance of the old masters."

"Well, then, you are a pre-Raphaelite," pronounced the smocked student, with a wondering laugh.

"Perhaps I am," Rossetti agreed with a smile, breaking the tension. The square echoed with the sound of the bells at St. Martin's. Rossetti counted them silently . . . seven, eight, nine. "Damn, I'm late," he said, nodding goodbye to the other students. He hurried down the steps and into the square. He thrust his hand into his pocket to see if he had a few shillings for a cab, but all that he came up with was a handful of old ticket stubs. No matter—his friends would surely not begin without him. It was he who had called the meeting, after all.

It had recently become fashionable among the students to form clubs around their artistic and political interests. Some were little more than drinking clubs with amusing names. A paper had recently been posted in the vestibule advertising for a Mutual Suicide Society, in which any member, weary of life, could call at any time upon another to cut his throat for him. This had caused a great deal of amusement, and garnered a fair number of signatures. But other societies were far more serious, with strictly observed rules and rites of membership. Tonight would be the first meeting of a new society, formed by Rossetti and his friends and fellow artists. By banding together, they hoped to give each other support in their pursuit of a new direction for British art. It was a bold plan, Rossetti knew. But what did he have to lose—besides his wits—if he had to endure any more tedious lessons at the hands of the old professors?

He cut across the wide expanse of Trafalgar Square and made his way through the winding streets toward the river and Blackfriars Bridge. He ducked down an alley where children scavenged in the refuse behind the shops, and factory men, fresh from the gin shop, staggered past him on their way home. Women with brightly painted faces and hollow eyes called out from the doorsteps, but Rossetti ignored them, intent on his purpose.

When he reached the foot of Blackfriars Bridge he stopped at the sight of a solitary girl at the far end of the bridge, leaning over the rail. For a moment it seemed that she meant to do herself harm, and he started toward her. But then he saw that she was only tossing something into the river, and he paused, curious. From where he stood he could see that she was plainly dressed, but a hint of red hair and the sweep of a high, perfect cheekbone were visible beneath her bonnet.

The fact that he was already late, and that a half-dozen men awaited his arrival, hardly crossed his mind. He was fascinated by the girl's graceful posture as she leaned against the rail and the porcelain-like curve of her cheek. It was like glimpsing the edge of a fine piece of stationery mixed among the dull pile of bills in one's mail, the creamy paper promising a glittering invitation or perfumed love letter. As a painter, he felt entitled—almost obligated—to indulge these romantic fancies, and tonight he imagined that he had spied a royal among the street rabble. A painting began to take shape in his mind: a girl on a bridge, but a bridge far from London. She was suddenly an Italian contessa, tossing an illicit love letter into the Arno in Florence.

He stood watching her, imagining the scene, and a line from Dante came to mind: "*My lady looks so gentle and so pure, when yielding salutation by the way . . .*" He was translating Dante Alighieri's love sonnets into English, and he couldn't help but be reminded of the moment when the poet had first seen his beloved muse, the lady Beatrice, in the streets of medieval Florence. The poet fell in love with Beatrice at first sight, and though the strictures of courtly love, and his own delicacy, prevented him from doing anything more than admiring her from afar, his passion lasted his whole life. Rossetti had often longed for such a love: a passion that would transform and inspire him, and give direction to his art.

But unlike Dante, Rossetti was under no stricture of courtly love, and so he began to cross the bridge, thinking that he would speak with the girl. As he drew nearer, he heard a faint cry. The fog was rolling quickly across the bridge, and it was difficult to see, but it appeared that there were now two figures at the end of the bridge. Rossetti could just make out the larger form of a man, his arms around the girl.

He blushed at his foolishness. The girl was not some saintly

Beatrice after all; he'd come upon a lovers' rendezvous, or something more sordid. Shaking his head, he kept walking, determined to pass them quickly. But he heard another cry, of pain, not pleasure, and realized this was no tryst. He could see now that the man had the girl pinned against the stones, and her pale hands were pushing desperately against his weight. Rossetti's chivalrous instinct was instantly revived. "Hello! What's going on here?" he demanded, stepping toward them.

The man turned in surprise and dropped his hands, and the woman broke free. She ran past Rossetti, and her red hair, loosened in the struggle, burned like a flame in the mist. He called out to her, and she paused, staring at him with wide gray eyes. She was beautiful, more perfect than he had imagined. With her flowing hair and flushed cheeks, she looked as if she had stepped from one of the medieval paintings that populated his imagination. He reached out his hand, but she turned and fled, disappearing into the night. He could not even be sure, for a moment, if she was real.

But the man was still there, and Rossetti turned to face him. He was leaning against the embankment, watching Rossetti with amusement. He let out a short, nasty laugh. "You needn't look so worried. Just a little slut, playing coy with me."

Rossetti didn't share his laughter. "I think that you should take yourself home," he said firmly, glancing over his shoulder to make sure that the girl had gotten clear. He was unsettled—the girl's sad and lovely face had pierced him to his core. "A girl like that is not to be trifled with."

The drunk raised his eyebrows, but chose not to argue. As he walked away, however, he called back over his shoulder: "Love and chivalry are a young man's game. Just wait and see."

Rossetti watched the man lurch back across the bridge, laughing at his own imagined cleverness. Once he was sure the man was gone, Rossetti began to search the shadows for some sign of the girl. He felt a sense of responsibility for her safety, and knew that he ought to go look for her.

But his better intentions were overcome by the sound of a single church bell. He swore again—he was now a full half hour late. With a shrug of annoyance, he looked around once more, but the girl was nowhere to be seen. This was really not his concern, after all. He had somewhere to be.

By the time he arrived at the meeting, his unease was forgotten. The evening held too much promise for the troubles of a girl by the river to worry him for long. He pushed open the door of the studio, and saw that his friends had all arrived ahead of him. They sat by the fire, their evening wear in various states of disarray. They were gathered around a book of Italian paintings, and Rossetti listened as they debated the merits of the frescoes in voices that rang with the ardor and grandiosity of men who were only lately out of their teens. Rossetti was pleased to see so many artists that he admired among those present.

John Millais sat at the center of the group. He was the rising star of the Royal Academy, and his prospects as a painter were good. He was talented and handsome, and not surprisingly, a favorite with society ladies eager for portraits. But despite his success, he professed to be bored by the austere style of the Academy, and he had thrown his hat in with the new movement.

Millais caught sight of Rossetti and rose to greet him. "You're late," he said, smiling. Rossetti was famous among his friends for having the best of intentions, but the worst resolve: he was always roaming through the city or dashing off a poem when he was supposed to be finishing a painting or meeting a friend. He was lucky that his friends found these qualities endearing; his charm had smoothed over many ruffled feathers. "But never mind," Millais said. "Everyone is here now, and it's a good group."

William Holman Hunt, a fellow student at the Academy, came over to them. Hunt was older than the others, but he had an unfortunately turned-up nose that made him look like a perpetual schoolboy. He had attempted to counteract this by growing extravagant sideburns that bordered on muttonchops, and the effect was slightly ludicrous. Hunt was, however, very serious about his work, and unlike Rossetti, he turned out regular pieces for sale.

Hunt shook Rossetti's hand. "It seems that we're really going to pull it off! I brought round a book of early Italian paintings. I think they're a perfect example of the spirit of simplicity that should regulate our movement, and everyone seems to agree."

"Yes, I saw," Rossetti said, bristling at Hunt's real or imagined intrusion on his authority with the group. It had been Rossetti's idea, after all, to look to the early Italians for inspiration. But he tried not to betray his annoyance. The point was to draw inspiration from each other, not to bicker over who came up with what idea.

Though the men were not generally drinkers, Millais poured out glasses of wine in acknowledgment of the occasion. Rossetti cleared his throat and the room quieted.

Despite their youth, or perhaps because of it, it was a serious occasion. The men knew that a movement was afoot, and each man felt the thrill of a private revolution, of being on the cusp of an important change in their craft. No one felt this more keenly than Rossetti, but he tried to dampen his excitement in favor of the solemnity that he believed such an occasion demanded. He stood to speak, summoning all his powers of poetry.

"Friends," he said. "I believe that I speak for all of us when I say that I have no more wish to paint according to formulas and prescribed proportions than I have to spend my days sitting over a ledger book. I wish to paint nature as I find it, not as the Academy believes that it would be prettiest. I wish to take my inspiration from the old paintings of saints and heroes, where beauty was prized above all. Together we can teach the British people to appreciate the true beauty of nature, and to reject the contrivance of the fruit bowl and the country lane. But if we are to succeed, we must band together and swear to be true to our ideals in art, and in life. We must guard our new movement closely, and fan up its small flame until it becomes a great blaze that will consume even the much-vaunted halls of the Academy! I know you all to be artists of the highest order, and I believe that we are the men to change the face of British painting. And why should we not distinguish ourselves in the process?"

"Hear! Hear!" cried the other men, nodding their heads vigorously in assent. What young artist present that night did not think of the glory that could be his if they were to pull this off?

"Then we are agreed. We shall paint beauty as we see it, in nature and in life."

"And in women!" called out Holman Hunt, lightening the mood. Everyone laughed, Rossetti as heartily as the rest. No one could deny that the chance to paint beautiful women was one of the draws of the field. For a fleeting moment, Rossetti recalled the girl on the bridge, with her wide eyes and shining hair, though now he could not be sure whether he was remembering her as she was, or as he had imagined her into a painting.

"Of course, we must paint beautiful women," he said. "But not just the pink-cheeked English roses. We must paint the more exotic beauties; the orchids and lilies of the foreign fields; the willowy women whose beauty harkens back to the age of saints and angels. Lord knows that we have enough paintings of plump and bonny-faced country girls."

"There are never enough bonny-faced English girls," said Holman Hunt. "I would take them by the two or three."

"Come," Rossetti said, his voice rising above the laughter of the other men. "If we talk all night of the beauty of women, we shall never get round to creating our own works of beauty."

"Amen to that. The most stunning woman will fade as sure as the sun will set," Hunt quipped, "but a beautiful painting may guarantee immortality to the artist."

"To the immortality of art," Rossetti toasted, raising his glass. The other men raised their glasses in cheers.

"And," Rossetti added, suddenly inspired, "to the Pre-Raphaelite Brotherhood!" The men laughed, not quite catching his meaning. "Tonight, after the lecture, one of the other students called me a pre-Raphaelite. Word has gotten around that we don't worship at the feet of the great master."

This news was greeted with delight. The men were pleased to think that their theories had gained some celebrity among their peers, even if they had been greeted with mocking. It was better, after all, to be known with contempt than not to be known at all.

"It's as good a name as any other," Millais said. He tried it out: "The Pre-Raphaelite Brotherhood. The PRB."

"The PRB," Rossetti repeated. "We can each inscribe our works with the initials, as a mark of our membership."

The other men nodded eagerly, liking the sense of intrigue and belonging that a secret symbol implied. Unable to contain himself any longer, Rossetti sprang from his chair and flourished a paper upon which he had been working. "Here, my friends, is our artistic creed: We hereby affirm our loyalty to Nature, Art, and Brotherhood."

"Agreed," affirmed the other artists, their young voices grave. They gathered around Rossetti to sign the statement, and then solemnly shook hands.

"To Brotherhood," cheered Millais, raising his hand in salute. His cry was echoed around the room. "To Brotherhood!"

CHAPTER 3

Despite the damp chill and fading light of the March afternoon, the scene in Cranbourne Alley was anything but subdued. Walter Deverell made his way down the alley from Leicester Square, pressing his way through the crowd with his mother on his arm. He should have been at his studio, painting, but his mother had begged him to accompany her on a shopping trip to the city, and he could hardly refuse her simple request. She refused him nothing, and spared no expense when it came to his training, his studio, or his supplies.

In the great current of commerce, it was all he could do to keep the two of them together. Genteel shoppers, companions in tow, sailed regally through the mass of working women. A crowd of children, beggars, and street hawkers spilled from the curb and into the street, and darted among the passing carts. Traffic snarled behind carriages that lingered outside of shops, while the shopgirls stood in the muck to show their wares to fine ladies who preferred to make their purchases from the comfort of their carriages.

Cranbourne Alley had its share of dressmakers and jewelers, but it was for the most part devoted to a wide selection of millineries, each showcasing the latest and most daring styles in ladies' bonnets. Through the dusty windows Deverell glimpsed an array of jewel-colored silks that rivaled the palette of paints in his studio. The better shops had new glass display windows presenting their finest wares: crown bonnets of deep blue taffeta trimmed with ribbon and Chantilly lace, shirred bonnets of olive crepe done up with paper roses and silk leaves, and, in one particularly sumptuous display, a burgundy velvet hat trimmed with ostrich plumes.

Each shop employed touters, wiry young girls who used flattery, charm, and, if necessary, force to solicit passersby into their shops. One of these touters, a pale girl in last season's faded silk bonnet, suddenly linked up with Deverell's free arm. Despite her small size, she managed to steer both Deverell and his mother back toward her shop, speaking all the while of the glorious wares within. Mrs. Deverell needed little convincing to enter the shop, and so, with a good-natured sigh, Deverell let himself be led, by both arms now, out of the cold afternoon and into the warmth of Mrs. Tozer's Millinery.

Inside the shop a quiet bustle prevailed. Pretty assistants stood at the ready behind glass cases, while the shoppers giggled and preened in front of the mirrors on the countertop. The shop was presided over by an older woman in purple satin, who kept order with a sweep of her eye and a wave of her hand, somehow appearing to be everywhere at once.

Deverell was forced into a waltz of polite bowing and stepping aside as the bells on the shop door jingled and women in cashmere coats and fur muffs paraded in and out, their slender arms laden with shopping bags. The shopgirls relieved them of their packages and helped them onto stools where their custom bonnets were fitted. The milliners set intricate frames of wire and straw upon the ladies' heads, and fluttered over them with deft hands, adjusting the shape here and there for a perfect fit.

Deverell observed these feminine rites with a smile. With their colorful silk dresses and wire bonnets, the fine ladies looked like nothing so much as songbirds caught in cages: well fed, well plumed, and perfectly suited to decorate a drawing room.

The scene would make for an amusing sketch, perhaps for a magazine. Deverell surveyed the room with a painterly eye, noting the lines and colors. But almost as soon as he had conceived it, the sketch was forgotten. At that moment, into the midst of this quotidian menagerie strode a most striking and luminous beauty.

She entered from the workroom behind the shop, but she was a lady in her bearing, and her simple beauty stood out among the studied prettiness of the shop. She was tall, with perfect poise and skin of the most translucent white, touched only by a hint of rose on her high cheekbones. But it was her hair, a great wealth of copper strands laced through with fine gold threads, that caught Deverell's eye. She reached for a bonnet on a high shelf and one long curl sprung loose from her chignon and lay against her cheek, revealing a natural unruliness. She was, as Deverell's friend Rossetti was famous for saying, a real stunner.

Deverell couldn't believe his good luck. He had been looking for a redhead to model for his latest painting for ages, and he hadn't seen anyone who would do. The picture was his most ambitious yet, and he'd taken painstaking care with every detail. The scene was from Shakespeare's *Twelfth Night*, and it depicted a melancholy moment of longing, as the young heroine Viola, disguised as a page-boy, pines for the love of the Duke, who hardly takes notice of her. But the success of the painting hinged on the figure of Viola, who must possess a classic beauty that would shine through her page's costume, but not make it ridiculous. The model would have to be young and slim enough to wear the page's disguise successfully, but at the same time reveal enough soft femininity to suggest the tenderness and yearning that she feels for the Duke.

The girl before him was absolutely perfect. Deverell watched her with the joy of the collector who has discovered a rare article and longs for its acquisition. It was as if she had been fashioned exactly to his order, and was now only waiting to be plucked from the shelves like one of the luxuriously trimmed bonnets.

He started toward her, smiling and holding out his hand in greeting. But the moment that she met his eye, she turned and slipped back behind the counter. She shot him one wary look and then quickly engaged another customer in conversation. She pursed her lips and nodded as the customer spoke, and for a moment Deverell wondered if he had judged her looks too quickly. She had to stoop to speak with the customer, and she suddenly seemed gangly rather than elegant. Perhaps she wasn't quite so beautiful as he first thought. But then the customer said something that made her laugh, and she tossed her head back with the graceful motion of a swan, her gray eyes wide and her smile betraying pure delight. Deverell decided that his first instinct was right: in any other setting, she might have been taken for a young noblewoman.

The girl would not catch his eye, and so Deverell turned to his mother, who was trying on a blue silk bonnet under the guidance of the imposing proprietress. He glanced down at the counter and saw that the woman had already taken down several orders.

"Mother," he whispered. "Look here, do you see that red-haired girl in the gray dress? The really lovely one, behind the counter?"

Mrs. Deverell stared critically at the shopgirl. "Yes, dear." She eyed the girl as if she were a horse for sale. "What an odd-looking girl—that hair! But I suppose that she has a certain grace to her." She paused and looked at her son. "You don't know her, Walter, do you?" she asked, raising one eyebrow over her spectacles. She knew that the young men were often in the shops to flirt with the girls.

"No, no, Mother, I don't know her. But, you see, I *must* know her. She's the girl—the girl that I've been looking for."

Mrs. Deverell's expression of amusement faded. She searched her son's face for the telltale signs of infatuation.

"As a model," Deverell explained, "for my *Twelfth Night* picture. You know that I've had a devil of a time finding a suitable model, and this one has just the right color hair. I really must convince her to sit for me."

Mrs. Deverell let out her breath. She might have let her darling boy flirt with shopgirls, but anything beyond that would be unthinkable. "She's awfully pale, dear. Are you sure she's quite right?"

"Absolutely. No one else will do."

Mrs. Deverell looked at the girl again. "I suppose that an artist looks for certain qualities in a model that might not be readily apparent to the layman's eye," she said, anxious to please her son, and to prove her understanding of his work. "And she can't be faulted for her posture, or for the delicate lines of her face. The right bone structure is very important to a model, isn't it, dear? If you must have her, I'll speak with her employer myself. That's the best way to go about these things."

Deverell kissed her on the cheek. "There's no one better than you, Mother, at managing this sort of thing. I can't imagine anyone refusing you."

Mrs. Deverell waved her hand to get the attention of the proprietress. "Dear madam! Allow me to introduce my son, Walter Deverell. He has told me that he quite likes the blue bonnet, and I shall add that to my order. Does that make three?"

"Yes, ma'am," Mrs. Tozer said. "That's three bonnets, all in silk, to be ready in two days' time."

"Very good. I'll send Walter round for them when they're ready, and I'll settle my account today." Having thereby smoothed the way, Mrs. Deverell set about making her son's request. "It's actually quite lucky that Walter is here with me today. He's a student at the Royal Academy, and he is at this very moment looking for a girl to sit for him for a portrait. He thinks that one of your shopgirls would be just right for the painting, if you could spare her for a few days. He has an extraordinary talent, and I can assure you that the picture will be of the highest order."

Mrs. Tozer looked dubious. It was a shopkeeper's duty to keep her girls respectable, and modeling for artists was hardly a suitable activity for a respectable girl. But it was also a shopkeeper's duty to sell hats, and Mrs. Deverell was proving a very good customer. Mrs. Tozer looked around the shop. "Which girl was it that he had in mind?"

Deverell discreetly nodded his head in the direction of the redhead, and Mrs. Tozer followed his gaze over to Lizzie. "Miss Siddal! Why, I never! Surely a girl such as Miss Evans would be more appropriate?" Mrs. Tozer pointed to a rosy blonde whose curls bounced as she fussed over her customer.

Deverell hardly gave the other girl a glance. "No. I'm quite certain. I must have the redhead. Miss Siddal, did you say?"

"Well, you couldn't have picked a less likely girl. She's a very quiet one. I really can't see that she would agree to sit for a painting by a stranger."

Mrs. Deverell wouldn't take no for an answer. "Let me assure you that there is no doubt as to the respectability of my son's studio! Miss Siddal would be chaperoned at all times. And," she added, almost as an afterthought, "the models are paid very handsomely for their work. I shall of course tell all my friends of your generosity in parting with her—and of your lovely bonnets! Surely there can be no harm in relating our proposal to her?"

"No, of course not." Mrs. Tozer was a shrewd woman, who had risen from a lowly shopgirl to proprietress of her own popular millinery. "So long as there's a chaperone, I have no objections. I'll speak to her myself, and to her mother if need be. I'm sure that she will see the advantage in your offer."

"We're very grateful for your assistance." Mrs. Deverell smiled with the easy satisfaction of a woman who is rarely denied the things that she wants.

"Please," added Deverell, "give Miss Siddal my compliments, and assure her that it would be an honor for me to paint her."

Mrs. Tozer bowed her head to hide a knowing smile. "I'm sure that you're anxious for her reply. I will speak with her today."

The shop closed for the day, and Lizzie joined the other milliners in the workroom. As usual, they gossiped as they worked. Lizzie rarely joined in, but when the talk turned to the lives of the shop's patrons, she found herself listening closely.

Mrs. Tozer's Millinery catered to a good class of women. Not the aristocratic ladies of the grandest Mayfair houses, perhaps, but certainly the fashionable ladies of the smart new townhouses in Belgrave Square. These lucky women spent their days roaming between country weekends at grand estates and the society of the city, with its balls, concerts, and literary salons. A yearly journey to the continent allowed them to take in a bit of culture and order the latest fashions in Paris before the start of the Season.

The customers were only too happy to tell their stories to the shopgirls as they sat for fittings. And the milliners, content to live vicariously through their clientele, felt their triumphs and slights as if they were their own. Lizzie collected their adventures, which often struck her as the stuff of fiction, like precious gems: stolen kisses in steamy conservatories, musical recitals in elegant drawing rooms, and leisurely walks over the bluffs and dunes at the coast.

And of course, there were the clothes. The shopgirls, whose business was fashion, after all, could describe in painstaking detail each of the gowns worn by their customers, from the cut of the bodice to the quality of lace in the trimmings. Listening to these stories, Lizzie longed for both the finery and the admiration that always surrounded those glittering women. But she was careful not to betray her desire—to do so would have invited ridicule from the other girls. Though each girl must have harbored some secret wish in her own heart, to admit such a thing would have robbed the delight from their talk, and put too plainly before them their own dingy prospects.

Lizzie sighed and looked down at the bonnet in her hands. The weak light made it difficult to see what she was doing, and the strain on her eyes was giving her a headache. When Mrs. Tozer bustled into the workroom and glanced over at Lizzie, her heart leapt with hope—perhaps she would be let out early again. She would much rather be at home, curled up in her bed with a book.

But to Lizzie's surprise, Mrs. Tozer only stood and watched her work for a moment with narrowed eyes. Finally she spoke. "When you've finished with that bonnet, Miss Siddal, I'll have a word with you."

Lizzie tensed, but the other girls burst into laughter the minute that Mrs. Tozer returned to her office.

"Well, well, I never thought I'd see the day!" said a plump girl at the end of the table. "Miss Siddal 'as gotten herself in trouble. Behind on your orders, are you, Lizzie?"

Lizzie colored but remained silent. She didn't know why Mrs. Tozer might want to speak with her.

"I think she has a beau," chimed in a thinner girl, with mousy brown hair. "I saw a fellow watching her in the shop this morning with eyes like a lovesick cow!"

"A beau!" the plump girl said. "I don't believe it. I never seen a girl that could cut a man down like Lizzie can. But I suppose even ice can melt."

"I've no idea what you're talking about," Lizzie said. She was proud that she knew how to keep unwanted attention at a distance, as her mother had taught her. A few of the other girls at the shop could have used such a lesson. They were always flirting with the clerks and errand boys who hung around the shop—boys who could offer them nothing but trouble. Lizzie turned back to her work, but the other girls had already seized upon the idea.

"Oh, come on," the plump girl pressed. "Don't keep us guessing! Who's your handsome lad?"

"He must have an eye for redheads—thinks her fiery!" called out another girl.

"Nonsense," Lizzie said, reaching up to smooth her hair.

"Well, maybe you don't have a beau, but you ain't so perfect as you would like everyone to think," the mousy girl pouted. "I seen you three times this week reading a book in the storeroom when you was supposed to be putting away the fabrics."

Lizzie bit her lip. She hadn't known that anyone had seen her little indulgence, glancing through a book of poems to break up the monotony of the day.

"What do you care?" Jeannie Evans snapped, coming to Lizzie's defense. "You're only jealous because you couldn't read a child's primer."

This elicited a roar of laughter from the other girls, and the mousy girl scowled. Before she could make a retort, Mrs. Tozer entered the workroom, all bustle and the swish of starched skirts. "That's enough, girls. Back to work. I want to hear nothing but the sound of flying needles." She looked over at Lizzie. "Miss Siddal, if you're finished, I'll see you now."

Lizzie stood and followed Mrs. Tozer into a small office at the back of the shop. Mrs. Tozer dropped heavily into a chair and indicated that Lizzie should sit as well.

"It feels good to sit for a moment," Mrs. Tozer said, kneading her hands against the small of her back. "It's hard work keeping after all you girls, you know! And the orders keep coming in, sometimes three or four for the same customer!"

Lizzie nodded, unsure why Mrs. Tozer should have called her aside. As far as she knew, her work had been satisfactory.

"Lizzie," Mrs. Tozer began, with a confidential smile. "I have a very interesting proposal for you. It seems that you've caught the attention of one of our customers, a Mrs. Deverell. She has a son, a painter, and he wishes you to sit for a portrait."

Mrs. Tozer's words caught Lizzie completely off guard. "A portrait? For an advertisement for the shop?"

Mrs. Tozer laughed. "No, dear, though that's certainly an idea! It's a proper portrait he wants."

"There must be some mistake," Lizzie said, thinking that she was being set up for some elaborate joke.

"No mistake, but between us, I was as surprised as you! I suggested that Miss Evans might be more suitable, but he seemed set on having you." Mrs. Tozer paused, perhaps aware that she had been unkind. "But really, you do have some nice features. It's a shame about your hair, of course—such an unfortunate color—but your complexion is lovely. Apparently this Mr. Deverell sees something artistic in you! So there it is." Mrs. Tozer did not seem to notice Lizzie's growing embarrassment. "His mother made a large order, and I couldn't very well refuse her request. And at any rate, you'll be paid seven shillings a day for your work; your mother can hardly turn her nose up at such a sum."

Lizzie was quiet. It was true that her mother could easily find a use for seven shillings a day. "But my position here? Don't you need me?"

"You needn't worry about that—I can spare you for a few days, though it will be a strain."

Lizzie had seen many portraits of ladies in exquisite gowns in the halls of the National Galleries. How many times had she imagined herself to be one of them? A slight smile passed over her lips and then faded. It was out of the question, of course—her mother would never allow it. And besides, having a society portrait done was quite a different thing from sitting as a paid model. The former was an honor afforded to wealthy ladies, while the latter was often done by women who wouldn't be fit to serve in their houses.

Mrs. Tozer sighed. "It's just like one of my girls, not to see a real opportunity when it comes their way! There's no need to look so scandalized, Lizzie. You'll be properly chaperoned at all times, Mrs. Deverell has assured me. And it's really very flattering! If he wants to paint you, he must think you beautiful. Perhaps it will lead to something more. At the very least, you're bound to meet some really refined people—artists, and perhaps others in their circle, their patrons. I've seen you glancing over your books and daydreaming when you thought no one was looking—not much passes in my shop without my knowledge. But of course you must do as you see fit."

"But if people should find out. It could ruin my chances . . ."

"It's not as if you'll be posing in your knickers! This is quite a different thing—you shall sit to Mr. Deverell as if you were his sister. He tells me that the subject of the painting is taken from Shakespeare—what could be scandalous about that? And really, my dear, what chances do you have to be ruined? I hope that you don't mind my being blunt, but that is my way. You really only have something to gain."

And yet, it seemed beyond foolish to Lizzie to risk what little she did have—her good reputation—on the slim chance for advancement that sitting for an artist might afford her. The thought was as terrifying as it was exhilarating. But Mrs. Tozer was right. If she didn't make a change now, she would soon have no chances at all, and each day would be just like the one before, with only herself changing: growing older and thinner, fading under the strain of the work. There was no future for her here.

She slowly nodded to Mrs. Tozer. She would try her luck, then, and see what came of it.

That night Mrs. Tozer walked Lizzie home, and for once Lizzie was happy for the company. The old drunk on the bridge had tempered her taste for lonely walks, and there was no chance of being accosted with that formidable lady by her side, parting the crowds with her stout frame, eliciting respectful nods with her sweeping gaze.

They reached the Siddal house and Mrs. Tozer looked it over with a sharp eye. It was a narrow structure wedged between a greengrocer and a chemist, with a shop downstairs and two perilously settled floors above, where the family made their home. Only the well-scrubbed front step and the window boxes set it apart from the other tired houses lining the street.

Mrs. Tozer glanced over her shoulder at Lizzie, with a look that asked how a girl who lived above a shop had come by such a fine accent. Lizzie Siddal obviously had designs above her station, much like Mrs. Tozer had at Lizzie's age. She paused at the door and turned back to Lizzie. "Let me do the talking, dear."

Lizzie nodded and showed Mrs. Tozer in, leading her up the narrow steps and into a neatly kept parlor. Lizzie stole a glance at Mrs. Tozer, trying to see what she made of the small house. Lizzie had nothing to be ashamed of—she wouldn't have been working for Mrs. Tozer, after all, if her family had been in better circumstances. But visitors always made her more aware of the house's shortcomings.

The Siddals fell into that class of persons who had gently, and almost without noticing, drifted downward from the comfortable middle class to the hardships of the London tenements. They had, several generations ago, been a family with a respectable income and various property holdings in Derbyshire. But any fortune that the Siddal clan could lay claim to was now long gone, chipped away at by each succeeding generation, with a profusion of claimants to an ever-dwindling stock. The remaining family property, Hope Hall, had gone to a distant cousin who ran it as an inn.

Mr. Siddal firmly believed himself to be the rightful heir to the Hall, and it had grown in his imagination into something far grander than it was. He often neglected his work as a cutler, making and sharpening knives, to go over the endless details of a lawsuit that he had brought to reclaim the family property. But his efforts had been thwarted by a legion of relatives, all as convinced of their own right to the property as he was of his, and so far the suit had rewarded him with nothing but solicitors' bills.

As a child, Lizzie had dreamed alongside him, imagining her triumphant return to the family's rightful home and all the finery that would entail. But now, at nineteen and almost a woman, the thought of the pointless suit just depressed her, and she would have preferred that her father put his mind, and his meager savings, to something more useful.

Lizzie glanced around the parlor, hoping that her father was out. He would be sure to talk Mrs. Tozer's ear off about the lawsuit, and Lizzie didn't want any gossip about it. She was relieved to see that he was still in the shop. She was about to call out to her mother when two of the younger children, a boy and a girl, rushed in from the back room and wrapped themselves around her knees.

"Lizzie, Lizzie!" they cried. "Will you read aloud to us? Oh, please?"

"Hush!" Her tone was serious, but her smile was affectionate. "I can't read to you now! Don't you see that we have company?"

The children glanced up at Mrs. Tozer, but, not recognizing her, they paid her no mind. The noise, however, brought Mrs. Siddal into the parlor. One quiet word from her and the children made a quick bow and curtsy before scampering back the way that they had come. Mrs. Siddal strode forward to greet her visitor.

"Mother," Lizzie said, "allow me to introduce Mrs. Tozer."

Mrs. Siddal nodded her head in greeting and gestured for Mrs. Tozer to take a seat in front of the fire. If she was surprised to find her daughter's employer in her parlor, her face did not betray it. "To what do I owe the great pleasure of your visit?"

Mrs. Tozer made herself comfortable and regarded Mrs. Siddal with interest. She had the same fine manners and impeccable dress as her daughter, and her hair, though somewhat faded, was of the same hue of golden red. Only her hands, the skin red and cracked, betrayed the hard work that it took to maintain appearances.

"Mrs. Siddal, so lovely to finally meet you. Lizzie has been such an asset to our shop. Her work is of the first order, and I can always depend on her to show the new girls their way about the workroom. She is a very talented seamstress."

A slight frown passed over Mrs. Siddal's face, and Mrs. Tozer paused. It was clear that Mrs. Siddal's pride weighed more than her purse, and that she was ashamed that she had to put her daughter out to work. Mrs. Tozer summoned up all of her saleswoman's powers of persuasion and started again: "What I mean to say is that I've taken a particular interest in your daughter, and in her prospects. She's obviously a girl of many fine qualities, very much apart from her talent at millinery."

The new tactic worked, and Mrs. Siddal instantly warmed to Mrs. Tozer. "She is indeed a girl of good qualities. Of course, she's had no formal education, but I tutored her myself. Lizzie can recite poetry, speak a little French, and draw. I raised all my girls the way I myself was raised."

Mrs. Tozer saw her opening. "Her artistic accomplishments are quite obvious in her work. That's why I'm so anxious for Lizzie to be further exposed to such . . . artistic elements."

Lizzie watched the exchange with barely suppressed excitement. Mrs. Tozer's words had done their work; Lizzie was beginning to see the opportunity as an adventure, rather than a sordid way to make a few extra shillings. But despite her growing excitement, she kept her eyes down and her head bowed. If she looked too eager, her mother would be suspicious.

"It will come as no surprise to you," Mrs. Tozer continued, her voice smooth and flattering, "that Lizzie has caught the eye of a painter who wishes to paint her portrait."

At the first mention of the painter Mrs. Siddal began to shake her head. "An artist paint Lizzie? No, no, I'm afraid that it's out of the question."

"What I meant to say is a *gentleman* artist. A graduate of the Royal Academy Schools. I would hardly bother you with such a request if I had any doubt that the situation would be advantageous to Lizzie. I feel strongly that this could be an opportunity for her to be introduced into a very genteel circle."

"I'm sorry," Mrs. Siddal said. "But I'm well aware of what sort of women pose for artists, and I won't have my daughter counted among them. Really, Mrs. Tozer! I'm surprised that you would allow such goings on among your girls!"

Mrs. Tozer gave a tight smile. She often said that she could sell a bible to a bishop or a sinner alike, and Mrs. Siddal was no different than any reluctant customer.

"You're right, of course. The respectability of my girls is of the utmost importance to me. As is their social advancement, when possible. I've had my eye on Lizzie for some time, and I'd like to see her introduced to some better society. Mrs. Deverell, the painter's mother, could be a great ally to Lizzie if she finds her agreeable."

"Of course I want the best for Lizzie. But a thing like this could do real harm to her reputation. If there were to be any improprieties . . ."

"Please, Mother," Lizzie broke in, unable to contain her excitement. "You always say that if only we had the right introductions, we would make the most of them."

"And how shall I introduce you if it gets around that you are posing for an artist?" Mrs. Siddal snapped. "It won't matter whether he's a gentleman or not, people will assume the worst. I'm sorry to disappoint you, Lizzie, but it will be said that a girl who will take money to sit for a painter will take money for other things as well. I'm only trying to protect you."

"But who would know?" Lizzie asked. "The people around here wouldn't know the Royal Academy of Art from the Royal Stables. And besides, I don't think that it's so bad as you say. Many young ladies pose for portraits, and so long as they have a proper chaperone, no one thinks anything of it! Please, Mother, I long for some little adventure. What's the point of speaking French and learning to draw, if I'm going to spend all my days in a workroom with girls who can barely speak the Queen's English?"

Mrs. Tozer raised her eyebrows, but chose not to reprimand Lizzie for her slight to the shop. Instead she turned to Mrs. Siddal. "You have my word, madam, that Lizzie will be properly chaperoned at all times."

Mrs. Siddal looked at her daughter and her face began to soften. "I've done my best with them, you know," she said, so quietly that it was almost as if she were speaking to herself. "But all of my plans, and all my little economies, have come to nothing so far. It seems that fine manners are worth very little without fine connections in society." She seemed to make up her mind and nodded once, very slowly, just as Lizzie had. Mrs. Tozer, who had not been blessed with any daughters, must have felt a twinge at how alike they were.

"Oh, Mama!" Lizzie cried, leaping from her chair and embracing her mother. "Thank you! I promise that I'll make you proud."

"But not a word to your father," Mrs. Siddal warned. "He'd be scandalized . . . I hate to even think of it." She glanced at Mrs. Tozer, who smiled back, no doubt thinking of the late Mr. Tozer, who, God rest his soul, was no longer around to stick his nose into her business decisions.

Mrs. Tozer rose to leave. "After all," she said, "it's only for a few days. And perhaps it will put Lizzie in the way of fortune . . . or who knows?" Mrs. Tozer spread her hands and raised an eyebrow. "She may even wind up possessed of her own fortune."

The thought of prosperity elicited a smile from Mrs. Siddal. She had raised Lizzie the best that she could—now it was up to her to go out and make something of herself.

CHAPTER 4

Ophelia ran down the forest path, her satin gown sweeping over the mossy ground with a soft whisper. She stopped for a moment to catch her breath, and looking up she saw the familiar turrets of Elsinore rising above the treetops. The light was dying, and she started again, anxious to reach the castle gates.

The fog that slid between the trees played tricks, forming into ghosts and turning twisted branches into castle gates. She reached out her hand, but the mist shifted to reveal that the castle was still far ahead.

A single purpose drove her steps: She must find her noble prince. Some whispered that he was mad, but she paid them no mind. For if he was mad, then so too was she, for giving herself to a madman.

At last she reached the gates and heard his voice, more clearly now, calling to her: "Ophelia, Ophelia!"

The words sent a shiver of pleasure through her, and her hands, prickly with cold, felt the warm sun upon them.

"Ophelia!" She heard the voice call again, and it was suddenly odd—familiar, but not quite right.

She glanced around, perplexed, and in her confusion she lost the path and slipped. The ground disappeared beneath her, and her crown of flowers slipped from her head, leaving a trail of columbine and rue in her wake. She cried out, afraid that she was slipping into oblivion.

But just as the shadow threatened to engulf her, a hand reached out and pulled her to safety.

Through the haze of sleep, she heard a voice: "Lizzie! Lizzie! Wake up!"

She opened her eyes and, still half dreaming, looked around. She blinked, surprised to see a cozy bedroom where she expected a dark wood. The shutters of her room were thrown open, and her younger sister, Lydia, stood over her, laughing and shaking her by the shoulder.

"What nonsense you were talking! Come on now, get up! You'll be late to sit for your artist!"

Lizzie sat straight up in bed, sending an open book in her lap clattering to the floor. The excitement of sitting for Walter Deverell had made it impossible to sleep, and so she'd spent the better part of the night burning down candles and leafing through an old volume of Shakespeare, trying to guess which of his heroines she was to sit for the next day. Now she scrambled out of bed, clutching her nightgown around her. The room was cold and the floor beneath her feet was colder. They couldn't afford to set fires in the bedrooms, unless someone was ill.

Lydia picked up the book that Lizzie had dropped. It was a heavy volume, with a faded cloth cover and only a suggestion of the gold embossing that had once graced its spine. Lydia barely glanced at it and threw it back onto the bed. "Were you up all night reading your fairy tales again?"

"They're not fairy tales. They're the works of the great playwright . . . oh, never mind." Lizzie could see that Lydia couldn't care less.

Lydia hadn't inherited the Siddal family's taste for literature. And it was just as well, Lizzie thought, since they had so few books to begin with, and she had no wish to share them with anyone else. Lydia preferred to spend her free time at cards or embroidery, and she only laughed when Lizzie asked her how she could bring herself to take up a needle for pleasure after sewing all day at her position at a dressmaker's. "It's no harder on my hands than reading would be on my eyes," Lydia said, ever practical.

Though she was two years younger than Lizzie, Lydia often assumed the role of an older sister: She was sensible when Lizzie was dreamy, quick to help their mother with the housekeeping while Lizzie was off daydreaming, and, though Lizzie was tall for a girl, Lydia was an inch taller, and had a fuller figure. She liked to joke that she would have to go to the country and become a farmer's wife, where a strong back was valued over a pretty face. But the whole family knew that she was really sweet on Robert Crane, the grocer's son from down the street, and that he must find her pretty enough, as he always asked for her when he was making a delivery. Lizzie had no doubt that as soon as he took over the business from his father, he would ask for Lydia's hand, and Lydia would move a few doors down, exchanging a small house above a cutlery for a small house above a grocery, and that she would be as happy with that as with anything. Well, that was fine for Lydia, but Lizzie wanted something different. And today, she hoped, might be her chance to see what a different life was like.

Lizzie sat down in front of her mirror, staring hard at her features and trying to see what it was that had made the artist notice her. She pinched her cheeks and bit her lip, calling forth an angry rose tint beneath her white skin. But the added color did nothing to quiet her fear that her nose was too long and her eyelids too heavy. Mrs. Tozer was probably right—Jeannie Evans would have made a more fitting model for a painting.

Lizzie turned to her sister. "What if this Mr. Deverell has made a mistake? What if, when he sees me again, he decides that I am not really what he needs after all? I would be too humiliated."

"Nonsense," Lydia said. "Here, let me. I'll brush your hair one hundred times for good luck." She took the brush from Lizzie's hand and began to brush her hair in long, regular strokes. Their faces in the mirror were variations on a theme; they had the same wide-set eyes, but Lydia's were a warm brown to Lizzie's pale gray, and she had dimpled pink cheeks instead of Lizzie's dramatic cheekbones. Lydia hummed while she worked, as if she were soothing a child. When she was finished, Lizzie's hair glowed like burnished copper. "There. You're as pretty as a picture now."

Their toilet complete, the two girls clambered down the stairs and into the kitchen. Lizzie stood before the hearth to warm her fingers and toes. "Any tea?" She glanced at the pot on the sideboard.

Lydia lifted the lid and looked in. "No," she said, wrinkling her nose. "Just the dregs. Father must have drunk it all and not refilled the pot. As usual."

They looked over at the table, where indeed their father had left an empty teacup and a pile of paperwork, some of it covered in rings where he had carelessly placed the cup on the papers, and none of it in too great of a condition to begin with. Lizzie could see that her father had been up early to look over the papers for his lawsuit.

"That can't be a good sign, can it?" Lydia asked.

"No. He only drags out that old pile of evidence when business isn't going well. What could be the problem now?"

Lydia sighed. Then, trying to make light: "Well, just think. If we lived at Hope Hall, we'd have our own fires lit every morning, and a maid to bring us our tea in bed!"

"And jam for our bread, and sugar for our tea," Lizzie responded with a smile. "But until that happens, I'm afraid that we must hurry to work."

On the stairs they met their father, who was coming up from the shop.

"As fresh as daisies, you two are!" he exclaimed, pinching their cheeks and leaving a smudge. He had an infectious smile, which had long ago charmed his young wife, and convinced her that he was a man with prospects. And it was that same smile that had later helped to smooth over some of her disappointment, when none of his plans had come to anything.

He'd been at work grinding knives, and a light metallic dust covered his shirtsleeves and blue work apron. In a misguided nod to the style of his clientele, he wore a shabby top hat, perched at a ridiculous angle. It was no wonder that the neighbors were always asking him how he was getting on with his lawsuit, and then laughing at him behind his back, calling him the Country Squire. "You'd better be off," he said, glancing at his watch, "or you'll be late."

"Yes, I know," Lydia said, annoyed. "It's Lizzie. She was up all night reading again and couldn't wake herself this morning.

Apparently the works of the *great playwright*—yes, Lizzie, I was listening, I'm not quite so ignorant as you think—were more important than rousing ourselves for work."

"Up all night reading, were you?" Mr. Siddal's eyes twinkled. "Like father, like daughter, I see."

"I should hope not," muttered Lydia. Louder, she said, "If Lizzie is up every night thinking of poetry, she will lose her place. She needs her sleep."

"My Lizzie has more brains and beauty than any of Shakespeare's heroines. I expect she'll be fine. Let her be, Lydia."

Lizzie could not be angry with her father for long, but his flattery solved nothing. Beauty and brains were quite all right when you were a fine lady in a play, but they hadn't proved of much use when you were a shopgirl from Southwark. She was tempted, for a moment, to tell him that she was going to sit for a portrait of one of Shakespeare's heroines, but then decided against it. Any pride that he would take in the thought would be far outweighed by his dismay that she was going to be a model.

"Goodbye, Father," she said. "I'll be late again tonight. Tell Mother not to wait up."

With that, the two girls brushed past their father and went down the stairs. They put on their cloaks and went out into the street. Before they parted, Lydia turned to Lizzie with some last advice. "Do be careful, Lizzie. And mind that there is always another lady present."

"As always, Lyddie, you're completely practical. If only I had a bit of your good sense."

Lydia laughed. "From what I've heard, good sense is not the quality that painters look for in their models." Then she became serious. "I've no doubt that they will be charmed by you, Lizzie. But do be careful that you're not too charmed by them. A painter is little more than a conjurer, after all. But you are so much more than a pretty girl in a painting. I don't want to see you sell yourself for a handful of beans."

Deverell's studio was situated in Kew, a green and elegant neighborhood west of the city. It was too far to walk, and the cost of a cab was well beyond Lizzie's means, so she boarded a horse-drawn omnibus and wedged herself in among the other passengers.

Anticipation made the trip seem longer than it was, but when she at last reached the house, her nerve almost failed her. It was an impressive redbrick mansion, three stories high, with white pillars at the door and a mansard roof. She checked the address twice before making her way up the path.

She rang the bell, and a maid in a starched cap answered and took her name. The maid went to fetch Mrs. Deverell and Lizzie stood awkwardly on the doorstep, unsure of whether she should have followed the maid into the house—the girl hadn't indicated either way.

Before she could make up her mind to enter, Mrs. Deverell appeared at the door. She looked Lizzie up and down, reminding Lizzie of her own mother. "My dear Miss Siddal," she said, in a voice that managed to be both solicitous and distant. "You are so very kind to sit for my son. I know that he is delighted to have your assistance. Please," she said, "follow me, and I'll show you to his studio."

Without ever having invited Lizzie into the house, Mrs. Deverell swept past her and went down the steps and onto the path. Lizzie followed her around the side of the house, her cheeks burning. Was she being shown to the servants' entrance? But to Lizzie's great relief, Mrs. Deverell proceeded past the kitchen door and through the garden to a studio set back from the house. She pushed open the door and gestured for Lizzie to follow her.

The studio was small but comfortable, with good light and a warm fire. The walls were hung with sketches that showed bodies in various poses and states of motion, and intricate studies of faces, hands, flowers, and trees. Deverell was sitting with his back to them, dabbing at a canvas on a large easel. When he heard the door open, he turned and jumped to his feet.

Lizzie recognized him from the shop. She saw that he was handsome, and not much older than she. His face had not yet lost its smooth, boyish aspect, and he had bright, curious eyes. He gave Lizzie a slight bow, and his dark hair fell playfully over his eyes.

Mrs. Deverell made the introductions, and they nodded shyly to each other, their greeting made stiff by Mrs. Deverell's presence.

"And this," Mrs. Deverell said, "is my daughter, Miss Mary Deverell."

Lizzie turned to see another girl, about her own age, whom she had not at first noticed. She was petite, with dark hair and eyes like her brother, and a sweet smile.

"Call me Mary," she said, taking Lizzie's hand. "I hope that we'll be friends. I'm quite grateful, you know, that you're to sit for Walter. That's usually my job, and now I'm free to work at my own poor little sketches instead!"

Lizzie returned the smile. "And you must call me Lizzie. I'm very pleased to meet you."

Mrs. Deverell returned to the house, and the three young people were left alone. Deverell stared at Lizzie for a full minute, and Lizzie shifted uncomfortably on her feet, unsure of whether she should meet his eye. She took his silence for disappointment, and wondered again if he had made a mistake in asking for her, or if she had somehow failed to prepare herself properly.

Finally he broke the silence. "You will make a perfect Viola," he declared. "Do you know the play? You are Viola, living and breathing."

"Viola? Yes, I know the play." Her cheeks burned. *Twelfth Night* had never been one of her favorites. She liked the tragedies, with their great romantic roles and heartfelt speeches. When Mrs. Tozer told her that she was to sit for one of Shakespeare's heroines, she had pictured herself as Juliet or Ophelia. Not Viola, who spends the better part of the play disguised as a lowly pageboy. It made sense to her now that Mr. Deverell had asked her to model, and she felt foolish for imagining that she was suitable to sit for anything more romantic. Mr. Deverell was still staring at her, so she tried to mask her disappointment. "I'm happy that I can be of some service to you," she murmured, looking down at her hands.

Mary saw Lizzie's discomfort and came to her rescue. "Walter! You're embarrassing the poor dear. Come, Lizzie, I'll show you where you're to dress while Walter gets his paints ready."

Mary took Lizzie's hand and led her over to a screen, behind which hung a pair of boy's britches, stockings, and a bright red tunic.

Lizzie looked at the clothes. "I'm to wear britches? Is that . . . is that something models often do?" Lizzie didn't know whether to laugh or to cry. She'd traveled across London, but it felt as if she had crossed into another world, where everything was topsy-turvy and she couldn't quite get her bearings.

"Didn't you know, my dear?" Mary laughed. "Oh my. Walter is painting Viola in her disguise as a page. You know the story? If not, Walter will tell you all about it—one of those things about the course of true love never running smooth and all that. Walter had me sew the clothes myself to his specifications."

Lizzie looked at the tunic and trousers with resignation. "It's just that I didn't realize that I had to wear a costume. I've never worn boy's clothes before." She swallowed hard, thinking of the satin gown that she had worn in her dream, and fighting her disappointment.

Mary was still smiling at her, and so Lizzie picked up the clothes, not wanting to appear unsophisticated by refusing. She stepped behind the screen, and for a moment she stood very still, fighting the urge to run from the studio and board the first omnibus back to Southwark. Daydreaming about sitting for an artist had been one thing; she had imagined herself lovely and serene, in a flowing gown. But now that she was actually here, she just felt embarrassed. It had seemed too good to be true, and it was: Deverell hadn't chosen her because she was beautiful, but rather because she would make a decent pageboy.

But, she told herself, if she left now, she wouldn't have another chance. She could picture Mrs. Tozer shaking her head, and sending a note to Mrs. Deverell to apologize for Lizzie's rudeness. Perhaps she would offer Mr. Deverell the use of another girl, like Jeannie, who wouldn't have Lizzie's qualms, but would be happy for the opportunity. And Lizzie would be back in the workroom, squinting at her needle and dreaming of knights and ladies.

The thought of the workroom made up her mind. She unhooked her bodice and shimmied free of her tight sleeves and heavy skirts. She stood, shivering in her slip and trying not to think of Mr. Deverell standing just beyond the screen. Then with a shrug she pulled on the costume. When she was fully dressed, she looked at herself in the mirror and almost laughed: But for her long hair, she could very well have been a medieval pageboy. She was as tall as many men, after all, and the clothes hugged her slim frame closely. She did a quick turn, enjoying the freedom of britches. Then she pulled her hair into a loose chignon and stepped out from behind the screen.

Deverell stopped setting out his paints. "You're a vision! A heroine of Shakespeare brought to life."

Lizzie blushed again, sure that Deverell must be making a joke at her expense.

"That's enough," Mary said, "or you'll have poor Miss Siddal scampering back behind the screen."

"When I see perfection, I must speak. And I never saw a more perfect Viola in my life."

Mary turned to Lizzie. "When Walter's on about a painting, there's no accounting for him. He goes quite off his head and forgets his manners, all in the name of art and the pursuit of beauty, or so he likes to claim. But you really do look quite the part."

Lizzie allowed herself a small smile. She knew that flattery was cheap, but if Deverell was half as pleased as he appeared, then perhaps she didn't look completely ridiculous. She admitted to herself how excited she was at the prospect of sitting for a painting, even if it wasn't quite what she had imagined. In the end, after all, Viola did marry a duke, despite her humble clothes.

Deverell offered her his hand. "Shall we begin? I'll show you where you'll sit, and we'll start with a few sketches."

Lizzie followed Deverell to the end of the studio. He asked her to sit on a stool, with her elbows resting on a table and her hands clasped. He used his hands to position her head, and Lizzie held her breath and told herself that it was no different from modeling a bonnet in the shop. Her profile was angled toward him, and she leaned slightly forward, her eyes upturned.

"Perfect." Deverell went behind his easel and began to sketch, glancing up occasionally and humming quietly to himself.

He seemed to be perfectly at ease, but Lizzie could not get comfortable. She tried to sit completely still, but she kept shifting, blushing every time Deverell looked up from the canvas. She was conscious that she no longer had a dozen layers of petticoats and skirts between her and the world, and she felt the absence of her high-necked gray work dress keenly. It was one of the few things that stood between her and the men who came to the shop to leer at the pretty girls. Now she was stripped of its shield, and she felt that not only her body, but her very self was on display, as if Deverell could read her every tortured thought.

But as an hour passed, and then another, she forgot her embarrassment. Deverell tossed off page after page of studies, and he stopped often to give her an encouraging smile or word. His attention was flattering, and Lizzie began to think that the work of modeling was rather pleasant, and that the studio was not at all the sordid place she had imagined.

A whisper from Mary Deverell recalled her from her thoughts. "Are you very uncomfortable? I always get so stiff when I'm sitting for Walter. He can draw for hours, and I don't think he notices that the time is passing."

"I'm used to sitting still. I don't mind. And I'd much rather sit in this lovely room than . . ." She trailed off. She didn't want to talk about the shop, not today. "Besides, it's so very interesting to me, to see an artist at work. I've never met a painter before."

"I also like to watch Walter when he's painting," Mary said. "My own watercolors owe so much to his instruction." She was sitting at a small easel near Lizzie, and she turned the easel so that Lizzie could see her painting, a half-finished watercolor of an iris, which sat in a jar of water on the table.

"Why, it's lovely!" Lizzie saw that the lines were clean and sure, the petals a velvety purple and the leaves a crisp green.

"Do you care for drawing?" Mary asked.

"Very much. But I've had no real training."

"Then you must ask Walter to give you a lesson!"

"Oh, no," Lizzie stammered. "I didn't mean to suggest . . . it's really just a hobby."

"I'm sure that he would be happy to critique your drawings. He never shies away from critiquing mine!"

The girls both laughed, and Deverell cleared his throat. Mary gave her brother a contrite pout and then smiled at Lizzie, her eyes twinkling. "I'm not to disturb you. I shouldn't be making you laugh. But don't worry; I won't let you be bored. I'll tell you all about Walter and his friends while you sit. They're quite a remarkable group—always coming up with schemes and grand ideas for paintings and literary magazines and the like. I'm sure that you'll like them very much, as I do. Unless, of course, you find them to be too bohemian, as Mother does. Of course you'll meet them before long. They pop in at all hours, and I can't imagine that Walter is going to be able to keep a girl like you a secret for long."

"You're too kind," Lizzie murmured. She thought that Mary must have been flattering her to put her more at ease. But Mary was so sweet, Lizzie was grateful for her company and attention.

Mary drew her chair closer and began to tell Lizzie stories, painting with her words a cast of characters that immediately sparked Lizzie's imagination. There was a secret brotherhood of artists which Walter may or may not have been nominated to join—she wasn't quite sure and he wasn't telling; lady poets who wrote daring verses and published them under noms de plume; and late nights at the Cremorne pleasure gardens, where painters and poets mingled with the lowest sort of women and the wealthiest of the aristocracy, drinking champagne under the many-colored lights.

The world Mary described was entirely new to Lizzie, and it didn't seem to exist in the same London that she knew, and which seemed very drab in comparison. She didn't care that her mother would have considered many of the stories shocking—she thought they sounded exotic and exciting. Here in Deverell's studio a different set of expectations seemed to apply, and Lizzie was free for a moment to forget the stricter rules of the world outside.

Mary wove her stories all afternoon. Deverell was intent on his work and hardly spoke, except to laugh or to utter an affronted disavowal of some rumor or other. But though he hardly spoke, Lizzie felt that she was beginning to know him through Mary's affectionate descriptions. When he finally stood and stretched with a loud yawn, it took Lizzie by surprise.

"I've done all that I can today," he said. "You must forgive my silence. I didn't want to waste a single moment. Would you like to see the sketches?"

Lizzie walked over to the easel. Deverell had drawn her in intricate detail, his pencil shading each shadow and tendril of hair. The girl in the picture was at once more beautiful and more serious than what Lizzie saw in her mirror. Could her profile truly be so fine? Or had Deverell been kind? Her chin seemed less pointed, her nose not quite so long as she believed it. She smiled.

"Are you pleased?"

"They're beautiful drawings. But I hardly recognize the girl in them; surely that girl is not me. She looks quite lovely."

Deverell laughed. "Haven't I made a good likeness?"

Lizzie knew that she had said the wrong thing—she'd insulted his work when she meant to do the opposite. "Oh, I didn't mean to imply . . . I only meant that your drawings are so lovely, I fear myself a poor thing in comparison."

"But you're wrong, Miss Siddal. It's my drawings that suffer by the comparison. Hasn't anyone ever told you that you're beautiful? I fear myself hardly capable of doing you justice."

Lizzie blushed and looked down, but Deverell gently raised her chin and held her eye for a long moment.

"I'm sure you'll try your best, Walter," chimed in Mary, bustling over to the pair. "Now, we mustn't keep Miss Siddal any longer, or she'll be too tired to sit for you tomorrow." She put a gentle hand on Lizzie's arm and led her back to the screen. "Come, dear. I'll help you with your dress."

"I leave you in competent hands," Deverell called after them. "And I look forward to tomorrow."

"As do I," Lizzie said, and it was the first time in as long as she could remember that she had something to which she could truly look forward.

"Gentlemen!" Deverell cried out, bursting through the door of Holman Hunt's studio. He slammed the door shut behind him, not noticing that the bang nearly upset a whole table of paints.

Holman Hunt was standing at his easel, and Dante Rossetti was sitting with his feet on a chair and his arms flung back behind his head, a barely begun canvas forgotten beside him. He waved a lazy greeting to Deverell.

"Deverell!" Hunt barked, glaring at the table of spilled paints. "Watch what you're doing!"

"I'm sorry." Deverell righted a few of the bottles and left the rest to lie where they were. He was humming to himself, and he seemed distracted as he walked to the window, flung open the shutters, and leaned out, inhaling deeply. Then he abruptly turned and collapsed into a chair next to Rossetti, leaving the window wide open and the cold air spilling in.

Hunt shut the window. "What on earth are you doing? There's a cold wind."

"Is there?" Deverell asked. "I suppose there is. I hadn't noticed."

Rossetti and Hunt looked at each other with raised eyebrows.

"Out with it, then," Hunt said. "You look like the cat that got the cream."

"Do I?" He stared dreamily around the studio. "I suppose that I *have* got the cream. You fellows won't believe what a stupendously beautiful creature I've found. A stunner, Rossetti, a true stunner, as you would say. She's like a queen, really. Nothing at all like the usual sort of girl—her features were made for painting, strong and true."

Hunt rolled his eyes, but Rossetti looked interested. "Does such a woman exist in London? Is she flesh and blood or goddess?"

"Goddess! A Phidian goddess, come to life," Deverell declared to laughter from Hunt and Rossetti.

"We were wondering where you'd gotten yourself off to," Hunt said. "I haven't seen you around in weeks. Between you disappearing and Rossetti moping about and neglecting his work, I was afraid that our movement might be done for before it had even started. And where did you find this goddess?"

"At a bonnet shop, of all places. She's really a wonder, though. Her friends are quite humble, I'm sure, but she behaves like a real lady. And the thing of it is that she seems to have no idea what a beauty she is! One gets the feeling that she's been passed over for commoner girls before. Most men in London wouldn't know true

beauty if it stepped off a Botticelli canvas and walked into Trafalgar Square. But she's charmed me, all right. She has grace and skill
quite beyond her class."

Hunt laughed. "I'm sure I know the sort."

"You may joke, Hunt, but you haven't seen her yet. The sketches
turned out perfectly, but I'm afraid that I've made a mess of painting her hair. The color is such a wonder, changing with the light,
and paint doesn't seem to capture it. She's coming again tomorrow.
You really ought to see her."

"How could I resist?" asked Rossetti. "I'll come by tomorrow."

"Tomorrow?" Rossetti's enthusiasm seemed to break through
Deverell's dreamy state, and he began to backpedal. "Maybe another day would be better. I'm just in the thick of it now."

But Deverell's reluctance only fueled Rossetti's interest. "I won't
be in the way at all. I'll just have a look at the painting. Perhaps a
fresh pair of eyes will help."

"You can't go tomorrow," Hunt said. He looked at Rossetti's
nearly empty canvas. "What of your painting? You're not going to be
finished in time to submit for the spring exhibitions. If we don't put
in our best work, the Brotherhood will be thought of as a joke. I
don't intend to have my career as a painter become a footnote to
the Brotherhood's failure."

"All in good time, Hunt, all in good time," Rossetti replied. "If
Deverell's new muse is as beautiful as he says, perhaps I shall have
some work for her myself."

"But only after I've finished my picture," Deverell reminded
him.

"Of course. I'll just stop in for a moment. I wouldn't dream of in-
terrupting your work."

But it was clear that Rossetti was very much looking forward
to getting out from under Hunt's watchful gaze, and the promise
of a beautiful woman was a welcome excuse. Rossetti smiled
broadly, but his two friends both frowned, each worried for his own
reasons.

Lizzie had only been sitting for Deverell for a few weeks, but
even in this short time she had begun to change, at first in small

ways—her accent growing a touch more refined to match Mary's soft speech, her head held a little higher as she walked down her street—and then the changes became more noticeable. If she had always possessed the necessary elements of beauty—a natural grace, a pale and lovely complexion—they had, as yet, somehow failed to coalesce into true beauty. But Deverell's admiring gaze acted like the sun upon a rosebud, and under its power Lizzie's beauty bloomed.

Away from the shop, the color returned to her cheeks and her expression softened. She no longer blushed whenever Deverell looked at her. Instead, she learned to return his smiles, and then to look away at just the right moment to preserve her modesty. When they took a break from painting, she walked around the studio, striking elegant poses in the best light and glancing back over her shoulder to be sure that he was watching, which he always was. Though she told herself that his compliments were nothing more than kindness, there was a part of her that could not resist his flattery, and began to believe his words.

To Lizzie's delight, Deverell became chattier as his picture progressed, and they spoke frequently of poetry, books, and art. At first Deverell seemed surprised at how widely Lizzie had read, and he would occasionally shake his head, wondering how he had found such a beautiful and charming girl in a bonnet shop. When Mary told him that Lizzie enjoyed sketching, he gave Lizzie a sheaf of paper and a few charcoal pencils as a gift. Whenever he stopped to mix his paints or let a section of the painting dry, he encouraged her to work on her own drawings, just as his sister did. She even wrote out a few verses, and when Mary insisted on reading them aloud, she was embarrassed and pleased in equal measure. The freedom of this arrangement was very new to Lizzie, and a welcome change from the rigid customs and long hours at the millinery.

Lizzie followed Mary's lead, sketching the flowers that Mary cut from the greenhouse garden. At first the pencil felt awkward between her fingers, which were more accustomed to holding a needle, and her first drawings were unsure and slight. But when she began a sketch of Mary, she gained confidence. As a child, she'd always loved to sketch her sisters as they sat sewing or reading, and her growing acquaintance with Mary lent the picture intimacy. In the sketch, Mary's face was happy and open, as if she had just looked up to see a friendly face at the window. Mary exclaimed at the likeness, and Deverell insisted on seeing it, despite Lizzie's embarrassed protests. She held her breath, thinking that he would laugh at her attempts at art, but to her delight and surprise he praised the drawing, and hung it on the studio wall.

For the most part, however, Deverell required Lizzie sit still in the pose as Viola, while he painted her in companionable silence. As she sat, she daydreamed, and her dreams became more immediate, as if she could almost touch the future that she imagined. What at first had seemed an impossibility, that she should be admired or accepted by these refined and talented people, became more real every day. The sudden sense of opportunity was intoxicating.

The days wore on in this agreeable way, until one afternoon when Miss Deverell excused herself to fetch the tea. Deverell and Lizzie were left alone, and Deverell gestured to her to relax her pose.

"Would you like to see the painting? I'm almost finished."

Lizzie walked over to the easel. She studied the painting closely, feeling Deverell's eyes on her. It depicted a medieval garden, with three figures lounging on a stone bench: a melancholy man in court dress, a jester in tights and a pointed hat with bells, and Viola disguised as the pageboy, for which Lizzie was sitting. Behind them, a crowd of musicians and merrymakers danced across a broad green lawn. Delicate vines climbed a stone column and sunlight fell across the grass in ribbons of light and pockets of deep shade. The brocades of the clothing were painted in painstaking detail, each brushstroke weaving together rich shades of crimson and gold. Of the main figures, only the pageboy was unfinished.

As she looked at the painting, Deverell told her its story: "The setting is Illyria. There has been a shipwreck, and Viola washes up alone on a foreign shore. The man in the center, who you will notice bears a striking resemblance to myself, is the Duke. Viola, in order to protect herself in this unknown land, dresses as a boy and enters the Duke's service as his page. A tangled affair of the heart ensues: The Duke is lovesick for the Countess, who refuses all suitors; Viola acts as their messenger, and in the process falls in love with the Duke herself. But she cannot reveal her love, for the Duke thinks that she is a boy."

The painting was done in such detail that it seemed to Lizzie as if she were looking into a mirror; she leaned forward, lovely and eager, and gazed at Deverell, who stared off into the distance, thinking of another. But of course it wasn't a mirror, and she wasn't in love with Deverell. Was she? She tried on the idea, as if it were a costume: Could she fall in love with him?

He was handsome and kind, and his family was well-off. Lizzie placed her hand over her heart to see if its beat quickened, but it was hard to tell. She felt like Viola, washed up in a strange land, unsure of her bearings.

"The third figure," Deverell said, "is the Duke's Fool. The Duke has ordered him to sing a song to relieve the torment of his unanswered love for the Countess. It's a melancholy scene—each figure suffers from love unrequited, and only the Fool is happy—as is the case so often in life, I'm afraid. But don't worry, it all works out in the end, somehow, and Viola marries her Duke."

"A happy ending," Lizzie said, "for such an unlikely pair. If only Shakespeare were the author of all matters of the heart."

For once, Deverell was the one who blushed. He looked like he was about to speak, and Lizzie didn't need to put her hand to her heart to know that it was beating quickly now. But the bang of the door caused them both to startle, and become flustered. Lizzie looked up to see the Fool, come to life.

A young man stood in the doorway, a look of sly amusement on his face that showed that he had been watching them. He was lightly built, with dark curls and an impish grin. His clothes looked well made, but rumpled, and mud had been allowed to cake about the bottom of his coat. He had an olive complexion, which gave him a continental appearance, and his eyes were gray, very close to Lizzie's in color. But though they were gray, they were bright and lively, catching the light as he glanced around, and changing quickly from near transparency to the color of coal. Right now they rested on Lizzie. "I would be careful what you wish for," he said. "Shakespeare was just as often the author of tragedies as of comedies. I don't know that I would entrust my own heart to him."

"Rossetti. You came." Deverell's tone was cheerful, if a bit thin. He made a sweeping gesture. "Behold, Miss Elizabeth Siddal, my model, my muse, my Viola, and a real stunner! Didn't I tell you that she was a beauty? Hair woven by the gods and skin to make a pearl jealous."

Lizzie knew that she should be mortified at the suggestion that Deverell had discussed her in such terms with other men. She could hear her mother's warning, that she must not become the subject of gossip. But her mother's cautions, much like the shabby parlor in Southwark in which they had been offered, seemed very far away right now. How could she chastise Deverell for his compliments, ridiculous though they seemed?

"Miss Siddal, allow me to introduce Mr. Dante Rossetti, painter, poet, and, as I'm sure you've noticed, your fellow model for my painting. Rossetti was kind enough to sit for my Fool, and one could not find a more perfect model."

"Slight praise!" cried Rossetti. "But I see that you were right on the mark regarding Miss Siddal." He stepped forward and took Lizzie's hand. He looked straight into her eyes, and then bowed his head and touched his lips to her hand.

Lizzie was unused to such displays; a simple bow usually sufficed in her circle. She pulled her hand back, eliciting an amused grin from Rossetti. Lizzie laughed to hide her embarrassment. She wanted to ignore him, as she would any insolent young man in the shop, but she didn't want to seem cold. She settled for a slight nod of her head. She may have been taught to mimic the manners of these people, but she didn't yet feel that she understood them.

Rossetti cocked his head and looked at Lizzie. "But surely we've met before." He squinted, as if he was trying to place her. "Though I can hardly imagine that I should forget a beauty such as yourself."

"I don't believe so. Unless you happen to frequent the shops in Cranbourne Alley." But she, too, was struck by the feeling that she had seen him before.

"No, no. I've no reason at the moment to call upon the ladies' shops at the moment. Though I hope now that may change."

Under Rossetti's stare, Lizzie was suddenly very aware that she was wearing nothing but britches and a thin tunic. She lowered her eyes and turned away from him.

Deverell watched Lizzie and Rossetti with growing dismay. "Miss Siddal is quite an artist in her own right," he said, abruptly changing the subject. "She's written some verses to amuse us, and a few of the students at the Academy could do worse than to look to the simple lines of her sketches."

"I have no doubt at all that Miss Siddal has talent," Rossetti said, not taking his eyes off her. "I can see an artistic soul behind her eyes. I'd love to see her work."

"Mr. Deverell is too kind," Lizzie said. "They're really just a few scribbles to pass the time."

"Then perhaps some other time. You really must meet my sister, Christina. She is a poetess, and I know that she is always pleased to meet a kindred spirit."

Lizzie looked out the window to see if Miss Deverell might be returning with the tea. Rossetti made her unaccountably nervous, and she hoped that Mary would return quickly. Deverell always treated her much like his own sister. But Rossetti was different, and her cheeks burned from the warmth of his greeting.

Rossetti stood behind the canvas, pretending to study Deverell's painting while he admired its model. Despite Deverell's enthusiastic descriptions, Rossetti was completely unprepared for the glorious woman before him. She seemed to be from another age, as if she had sprung to life from an antique painting of an Italian saint. Seated before the window, her hair cast a slight golden glow in the afternoon sun, like a halo. She could not have been more perfect if he had sculpted her from marble with his own hands. Deverell claimed that he had found the perfect Viola, but this girl was far too beautiful to pose as some lovesick page. She was clearly meant to sit for the great heroines of history and myth, and Rossetti vowed to paint her as a queen. The moment that Deverell was finished, he would claim her for himself.

"Miss Siddal, has anyone ever told you that you were surely crafted by the gods in order to be painted?" Rossetti looked at Lizzie, expecting to see the glow of pleasure that such compliments normally elicited from his models. But instead, Lizzie's face fell.

"Please don't, Mr. Rossetti," she said, once more looking down at the floor. The flattery of the two men had reached such a peak that she suddenly realized that they must be in jest. "No doubt you think that because of my circumstances I am simple, or perhaps silly, but I assure you that is not the case. I imagine these false compliments turn many girls' heads, but mine will not be among them."

"You're right," Rossetti said, so stridently that it took both Lizzie and Deverell by surprise. "Your beauty is beyond my poor powers of description, and you are right to be angry. But if you don't believe that yours is a beauty for the ages, you underestimate yourself."

The force of his words struck Lizzie, and she wondered if he was serious, and if it could be true. Was this the thing that she had always been waiting for? Was she really meant to inspire great artists? Her head buzzed with the possibility, but the very allure of the idea felt dangerous. She didn't know what to say, and she was grateful when Rossetti at last turned his gaze from her and began to examine Deverell's painting in earnest.

"Ah, the lovesick Duke. I think that you've got his features right, my friend. He looks absolutely, miserably in love. Pining for the ideal, unknowable Countess, when right before him is a lovely young girl, completely taken with him. But alas, he's blind to her charms." He glanced up at Lizzie and then looked back down at the canvas. "And how goes the young page, the lovesick Viola?"

Deverell nodded to Lizzie, signaling that she could take a break from her pose. With Rossetti in the studio the conversation was sure to flow, but the painting would have to wait. "I'm happy with the hands, and I'm on my way to getting the face just right. It's the hair that troubles me. Miss Siddal has such wonderful auburn locks, just what I wanted. They're an inspiration, but I'm having trouble capturing them on the canvas."

"May I?" Rossetti grabbed a clean brush. It was common practice for the friends to work on one another's pictures as a favor when frustration or boredom set in. But Deverell didn't look pleased.

"Oh, no. It's really not necessary. I'll make a fresh start of it tomorrow."

"It's no problem at all." Indifferent to Deverell's protests, Rossetti began to add paints to a clean porcelain tablet. "It would be my pleasure."

"Yes, I'm sure it would," Deverell muttered. He ceded his place in front of the canvas to Rossetti with a reluctant sigh. If he was angry, he kept his face smooth. To do otherwise would have caused a scene, and implied a claim on Miss Siddal that he did not have.

Rossetti set out his colors and began to test them on a spare bit of canvas. "Miss Siddal, if you could do me the great favor of resuming your pose?"

Lizzie looked to Deverell, who nodded his head. She sat down, smoothed her hair, and stretched her neck like a swan. She let her eyes go wide and dreamy, and folded her hands delicately in front of her. She took all of the stirred-up emotion of the last few moments and channeled it into her character—inhabiting Viola's distress and longing so completely that her body seemed to strain forward even as she sat perfectly still, yearning for the Duke, inviting his notice.

Rossetti began to work. He applied the paint with feathery strokes; first a rich dark brown, next yellow, the paint the color of honey. For the slight curls at the brow, he used a lighter brown and a deep red. He did not mix the colors on the palette. Instead he used small, light brushstrokes to layer the paint directly onto the canvas. He looked up at Lizzie again, made a few more strokes, and then stepped back to allow the paint to set.

While he waited, he picked up a tattered copy of *Twelfth Night* from the table, which was opened to the scene depicted in the painting. "Would you allow me, Miss Siddal, to entertain you with a little poetry while you maintain that lovely pose?"

"That would be very kind." Though she often recited poetry herself, Lizzie had never had a man read it to her, other than her father.

"Then I'll read to you the words of Viola, who loved the Duke, and sought to teach him a lesson about the depths of a woman's love. Here, the fair Viola concocts a story of a lovesick sister to disguise her own feelings for the Duke."

Paging through to the speech, Rossetti began to read:

She never told her love,
But let concealment, like a worm i' the bud
Feed on her damask cheek. She pined in thought,
And with a green and yellow melancholy
She sat like Patience on a monument,
Smiling at grief. Was not this love indeed?
We men may say more, swear more, but indeed
Our shows are more than will; for still we prove
Much in our vows, but little in our love.

Rossetti recited with feeling, and Lizzie was moved. "It's true," she said. "Men will write a thousand words about a girl whose face they have only glimpsed in the street. But for all that passion, having hardly known her, they are so easily caught by the next passing fancy. But a woman, once she loves, is true to that love, whatever may come."

"I must defer to your expertise," Rossetti said. "But in defense of our sex, I can point to the example of the poet Dante Alighieri, whose sonnets I'm translating. His famous love for the lady Beatrice was no passing fancy. Having seen her once, it consumed him completely, and transcended even her early and tragic death."

"In that sad story, I shall have to defer to you," Lizzie replied. "But is it not easier to love one who has died young and beautiful, than one who has grown old and nagging by your side?"

Rossetti stared. "Perhaps that's true of mere mortals, but I can't believe that there is a purer love than the passion that inspired Dante's great verses." Then he smiled, trying to take Lizzie's words in the spirit of jest in which they were intended. "But what does youth know of such things? Nothing that you could say would convince me that a shining beauty such as your own could ever be tarnished, even by the passing of time."

"We are only servants to such beauty," Deverell added, clearly not wanting to be left out. "Plying our trade in poor reflections of its glory."

Lizzie's heart was racing; the attention of Rossetti and Deverell was exhilarating, almost overwhelming. For one moment she felt the strangeness of her position, sitting alone with two young men, talking of love. But Deverell and Rossetti seemed entirely at ease; why should she borrow trouble? It was far easier to enjoy their company than to doubt their motives. She turned her profile to its best advantage and smiled.

Rossetti turned back to the easel, but he couldn't resist one more riposte. "If you're interested in the subject of love, I would be honored to send you a copy of my translations of Dante's poems. Perhaps they'll change your mind."

"I'd like that very much." The offer was bold, but Lizzie told herself that there was no harm in accepting his gift. Deverell, she noticed, was looking more and more deflated since the arrival of his friend.

"Rossetti, don't you have some work of your own that you need to be getting back to?" Deverell asked. "I want to finish before I lose the light. I think that you've made an excellent start of the hair, and I'm sure that I can take it from here."

"As you wish." Rossetti nodded to Deverell and took Lizzie's hand once more before he left. This time she offered it readily, and she did not draw back when he kissed it.

CHAPTER 5

Rossetti left Deverell's studio full of energy and feeling that he was greeting a new day. It was a welcome change. The last few months had not been productive; he had been distracted, and had made little headway in his painting. He couldn't blame a lack of enthusiasm—he often felt the impulse to write or to paint. But the brilliant idea of one moment often felt stale and trite the next, and he would abandon one work for the next, leaving behind him a trail of couplets lacking quatrains and plans for paintings that would never see a gloss of paint. And then there was the doubt, eating away at him as he saw others from the Academy gain fame and success, while he did nothing of consequence. But now that doubt receded, a ghost at dawn.

The simple act of being near Miss Siddal filled him with the desire to paint. The urge to create, which raged like a storm inside him, stopped its pointless churning and thrashing. He felt it gather strength and form itself into a powerful tide, pulling him toward his purpose: He would paint real beauty. He would paint Miss Siddal.

If destiny was real, he thought loftily, then his was now defined. He would paint her as Beatrice, and as a hundred other beauties, real and imagined. His mind, so recently a blank canvas, was now brimming with images: a narrow alley of medieval Florence, a hidden window seat beneath jewel-toned stained glass, a candlelit chapel. And through each of these settings floated a woman with the radiance of an angel and the bearing of a noblewoman. He could see her as clearly as if she still stood before him: white skin with a hint of rose, and wide eyes like the pools of a shaded courtyard. He was not an overly religious man, but he couldn't help but feel that the sight of Miss Siddal had been a moment of grace.

Yet perhaps the most amazing thing was that she had appeared completely unaware of her effect. She had none of the showy confidence of the ladies who populated London's drawing rooms. She seemed untouched by the world, above its vanities and desires, and he was as dazzled by her innocence as by her beauty.

Deverell had called her his "muse," and Rossetti seized upon the word. Until this moment, he had always used it half in mocking—it never seemed to apply to the models whom he knew, who laughed too loudly and wore too much rouge on their cheeks. But seeing Miss Siddal, he finally felt that he understood how the quality of a poem or painting might depend not only upon the skill of its author, but also upon the beauty of the muse.

His mind still on Miss Siddal, he walked up Kew Road, hardly noticing the stately homes that he passed, or the snug cottages that replaced them as he drew nearer to the high street. In this quiet suburban quarter the road was no busier than a country lane. He waited for a carriage to go by and then crossed the street, cutting through a churchyard where March's first daffodils and crocuses were just beginning to push up among the gravestones. The view opened onto Kew Green, where a few boys were shouting and running after a kite. Rossetti paused for a moment to watch them.

He thought of going straight to his studio, to begin sketching Miss Siddal while her image was fresh in his mind. But he had promised her a copy of his translations. He would go to Charlotte Street instead, to his study at his mother's house, where the sonnets lay on his desk, unfinished. The moment that they were complete, he could use their delivery as an excuse to see Miss Siddal again.

He took off toward the high street and climbed aboard the first omnibus he saw. The open-air seats on the roof were already full, and he had to take a seat inside with the women and children. The driver tapped the horses and the carriage lurched forward, joining the traffic flowing into the city. Someone had left a newspaper on the seat, and he paged through it, happy for the distraction. But the whiskered man across from him took this as an invitation to discuss politics, and he soon gave up trying to read. The carriage stopped frequently to load and unload passengers, and soon it was full of quarrelling children and their indifferent nannies. He fidgeted in his seat until they finally reached the corner of Hyde Park, where he stepped over the boots and skirts of the other passengers and leapt from the vehicle. He tossed a shilling up to the driver and set off, meaning to walk the rest of the way to Charlotte Street.

He entered the park down a wide alley of elms and passed through an iron gate onto a narrow path. Two young ladies in white fur muffs and silk gowns walked by, and Rossetti made them a deep bow and tipped his hat. The girls giggled and hurried on, and a woman pushing a baby pram shook her head and smiled. He made her a bow as well, and then continued on his way. The afternoon sun warmed the path, and the scent of fresh earth tempted his senses with the promise of spring. He inhaled deeply.

The path joined with a larger road, and Rossetti fell in among the other fashionable Londoners who paraded slowly down the road, enjoying the long-awaited sun and the chance to see, and be seen. Gentlemen on horseback and ladies in open carriages went by at a slow trot, nodding and waving to each other as they passed. Everyone was in their best dress: the women in the newest styles from Paris and the men in silk waistcoats and hats. The road led toward the Serpentine Lake, and small boys raced toward its edge, clutching wooden sailboats and fishing rods under their arms. Their sisters, some of them in long skirts for the first time this spring, looked on with envy, but walked primly alongside their mothers.

Rossetti followed the road toward the half-finished structure of the Crystal Palace, which was rising quickly beside the lake in anticipation of the Great Exhibition, due to open the next spring. It was a massive building, constructed almost entirely from iron and glass, and it sprung from the fields of Hyde Park like a glittering mirage. The central gallery, still just an iron skeleton, soared skyward like the transept of a great cathedral, but a small army of workmen was busy affixing thousands of sheets of plate glass to its grid. The glass shimmered in the afternoon light, and Rossetti joined a crowd of onlookers who stood marveling at it.

Turning away, he continued down the path and across the Serpentine Bridge. Under the spell of his own thoughts, he failed to notice the approach of two familiar forms until a friendly hand caught him by the shoulder.

"Rossetti! Hello! You must really be a poet at heart. Didn't you see us waving?"

"Hunt, Ford." Rossetti nodded. "You've caught me daydreaming, I'm afraid. I was enjoying the air before I lock myself up to work."

Ford Madox Brown, who at thirty was a few years older than Rossetti and Hunt, was a fellow painter who often served as a mentor and tutor to them. Ford hadn't officially joined the Brotherhood—he was already an established, if often impoverished, painter—but the style of his work was an inspiration for their methods. Ford looked amused by the genuine surprise that his approach had elicited. "Dante Rossetti choosing work over the pleasures of a fine afternoon? I never thought that I'd see the day. Either your model must be very beautiful, or the bill collectors must be at your heels."

Rossetti blushed, and Ford gave him a searching look. He turned to Holman Hunt with a devilish smile. "Is it possible that Rossetti's eyes are glowing a little too brightly to be chalked up entirely to the fresh air and a brisk walk? If I didn't know him so well, I might be inclined to think that he is in love."

"I doubt it," said Hunt. "Rossetti is too great a flirt to fall for any one girl. Perhaps he's in love with a design for a painting. Or the undertaking of some new literary circular. It's grand ideas that Rossetti truly loves."

"Perhaps," said Ford, but he didn't sound entirely convinced.

Rossetti laughed. "I swear to you both that my heart still belongs to Art; she's not had a worthy contender yet." He said nothing about Miss Siddal. With Deverell blabbing around about what a stunner she was, the other artists of their group were bound to find out about her without his help. If he wished to secure her for himself, he would do better to keep mum. Besides, Hunt and Ford were in a joking mood, and Rossetti had no wish to have his feelings for Miss Siddal made a subject of their jibes.

Ford gave Rossetti one more close look and then shrugged, letting the matter drop. "If you were in love, you would be in good company. I'm afraid that we've completely lost Hunt to his newest conquest, the barmaid Annie Miller."

Ford's tone was light, but Hunt flushed with anger at his words. "I told you," he snapped, "not to call her the barmaid. She's a lady of uncommon kindness and beauty, and if she's had to work for her living, it's no fault of her own. She's lived in hard circumstances."

"I didn't mean anything by it," Ford sighed, turning to Rossetti. "At any rate, Hunt's *lady of uncommon kindness and beauty,* most certainly not a barmaid, has been sitting for him for his latest painting. Have you seen the sketches? She's the girl with the great head of golden hair. She's charmed him completely and stolen his heart. I don't think that he shall ever get it back to give to his next model."

Rossetti smiled, thinking vaguely of some sketches that he'd seen lying about Hunt's studio. The girl was no match for Miss Siddal.

"Ford!" Hunt barked. "This one is different. I'm determined to make her my wife, after her education has been looked to, so you'd do best to be careful of what you say about her."

"You mean you'll marry her after she stops dropping her aitches?" Ford laughed, and then, seeing that his friend was in no mood to joke, he put a conciliatory hand on his shoulder. "I'm sorry, Hunt. Miss Miller really is quite lovely, and friendly as can be. You couldn't have picked a nicer girl. I'm sure that all the members of the Brotherhood will be having her to sit before long. But don't leave her alone with Rossetti—if he isn't already in love, he certainly looks ripe for the picking."

Hunt flushed again, and this time it was Rossetti who laid a calming hand on his friend's arm. "Come, friends," he said, changing the subject. "I'm just on my way to Charlotte Street to work on my translations. Walk with me and I'll tell you about a plan I have for a magazine, to be published monthly, which will showcase the works of the members of the Brotherhood and our friends."

"I told you that it would be some new plan," Hunt said. "I

suppose that we had better go along and hear all about it. No doubt we will all be caught up in it before long. Who can resist Rossetti's schemes?"

He threw his arm around Rossetti's shoulders and the three friends resumed their walk, leaving the touchy subject of love behind, and speaking instead of their work as they made their way down the path and out of the park.

Rossetti burst into the parlor of his family's small but respectable home in Charlotte Street and threw his jacket onto a chair. His sister, Christina, was sitting at a writing desk in the corner of the room, her head bent over her work. She had dark hair, simply parted, and a naturally serious face, made more so by her devotion to her poetry and her church. But when she saw her brother she smiled, and she was pretty.

Rossetti strode over to her, swept her from her seat, and began to waltz her around the room. Christina threw back her head and laughed, hardly able to keep up with his steps.

"Dante!" she cried as he released her. "You're certainly in a grand mood! To what do we owe the honor of your visit?"

He'd been staying at his studio more and more lately, and he knew that he was missed at home. He depended upon his sister's great affection for him to keep her from scolding him for his rare visits. "Why, only my wish to see my darling sister. Is Mother at home?"

"No, I'm afraid that she's out on a visit." Christina settled onto a divan and patted the seat next to her.

"All the better, then." Rossetti sat beside her. "I'll have you all to myself, and you can tell me how your writing is getting along. By the way, Ford sends his compliments on your last contribution to *Athenaeum*. He said that it was quite as good as anything you've ever published, and I agree wholeheartedly."

Christina glowed under her older brother's praise. "I would love to have your opinion on my new sonnets."

"It would be my pleasure. And I may have another reader for you. Another student of poetry—perhaps a protégée."

"Indeed? I always love to meet your friends."

"Her name is Elizabeth Siddal. She's modeling for Deverell at the moment, and he says that she shows a great aptitude for drawing and verse. I met her today and I think that with your guidance, perhaps her talents could be encouraged."

"Oh yes?" Christina's tone grew more formal. "And has she published?"

"No, I don't believe so. But be kind, dear sister. This girl has not had your advantages; her origins appear quite humble. But she has a very artistic manner, and an excellent knowledge of poetry. Deverell found her working at a millinery, but you would never know it. She was exceptionally beautiful—I'm going to paint her as Beatrice." Caught up in his thoughts of Miss Siddal, he was oblivious to Christina's fading smile and darkening brow.

"I see. How charming."

"I told her that you would be very pleased to meet her. She is really more of a lady than the usual model, and I think that it would set her at ease if you could take her under your wing. Deverell's sister is quite taken with her. I have no doubt that you will be as well. I'll bring her around to the house to visit as soon as she is free."

Christina fingered the heavy cross at her neck. "A model? You want to bring her here, to visit with Mother and me? Dante, you can't believe that we can receive such a person!"

"Don't be a snob. Where's your Christian charity, dear sister?"

Christina was quiet for a moment. Then she gave Rossetti a resigned smile. "Perhaps it would be best if I came to see her at your studio."

"Yes, that's just the thing. I have a number of sketches that I'd like to show you anyway. Once you meet her, you'll love her just as I do."

"Love her? Dante, you've only just met her!"

"No, of course," Rossetti laughed, embarrassed by his ardor. "I only meant that you're sure to see the same promise in her that I do." He kissed his sister on the cheek and rose from the divan, cutting the visit short. "I'm off to work in my study. Can you have tea sent up?"

"Of course," Christina said, glancing over at her unfinished work on the desk. "I'll bring it up myself. It's the maid's day off."

But Rossetti didn't hear her—he was already on the stairs, eager to begin work on his translations.

Dante Rossetti was not the only man determined to court Lizzie with poetry. Deverell, who didn't like being upstaged by Rossetti, had taken a page from his friend's book and purchased a little volume of Alfred Tennyson's poems as a gift for her. He presented it on the last day that she came to sit for him.

He handed her the book, not quite meeting her eye. "A little token of my appreciation for your help. It's a volume by our new poet laureate. It's not his most recent work, but there is a poem in it that reminds me of you."

Lizzie glanced down at the book, which was bound in soft leather and felt heavy in a satisfying way. "I very much admire the works of Tennyson," she murmured. Without opening the book, she began to recite:

> *There she weaves by night and day*
> *A magic web with colours gay.*
> *She has heard a whisper say,*
> *A curse is on her if she stay*
> *To look down to Camelot.*
> *She knows not what the curse may be,*
> *And so she weaveth steadily,*
> *And little other care hath she,*
> *The Lady of Shalott.*

Deverell looked disappointed. "You already have it."

"No!" Lizzie laughed. "Certainly not. We hardly have any books at all, I'm afraid." She stopped, anxious that her words had revealed too much. But Deverell didn't seem embarrassed by her admission, and so she went on: "I first read Tennyson's poems only by chance. One morning I unwrapped a pat of butter for my mother, and the newspaper that it came in was printed with one of his verses. I read it right there on the kitchen floor, and ever since I've collected his works whenever I can. I cut them out of my father's magazines and paste them into a little book."

Deverell smiled. "How sweet you must have been. I can just imagine the young Miss Siddal hiding away her book of poems."

"And now I have a beautiful copy of them to treasure. I'm very grateful."

It looked for a moment as if Deverell meant to take her in his arms and test out her gratitude. But he stayed put behind his easel.

Lizzie felt relief tinged by disappointment. Her month in the studio had passed like a pleasant dream. For a few weeks she had played a small part in the creation of something beautiful. And Walter Deverell, with his excellent manners and kind words, had treated her as if she belonged there.

She swallowed, realizing how hard it would now be to return to the long hours at the millinery, to once again spend her days fending off the obnoxious young men in the shop and enduring the silly talk of the other girls. And despite Mrs. Tozer's predictions, it didn't seem that her time here would lead to anything else. If Deverell had any real feelings for her, the gift of the book of poetry had been the first and only definite sign, and he had said nothing about having her come to sit again. It would have been better, she thought churlishly, if he had never asked her in the first place—then she wouldn't have known what she was missing.

As if reading her thoughts, Deverell said, "You remember my friend, Mr. Rossetti, I'm sure. He mentioned that he might want you for a painting. If your employer can spare you again, of course."

"Did he?" Lizzie smiled. If Rossetti were to ask her to sit, she might be able to linger a little longer in this dream. Though whether her mother and Mrs. Tozer would allow it was another matter. Rossetti had projected none of the stodgy respectability that the Deverells possessed. "Is he any good? He was very forward. I don't know if I would be quite as easy in his studio as I am in yours. But of course I'd be honored to sit for him, if he asked me."

Deverell gave Lizzie a close look and then turned back to his canvas. "It might be best to take a chaperone. And you'd do well to ask for your wages up front," he added, with a peevish note. "Dante is always short of funds."

"Is that so?" Lizzie had assumed that all the young men in their circle were well off, or at least had good expectations. "But he chooses to paint, rather than take up some more steady profession?"

"That was unkind of me. I shouldn't have spoken so of a friend. Rossetti's family is very respectable. I didn't mean to imply that he would leave any debt unpaid."

Lizzie nodded, feeling reassured. It didn't occur to her that a respectable family might, like her own, be hanging on by a thread to pretensions that their accounts could only barely support.

Deverell stepped back from his canvas to get a better view of his work. As he did so, he winced and grunted with pain.

"Are you well?" Lizzie rose to her feet. Deverell's face was pale, and his cheeks burned as if he had a fever. "I'll get your sister."

"No, no, please don't bother, I'm fine," Deverell muttered, making his way over to a sofa and lowering himself gently into a seat. "I'm just tired. I've spent too many hours this week bent over the canvas." He looked at the painting and then out the window, to the garden beyond. "It's very important to me that it be accepted for the Royal Academy Exhibition this spring. I think that it might be my first really good painting. And of course, I have you to thank. I wouldn't have had my Viola without you. I hope that you will accept my humble thanks, and come to sit for me again soon."

"I would love to. These last days have been the most pleasant of my life."

As Deverell rose to fetch Lizzie's cloak, he winced again. "I'd better go lie down. Please, allow me to call you a cab. It's late, and I know that you have a long ride home."

Deverell rose from the couch and took Lizzie's arm, escorting her to the front of the house and calling for a hansom. When the cab pulled up, he handed Lizzie up onto the seat and paid the driver. Lizzie turned to wave, and Deverell stood on the curb and watched her go.

It was her first ride in a cab. The expense had always been too much for her, but tonight she was one of those lucky women being spirited through the streets in ease and comfort. She drew the blanket over her lap as the cab raced through the darkening streets of Kew, passing quickly down its broad avenues.

As they drew nearer to the city, the streets narrowed and filled with carriages and carts. The London fog lay thicker here, and coal smoke swirled outside the windows of the cab, leaving only the dark outline of rooftops visible against the sky, and rendering the figures that darted past in the street little more than their own shadows. But Lizzie was safe and snug inside the cab, a bubble of luxury impervious to the cold night and the crowded streets. It was quite a change from the omnibus, where one was pinched in among so many other travelers. It was, Lizzie knew, just another small extravagance of which some in London thought nothing.

Lizzie's cab traveled swiftly toward Blackfriars Bridge and clattered over the muddy cobblestones of Kent Place. When the driver opened the door, she saw that she was in luck: Her father had closed up the shop early, and there would be no questions about where she had come from, and how she had been able to afford a cab.

She found her father and several of the younger children gathered before a warm fire. The room was tidy, with flowers in a vase and bits of lace over the tables. But the furniture was shabby, and the walls were blackened by smoke that had never quite come clean, despite repeated scrubbing. She knew that it was her eyes, and not the room, that had changed, and that she should be grateful for what they had. But her feeling of distaste clung stubbornly, like the soot from the fire.

She could hear her mother and Lydia preparing supper in the kitchen, and she put on an apron and went in to help. Neither woman looked up at her as she entered. Mrs. Siddal threw an oilcloth over the table and Lydia set out the dishes, banging them as she put them down.

Lizzie was still giddy from Deverell's compliments, and from the unexpected treat of the cab ride. She hummed as she helped Lydia to set out the dishes. "It's certainly dreary in here tonight! Are we preparing for a funeral or for supper?"

"Lizzie!" her mother scolded. "Such crassness may pass for conversation at the Deverells' house, but it certainly will not be tolerated here."

"I'm sorry, Mama. I didn't mean anything by it." She paused and looked at Lydia, who avoided her gaze. Something wasn't right—there were no smells of cooking, and her mother's face looked pinched and white. Lizzie walked over to the stove and peered in. The coals weren't lit. "I thought that we were going to use my extra earnings this week for a roast! We've had nothing but toast and drippings all week."

"There will be no roast."

Lizzie looked back into the parlor and frowned as she watched her father read to the children. "Why is Father home early? I thought that he took on extra help for the order from the wharf house. Why isn't he in the shop?"

Her mother sighed and sat down at the table. "He lost the order. And with it the money for our rent. And there are bills, solicitors' bills . . ."

Lizzie dropped into the chair next to her. Her mother's face was pale, and her usually perfect posture drooped, as if all the air had gone out of her.

"Oh, Mama," Lizzie said, putting her hand over her mother's. "What will we do?"

"I'll tell you what we'll do first," Lydia burst out. She opened the sideboard and gathered Mr. Siddal's legal papers into her arms. Then she strode over to the hearth, ready to throw them in.

Mrs. Siddal jumped to her feet. "No! You mustn't! Your father will be livid!"

Lydia stood irresolutely by the fire and looked at Lizzie.

"Don't look at me to stop you. I say throw the whole lot in. They'll do us more good as kindling than they will as a lawsuit."

"That will solve nothing," Mrs. Siddal said, regaining her composure. "Now, all's not lost. We can use Lizzie's extra wages for the rent, and the lawyers can be put off. But there will be no little extras, I'm afraid. We'll all have to make do with what we have for a bit. I know I can depend on you."

Lizzie bit her lip. She'd been planning to ask her mother for a few shillings for a new shawl. Now, as always, everything would have to be spent on the bare necessities. She thought of the tea she had just taken at Deverell's studio. There had been a tiered tray of sweets and sandwiches, strawberry preserves and clotted cream for the scones, and a plate of fresh fruits. It had been enough for a dozen people to enjoy, and it had been served to just the three of them. And now there was to be nothing but toast and tea for the children for dinner. And they were lucky to have even that. Without Lizzie's extra wages, it might have been worse. But there was nothing that she could do. "Yes, Mama," she said with resignation. "You may depend on us."

"Now, Lizzie, is there any chance of your sitting for Mr. Deverell again? He paid you very well."

She sighed. "Not at the moment, I'm afraid. He's all done with the picture."

"And I don't suppose," her mother began, her tone delicate, "that he gave you any indication of wanting to see you for any other reason?"

She paused. The book of Tennyson was in her cloak pocket. But it was hardly a declaration of love—it could just as easily have been a parting gift as a sign of his affection. "No. He was very kind, but he gave me no reason to think that he wanted me for anything other than my red hair."

Mrs. Siddal turned, but not quickly enough to hide her disappointment. "Well, there's no reason to lose hope. He's a gentleman, after all, and he could hardly be expected to make any declarations to you while you were under his employment."

Lizzie didn't have to guess what her mother was thinking: If Lizzie could make a good marriage, it would solve many of their problems. One daughter married well meant that the others could be introduced into good society, and make advantageous matches of their own. And well-married daughters didn't need to be supported, and might even be depended upon to look after their parents. Lizzie was sorry that she didn't have anything more hopeful to tell her.

"There may be another artist," she said carefully. "I met him at the studio, and Mr. Deverell thought that he might ask me to model as well."

"A different painter?" Mrs. Siddal asked. "Do you know anything of his family? We must be careful."

"If the fate of the family is to rest on my shoulders," Lizzie snapped, "I can't very well turn down good work if a man's family isn't up to your high standards."

Mrs. Siddal looked near to tears, and Lizzie regretted her tone. "I'm sorry. Please don't worry, Mama. He's from the Royal Academy, and a gentleman as well. But he hasn't asked me to sit for him yet, so it's hardly worth fretting over."

"In the meantime, then, you'll have to go back to Mrs. Tozer's."

"Yes, Mother." But as she turned she muttered to herself, "But you might as well send me to a nunnery, for all the luck I'll have finding a husband in the back room of a bonnet shop."

When Lizzie returned to the shop the next morning, Jeannie Evans greeted her warmly, but the other girls stared at her and gave each other meaningful looks. Mrs. Tozer had done her best to keep Lizzie's absence discreet, but in the midst of so many girls, it was impossible to prevent all gossip. As usual, Lizzie ignored them and focused on her work. She had just finished trimming a bonnet when she looked up to see Jo, the new apprentice, approaching her with a nervous smile. Jo cleared her throat, and the other girls stopped working and watched them, waiting to see what might happen.

Lizzie regarded the apprentice from under raised brows. The girl was nervous, and had obviously been put up to something by her friends.

"Miss Siddal," she said. "Is it true that you've been married to one of the customers? That you . . . eloped?" She giggled and shot a glance back at the other girls to see if they were watching, which they were—work in the shop had nearly come to a stop.

Lizzie was shocked, but she let out a short, derisive laugh and leveled her haughtiest stare at the apprentice. Then she very deliberately reached for her bonnet frame and began to check the shape. She would not engage the impertinent girl. No good could possibly come from adding grist to the rumor mill.

"Well, that's what's been said, anyway," Jo continued. "That you ran off with a bloke and now he's left you, and you had to beg Mrs. Tozer for your place back."

At this, several of the girls began to giggle, their mouths hidden behind their hands. When Lizzie still didn't reply, Jo turned and walked sheepishly back to her seat, as if she suspected that she might somehow have become the object of the joke.

Lizzie kept her face calm, but she was breathing rapidly. If one of the new girls felt that she could treat her that way, the rumors must have been bad. Lizzie was worried. A reputation was such a fragile thing, and the other girls were bound to talk, as much out of boredom as out of any real viciousness.

"That's not it at all," said another one of the milliners, the plump girl who had never taken to Lizzie. "I have it on good authority that Miss Siddal 'as been sitting for an artist."

"Who told you that?" Lizzie snapped, surprised.

"It's true then, is it?" The girl looked up from her work with a smug smile. "I'd be very careful if I was you, Lizzie. Once a girl starts taking off 'er clothes for money, there's not a long way to go before she'll take money for anything. And I, for one, don't fancy working alongside that sort of girl."

All of the color drained from Lizzie's face. She had sat for Mr. Deverell as chastely as if she were his own sister, but her mother was right: It didn't matter what she did, only what people said. "I haven't the least idea what you're talking about. But you ought to pay more attention to your work." Lizzie pointed at the bonnet that the girl was working on. "You've made the seam crooked."

They stared at each other coldly, but said nothing further. The other girls, who had followed the exchange as high entertainment, turned back to their work when Mrs. Tozer appeared at the door, looking flushed.

"Miss Siddal!" she said, her voice high and strained. "Please come out to the counter at once. There is a customer here who wishes to speak with you."

At this the girls resumed their giggling. This was very unusual; Mrs. Tozer never fetched a girl by request. It was known that she didn't mind a little flirting in the showroom—it was good for business. But she was adamant that the young men not treat the shop like an open hunting ground. It was unseemly, to say the least. At the moment, however, a very insistent young man was at the counter, demanding to see Miss Siddal. He would not be put off, and Mrs. Tozer could not permit an unpleasant scene in the shop.

Lizzie stood and smoothed her dress and her hair. Surprised by her own agitation, she took a deep breath to calm her nerves. Perhaps Mr. Deverell was not finished with his painting after all, and had come to ask her to sit again. Her excitement outweighed the embarrassment that she felt at having the other girls' suspicions confirmed.

She went into the shop and looked around expectantly, but she saw no sign of Deverell. Instead, standing at the counter with his face full of expectation, was Mr. Rossetti.

"Good day, Miss Siddal," he said with a slight bow.

"Mr. Rossetti." She nodded and tried to keep her voice even. "I didn't expect to see you here. I rather thought that it might be Mr. Deverell." But she was not disappointed.

Her pleasure in their meeting was marred, however, as she watched him look around the shop. When they met in Deverell's studio, she had been able to imagine herself, if not exactly his equal, then at least a person of elegance and interest. She had, after all, been sitting for a portrait. But in the shop the modesty of her position was clear.

Rossetti, however, noticed nothing of Lizzie's discomfort. If he thought at all of her position, it was only that her noble features stood out all the more so in the humble setting of the shop. She had been on his mind constantly as he labored over his translations of Dante's sonnets. In his imagination she had grown more beautiful, and more modest, with each passing day. Now she appeared like a shining saint tending to the poor, or as the lovely Beatrice herself, promenading through the crowded streets of Florence. If her dress was simple, it only set into relief the delicate modeling of her face and her large gray eyes. She needed no adornment—her rich auburn hair was her crown. Such beauty spoke to him of inner depths of virtue and poetry—it must be only the blossom of an intricate and flawless system of roots. Though he had hardly met her, he felt that he already knew her.

Rossetti wanted to reach out and brush a loose curl of hair away from her face. He wanted to take her hand and lead her away from the shop without another word. But he resisted, denying himself this impulsive pleasure, and instead cleared his throat and pulled a package wrapped in brown paper from his pocket. "As I promised you. A translation of Dante's love poems, from *The New Life*."

"Thank you," Lizzie murmured, pleased that he had remembered. "You are so kind. I very much look forward to reading them."

They stood awkwardly for a moment, smiling at each other, but not speaking. Lizzie hated to end the interview, and she groped around for something to say. "And how does Mr. Deverell get along with his painting?" she asked.

"Deverell? I'm sure that he gets along fine. It's a very good painting; no doubt it will be accepted for the Exhibition this spring." He paused. "But I didn't come here to speak of Deverell's work. I'm afraid that my gift was not entirely unselfish. I had hoped that you might consent to come sit for me, for a painting based on one of the poems. Please say that you will."

Lizzie could feel the eyes of the other girls in the shop on her. There would be no denying the rumors now, if she were to say yes. "I don't know . . . I've already been away from the shop for several weeks."

Rossetti looked around as if he had just now realized that he was in a shop. Then he waved his hand impatiently, dismissing it from his notice. "Your beauty must be painted. You wouldn't deny me if you knew how important you will be to my work. Already you begin to inhabit my poems."

Lizzie laughed at Rossetti's excessive praise, but she was not immune to it. Why should she suffer for the small-mindedness of the other girls? The feeling of being watched by them now only made her answer more exhilarating. She glanced down at the poems in her hands. "How could I deny your request? I'm in your debt."

She glanced over at Mrs. Tozer, who glared back at her, clearly on the verge of turning the young man out of the shop. She jotted down her address on a scrap of wrapping paper and handed it to Rossetti. "If you send a note round with your address and the time, I will try to settle with Mrs. Tozer for a few more days off."

"I'm honored," Rossetti said, ignoring the red-faced proprietress. He made a small bow at the door of the shop. "I'll await your visit with bated breath."

Lizzie blushed and, avoiding Mrs. Tozer's eye, she gathered up the poems from Rossetti and hurried back to the workroom. Mrs. Tozer might be angry at the moment, but surely she could be reasoned with. After all, it had been her idea for Lizzie to try her hand at modeling.

She sat down and placed the packet of poems on her lap, unwrapping them and examining Rossetti's bold scrawl. She took no more notice of the muttered comments of the other girls than she would have of the wind whispering through the trees. For the rest of the afternoon she stole glances at the poems as she worked, silently mouthing their antique words. Her hands may have worked on the bonnets with practiced skill, but her mind was consumed by a fifteenth-century romance, the words of the poems an incantation, an invitation.

CHAPTER 6

Rossetti leaned out over the balcony of his studio in Chatham Place. The road below his window sat snug against the Thames, at places nearly spilling over its banks. A mass of carts and carriages surged up the narrow passage, keeping time with the rising tide, and crossed over Blackfriars Bridge, bound for the markets and offices of the city. The sound of the traffic floated up to him, but he barely noticed the pushing crowds below. They were nothing to him but a sea of bent heads and ordinary cares. His eyes were on the river, which shone like dull silver under the gray sky, a hazy mirror of the steeples and domes that lined its banks. If he squinted, he might have been gazing over the Arno from a Florentine palazzo.

His studio was located in an out-of-the-way corner south of the Thames, a good walk from his home in Charlotte Street. But any inconvenience was more than made up for by the painterly light and constantly changing view of the river, and it was an added pleasure when he discovered that his new model, the incomparable Miss Siddal, lived only a few minutes away in Southwark.

The first day that Lizzie came to sit for him, she arrived with his translations in her hands, and the poet's immortal words on her lips: "Here beginneth the new life."

Hearing her speak the line touched him as deeply as if she had laid a hand upon his heart, and it was all that he could do to usher

her in, an answering line playing silently on his own lips, though he did not dare to speak it aloud:

> *I felt a spirit of love begin to stir*
> *Within my heart, long time unfelt till then;*
> *And saw Love coming towards me, fair and fain . . .*

The memory of that first morning was still enough to cause his cheeks to burn. And to his surprise, the feeling did not fade. Her beauty was a fresh surprise to him each day, as if it were too great and too intricate in its detail to be committed to memory. It was an unsolvable puzzle that he worked at incessantly, trying to capture it in sketch after sketch, churned out with a single-minded devotion. At night, after she left, he asked himself whether she wasn't an apparition, called forth from an old painting by his imagination. In his dreams she was life breathed into a marble statue, a goddess who held the secret of fire in the flames of her hair.

Now Rossetti looked down into the street below, searching among the dusty bonnets for a glimpse of Lizzie's red hair. But the throng below pushed on, with no rose among its thorns. He was just turning away when a single upturned face in the crowd caught his eye. There was no mistaking her ivory skin and brightly trimmed bonnet. She held up her hand to shade her eyes as if she were searching among the windows for the one that belonged to him.

Rossetti waved, but she did not return his greeting. He waved again and then, realizing that she could not see him in the glare from the balcony windows, he continued to watch her, unobserved in his worship.

Lizzie separated herself from the bustle of Chatham Place and slipped into number 14. In the downstairs hall she stopped before the mirror to take off her bonnet and pinch her cheeks, which hardly needed the attention—they were already pink and glowing.

Satisfied, she started up the narrow stairs to the studio. She stepped carefully on the creaking boards, but before she reached the first landing she heard a door open above her. With a sigh she prepared herself for the appearance of the landlady, who had taken an unwelcome interest in her comings and goings over the last week.

Sure enough, Mrs. Wright was peering out from behind her door at the end of the hallway. She wore a plain black dress with a high neck, and her silver hair was twisted into a tight bun at the crown of her head. When she saw Lizzie, she glared at her with narrowed eyes, and her mouth puckered into a grimace. Like many older women of her sort, she had an active imagination for scandal, and an even greater fondness for voicing her disapproval. Lizzie knew that Mrs. Wright believed her to be Rossetti's mistress, or something worse.

Mrs. Wright's cold gaze wasn't the only humiliation that Lizzie had encountered on the stairs. A few other tenants had smirked and even leered at her as she made her way up to Rossetti's studio. She did her best to ignore them, but their looks stung. She knew that she had nothing to be ashamed of, that she was different from the other girls who modeled for artists, but the world did not generally make such fine distinctions.

Lizzie did her best to maintain her composure. "Good day, Mrs. Wright!" she called out with false cheer.

The landlady drew in her breath and returned Lizzie's greeting with a silent glower, and Lizzie bowed her head and hurried past. As she started up the next flight of stairs, she heard the old woman mutter, "If it weren't for the good rent that he pays," before the door shut with a bang.

The words cut Lizzie to the quick. She wondered, not for the first time, how exactly she had found herself here. Rossetti's studio was only a short walk from her home in Kent Place, and yet it was as alien to her as if she had sailed for a foreign land. She recalled with lingering shame how, on the first day that she sat for Deverell, his mother had led her around to the studio by the garden path without ever having asked her into the house. She had known, at that moment, where she stood. But the respectable domesticity of the studio, and the genteel company of Mary Deverell, had convinced her that there was nothing really untoward in sitting for an artist.

Rossetti's studio was different. It was a rented space, far from his mother's house, and on her first visit, Lizzie had been dismayed to find that there was no other lady present when she arrived. Rossetti had mentioned a sister, and Lizzie assumed that she would join them. But Rossetti appeared unconcerned by the situation, and Lizzie could think of no way to insist on a chaperone without implying that she could not trust him to behave as a gentleman. In the end she had decided not to make a fuss. She had lived her entire life under the stern gaze of one lady or another, after all, and she could not deny the appeal of the relative freedom of Rossetti's studio.

She tried to put the landlady's glare from her mind as she entered the studio. The room was lined with bookcases, filled to bursting with hundreds of volumes of poetry, history, and myths. Canvases were everywhere, leaning against tables and easels, and propped up on chairs. A desk in the corner was piled with sketches, and an entire table was devoted to glass pots of paint in an array of colors: cerulean blue for painting the sky on a perfect summer day, viridian green for the shoots of new leaves, and madder rose to tint pouting lips.

To a more sophisticated eye, the studio may have appeared humble. The room was large but cluttered, with yellowing wallpaper and an unmade bed that could be glimpsed in a side chamber. But to Lizzie it was like something from a novel—the Parisian garret of a romantic poet.

Lizzie glanced around the room, and dozens of her reflections stared back, her image captured over and over in the sketches that festooned the studio. Her face peered out from every wall: There she was reclining in the divan by the window; over there she rested her face on clasped hands. Piled on the mantel and the desk were still other Lizzies, some quickly drawn in charcoal, and others more detailed and shaded with jewel-toned strokes of watercolor. Rossetti never seemed to tire of drawing her, though Lizzie couldn't imagine what it was about her that so fascinated him.

And then she saw him, standing among the paintings with the confidence of a king among his subjects. He smiled and reached out his hand in greeting.

"Dante," she said, using his Christian name and giving him her hand to kiss. The gesture, which had at first embarrassed her, now felt more natural, just another part of the glamorous role that she took on when she entered the studio. "I feel as if I never left, with so many reflections here to greet me."

"If only you never did leave, I should never have to stop drawing."

Lizzie walked over to the divan by the window and threw herself onto it. If it were up to her, she never would leave, but some propriety and restraint must be maintained, and she didn't think Rossetti could be depended upon in that regard. She enjoyed playing at the sophisticated bohemian, but such games could only be taken so far. "If you never stopped drawing, you might never sleep or eat, and then what would become of you?" she asked.

"What sustenance do I need, other than your presence?"

"Do be serious for a moment!" she laughed. "You know that your habits are irregular enough to begin with. Has that horrid landlady been bringing up your meals?"

Rossetti sat down beside her on the divan. He did not quite touch her, but Lizzie blushed at his closeness. "You're a dear to worry, but there's no need. I've been taking my suppers with the Brotherhood, and I could hardly be called a starving artist."

Whatever secrecy the members of the Brotherhood had sworn to in the excitement of the moment had in practice been loosely applied. Whispers of its existence had spread out to trusted friends, and Rossetti had wasted no time in telling the story to Lizzie, and recounting his own speech in particular detail.

Lizzie smiled, happy to be in on the secret of the Brotherhood. "How are the plans for the literary circular coming on?"

Rossetti became serious. He was always serious when he spoke of his art. Lizzie liked to watch the way emotion passed over his features, his face as changeable as the spring sky beyond the balcony doors.

"It goes to the printer tomorrow. I've put in a poem, and we've gathered a few essays that should begin to shape our ideas for the public. But the true test of the Brotherhood's fate will be the upcoming exhibitions. I'm submitting my painting of the Virgin Mary, modeled on my sister, Christina, and Deverell is sending in his painting of you as Viola. Did he write to you? No? Oh, well, no doubt he will. Millais also has something ready to submit. This is our chance to put the proof of our theories before the world, in the beauty of our paintings."

"I'm sure you'll do wonderfully," Lizzie said quietly. She knew that it was unreasonable, but she was disappointed that Rossetti would not be submitting a picture of her for the exhibition.

Rossetti saw the unhappiness on her face. "Don't despair—this is only the beginning, and I haven't had time to do you justice yet. For the next Exhibition I will submit a painting of you—of you as the fair Beatrice. You, Lizzie Siddal, will be the face of the new British art."

"You go too far, Dante. What do I have to offer art?"

"You don't see it, do you? Lizzie, you could be the queen of a Renaissance court, adored by knights and noblemen alike."

Lizzie shook her head. "Then perhaps I should have been born in another era. My looks have never been mistaken for beauty in this one. I can't help but wonder at your flattery."

"This is a new era, Lizzie. A new era for art, and a new era for beauty. The age of tailored young ladies with plump cheeks and plump poodles on their arms is coming to an end. True beauty—the classic, strong beauty of Eleanor of Aquitaine and Beatrice Portinari—will prevail. I see you as their heir, Lizzie. You are beautiful to me, and when I paint you, the world will see what I see."

He leaned a little closer and Lizzie smiled with pleasure. "You flatter me, Dante. I only hope that I am equal to the task. Beatrice inspired such poetry. I can hardly imagine that such a woman was flesh and blood."

"Perhaps she was like you. Part woman and part angel."

Lizzie laughed, but Rossetti's face was serious. "I am afraid that you see more in me than is really there. I know of women of great beauty and great virtue, but true angels are only born of the grave."

"I see only what is right before me." As they spoke, Rossetti's voice became more urgent, and he peered at Lizzie with eyes that were unnaturally bright. "Angels do walk the earth, but only the true artist can recognize them. Dante saw his fate in the beauty of Beatrice, and I see mine in yours."

Lizzie blushed, feeling the pull of Rossetti's enthusiasm. No one had ever spoken to her in such terms before, though she had many times imagined herself as a romantic heroine, a Juliet or Queen Guinevere. But she was troubled by the sense that he must be speaking to someone else, someone just past her shoulder, who was truly worthy of such praise and poetry. If she were to give herself over to his vision, she worried that he would only laugh and say, oh, I didn't mean you, dear, and she would be humiliated.

She shook her head again and tried to pull away, but this just seemed to encourage him. Undaunted, he spun his glittering web of flattery. "You are so much like her. No true Beatrice would be vain, or easily won. She was the ideal woman—a queen of virtue, blessed in every way. Dante's love for her was entirely pure, fed by nothing more than a few brief glimpses of her in the street. To Dante she was everything: love, art, salvation."

"But they never married?"

"They were both promised to others. But if he had known her as a wife, he might never have known her as his divine muse."

"It must be a wondrous thing, to play such a role in the creations of a great master," Lizzie said, allowing Rossetti to draw her closer. "To know that one's very existence can inspire such poetry."

"You will certainly be equal to sitting for Beatrice," Rossetti whispered, almost to himself. "You have already begun to inspire me." They were face-to-face now, and Rossetti's eyes were slightly unfocused, as if he saw beyond the present, to the finished canvas.

Lizzie sat very still. For a moment she saw herself through Rossetti's eyes: She was a thing of beauty, inseparable from the paintings in which he saw her. The vision worked a sort of alchemy, as if her imagination could teach her body the secret of beauty. She let the feeling wash over her, and smiled the enigmatic smile of a Renaissance portrait. Her eyes grew wide and bright, and she sensed that their light was capable of drawing Rossetti to her with a single glance. She ran her hand through her long hair, and the enchantment of the movement was not lost on either of them.

Rossetti watched her carefully. She seemed to have gained a greater sense of presence, like a figure in a painting to which he had just applied the final wash of color. "Yes, you are Beatrice." He cleared his throat and spoke directly to her: "To complete the picture, all you need is her gown."

From a wardrobe in the corner he produced an elegant gown of deep green velvet. It was simply cut, with a loose velvet bodice that hung like a tunic over sleeves of royal blue silk.

"It could not possibly improve you—but perhaps you will find that it transforms you."

He handed the gown to Lizzie, and she held it to her body, feeling the luxurious pile of the velvet. She had never worn a dress so fine. She smiled, thinking that she already felt different. Rossetti had led her to the edge of a new world, and she could sense in it the beginnings of a new self. He was right; all she needed was the dress.

To Lizzie and Rossetti, the studio in Chatham Place was a retreat. It floated above the city, a place without prying eyes or ticking clocks. As long as they stayed within its book-lined walls, they felt no need to answer to anything besides the cause of art, and the demands of their own happiness. They were free, and surprisingly innocent—like children playing in a garden, with no thought of the world beyond its walls. This purity found its way into Rossetti's sketches, which showed Lizzie in simple lines: her lips curved in slight smiles, her eyes lowered from nothing more provocative than the languor of a warm afternoon.

The new painting changed that. Lizzie donned the gown, and the studio became a stage.

Draped in velvet and with her hair loose and flowing, she looked every inch the part of Beatrice. It wasn't difficult to go a step further, to believe that she was assuming that medieval maiden's grace and charm along with her attire. In her heart, Lizzie knew that it was nothing more than an illusion, a trick of the studio's enchanting light, and that underneath the gown she was still Lizzie Siddal, milliner. But it was a powerful illusion, and Rossetti seemed to feel its effect as well.

The room, which once felt safe from the sordid implications that the world attaches to even the most innocent of gestures, was now full of undiscovered possibility and hidden meaning. Each of

Lizzie's movements, and each of their shared glances, were now weighted with the echoes of Dante's poems: She was the untouchable muse, he was her knight-errant; they were lovers, in body or in spirit; they were souls, swirling in the inferno. Their possibility was limited only by what Rossetti could render on the canvas.

The painting of Beatrice was small and jewel-like, painted in rich reds and greens. The Poet gazes upon his beloved as she passes by him on her way to a wedding feast. Beatrice is pale and lovely, with her head held high and her body still for a moment in the middle of the revelry of the other guests. She has heard that Dante loves another, and she looks down on him, her gaze cold. He leans toward her, his jaw tense and his hands hanging irresolute by his sides. Desire and restraint, equal and opposite forces, hold them rooted to the spot, while the crowd flows around them and a fresco of angels regards them mournfully from the walls above.

As he painted, Rossetti tried to maintain the measured practices of courtly love that he so wished to emulate. But the privacy of the studio was a very different place from the crowded streets of Florence. Rossetti began to wonder how Dante would have fared if he had ever had the pleasure of a private interview with Beatrice.

He placed a crown of fresh flowers on Lizzie's head, barely letting his fingertips brush against her hair as he guided her pose, and Lizzie blushed.

"Your modesty is becoming. Remember, I must have your most proud expression for this painting. Beatrice believes that Dante loves another, and in her anger denies him her salutation. You must look down upon him with disinterested eyes, like a queen upon her subjects."

He placed his fingers under Lizzie's chin and raised it up slightly. The unexpected touch sent a shiver across her skin, and he let his hand linger for a moment against her cheek. "That's right, just a bit higher."

He stepped back and slowly took her measure. She purposely kept her eyes down, avoiding his gaze, but Rossetti continued to stare at her.

"It is the height of cruelty, and coquetry," he finally said, his voice taking on a raw edge that she had not heard before, "for a woman to feign disinterest in a man whom she knows to love her deeply. Dante Alighieri had great control of himself. I don't know if Beatrice would have been so fortunate with another admirer."

Lizzie did not need to look at Rossetti to know that his eyes were still on her. She tried to look down, but it was impossible not to return his gaze. When their eyes met, his were dark and focused. He held her gaze for a moment, and then let his eyes roam deliberately over her body.

The air in the studio changed. It became heavy and still, with the scent of earth, like a field before a storm. Lizzie struggled to hold her pose, trying to radiate Beatrice's chastity along with her beauty. Their eyes met once again, and remained locked; Lizzie was magnificent in her velvet robes and Rossetti was rapt before her. Then, exhaling, he turned away. Without a word he retreated to his easel and began to paint.

His movements were quick and focused, almost angry. He stabbed at the canvas with fast, precise brushwork and long strokes. His whole body moved as he painted, as if he were dancing, the easel his partner. He worked furiously, seeing nothing now but the canvas.

Lizzie let out a breath that she did not realize she was holding. Electric traces danced along her skin where his eyes had moved over her. She stood and started to move toward him. She was drawn to him like a pin to a magnet, a sudden motion without determination. "Dante," she whispered, calling him back to her, away from the painting that seemed to consume him.

He looked up, surprised, and then in a second he was next to her. "Beatrice," he whispered, and Lizzie did not correct him.

He kissed her, his lips biting hard against hers, as if he were drinking after a long thirst. She closed her eyes and he kissed her eyelids, and then her brow, while the studio spun around them, a whirl of dusty sunlight and paint and shadow. He ran his hand lightly from her shoulder, over the bodice of her dress, to her waist. He held her like that for a moment, and then took her hand and began to lead her across the room, to a small sofa.

She followed him, as if in a trance. But the sight of the sofa recalled her abruptly to her senses. The spell was broken, and she drew her breath in, shocked at her daring. As she turned away, she was aware only of a vague and unnamable frustration, and a sense that things were happening very much out of order.

She pulled her hand back and stood still, and Rossetti saw at once that he had made a mistake. "Please forgive me," he muttered, red-faced. The girl before him was as pure as a dove. He couldn't be the instrument of her downfall. And yet—even now he wanted nothing more than to take her back into his arms. He stood uncertainly, his hand reaching toward her.

They were still standing like that when a knock on the door caused them to jump apart.

Before Rossetti could call out, the door swung open and William Holman Hunt strode into the room. He stopped when he saw Rossetti and Lizzie standing flushed and silent. "Well, hello!" he said, with a knowing smile. "I didn't mean to interrupt anything!"

Rossetti recovered first. "Not at all, Hunt. Miss Siddal was just obliging me by posing for my new watercolor."

"Yes, obliging you. I quite see what you mean."

Lizzie stared at the floor, mortified. The rose tint of her cheeks was gone, and her face was pale and drawn. She tugged clumsily at her dress, trying to pull up the sleeve where it had slipped from her shoulder. If Hunt had caught a glimpse of the stunning beauty who had just been posing as Beatrice, she was gone now, and an ordinary young woman had taken her place.

Rossetti glared at Hunt and then turned to Lizzie, begging her forgiveness with his eyes. "That will be enough for today, Miss Siddal."

Lizzie nodded without looking up and hurried into the back room.

Hunt watched her go. "I would ask you where you've been, but I can very well see what, or should I say who, has been occupying you." He looked around the room at the dozens of sketches of Lizzie that lined the walls.

Rossetti followed Hunt's gaze. He shrugged. "I can't stop drawing her. She's the most beautiful woman that I have ever seen."

"Aren't they all?"

From the back room, Lizzie could hear the men speaking about her. She struggled to free herself from the velvet gown, which now looked cheap and tawdry to her eye. How easily she had let herself slip into Rossetti's fantasy! She was relieved to put her plain gray dress back on, and she pulled her hair into a simple bun. Embarrassed, she tried to slip quietly out the door without Rossetti's notice.

"Wait, Miss Siddal! Allow me to introduce Mr. Hunt. A fellow artist."

Lizzie wished nothing more than to be free of the studio, but she turned and tried to present a smooth face to Rossetti's friend. "How do you do?" she asked, the coolness in her voice a rebuke.

Hunt smiled gallantly. "Exceedingly well, now that I've seen Rossetti's new painting and his lovely new model."

"You're too kind," Lizzie murmured. If she did not quite forgive him for his insolence, she was practical enough to be grateful for his interruption. Who knew what may have happened if he had not come in at that moment?

Rossetti accompanied Lizzie to the door of the studio. On the landing, he took her hand and spoke to her quietly. "Please don't take Hunt's jokes too seriously. No one else does. You will come again tomorrow, won't you?" He smiled, and Lizzie reflexively returned his smile, failing to maintain the haughtiness that she knew that he deserved.

She hesitated for only a moment. "I'll come again tomorrow. But only to sit for your painting. I'm already taking a risk in coming here alone, and I must know that I can trust you."

Rossetti looked relieved. "What a sweet little dove you are. Please don't worry, you have nothing to fear from me."

Lizzie waited for a moment, as if there were something else that ought to be said by one of them. The silent, shared knowledge of their quick embrace hung between them, more intimate than any touch. But perhaps it was better not to put words to such things, and so Lizzie turned with a last shy smile and made her way down the stairs.

In the vestibule, she stepped aside to make way for another woman who was just coming in from the street. The woman was plainly dressed, a servant of some sort. But something about her careless knot of thick blond hair and the unnatural rouge of her cheeks caught Lizzie's attention. As the woman passed, she looked slyly at Lizzie and then smirked, as if she recognized her.

Lizzie was sure that she didn't know her, and so she let her pass with a shrug. But she paused in the vestibule and listened to her footsteps as she mounted the stairs, counting off each flight until they stopped on Rossetti's floor. Or was it the floor below? Lizzie couldn't be sure.

For a moment, she toyed with the idea of going back up to Rossetti's studio on some pretext—a forgotten glove, perhaps. Then she laughed, acknowledging her own foolishness. No good ever came of listening at keyholes. Besides, Rossetti's visitors, real or imagined, were no business of hers.

Despite Rossetti's promise that she could trust him, Lizzie spent a restless night thinking of how close she had come to forgetting herself. She had always looked down her nose at girls who gave themselves up for the flimsiest of promises, or for nothing at all. How could they put themselves in such a position, Lizzie had often murmured to her mother, watching as a neighborhood girl was rushed down the aisle, already showing her shame. And far worse were the girls who had to leave home and take up in some obscure town to have their babies alone, after the lad took off.

Lizzie knew this, and yet she had still found herself alone in Rossetti's studio, letting him take liberties with her that she could hardly have imagined a few months ago. No, not just letting him. When she was honest with herself, she knew that she had willed him to kiss her, had wanted him to take her in his arms. The feel of his gaze was a strong breeze; his touch was the storm.

She knew that she should not go back to his studio, at least not alone. But when she thought of the alternative—the tedium of the millinery, the plain gray work dresses, and the men who hung about the shop and confused their crude jokes with compliments—she knew that she would return to Rossetti. She had to see him again.

She told herself over and over that he was a gentleman, different from the men whom she knew; that he would never put her in an impossible position. In the studio he spoke to her of Dante's chaste and perfect love for Beatrice. But his voice, as he spoke, seemed to say something else, to hint at a deep current of desire unbound from any code of chivalry. Lizzie sensed the same danger in his paintings, a worship of love and beauty that owed no obedience to ordinary notions of right and wrong. His paintings, and his studio, were a romantic dream, and Lizzie was drawn to them even as she sensed the peril that lay beneath their shimmering surfaces.

And so she returned to his studio, assuring herself that now that she was aware of the temptation, and of her own weakness, she would be better prepared to resist it. But she need not have worried. The next afternoon Rossetti greeted her at the door, his hat already on. The brim was low enough that Lizzie could not quite tell whether the rosiness of his cheeks was due to embarrassment, or merely the warmth of the studio. "It's far too fine a day to stay inside painting," he said. "Let's go for a walk."

Lizzie didn't stop to examine whether the quick surge of emotion that she felt was relief or disappointment. She gave him her arm and let him lead her back out into the street.

Rossetti was right; it was too beautiful to stay indoors, if one could help it. It was a perfect May afternoon, the sun's warmth kept at bay by a pleasant breeze. The streets were full, as if all of society, from the errand boys of the city to the young lords of St. James's Park, had emerged to enjoy the good weather in a spirit of thanksgiving for spring and goodwill for humanity.

In the anonymous crowd, Lizzie felt that she and Rossetti could be anyone. Who was to say that they were not newlyweds, perfectly free to walk alone through the sunny streets? Rossetti kept up a steady discourse on the poems that he was translating, and Lizzie held her head high and smiled at the men who tipped their hats to her. She was a different girl, after sitting for Deverell and Rossetti, from the one who had only a few months before scurried to and from work with her bonnet pulled low and her eyes down. Her new confidence was more flattering than any new gown, and she basked under the admiring glances thrown her way as others basked under the spring sun.

But the fine weather did not hold. A stiff wind blew in the clouds that had hovered at the horizon, and they settled quickly over the city, turning the air damp and chilly. Lizzie wore only a shawl, and Rossetti threw his coat over her shoulders. When a light rain began to fall, they made a dash for the cover of St. Saviour's. They stood on the steps of the cathedral, laughing and shivering under the watchful eyes of a stone saint.

Rossetti reached out to smooth Lizzie's hair, which had come loose as they ran. His touch was gentle, and here on the church steps Lizzie felt none of the confusion and unease that she had felt in the studio. They were no different from any other couple caught in the rain, sharing a moment of the most ordinary intimacy in the quiet alcove of the church stairs. Rossetti let his hand linger on her cheek, and smiled at her sweetly.

From beyond the heavy oak doors of the church, they heard music. First the low rumble of the organ, and then a high clear note, the sound of angels singing.

"Evensong," Lizzie murmured. Rossetti pushed open the door, and the music swelled and filled the entryway, the chorus of voices carrying them into the cathedral on its tide. They passed into the nave, a soaring space of arched columns that rose to form a high tower. Above the altar, the last pale light of the afternoon illuminated the jeweled panels of a stained glass window. There were only a few worshippers, crowded into the first few pews and scattered toward the back.

The rising notes of the choir echoed from the stone columns, and Lizzie shivered with pleasure. They walked down the aisle that flanked the nave, passing small chapels and racks of candles that testified to the prayers of those hoping for solace, healing, and luck. When they came to the chapel of the Virgin Mary, Lizzie slipped a coin into the wooden box and took a long white candle, which she lit and placed before the altar. She knelt down and lowered her head in prayer.

Rossetti stood and watched her pray. Behind them, the choir began a quiet chant, a whisper no louder than a breeze that slowly built strength until it resonated in a high, clear note, the innocent voices of the children offering their glory to God. In the half light of the chapel, Lizzie, with her porcelain skin, looked no different from the carved stone saints that surrounded her. Rossetti saw that it was not some spell of the studio that drew him to her—she had the power to transform any landscape into art, as if her presence could convert the ordinary into the sublime.

The scene was perfect: the pious, innocent girl, the curve of her neck mirrored by the bent head of the Virgin; the rich embroidery of the altar cloth and the gold of the saints' halos; the warm light cast by the candles. Lizzie was so beautiful at that moment that Rossetti didn't know whether he ought to go to her or paint her. He hesitated. He knew instinctively that to enter the scene was to change it, subtly but definitively. Alone she was a praying saint; together they would be a man and woman, kneeling at the altar.

But he had no brush and no easel, and so he went to her, kneeling down beside her and assuming his role, unable to resist adding the necessary detail that would bring the painting into harmony. "What do you pray for?" he asked her.

Without looking at him, Lizzie lifted her face toward the statue of the Virgin. She too could feel the weight of the moment, the rush of emotion that built toward some end as naturally as the crescendo of the choir rose to a transcendent finale. "I pray that I am worthy of you. Of your talent."

She could not have chosen words better calculated to entrance him. "Then you have wasted a candle. Your beauty requires no further grace."

"And am I worthy of your regard?"

"Lizzie." He took her face in his hands. He could feel the beat of her pulse against his palm, like the quiver of a dove. He leaned in to kiss her, but she stood suddenly, jarringly, and put her finger to his lips.

"Would I be worthy of your regard if I let you kiss me here, in this church?"

He hesitated. In the studio he might have grabbed her hand and pulled her back to him, but here before the Virgin such gestures rang a false and empty note. He knelt before her and took her hand. "Is there a more perfect place to kiss you, than in a church? I should like to be able to kiss you freely before God and all the world."

Lizzie's face lit up and he could see, within the young woman before him, the little girl who had dreamed of knights-errant. The power to please her was a potent aphrodisiac, and he continued in a rush, his spirit stirred by the sound of the choir and the perfume of the candles. His words tumbled out, unplanned and heartfelt. "Lizzie, you may trust me. I know that you haven't had an easy life, and I won't add to your troubles. I can offer you nothing now but to paint you. But if my work succeeds, when I gain a name for myself . . . there will be no happiness that can be denied to us. There is something that I would ask you, if I could only be sure of being worthy of your answer."

"Then kiss me once," Lizzie said, her smile beatific. "And then let us go, before Evensong ends. I want to carry this music, and this moment, with me for the rest of the night."

CHAPTER 7

Charlotte Street, London, May 22, 1850
Dear Lizzie,

I write with happy news—my picture of the Virgin Mary has been accepted for the Summer Exhibition. Will you do me the honor of accompanying me to the opening reception? I can hardly sleep for thinking how, in one night, my career may be either set on a path for glory, or else tossed onto the ash heap. But if you are on my arm, I'll be able to face whatever might come. If you will allow me, I will call for you at six o'clock, the fourth of June.

Your friend,
D. G. Rossetti

Lizzie received the invitation, written in Rossetti's now familiar scrawl, and accepted at once. When a similar note arrived from Walter Deverell the next day, she declined with only a tinge of regret, adding a friendly note that she looked forward to congratulating him on his success in person.

In the days leading up to the reception, she could think of little else. The Artists' Reception was a bohemian highlight of the city's social calendar; a much-anticipated chance for the wealthy patrons of the arts to mingle with the more artistic set whom their purchases supported. In her days at Mrs. Tozer's, she had worked on special orders for the event, and she knew that many fashionable ladies would be there. She knew that any dress that she had would be very poor by comparison, and when she and Lydia looked over her best dress, the dove-gray silk, with an eye to re-trimming it, they found it hopelessly plain for an evening gown.

There wasn't much time before the reception, but Lizzie's work at the millinery had made her a quick and competent seamstress, and she thought she might be able to design something original in time for the party. There was no time, and not nearly enough fabric on hand for her to sew a full ball gown. But she thought she might be able to do something simple, in the style of the dress that she wore as a model for Beatrice. The costume's high waist and flowing skirt was much more becoming to her tall and slim figure than the modern style of corsets and crinolines, which emphasized curves she did not in fact possess. She had begun to take her role as muse to Rossetti seriously, and she was excited at the idea of wearing a medieval-styled gown and entering the reception as if she were stepping from one of his paintings.

Mrs. Tozer was willing to part with a length of sapphire blue velvet for ten shillings, a good price that still required Lizzie's entire savings. Using long, simple lines, she cut a dress from it that fell straight from a high waist to the floor in an elegant column. She added long sleeves and a square neck, and at the shoulders and waist she attached a gold lace trimming, leftovers from the shop. Mrs. Tozer, despite her initial annoyance at Rossetti's appearance in the shop, had been exceedingly helpful, letting Lizzie work only a few hours a week in the shop while she sat for Rossetti, and lending her a fashionable new bonnet to wear to the reception.

On the evening of the party, Lydia fixed her hair, pinning the front pieces back to frame her face and letting the rest fall down her back, loose. "Promise you'll remember everything, so that you can tell me what all the ladies wore, and what sort of punch was served, and all the witty things that were said. Then I won't be so jealous that I wasn't there."

"Of course I will! Though half the witty things that are said are like Latin to me. Rossetti and his friends are so clever that I can hardly keep up." Lizzie laughed, trying to disguise her anxiety. It was one thing to speak with Rossetti in the intimacy of his studio; it was quite another to mingle with so many strangers, most of whom would not ordinarily give her the time of day.

Lydia gave Lizzie's hair a last brushing. "There. You look lovely. Mr. Rossetti is sure to be smitten."

"Do you think?" Lizzie asked, a little too quickly.

Lydia raised her eyebrows. "Then you *are* in love with him."

"I suppose that I am. Why shouldn't I be? He's the most handsome and talented man in the world!"

"And does he share your feelings? Will he ask you to marry him?"

"If he did, I would accept."

"But he's said nothing yet?"

Lizzie hesitated. She had thought of little else in the last days besides Dante's words to her in St. Saviour's. It had not been a proposal, but it was a promise of one, she thought. He had looked at her with such love. But she wasn't sure that Lydia would understand. She knew what Lydia would say: Either he proposed or he didn't.

Finally Lizzie answered, "If you're asking if he has proposed, he hasn't. But I have reason to believe that he will soon. You should hear him talk—it's pure poetry. He's very different from the other men whom we know. He doesn't care a whit for any of the petty things that pass for life around here."

"Like making a decent living?" Lydia asked, and then blushed, embarrassed.

"Why would you say such a thing? Are you repeating something that Mother said?"

Lydia hesitated. But Lizzie stared at her hard, and she made a grudging answer: "Mother only said that she thought that perhaps Mr. Deverell might have made a more suitable match. She made a few inquiries, and Mr. Deverell's family is very well off, while the Rossettis . . . well, they're quite respectable it seems, but there's very little to live on. A man of leisure who paints is quite a different thing from a man who must make his living by his painting."

Lizzie turned on her sister. "How dare you speak with Mother behind my back about such things! She knows nothing of these people. Has she forgotten that our family is currently living off of the wages paid to me by Mr. Rossetti, and on very little else?"

Lydia looked stung. "Well, you must be practical. You haven't anything of your own—he must be able to support you. We only want the best for you, Lizzie."

"Don't be jealous, it's not becoming." Lizzie's words came out sharper than she intended, and Lydia's eyes filled with tears. "Oh, I'm sorry, Lyddie, I didn't mean that. Of course you're right; I must be practical. But I'm not at all worried, and you mustn't worry, either. He wouldn't have asked me to accompany him on such an important night if his intentions weren't serious. Don't say a word to Mother, but I believe that the only reason he hasn't yet proposed is that he despairs of supporting me on a painter's income. But he's beginning to do very well in his work, and people, important people, are taking notice. It's only a matter of time. And when I'm married, dear sister, there won't be any question of my telling you about a party—you will be by my side at every one."

She stood and kissed Lydia on the cheek. "Don't worry about me," she repeated, as much to herself as to Lydia. "I have no doubt about his intentions, or his chances for success."

Lizzie told her father that there was an entertainment at the local women's club, and if he noticed anything different about his daughter, it was only that she looked more lovely than usual. She walked to the top of Kent Place and tentatively reached out her hand to hail a cab. She could barely afford the expense, but finding the extra shillings was easier than trying to explain to her father why a man he'd never met was fetching her in a coach. The Siddals may have been poor, but Rossetti was an artist, and in Mr. Siddal's estimation artists were one step above criminals. It would have been impossible to invite him inside, and besides, Lizzie had no wish to entertain Rossetti in their shabby parlor. She suspected that the image Rossetti had of her home was much more becoming, in its simplicity, than the reality of too many children in too few rooms, and her father eating dinner in his rolled up shirtsleeves, the metal dust from the grinding shop still glistening on his brow. For the time being at least, it was better to keep her two worlds as far apart as possible.

A cab pulled up and the driver helped Lizzie onto the seat. She saw him glance sideways at her strange gown, but his face remained impassive. If they were at it long enough, the London cabbies eventually saw everything, and a girl wearing a fine dress in a seedy street was nothing new to him. He put his crop on the horse and they took off, moving in fits and starts through the narrow streets of Southwark.

The roads were clogged with merchant carts delivering their goods: whole carcasses of pigs and lambs to the butcher, baskets of watercress and potatoes to the greengrocer, and load after load of coal, hauled off the cart in sacks and sent ricocheting down the coal hatches with a hammering sound like a stampede of horses. Little boys no higher than Lizzie's knee followed the coal cart at ten paces. They leapt upon any piece that tumbled from the back of the truck, placing the precious bits into sacks slung over their shoulders. The air was thick with smoke, making the streets feel closer than they were, and carriages emerged without warning from the mist, their lamps like the beacons of lighthouses on a dark sea.

They passed over Blackfriars Bridge and cut west toward Trafalgar Square, where the streets were lined with shops and cafés. Light spilled from plate glass windows, seeping into the puddles in the cobblestone streets. The houses here were larger and more regular, set behind fortifications of iron gates and heavy velvet curtains.

Lizzie's cab slowed and prepared to join the fray in front of the exhibition hall, where carriages and cabs jockeyed for position at the curb. The driver pulled in as close as he could, and Lizzie paid her fare and alighted. She watched as women in the latest fashions stepped from their carriages and into the waiting hands of their top-hatted escorts. Their fine silk dresses, in shades of emerald and ruby, emerged from the carriage doors first, the skirts buoyed by full crinolines and edged in lace. Next came their delicate hands, sheathed in white gloves, and then a glimpse of a boot in kid leather. With a last graceful hop they stepped into the street, and the full measure of their finery was revealed, like exotic butterflies spreading their wings. They tossed their heads and clutched their velvet capes around their shoulders, crying out greetings and compliments to old friends.

The crowd made its way up a wide set of stairs and into the hall through a series of arched doors, but Lizzie hesitated on the sidewalk. She put a hand up to her hair, now feeling that its loose style was childish rather than romantic, as she had hoped. The ladies around her had clearly spent the last several hours with a maid or two and a hot iron; their hair was sculpted into elegant piles of braids and ringlets. And her dress, perhaps it wasn't right after all. In the midst of so many bright silk gowns trimmed in yards of lace and ribbon, it seemed to stand out more for its plainness than anything else.

Her face burned. Had she really thought that she belonged here, among these people? She stood biting her lip as the sea of finery flowed around her and into the gallery. She was on the verge of turning around when she felt a pair of eyes on her. She turned to see a woman staring at her with open curiosity. Lizzie returned her glance, and to her surprise, the woman gave her a nod and a smile, rather than a sneer. That one kind glance was enough; with a nervous smile of her own, Lizzie joined the crowd making its way through the doors.

Inside she scanned the room, trying to get her bearings. The hall was large and airy, with a gleaming parquet floor and a tall gilded ceiling. Groupings of velvet settees and palms in Chinese pottery punctuated the vast space, and a massive chandelier cast a rosy light over the guests. Most striking, however, were the walls, which were covered in hundreds of paintings, stacked one above the other, reaching almost to the ceiling. Lizzie ran her eyes over them, looking for Rossetti's and Deverell's paintings, but it was impossible to pick them out from the hundreds of others.

At first she didn't see any familiar faces in the crowd, either, but then she spotted Rossetti, surrounded by a knot of friends and admirers. He was gesturing grandly with his hands, a pleased smile on his face. But when he saw Lizzie, he stopped still and looked at her with unmistakable admiration, his eyes taking in every detail of her gown. She saw that she had done well to make her own dress.

He greeted her warmly, whispering into her hair: "You are a vision."

"Even in the midst of this splendor?" Lizzie asked, looking around.

"Yes, even here. Especially here."

Lizzie blushed. "And your picture? Is it a success?"

"I don't want to boast, but I've received many compliments. But of course one hears nothing but compliments at these parties. The real test will be in the reviews, and those won't be out for a few days at least. Where the critics lead, the buyers follow. But tonight we celebrate. Now come, I can't wait any longer to introduce the lovely Miss Siddal as my escort."

While Lizzie was being introduced to Rossetti's friends, she heard a familiar voice, high and girlish, call out her name: "Lizzie! Lizzie Siddal! Is that really you?" Then a whirl of pink satin and black lace was suddenly upon her, embracing her and peering at her with disbelief.

"Emma! What on earth are you doing here?" Lizzie stared into the face of Emma Hill, an old friend from her neighborhood whom she'd lost touch with as Lizzie's family had moved from house to house. She hadn't seen Emma in years, but she was just as Lizzie remembered her: petite, with slender shoulders and white skin, glossy dark hair, and dancing eyes. Her figure was a bit fuller now, and her smile had softened, but otherwise she was unchanged from the girl whom Lizzie had played hopscotch with in the street as a child.

"Why, Lizzie!" Emma exclaimed, all excitement and fluttering hands. "I had no idea that you knew Dante!" She turned to her companion, a man with a serious face and kind eyes. "Ford," she scolded him. "You didn't tell me that Dante's new model was Lizzie Siddal!"

"I'm afraid that I haven't had the pleasure of meeting her," Ford said, stepping forward and taking Lizzie's hand. "Ford Madox Brown. I'm always enchanted to meet friends of my wife, and of course friends of Rossetti."

"Your wife?" Lizzie asked, turning to Emma.

"Yes, I'm Emma Brown now!" Emma turned a beaming face on her husband and laid her hand on his arm. "Just married last month! Oh, Lizzie, this is too wonderful. I'd heard the rumor, of course, that Dante had discovered some stunning new muse, but I had no idea that it was you. If I had, I would have had Ford bring me over to the studio at once!"

"It's so lovely to see you," Lizzie said. "And congratulations on your marriage."

Emma glowed. "Yes, well, we had to get round to it one day! And it wasn't a moment too soon." She winked, discreetly patting her stomach.

Lizzie looked down and saw a gentle roundness beneath Emma's loosely corseted dress. She could see that, despite having only been married a month, Emma would be welcoming a child before the summer was out. Lizzie blushed. "I'm so happy for you."

"I can see that you're shocked," Emma laughed. "But you mustn't be. Ford, Dante, all of their friends—they live as true artists, and with no apologies. They're all very wicked, you know, not at all what you're used to. I don't mind saying that I was Ford's model for a long while before I was his wife." She paused and gave Lizzie a knowing look, causing Lizzie to blush again. "But you'll come round to it—it's such a lot of fun. You see, they care only for the really important things in life—love, art, beauty. And we are so very lucky to be a part of it."

"I do feel lucky." Lizzie glanced at Rossetti. Emma had put words to the breathlessness that Lizzie felt when she was with him; the sense of possibility, as if the drab surface of London could be peeled back like the rind of an orange, revealing a feast for the senses. Sometimes it was easy to forget that the real London, the one that she had to return to each night, had standards that must be met if a girl wished to walk with her head up in decent society. But in the excitement of the moment, Lizzie didn't have time to dwell on such thoughts. Perhaps Emma was right—the art was the important thing; the rest was just the dull realm of the uninitiated.

Rossetti caught her eye and walked over to them. "Come, ladies," he said, offering an arm to each woman. "Let's find Deverell and congratulate him on his success. I see that there is quite a little crowd gathered around his *Twelfth Night*."

Lizzie squeezed Rossetti's arm, and he steered them through the crowd. Heads turned as they sailed past, and women whispered behind their fans. Rossetti had promised to make her the envy of London, and it seemed that he was as good as his word. She drank up the crowd's approving looks, threw her shoulders back, and allowed herself a moment of triumph. Rossetti murmured, "All eyes are on you," and she shivered at his compliment, and his closeness.

But Lizzie's beauty, and the spectacle of her dress, wasn't the only thing causing a stir. Rossetti's painting *The Girlhood of Mary Virgin* was the talk of the Exhibition. It showed Mary as a child, at work on a bright scarlet piece of embroidery, with her mother by her side. It was done in the style of an early Italian religious painting, rich in both color and symbolic detail. Mary and her mother were crowned by golden halos, and a vase of white lilies suggested Mary's purity. The current fashion was for muted domestic scenes, but Rossetti's painting took the divine as its subject, and its bright hues stood out from the other paintings. A crowd had gathered in front of it all day, and whether they had adored it or detested it, no one had failed to notice Rossetti's painting, or the mysterious initials "PRB" that followed his signature.

Many in the crowd had connected the letters with the matching initials on paintings by John Millais and William Holman Hunt. The public loved nothing more than a good scandal, and the possible meanings of "PRB" had been on everyone's lips since the exhibition's opening. Despite the vow of secrecy, many friends had been let in on the Brotherhood's existence and its revolutionary goals. These insiders now found themselves surrounded as they recounted the tale of a secret meeting, the plot to overthrow the supremacy of the Royal Academy, and the pact among the seven audacious brothers in art. This buzz followed Rossetti as he moved through the room.

At the end of the hall, Lizzie finally saw Deverell's painting. She felt a thrill of recognition at seeing her own face peer back as the pageboy. The picture had earned a good place, and she felt as pleased as if she had painted it herself.

She knew from Rossetti's stories how fraught the submission process could be. Having a picture selected for display was an achievement, but the location of the picture on the wall made all the difference. The pictures were stacked three and four on top of each other, starting at eye level and ascending the wall. Some pictures were hung so high that a man would have needed to stand on his neighbor's shoulders to get a good look at them. On Hanging Day, when the jury made its final selections and the work went up, each artist was frantic to find out whether his picture had earned a good place. Deverell's picture was hanging in the center of the wall, right at eye level. It was quite a coup.

A small crowd was gathered in front of Deverell's painting, and it seemed that some of the Brotherhood's celebrity had shone on him. The keen eye of the crowd was quick to make the connection in style between the paintings.

"Deverell!" Rossetti cried, clasping his friend by the shoulders. "The picture is extraordinary! And I don't say that just because it features the lovely Miss Siddal and myself—you have done us more than justice. It's been surrounded all evening, and rightly so. May I offer my congratulations on a very auspicious beginning to what is sure to be a long and distinguished career?"

"My thanks, and the same to you. The talk tonight has been of nothing but your *Girlhood* painting and the mystery of the PRB." He turned to Lizzie. "Miss Siddal, it's been entirely too long. When I last saw you, you played the lowly page, but now I see that you are more like a countess." In a move more in keeping with Rossetti's extravagant behavior than his own very English comportment, Deverell took Lizzie's hand and brushed his lips against it, holding her eye as he raised his head. Emma giggled and gave Lizzie a sly look before she offered her own hand to Deverell.

Lizzie was happy to see Deverell. Success agreed with him—he looked as flushed and proud as a new father. In the excitement of sitting for Rossetti, she had almost forgotten how pleasant her afternoons sitting for Deverell had been. Now she embraced him as a friend and murmured her congratulations. "It's a very fine painting. I'm honored to have played some small part in its success."

"I couldn't have painted it without you. And how does your own work get on?"

"My own work? Do you mean Dante's new painting? It's nearly finished, I believe."

"No, not Dante's painting. What of your own sketches and

poems? The drawing that you made of my sister Mary still hangs on my studio wall. As I told you then, it showed great promise."

"You're too kind—I'm afraid that I've done nothing more than dabble in drawing lately. I do a little sketching here and there, mostly while Dante is working. But I would love to really learn to paint." She colored a little at this admission, embarrassed to talk of her own wish to paint in such a setting. But Deverell didn't laugh at her.

"Well then, Rossetti must give you lessons. Or perhaps I could do so myself. In fact, I've been meaning to send you a note. I'm planning a new picture, and I was hoping that you might come sit for me again. Mary is eager to have your company. She speaks of you often."

Before Lizzie could reply, Rossetti broke in. "I'm afraid that Miss Siddal is very much occupied with my own work at the moment. I couldn't possibly spare her."

"Oh, come now, Rossetti! You can't mean to keep this lovely creature all to yourself? Miss Siddal says that you're almost finished with your picture, and I've planned my picture around her—no one else will do."

"As I said, Miss Siddal is occupied at the moment," Rossetti said sharply. "I really can't spare her—she's absolutely essential to my work."

Lizzie stared at Rossetti in surprise. He was nearly finished with the Beatrice painting, and she had taken on extra days at the shop, knowing that he might not pay her to sit again for a few weeks. It seemed odd that, knowing that she must make her living as a model or else return to Mrs. Tozer's, he would wish to prevent her sitting for Deverell. But perhaps he had some something besides painting in mind. If he was planning on proposing soon, of course he wouldn't want her sitting for other painters.

Deverell was frowning, and Lizzie sought to smooth over any ruffled feathers. "My dear Mr. Deverell, I'm busy at the moment, but I'll write to you as soon as I am free."

"Yes, of course." He looked questioningly at Rossetti. "Some other time."

"Well, we must make the rounds," Rossetti said, drawing the conversation to an abrupt end. He seemed embarrassed by his outburst, and eager to get away from Deverell. He took Lizzie's arm and steered her into the crowd, leaving her no choice but to shrug and smile at Deverell over her shoulder.

Deverell stared after them as they crossed the room arm in arm, their heads inclined toward each other as Rossetti whispered some little comment in her ear. His eyes lingered on the pair as they joined another group, Rossetti joking with friends and Miss Siddal smiling her serene smile, her eyes locked on him. If Deverell was uneasy at the sight, it would have been difficult for him to say why. Perhaps it was only jealousy that Rossetti had lacked his scruples in the matter of Miss Siddal. Or perhaps it was a more instinctive alarm at the way Miss Siddal's radiance seemed to dim in Rossetti's company, as if her light reflected off of him to greater effect, leaving her somehow depleted.

Rossetti led her into a private alcove at the far end of the gallery, and Deverell at last turned away, shrugging and muttering under his breath, "If they are in love, or lovers, what business, really, is it of mine?"

Rossetti pulled Lizzie onto his lap and loosened the velvet curtains of the alcove so that they were hidden from view.

He was in his element, his sudden celebrity a more powerful intoxicant than the fine champagne, though he'd drunk plenty of that as well. He thought of all the hours spent in his studio, choosing just the right paints, working and reworking his figures; the labor so draining that it sometimes felt like a bloodletting, as if the paint came not from a pot but from his open veins. And the other moments, when he sketched Lizzie as if he had been born to do nothing else, each drawing engendering the next; the desperate need to capture every telling glance, his hand racing across the page for hours until he fell back, spent. The exhaustion and the exhilaration had all culminated in this, his moment of victory.

He felt as rich men must feel—the reckless abandon of a heavy purse. Tonight London was his, and he saw what he wanted: Lizzie, resplendent in her rich velvet gown, no longer of this age or place. She was Beatrice, as if he had conjured her from Dante's sonnets with a sorcerer's spell. She was a *tableau vivant* staged only for him, poetic verse given the warmth and weight of a body. "You look divine," he said, running his fingertips over her cheek and down her white neck.

"But who will see me back here, in this alcove?" she laughed.

"Who could look at the paintings when you are in the room? I'm doing the other artists a favor by taking you aside."

"Promise me," Lizzie whispered, taking his face in her hands, and feeling her power over him at this moment, "you will paint no one but me."

"No one but you," he said, kissing her. "There's no one else worth painting." He slipped his hands around her waist, and she was instantly pliant, leaning against him and sighing. He wanted to whisper poetry into her hair, but none of Dante's verses felt right. Such carefully constructed lines, love tempered by restraint, felt pale and stilted in the face of his desire for Lizzie at this moment. His lips mute, he kissed her neck and her shoulders, pulling at the sleeve of her dress as he searched for more of her white skin. All of his art seemed to fall away; he would worship her not with verse but with a love so pure that it would transcend all words. Was not love an art in itself? But Lizzie drew back with unexpected force and put a restraining hand on his chest.

"Somebody might see us, Dante! And what will they think?"

"Our friends will think that we are in love, and what should I care what anyone else thinks?" he said, renewing his efforts.

"Are we in love?"

"Yes, of course we are, you silly girl. If this isn't love, what is?" Rossetti stopped trying to kiss her for a moment, and looked at her with tenderness and amusement.

Lizzie smiled, but she kept a hand firmly between them. "You may not care what people think, but I *must* care. Already people are talking. I can't be seen back here, alone with you. Unless, of course, there was some reason . . ." She let the suggestion hang in the air.

Rossetti released her and sat back. Thoughts of marriage, and its attendant concerns—houses to be let, visits to be made, the cries of babies outside the studio door—were so far from his mind that it took him a moment to catch her meaning. "Lizzie," he murmured, but no further words came to his lips, and his brow furrowed. Had he not, just a moment before, thought his love for her a thing more perfect and pure than Dante's sonnets to Beatrice? And yet . . . the practical concerns of marriage and family seemed to have little to do with such a love. That day in St. Saviour's he had nearly proposed, but something had held him back. He wanted to savor what they had, and was in no rush to change it. He desired the Lizzie who walked among other women like a goddess, who fed upon nothing more than love and poetry, and demanded nothing more, or less, than worship.

The moment stretched on in excruciating silence, and Rossetti saw Lizzie's face fall. She turned from him ever so slightly, looking past him and pressing her lips together. "Please excuse my silly behavior," she said, her voice small and cold. "I'm afraid that I've misunderstood you. Shall we rejoin our friends?"

He had disappointed her. It was an unwelcome feeling, crowding out his joy in the success of the exhibition. He roused himself to speak. "Lizzie, there's no misunderstanding. I love you. We won't always have to hide ourselves in alcoves and behind stairs. But I must put all of my effort right now into my work—it's of the utmost importance. Once I've made my reputation, we can plan our future. You have my promise. Until then, you must be my muse, and my inspiration. Come, you're right. We shouldn't be hidden here, alone, when there is an admiring public awaiting a glimpse of you. You must help me charm the wealthy guests who might make my fortune."

Lizzie's face had softened, but her next words were uttered in a tone almost of warning. "Yours is not the only reputation that I must consider, Dante. The longer that I'm your model, but not your wife, the more the world will look at me as if I am something else altogether. But let us speak no more of it tonight."

He nodded. He knew that she spoke the truth. But it was a truth that could be considered tomorrow, in the more practical light of day. Tonight was a night for celebrating.

Before they could stand, the alcove curtain was pulled back with a flourish, and Emma Brown greeted them with a peal of laughter. "I was wondering where you two slipped off to."

Lizzie blushed, but Rossetti only smiled. "Be careful, Mrs. Brown," he joked, "or I'll be forced to whisk you off behind some curtain as well."

Lizzie tried to join in with their laughter, but she could only manage a stiff smile. Emma rolled her eyes, and Lizzie told herself that Emma was a friend, not a rival. She was beginning to realize that she would have to get used to the easier ways of this crowd if she was to survive in it. And she must put her worries aside, if she was to enjoy the evening. After all, Rossetti had assured her that she had nothing to worry about.

"Ladies," Rossetti said with a mock bow. "May I escort you on a tour around the paintings?"

"There's nothing that I'd like more," Lizzie said, determined to enjoy herself. She turned to Emma. "And you must tell me everything that's happened since I've last seen you. I'm so happy to find you here, among all these strangers."

"Not to worry, my dear. They may be strange, but they will not be strangers for long. Stay close by my side and I'll whisper all the most amusing stories about each of them in your ear as we walk."

If Emma noticed Lizzie's red cheeks and the agitated way she pulled at her dress, she said nothing. They left the alcove and rejoined the crowd. Rossetti stopped short, however, at the sight of a man who was holding forth to a group at the center of the room. The faces around him ranged from reverence to thinly masked contempt, but they all appeared to be listening closely, like pupils at a lecture.

"That's John Ruskin," Rossetti said. "The critic and collector. And, incidentally, the man who's kept me in my meals and lodgings these last few months. I must go speak to him."

Lizzie studied Ruskin. He was tall and slender, with a thick shock of light brown hair, a thoughtful expression, and eyes that darted around the room as he spoke, taking everything in. Whenever he gestured or turned toward different paintings, the group shifted with him, as if he held them on marionette strings.

They joined the crowd around him and Lizzie heard him speak: "The question here is one of truth to nature." He let the pronouncement hang in the air for the moment, as the group murmured their assent. "That is, is the artist painting life and nature as they truly exist? Or is nature no different to the artist than the scenery at the opera, a pretty setting for his composition? And if it is a mere setting, what does that painting teach us about life, about beauty? No, sir, don't answer, it's a false question. Such a painting teaches us nothing! It is useful only as a decorative item, and nothing more."

The gentleman who had been quieted by Ruskin put his hand up, as if he was asking for permission to speak. "Then I take it that you disapprove, Mr. Ruskin, of the charming domestic scenes displayed to such great effect tonight?"

"As a matter of fact, I do. These charming domestic scenes, as you call them, lack the very essence of art, as it should be. They reveal nothing; they ask nothing. They are meant only to be hung above the mantel in a nice home, and never to give provocation or offense. They are fashion and decoration only; no better and no worse than a nicely trimmed bonnet."

A shocked whisper went through the crowd at these words, and Ruskin looked as pleased at their distress as if they had cried out their approval. Rossetti alone nodded his agreement, and spoke up. "Mr. Ruskin has hit the thing on the nose. Our art is stagnating in its own sentimentality. The modern artist celebrates the humble— the adored wife or pet, the country landscape—and fails to elevate it with either skill or beauty."

"Here, perhaps, is our answer to this dilemma," Ruskin said, ushering Rossetti to the center of the group. "Allow me to introduce Mr. Dante Rossetti. No doubt you've seen his very fascinating picture of the Virgin Mary as a child." He glanced around the room and located it. "This way, please, right over here."

"The first thing that you'll notice," he began, settling again into the role of professor, "is the elevated subject matter: the mother of Christ. This is no mere portrait of a beloved aunt at a country gate. Now, the Virgin Mary is a familiar subject, but one that is presented here in a wholly unique way. We see her as a child, but not, as is the usual way, studying a book under the watchful eye of her mother, Saint Anne. What, really, is the chance that a female child of her day and age would often, if ever, be reading? No, instead

Rossetti has portrayed her at her embroidery, leaving the books to the side as a symbolic gesture only, representing the lessons of charity, faith, and hope. The coloring and the use of light should also be noted. The painting is radiant; there is little shadow. And why should there be? The classical proportions of light and shade have no place in this picture. The purity of Mary, and of the saints and angels who surround her, banish any such shadows. Mark my words, this is the new direction of the modern painter. He will paint things as they truly are, or as they might have been, irrespective of any conventional rules of picture-making."

Rossetti gave Ruskin a deep bow. "That is kind praise. I only hope that it's deserved."

"It most decidedly is, and you would do well to remember it. If I am not much mistaken, the other critics will not be so easy on your work, and on that of your friends, in the coming weeks."

Rossetti seemed surprised. "But the pictures have had a very good reception!"

"Yes, but in circles such as these, a little scandalous gossip and a lot of good champagne will go a long way toward endearing the public. In the sober light of the coming weeks, however, I'm afraid that other critics may make a feast of your revolution, and leave nothing but scraps upon the table. We critics are known to be set in our ways, after all, and you have made a bold statement against the current fashion." He paused to give Rossetti a sympathetic smile. "But do not concern yourself with their words, and do not, by any means, take them to heart. I have faith in your Brotherhood, as they are calling it, and I expect that in time the public will be swayed to see things as I do."

"Then I may count on you as a friend?"

"You may indeed. In fact, I've been meaning to visit your studio again—I'd like to see what you're working on, and I might have a few buyers for you." Ruskin looked past Rossetti, and caught sight of Lizzie, who had hung back. He studied her for a moment before speaking. "Is it?" he asked, hesitating. "Could it be Deverell's page, the lovely Viola?"

Lizzie smiled, pleased to be recognized, and nodded her head.

"May I present Miss Elizabeth Siddal?" Rossetti asked.

Ruskin bowed to Lizzie. "What a pleasure. Deverell's portrait is very fine. But it does no justice to the real thing. Are you sitting for Mr. Rossetti?"

Lizzie opened her mouth to speak, but Rossetti cut in. "Yes, she is. I've done a number of studies of her, some in watercolor, and one or two in oil. She's proven a very capable model."

"I have no doubt," Ruskin said, gazing at Lizzie long enough that she had to look away. "With her cheekbones and your talent, the work must be very fine."

Rossetti laughed, and Lizzie heard nothing forced about his laughter. To the contrary, he seemed pleased by Ruskin's attentions to her. It was a surprise, after his shortness with Deverell, but of course Ruskin was an important man, and Rossetti would want to court his good opinion, and his checkbook.

"Why don't you come round to the studio next week? If you like what you see here"—Rossetti nodded in Lizzie's direction—"then I have more than a few sketches of her that you might want."

"You may depend upon it. I'm anxious to see the new work." Ruskin turned to Lizzie. "And I look forward to seeing you as well, Miss Siddal."

Lizzie gave Ruskin her hand as he took his leave, but she could not summon more than a slight smile for him. She knew her role tonight was to aid Rossetti in bringing notice to his paintings; he had made that very clear. But Rossetti's compliments had sounded to her ears more like the cries of a street hawker, lavishing praise on her beauty as if she were a particularly juicy apple for sale. She thought of her distaste at being called out into the shop to model bonnets for a wealthy customer, the feeling that she was no different to them than a wooden hat block. As Ruskin walked away, she realized that she had not spoken a single word to him.

But Rossetti was in high spirits. He smiled at her, oblivious to her discomfort. "You've charmed John Ruskin, and that can only be good for both of us. He could be a powerful ally, and a champion for the Brotherhood. He seemed very keen on seeing my portraits of you. You are an absolute dove, Lizzie. I don't know what I would do without you."

Now that they were alone again, his words felt more sincere, and once again she put aside her misgivings. She must learn not to take things so personally—she herself was not for sale, after all. When they spoke of her, they were really only speaking of Rossetti's paintings of her, which was a different thing altogether. It would serve her well, she thought, to remember the difference.

Rossetti plucked two glasses of champagne from a waiter's tray and handed one to Lizzie, who drank it quickly. The champagne made her giddy, and she was happy to let Rossetti lead her from group to group, where ladies inquired after her dress and gentlemen demanded that Rossetti paint her portrait for them. As the night wore on, the room seemed to open its arms to her, and she imagined for herself a future filled with champagne, parties, and fine dresses. Rossetti never left her side, and at last she gave herself over fully to the pleasure of the evening, as all about them whirled the glowing faces and glittering smiles of those who admired them and wished them well. She had arrived.

CHAPTER 8

After the success of their evening at the Exhibition, Lizzie knew that it would be madness for her to steal off to see Walter Deverell behind Rossetti's back. After all, Rossetti had made it perfectly clear that he objected, and why shouldn't she honor his simple request? It wasn't unreasonable—he might need her at any moment to sit for one of his own drawings. And if they were going to be married soon, it really wasn't proper for her to sit for other artists. And yet, despite all the reasons why she should not be on the omnibus to Kew, that was exactly where she found herself on a brisk September morning.

If Rossetti had been less insistent, less sure of her affection, she may have let the matter drop. But several months had passed since the night of the Exhibition, and Rossetti had not mentioned their talk, or the possibility of their engagement, again. He seemed happy to let things go on as they were, and Lizzie was losing patience. It didn't help that her mother peppered her with questions about his intentions whenever she could get Lizzie alone, and that even the usually imperceptive Mr. Siddal seemed to suspect that Lizzie was up to something other than making bonnets at Mrs. Tozer's. Lizzie wouldn't be able to hide the fact that she was modeling from her father forever, and when she did tell him, she wanted the news to be cushioned by the announcement of her marriage.

Rossetti's refusal to give her any real promises in return for her obedience was maddening. She had all but given up her position at the millinery for him, and now he was preventing her from sitting for other painters.

Her old obstinacy, tamed only in part by her desire to please Rossetti, resurfaced. Didn't Rossetti allow himself to be carried along by every impulse and romantic notion that crossed his mind? Why shouldn't she enjoy the same liberties?

When, at the beginning of September, Rossetti went to Birmingham to meet with a new patron, Lizzie seized on his absence as a chance to visit Deverell without deceit or explanation. If she was guilty of anything, she told herself, it was only of an omission, and a small one at that. She wasn't going to sit for a painting, after all, but only a few sketches.

The studio in the garden was just as pleasant as she remembered, though now its cheer came from vases full of early autumn blooms, rather than the fire that had first greeted her. Through the door she glimpsed Deverell at work at his easel and Mary sitting nearby. Lizzie tapped on the glass and then let herself in. Deverell rose at the sound of the door, and Lizzie was brought up short. He was pale, his face almost white, and the skin below his eyes was as dark as a bruise. His wan face was not the only change—his eyes, once bright, now seemed faded, though no less kind, and his hand trembled slightly as he held it out to her.

"You've been ill!" she exclaimed. "I shouldn't have come."

Deverell stepped closer and took her hand. "Nonsense. I haven't been well, it's true, but I'm fine now. When I received your note, I knew a visit from you would be just the thing to restore me completely."

Lizzie was relieved to hear that his voice was still as she remembered it, low and hearty. She glanced at Mary, who carefully avoided the question in Lizzie's eyes, instead rising to embrace her.

"It's so good to have you here, Lizzie. Walter and I were a drab pair without you! I'll just run up to the house to fetch some things for tea, and then you have to tell me everything that's happened since we last saw each other. I heard that you made quite an impression at the Exhibition." Mary bustled out of the studio and Lizzie and Deverell were left alone.

"I am glad that you're better," Lizzie said, "and glad to be here."

"So Rossetti has come around?" Deverell asked. "I thought I'd have to give you up, after that little scene at the reception. He seemed determined to keep you to himself."

"Dante's away on business, and can't possibly need me today. I couldn't see any harm in coming to see an old friend."

Deverell's smile faded, and the coldness of his next words surprised Lizzie. "You came here behind his back? I wouldn't have thought you capable of such artifice." He paused and frowned. "What hold does he have over you?"

Lizzie thought that there must be some very great change in Deverell, or in herself, for him to speak to her this way. "Please, you must not think ill of Dante—it's only that he's so serious about his work, and he never knows when inspiration might strike. It makes him easy to know that I'm there if he needs me. And I hope you won't think ill of me, either. I'm a free woman, after all, and I may come and go as I please."

"You didn't seem so free when I saw you at the Exhibition."

Lizzie blushed, hating to admit that Rossetti had given her no real reason to answer in the negative. She forced a laugh and tried to hide her embarrassment with light banter: "Oh, but I am free! No man can claim my obedience besides my father, and he takes little interest in such claims." But the words rang hollow in the silence that followed. That sort of talk had no place between her and Deverell, with whom she had always felt at ease being herself. "My heart," she finally said, "is not quite so free. You asked me what his hold was. I'm not sure if I know. But I love him. I feel as if I never knew myself until I knew him. When he paints me, I am a holy thing to him. What woman would forsake the chance to become a goddess?"

Deverell started to turn away again, but then changed his mind and stepped closer. His next words were quiet, but their softness in no way detracted from their force. "Be careful, Lizzie. Rossetti is not a god, and he is certainly not a monk. He won't always be content merely to worship at your altar. If he doesn't keep you as his wife, then he keeps you as a pet, and you are far too fine a creature to be kept like a songbird in a cage, petted and kissed, when you should be free."

"Deverell, please don't."

They stood in pained silence for a moment, and both were relieved when Mary returned with the tea tray.

"Walter?" Mary asked, looking at Lizzie's white face. "Why are you upsetting dear Lizzie?"

"No, no, it's nothing," Lizzie said with forced cheerfulness. She moved past Deverell and began to help Mary with the tea.

"I know you adore Shakespeare," Mary said. "So you'll be pleased to hear that Walter has planned another beautiful picture of you from one of the plays. I've looked over the sketches and they're lovely."

"No," Deverell interrupted his sister. "I changed my mind. I have something quite different in mind for Miss Siddal."

"Oh, well, of course, you're the artist," Mary said, surprised.

"I'm happy to sit for anything you like," Lizzie said. "But I'll only be able to sit for a few sketches. I don't know when I might be able to return again."

"It's no matter." He had decided, it seemed, not to quarrel with her. "I'm happy to have you here for however long you can stay. I have a painting in mind that will require only your spirit. For the rest—the hair, the cheek, and so on—Mary will do as well as anyone."

"Well! I'm glad that I'll do for something!"

"Mary, don't listen to me. You'll do quite nicely, is what I mean. And indulge me once more, darling sister, by being a dear and running up to the house to fetch your gray parrot for me. I need him for my picture."

Mary went up to the house for her parrot, and Deverell turned once more to Lizzie. "I'll give you no reason to fear upsetting Rossetti. In fact, I'll paint your hair as black as a raven, and no one shall know you, unless they guess by the fineness of the sentiment."

"Thank you." Lizzie saw that Deverell understood, and that he would treat her with sympathy, rather than scorn. Her face brightened. "I almost forgot! I've brought you a little present."

She opened her small portfolio and took out a sketch, which she handed to Deverell. It was a drawing of a woman sitting at a loom. In it, the woman stares steadily out of her window, while behind her the threads of her weaving fly wildly from the loom and a great mirror on the wall cracks to pieces. "It's my poor rendering of the Lady of Shalott, at the moment that she turns to see Lancelot through the window, and brings the curse upon herself by leaving off of weaving her magic web. I hoped it might serve as a remembrance of your kind gift to me of Tennyson's poems."

Deverell examined the sketch and then smiled, his eyes regaining some of their brightness. "It's very well done! You've made progress since I last saw your work. Has Rossetti been giving you lessons?"

"You're very kind. No formal lessons, I'm afraid, but of course I learn so much just being in the studio with him. And I always think of your encouragement, and practice whenever I have a spare moment."

The door rattled and Mary entered, carrying two wicker birdcages. "I've brought the gray, as well as the canaries. I hope that you don't mind, but they could use the change of scenery. They drive Mother mad with their chirping and chattering all day in the drawing room."

Deverell began to set his scene. He propped open the door to the studio, beyond which was a neat gravel walkway and border of boxwood and geranium. He hung the canary cage from the doorframe and placed the parrot's cage just outside the open door. Then he opened the little gates of the cages.

"Won't they fly away?" Lizzie asked.

Deverell shook his head. "No, they're quite domestic. They've been fed by Mary's gentle hand for far too long to dream of taking to the open skies. We call them lucky, of course. Their fine feathers and pretty songs have bought them comfort and ease, of a sort. Now, Lizzie, if I could ask you to pose in the doorway as well? With your profile toward me, and your attention on the canaries, as if you were feeding them. Or must I worry that you will fly away if I leave the door open?"

Lizzie laughed. "No, I won't desert you. I'm afraid that I'm quite as domesticated as these gentle birds."

Deverell drew his easel closer to the door and began the sketches. Lizzie cooed at the birds and they sang back to her. Mary filled a teacup with seeds for them, and Lizzie fed them from her fingers, laughing with delight when one jumped from its cage onto her shoulder and settled itself happily just below her chignon. She knew that she made a charming sight.

Deverell's sketches took the better part of the day, and he didn't take a break until well into the afternoon. The weather was fine, and the days were still long, so they took a turn in the garden when they were done, not wishing the visit to end. When it was at last time for Lizzie to leave, Mary gathered the birds into their cages and returned to the house.

"I hope that you'll come again, if you can get away," Deverell said.

"Then we are friends?" Lizzie asked, holding out her hand to him.

"Yes, of course we are friends. And I hope that you'll remember that friendship if you're ever in need of it. I feel some responsibility for you, you know."

They smiled at each other, and Deverell's smile was tender, not like Rossetti's, which dazzled her with its brilliance, but left her blind to everything else. Deverell's friendship, on the other hand, felt like a real thing, something that she could put into a carved box and hide away for later.

"Come," Deverell said. "We'll share a cab. I'm on my way into the city." As they left the studio, he pressed some money into Lizzie's hand. "Your fee, for your excellent work today."

Lizzie could tell, without looking, that it was far too much for a single day of work. "It's not necessary. I came to you today as a friend."

"I'll hear no arguments. Think of it as a present, and buy some pretty trifle. A woman of your beauty should have things as lovely as herself."

Lizzie smiled and slipped the money into her pocket. She could never resist a gift, and she knew exactly where she would spend it. "In that case, would you tell the driver to take me to Cranbourne Alley?"

It was nearly six o'clock when Lizzie reached the doorstep of Mrs. Tozer's Millinery. Deverell helped her down from the cab and made her an elegant bow, then jumped back in and rode on with a last wave of his hand.

Jeannie Evans stood on the doorstep, greeting the last of the day's customers, and she waved her hand and called out: "Lizzie! Is that really you? Why, the girls will never believe it!" She took Lizzie's arm and led her into the shop.

The girls didn't have to believe it—a few of them had seen Lizzie through the window, and now they gathered around her, exclaiming over her dress and the glow in her cheeks. Even Mrs. Tozer joined them in their admiration. She held Lizzie out at arm's length and looked her over, eyeing Lizzie's dress with a seamstress's practiced eye. "Just look at our Miss Siddal—it *is* still Miss Siddal, isn't it? I suppose if it weren't, you would have called on me to do the wedding bonnet!"

"Yes, it's still Miss Siddal—though perhaps not for long." Lizzie blushed, touching off a wave of giddy laughter from the girls. Whatever they'd thought of her before, she was now worthy of their interest, and they had only to see whether she might also be worthy of their jealousy.

"Now, now, girls," Mrs. Tozer said. "Let her be. A lady hardly speaks of such things." She smiled at Lizzie, as if the two of them were now of the same breed, with the other girls to be indulged only up to a point. "Are you here for a social call only? Or for a new bonnet to hide those blushing cheeks?"

"You did say, Lizzie, that you would only come back here to order your new bonnets, as I remember!" Jeannie chimed in.

"And so I am," Lizzie said, not bothering to keep the satisfaction out of her voice. She turned to Mrs. Tozer. "Do you still make the brown silk, with the ostrich trim?"

"Certainly, and it's a fine hat. But for you, my dear, something better is in order. Even in our little corner, we heard that Mr. Deverell's picture caused quite a stir at the Exhibition—no doubt your beauty is being celebrated in all the best quarters! We must make something fit for your new position. And of course you can tell all of your new acquaintances where it came from."

Mrs. Tozer tugged at the chain around her neck and produced a key from her bosom that unlocked the cupboard where the finest materials were kept. She rummaged about for a moment and then pulled out a bolt of black velvet and a box of iridescent blue-green peacock feathers. She began to trim the feathers herself, separating out the most beautiful part, the eyes, and arranging them in a fan shape, which she held up just above Lizzie's ear. In the mirror, the feathers shone brightly against her red hair.

"That will do quite nicely," Lizzie said, allowing a hint of imperiousness to creep into her voice.

"I should say so!" Mrs. Tozer laughed. "They're our finest trimmings."

Lizzie laughed, too, unable to mask her pleasure with indifference. While Mrs. Tozer wrote up the order, the other girls gathered around, asking questions so quickly that she could hardly answer one before the next was put to her. When Mrs. Tozer finished, Lizzie proudly placed her money on the counter. Jeannie gave a low whistle and shook her head. "You've really come up in the world. And there I was thinking that you was half mad."

"Yes, girls, our Lizzie is quite an example," Mrs. Tozer said. "You could do worse than to cultivate yourselves in her style." She turned to Lizzie. "Didn't I tell you, my dear, that this was your opportunity to make something of yourself? Now mind, when it's time to order your trousseau, you come straight to me. I can help you at all the better shops."

Lizzie blushed, thinking of the day—soon, she hoped—when she would be buying the things that she would take to her new home as a married woman. "I wouldn't dream of going anywhere else."

When she was finally able to leave the shop, she did so with a light heart, pulling the door closed behind her with hands free of the ache of work. Jeannie was right: She had come up in the world.

But a new gown and the means to buy a pretty bonnet were only the trimmings. As she walked down Cranbourne Alley, she promised herself that she wouldn't come back until she came to order her wedding bonnet. It was only then that her new position would truly be established.

CHAPTER 9

Rossetti spent the next few days after his return from Birmingham in a state of high agitation. Whatever good cheer he'd found in his new commissions had been lost on his return to London, when he opened the papers to read the reviews of the latest exhibitions.

"Just listen to this, Lizzie," he bellowed, a newspaper clasped in his hands. "That underhanded bastard, Charles Dickens, writes here that we are nothing but a class of juvenile artists who, with the *utmost impudence,* style ourselves the Pre-Raphaelite Brotherhood! He says, and I quote, that we have an absolute contempt for perspective and the known laws of light and shade, and an aversion to beauty in every shape. And in a letter to the *Times,* no less!"

Lizzie murmured sympathetically, knowing that Rossetti's rage must wear itself out.

"And all the while," he went on, "Dickens is turning out populist drivel that is no more art than the lowest sort of comic. This is a disaster, Lizzie, mark my words. Who in London does not worship at the feet of the great Charles Dickens? There won't be one among us who can get a commission to save our lives after this."

He threw the paper down and Lizzie picked it up and glanced over the review. She sighed. The paintings had been popular at the Exhibition, but in the end the critics had come down very hard on anyone associated with the Scandal of the PRB, as it was being called, and of course it was the opinion of the critics that mattered.

Rossetti rose and began to pace. "The damned critics have rallied round the Academy, just as Ruskin said they would. It's as if every English artist, upon receiving his first sketchpad, must swear his loyalty to God, the Queen, and the Royal Academy. No matter that the artists at the Academy turn out nothing but sentimental rubbish. The critics fawn over them, and then turn and cast insults at the first really interesting—the first really beautiful—paintings to be shown in decades. I despise them—they are nothing more than failed painters themselves, and they will not be happy until they drag us down to their own level!"

Lizzie laid a gentle hand on Rossetti's arm. "You've thumbed your nose at the Academy—you can't be surprised if people call you arrogant. They're scared, as people always are of something new and bold. In a few years they'll all be swearing up and down that they were the first to admire your work. And there have been some good reviews. John Ruskin has come to your defense, and his words surely carry as much weight as those of Dickens, when it comes to art?"

"Ruskin has stood by us, thank God. But it will take more than one man's opinion to make a success of this movement."

Lizzie wrapped her arms around his shoulders and rested her chin on his shoulder. "Pay them no mind. I know how talented you are. I can see that you paint dreams, while others paint only what they can see. What sane man would prefer a painting of a fruit bowl, when he could instead look upon the divine visions of the great poets? The public will come around in due course. One day you won't be able to paint fast enough to satisfy all of those who clamor for your work."

"If you see beauty in the paintings, then I don't care what anyone else thinks. I'll just have to keep painting, Charles Dickens be damned." He turned to her. "I can never be gloomy for long when you are here, my little dove."

"Then I won't leave your side. But Dante . . ." She hesitated. "There is something that I want." Deverell's praise of her drawing had made her bold. "I want to learn how to paint. I mean, really paint, not just the little drawings that I've been doing. I want you to teach me."

She was afraid that he was going to laugh, but he didn't. Instead, he looked at her thoughtfully. "Then I'll teach you. Your drawings show talent, I've told you that before. But before you learn how to paint, you have to master the basics: the human figure, the hands, the face, and trees, flowers, petals. Those are your tools, no different from the spangles and ribbons you use to fashion a bonnet. The beauty in any painting comes from a hundred tiny decisions of color and shade and detail, but the basic framework must be there first, the roots that feed the blossom. Come here."

He motioned to his easel by the window, and Lizzie sat before it, very aware of being in his seat. He fastened a large sheet of drawing paper to the easel, and handed her a charcoal pencil. "We'll start with life drawing. Your figures are good, but you need practice. The drawing you did of the Lady of Shalott sitting at her loom, where is it? Not around? It would be a pity to lose it—it had a lot of promise, and the figure was well proportioned. But if I remember right, it was a bit stiff. Don't look so hurt! If we are to make you into a real artist, you must set aside your vanity."

She nodded, encouraging him to go on, and Rossetti began to draw, sketching a quick series of figures in various poses. He was focused and energetic, taking to his new role as teacher with relish. He pointed to the first figure. "This man, Lizzie, what is he doing?"

"Sitting?"

"He's seated, yes, but what is he doing?"

She hesitated for a moment, studying the figure. There were no other details to give her a clue, not even a chair, and the lines were rough, more a suggestion than a true rendering. But as she looked, she noticed that while the curve of his back implied indolence, the tilt of his head suggested that he might be daydreaming, rather than sleeping, and his outstretched foot looked ready to tap a beat. "He's listening to music," she said, suddenly able to imagine a small band of musicians and the park bench where the man sat.

"Exactly!" Rossetti cried. "And this one?" He pointed to the standing figure, done at a slight angle, his arms folded and one foot crossed over the other.

"Is he waiting? Waiting for his lover, perhaps, and leaning against a building, or a tree."

"Precisely. Do you see, Lizzie, how important a few little lines can be? How they can tell a story as easily as an entire canvas? A woman sitting at a loom sits differently from a woman at her mirror, or a girl at a workroom table in a millinery. We shouldn't have to see the loom to know that the girl is a weaver. We should be able to read it in the grace of her arms, the delicate movement of her fingers, and the strength of her back. The lines of the figure are not mechanical things; they are creatures of emotion."

"I see," Lizzie said, although she wasn't entirely sure that she did. But she sensed the beginning of an understanding, a new awareness of the unseen elements of a painting.

"It takes time—it can't be learned in a day. You must draw, every day, and practice. When you're not sitting for me, that is. But today I will sit for you." He tossed aside the sheet that he had drawn on and fastened a fresh paper to the easel. Then he sat in the chair that was normally hers, leaned back, and crossed his legs.

It was difficult to begin. Her hand was unsure, as if she had never held a charcoal before. Her first effort was stilted, even to her eyes, with the shoulders too square and his face blank, like a mask. She tossed it aside and began again. The second one was better, but not by much. This too she crumpled up.

Rossetti laughed. "You're trying too hard. If you worry too much about what I'll see when I look at it, you won't be able to concentrate on what you see. I promise that I won't even peek. Just draw what you see, and be honest."

The result this time was better. Not good, she knew, but better. It caught something of his amused grin, the relaxed slouch of his shoulders. She put down the charcoal, and her hand ached as badly as it did after a long day sewing bonnets. She'd started after lunch, but now the light was nearly gone from the studio.

"May I see?" Rossetti asked, standing and stretching.

"No! You promised that you wouldn't look." She clutched the paper to her chest as he tried to grab at it.

"What kind of teacher would I be if I didn't give you a critique?" He snatched the paper from her and looked at it for a moment. "Not bad at all. In fact, it's rather good. You're going to be very good." He kissed her once, hard, and she felt her cheeks flush, from his praise and his touch.

"Come with me tonight," he said, turning to his desk and rummaging through a pile of correspondence. He found what he was looking for, an invitation, and slipped it from its envelope. "I've been asked to a soirée at the home of Lord Lamberton."

"Lord Lamberton?" The name sounded familiar. "The collector?"

"Yes. He buys up paintings the way some buy bread."

Lizzie didn't pause to wonder why Rossetti was just now asking her to accompany him. An invitation to such a fashionable party was too exciting to question. "But my dress!" She looked down at her plain gown. "I dressed for a day of sketching."

"You look splendid as you are. Your gowns are proving more popular than my paintings. I've already seen several ladies of our acquaintance adopt your style. And besides, I have something for you."

He reached into a drawer in the desk and brought out a little velvet bag. The bag contained a long strand of luminous seed pearls, which he looped carefully around Lizzie's neck. She fingered the lovely pearls, which were smooth, with a slight graininess reminiscent of their seabed home. "Dante. How on earth? With all of your expenses, and I know that the rent is still to be paid. . . ."

"Hush. They're just a trinket, a little souvenir from my travels. I wish that I could buy you the finest pearls of the Indian Ocean. And perhaps someday I will. But for now I hope that you will accept this token of my affection."

She nodded and turned away to hide the tears that welled up, unbidden, in her eyes. "It's the finest gift I've ever received. I wouldn't wish them to be any different."

She turned to admire herself in the glass. The strand of pearls transformed her simple blue dress. She loosened her hair and let it fall around her shoulders, then smiled at her reflection. "I would be honored to accompany you tonight."

Rossetti hailed a cab and they clattered into the night, the streets of London slipping by in a series of gaslit vignettes as they made for the leafy streets near Holland Park. Rossetti took Lizzie's hand and kissed it. "You'll be the most beautiful woman at the party. And don't worry, you won't feel out of place. Lord Lamberton's parties are never stuffy."

Rossetti's words touched off a wave of anxiety that Lizzie had been trying to ignore. She knew that he went out often without her, in the evenings when she was at home with her family, and she had begun to wonder why he didn't at least ask her to come along. She worried that he hesitated to introduce her into society because her family and position embarrassed him. "Stuffy?" she asked sharply. "By stuffy do you mean respectable? I'm perfectly fit to associate with genteel people, you know. Or are you ashamed of me?"

Rossetti sighed. "As far as I'm concerned, you're fit to associate with the Queen. I only meant to say that you would know some people there. Ford and Emma Brown are coming, I believe. They haven't been about much since their little girl was born, and it will be nice to see them. And Lord Lamberton likes to keep his parties lively. He always invites poets, painters, singers—even dancers. But of course there will be people of his own sort there as well. There might even be a few people who are interested in my work."

"Oh. Of course I'll be very pleased to see Emma," Lizzie said, regretting her touchiness, and the anxiety that it revealed.

They rode the rest of the way in silence, and in the quiet streets of Holland Park, the only sound was the carriage wheels and the crack of the driver's whip. They pulled up in front of a grand red-brick house surrounded by a high hedge. A gravel path led to the front door, which opened as if by magic as they approached, and a silent butler took their cloaks and waved them into the hall. The door closed behind them, and the spicy scent of incense filled Lizzie's nostrils.

When their eyes adjusted to the low light, they saw that they were in a long hall of iridescent blue tiles, which glinted like the sea under a noon sun. Above them, marble columns stretched grandly up to a gold leaf ceiling. Bronze sculptures lined the walls, and Lizzie recognized among them a small statuette of Narcissus, peering at himself in the pond. She laughed, wondering how he could be expected to fall in love with his own image in the midst of so much beauty.

Arm in arm, they walked down the hall toward the muffled sounds of the party. The hall opened into a cavernous room, where the soaring walls were inlaid with thousands of tiles and bits of glass in shades of cobalt, sapphire, and indigo. White Arabic script wove its way across the tiles, its unfamiliar letters twisting seamlessly into flowers and snakes, which climbed the walls as if they were a garden trellis. In the center of the room, a black marble pool shone with the soft light of candles that floated on its surface like lily pads. Lizzie had never seen anything like it.

The room was full of people. The women were intimidating in their collective beauty and style, and they lounged on window seats and fainting couches in poses of studied nonchalance. The gentlemen roamed among them, laughing loudly and blowing great plumes of cigar smoke toward the arched ceiling. A band played a strange and keening music, and servants clad in silk headscarves and kohl-blackened eyes threaded their way through the crowd, pouring fragrant teas and wine into jewel-toned glasses.

Lizzie looked at Rossetti in wonder, and he smiled and nodded his head as if to say yes, this is all real, you're not dreaming. She shook her head in a pantomime of disbelief, but her eyes traveled over the room, taking in every detail. She felt that she had at last drawn back the heavy curtain of the city's most fascinating drawing room, and what she saw was more wild and beautiful than she had ever imagined.

She heard a familiar voice behind her and turned. "Lizzie! Dante! There you are!" Emma Brown trilled. "Isn't it too much?" She gestured around the room with her fan and then opened it with a flick of her wrist and fluttered it in front of her face. Above her fan, her eyes sparkled with amusement. "It's all very grand and mysterious. The costumed servants are an exotic touch, I dare say."

"Lord Lamberton never does things by halves," Rossetti said, looking around. "The house is a work of art in itself. Say, have you seen Holman Hunt? He's supposed to be here."

"Yes, he was just over there. . . ." Emma scanned the room. "There he is! Hunt! Hunt! Over here!" She waved her fan.

Holman Hunt caught her eye and came over. He shook hands with Rossetti and nodded to Lizzie. "Lord Lamberton certainly has a taste for the East. I'm thinking of trying to get him to put up some funds for my painting trip to Palestine. What do you think? I bet that he'd be game to commission a few pictures."

"He might, at that," Rossetti said. "When do you leave? I hate to think of the painting that you'll do there without me."

"Not for a few months. And you know that I would love nothing more than to have you come with me. The light there is supposed to be the most beautiful in the world. What do you say?"

Rossetti's eyes took on a faraway look at the suggestion, as if he were already among the desert dunes, the flat light reflecting off of the sand. He'd mentioned to Lizzie several times that he was thinking of joining Hunt on his travels, but Lizzie had done everything in her power to gently discourage him. She hated the thought of his leaving for so long. A trip to Palestine would take at least a year, and if they weren't married, or at least engaged before he left, it would be ridiculous for Lizzie to wait for him. She would have no means of support, except to go back to Mrs. Tozer's, if Mrs. Tozer would take her back, and no reason to think that he would return to her. She slipped her hand into his and squeezed it, willing him to remember that she was a reason to stay.

Rossetti glanced over at her and seemed to snap to attention. "No, no, it's very tempting, but I have all the inspiration that I require right here."

"I see," Hunt said, looking at Lizzie with somewhat less affection. "Of course I understand. I myself am loath to leave my fiancée, Miss Miller. But I have our marriage to look forward to on my return, and the thought of that happiness must sustain me."

"And when do I get to meet the beauty who finally tamed you? I've heard so much about her from Ford."

"You can meet her now," Hunt said, looking over Rossetti's shoulder. "Here she comes."

The little group turned toward the approaching woman, who moved through the room like a siren, turning heads as she went. Her hair was golden, and she wore it loose, like Lizzie's. Her gown was daringly low cut, and the men in the room took no pains to hide their admiration of her gifts, despite the sizeable pearl engagement ring on her finger.

Emma leaned toward Lizzie and whispered in her ear: "Don't be fooled by the new dress—Annie Miller's as low as they come. Hunt may have taken her out from behind the bar, but I don't think that he's quite managed to take the taste for the bar life out of her."

Hunt beamed at his intended as she joined the group. "Miss Annie Miller," he said, taking her hand. "Allow me to present Mr. Dante Rossetti."

Miss Miller made an exaggerated curtsy and smiled at Rossetti. Her cheeks were flushed from drink, and she tossed her head and simpered, aware of her effect on the men in the room. When she began to speak, Lizzie wasn't at all surprised to hear the thick accent of the lower classes. She shuddered at the harsh tones, though she knew that it was only with great effort that she had avoided such an accent herself. But Miss Miller clearly couldn't care less what people thought. Lizzie shifted away, not wanting to be associated with the fringes from which she had somehow made her way here.

"Mr. Rossetti," Miss Miller said, ignoring the two ladies completely. "Very pleased to meet you! Hunt 'as told me all about you, you know." She smiled and placed a light finger on Rossetti's chest. "A great painter and a great rascal, he says! Well, I like a man with a little fire in him. Keeps life interesting, I say."

Hunt cleared his throat, and Lizzie saw him flush, but Miss Miller took no notice of his discomfort.

"The pleasure is all mine." Rossetti looked at Miss Miller appraisingly. To Lizzie's surprise, he seemed impressed by what he saw, rather than repelled. "Now I know why Hunt has kept you to himself for so long—you must be a great asset to him in the studio. But I insist that he bring you round to my studio at your earliest convenience, so that I might paint you as well."

"To be sure!" Annie giggled, enjoying the attention. "But nothing naughty, mind you. Now that I'm to be married, my dear Hunt tells me that I'm only to sit for portraits of the highest kind!" She let out a peal of laughter and Rossetti laughed right along with her.

Lizzie's eyes went wide. The man she saw before her was very different from the serious painter and poet whom she knew, the one who had promised to paint no one but her. That man never would have been amused by Miss Miller's crude jokes.

Lizzie wasn't the only one made uncomfortable by Miss Miller's easy manner. "Annie, dear," Hunt hissed. "You're making an exhibition of yourself." He turned to the rest of the group. "Miss Miller is a great one for jokes."

Lizzie leaned in to Rossetti's side. "Dante, it's a bit close in here—I need some air."

"It is warm," he agreed, not taking his eyes from Miss Miller. "There's a lovely terrace right through there." He pointed to the doors that led out to the garden. "Why don't you step outside, and I'll join you in a moment."

Lizzie had no choice but to smile tightly and make her way alone onto the terrace. She had no wish to watch Rossetti fawn over Miss Miller. Emma shot her a sympathetic smile as she left, but didn't offer to accompany her, either—she was enjoying the spectacle of Hunt's fiancée far too much to leave.

The terrace was breezy and dark, and Lizzie found a bench sheltered from the noise of the party by a low hedge. The night air cooled her jealousy. She knew that she shouldn't let Rossetti's flirting bother her. After all, she had to admit that it wasn't really the flirting that annoyed her, but the sight of the showy engagement ring on Annie's finger, while her own finger went bare. But it was useless to fret over such things; Rossetti had promised her that he would propose as soon as he had the means to support her, and his work was going well. It wouldn't be long, surely, before she had a ring of her own.

She inhaled the cool September air, relishing the heady scent of night-blooming jasmine, and felt refreshed. The glow of the party beyond the terrace doors beckoned to her, and she was just rising to rejoin her group when she heard her name spoken by a familiar voice behind the hedge. There was a moment of silence, and she heard the sounds of two men cutting and lighting their cigars. Intrigued, she paused for a moment to listen, but she couldn't quite place the voices.

"Yes, she is very beautiful, but her beauty is nothing in proportion to this madness that Dante has for her."

"They're saying she's an enchantress, that she's cast a spell on him and now the poor man can draw no one but her. Have you been to his studio lately? The walls are papered with her image—he'll have to find a buyer as taken with her as himself if he hopes to make a living. But perhaps John Ruskin is his man—I heard he bought a whole sheaf of them. And now Rossetti has brought her here, to Lord Lamberton's. I do think that he means to marry her."

Lizzie heard laughter. "Marry her? I should think not, though I've heard they're lovers. No, he'll never marry her. She plays at gentility, but you know she's got no money and no family. Just like Miss Miller, though Hunt doesn't seem to care."

"Is that so? When I was introduced to her at the Exhibition she looked down her nose at me as if she were the Duchess of York. For my own part, I much prefer Miss Miller—for all her coarseness she seems a great deal more fun."

"That she is. And of course, Hunt may marry as he likes. His family has no pretensions and he makes a fine living. But Rossetti would do better to meet some girl of property, with an interest in supporting the arts . . . and supporting an artist."

The two men laughed. "Rossetti isn't the only one who's come under her spell. Walter Deverell was quite gone on her as well. When he hinted as much to his mother there was an awful row. Can you imagine the very prim and proper Mrs. Deverell welcoming a shopgirl as a daughter-in-law? She sent poor Deverell off to an uncle in Sussex to get him out of the city and away from her."

"Probably for the best. Shall we?"

Lizzie listened as the men stubbed out their cigars and walked back toward the house. She'd stood frozen behind the hedge, but now she sank back down onto the bench, her head bowed under the weight of the men's words. So that was what was said of her: that she was Dante's whore.

It hardly mattered that it wasn't true—if it was said, it was as good as true. She slapped her hand against the bench in frustration. How naïve she had been, to think that she was making a success of herself. They had seen through her, and easily. She tried to fight back her tears, but they came anyway. She dropped her head into her hands and sat on the bench, unable to move. That was how Emma found her a few minutes later.

"Lizzie? Are you unwell?"

She wiped her eyes on her sleeve. "Oh, Emma, I'm such a fool."

"What's happened?" Emma asked, putting an arm around Lizzie's narrow shoulders. "Surely, my dear, this can't be about Annie Miller. Dante's flirting means nothing. He's just humoring Hunt. You mustn't take it to heart."

"No, no. It's not that, though I have just heard myself compared with her, and not favorably. I overheard two men making sport of my reputation."

To Lizzie's surprise, Emma laughed. "Is that what all this fuss is about? The men always chide us for our gossiping, but I do believe they love a scandal as much as we do. Dry your eyes, Lizzie, that's nothing to cry over. You've no idea what they used to say about me. But now that Ford and I are married, it hardly matters, and they are on to the next scandal."

"But what if it's true? What if they all look down on me?"

"I've never heard anyone say a single unkind word about you. Whoever said that doesn't know what they're talking about, and you shouldn't pay them any mind. Now come back inside, dear. I was sent to fetch you. John Millais has just arrived, and he's looking for you. Do you know him? He's the most successful of the bunch, I should say. He spoke to Dante about you—flattering things, dear, don't look so worried! He wants to have you as the model for his new painting, and he won't take no for an answer. It's to be a painting of Ophelia—on a grand scale and very romantic."

The faint memory of a dream—a heavy satin gown and the twisted gates of a castle—tugged at Lizzie's memory. "Ophelia? He wishes to paint me as Ophelia?" She paused. "But Dante will never allow it. I'm sure you remember how he put poor Deverell off of painting me at the Exhibition. He seems determined to have me sit for no one but him. And I've no wish to cause a row."

"I don't think Dante would dare to refuse him. Millais has been very kind in sending ready buyers in Dante's direction. And, besides, I heard from a little bird that Dante's warning didn't put you off of sitting for Deverell at all." She laughed at Lizzie's shocked face. "Very little happens in this circle that I don't hear about. But don't worry—I'm sure that Dante doesn't know, and besides, it's my opinion that he may tell you what to do as soon as he marries you, and not a moment before." She stood and held out her hand to Lizzie. "Now put on a brave face, and let's go inside. This is a party! You mustn't take everything so seriously."

"You're right." Lizzie smoothed her hair and dress, but she could not so easily smooth over her ruffled feelings. Everything had worked out for Emma, but Lizzie had no such guarantee—no promise from Rossetti. Still, she had come so far, and she would not give up yet. She linked arms with Emma and went in to find John Millais.

Millais waved as they entered, and then came forward and made Lizzie a little bow. "The celestial and my soul's idol, the most beau- tified Ophelia!"

"Mr. Millais," Lizzie said, giving him her hand and glancing side- ways at Rossetti, who was doing his best not to look put out.

"I've been waiting patiently for my chance to paint you. And now I have a picture for which no one else will do. Do say that you'll sit for my portrait of Ophelia."

She turned to Rossetti, and tried not to sound too eager. "Can you spare me?"

"It will be a great difficulty, but if I must, I can spare you." His tone was friendly, but she could tell that the effort cost him some- thing. "I can't deny a favor to a friend, and you will make a fine Ophelia."

"Then I would be happy to sit for you," Lizzie said to Millais. "Just name the day."

"While the weather's still fine, I'll paint the background, in Sur- rey. As soon as that's finished, I can begin to paint Ophelia. We can work through the winter at my studio." He offered her his arm, and paraded her around the room as he told about his plans for the paint- ing. Rossetti and Emma followed behind, and Lizzie felt a little tri- umph at knowing that Rossetti was sure to be jealous of Millais's attentions. It would serve as a reminder that he had no real claim on her yet.

Millais's compliments helped Lizzie to forget the ugly gossip that she'd overheard, and soon she was laughing and gossiping with Emma as if nothing had happened. As the clock approached mid- night, the older guests left and the revelries became more spirited. Lizzie watched the men pass around long black pipes, and the room filled with opium's sweet, sticky smoke. Faces and jeweled hands seemed to float unattached in the mist, and the figures before Lizzie moved slowly, smiling and laughing at everything and nothing.

Voices echoed from the tiled walls in crescendos and diminuendos of sound, like waves crashing against the shore and receding back into the fold of the ocean. A high voice pierced through the din, and the guests turned as a singer began a slow, haunting song that wound its way through the smoky air and filled the room with long and eerie notes. A drum and guitar provided a spare accompaniment. As the tempo quickened, an oboe joined in, followed by a tambourine.

Without warning, the music stopped and the room went silent. The lights dimmed and a murmur went through the crowd.

Suddenly, the tambourine started again, high and fast. Two kohl-eyed servants threw open a curtain in the wall to reveal a beautiful woman with her arms raised above her head and her hips thrust to one side. The band started up again and she began to dance, swirling through the room, her gold-threaded skirts floating around her and the bells at her ankles and wrists keeping time with the music.

More dancers appeared at the door and made their way into the crowd, drawing the guests into an impromptu dance and filling the room with twirling couples. Even Lizzie allowed herself to be pulled out onto the floor by Rossetti, and together they danced across the room as the music urged them on.

They no longer seemed to be in London, or in any real place. The night was a mad dream, and it would be remembered as dreams are: in shards of light and color, the echo of a whispered aside, a haunting scrap of melody. Lizzie spun in Rossetti's arms, letting her hair and dress fly around her. Annie Miller danced past her, moving her hips as expertly as the dancing girl and trailing a wide-eyed Hunt behind her. But amidst so many wonders Lizzie hardly noticed. She pulled closer to Rossetti, abandoning herself to the call of the strange and intoxicating music.

It was nearly morning when the last guests took their leave. Rossetti stumbled a little on the path. "Should we walk?" he asked. "I need to clear my head."

Holland Park was quiet, populated only by servants and deliverymen who scurried up to the back doors of the grand houses before the families awoke. As they drew closer to the river, however, the streets narrowed and came to life. Poverty kept no hours, and in these crowded alleys the poor moved like wraiths through the morning's long shadows.

Children were everywhere: collecting rags to sell, or sitting bundled in doorways with younger babes asleep in their arms. Glassy-eyed men stared at Lizzie and Rossetti, gauging whether they might have anything worth taking, and women in cheap gowns called out to Rossetti as they passed, paying Lizzie no mind.

She pulled in closer to Rossetti's side. She was not afraid—she was used to such scenes, had passed them countless times outside her own door. But it was shocking to see so much suffering after the splendid excesses of Lord Lamberton's house. She felt for a moment that she had lost the physical presence that pegs a person to time and place, as if she were a falling leaf that could either ascend to the heavens or drift down to settle in the mud, depending on the breeze. She buried her head deeper into Rossetti's shoulder, wishing to pin herself to something real. But as she turned to him, the sight of a woman in a doorway brought her up short.

The girl was crouched on the step, her head tipped back to rest against the door and her arms crossed. Her dress, once grand, was dirty, and her skin and hair were the sallow color of moth wings. She stared out at the street, but she didn't call to passersby like the other girls. The girl's eyes caught Lizzie's attention. They were an unusual shade of pale blue, watery but still distinctive, and Lizzie thought that she would know them anywhere.

She broke away from Rossetti and went over to the girl, motioning to Rossetti that he should wait for her in the street.

"Bess?" she asked, suddenly unsure. The girl looked like a milliner from Mrs. Tozer's shop, but her face was badly wasted, and on closer inspection Lizzie thought she might have made a mistake. "Elizabeth Bailey? Is that you?"

The girl in the door stared at her for a moment. "Lizzie Siddal? My God, I'd never 'ave thought to see you 'ere." She looked Lizzie up and down. "But you look very well. What are you doing out here?"

Lizzie glanced back at Rossetti, who was still standing in the middle of the street. "No, no. I'm not . . . I'm just . . ." She trailed off. She couldn't think how to explain to Bess why she was walking in the street in the middle of the night with a man who was not, in fact, her husband.

Bess reached out and fingered the strand of seed pearls around Lizzie's neck. "Well, anyway, it looks like you've done very well for yourself."

Lizzie blushed, but she was too worried by Bess's state to feel much shame at her own situation. "Bess, you don't look well."

"I been ill since last month. I went to the hospital but they was short on beds and sent me off. The gentlemen won't have me looking like this, but if I don't work, I don't eat." She looked down at the ground and then back at Lizzie with a smile that was more like a grimace. "It's a far cry from Mrs. Tozer's, where I've found myself, ain't it?"

"Lizzie?" Rossetti called. She glanced back at him and held out her hand, asking for one more moment.

"You'd best be off. You don't want to keep your gentleman waiting. But it warms my heart to see that one of Mrs. Tozer's girls has made good for herself."

Lizzie could have cried. She felt that she had failed in some way, though she couldn't say how. She reached into her pocket and pulled out the few coins that she had, pressing them into Bess's hand. She was afraid that Bess might refuse her charity, but she didn't protest.

"Lizzie!" Rossetti called again, angry now. He started to walk over toward her.

"I must go, but I'll come back to see you."

She turned and ran back to Rossetti. He looked at her, and his eyes had a strange sheen to them. "Who was that? Was that . . . a friend of yours?"

"Of course not," Lizzie said, thinking quickly. She couldn't let him connect her in any way with that sort of girl—her position was already so precarious. "A charity case. A poor unfortunate I helped at the church. I'm afraid that she's not been reformed."

When she looked at Rossetti again, his eyes were kinder, the light of suspicion extinguished. "You're an angel of mercy," he said, pulling her close. "Let's get you home. The streets at night are no place for a lady."

CHAPTER 10

Rossetti paced back and forth in his studio, glancing at his watch at every turn. What was keeping Lizzie so late? It was long past the hour when she should have stopped by on her way home from Millais's studio.

An image of Millais and Lizzie entwined on the sofa, the painting forgotten, came unbidden to his mind. Would Millais dare to take the liberties that Rossetti had, for the past year, denied himself? He tried to banish the thought, but it only grew more insistent. Finally he cursed and threw on his overcoat. He would go to Gower Street to check on her.

The January night was so cold that his back ached from shivering and each breath was painful. He flipped his collar up against the bite of the wind, but he had no defense against the creeping chill of his own thoughts. He imagined them, alone for hours on end, sharing the intimacy of jokes and compliments that should have been his.

In the two months that Millais had been painting Lizzie, Rossetti's jealousy had become constant, seeping up like bile and spoiling his taste for food and drink. He was too restless to paint and his verses sounded stilted to his ears. Worse yet was the thought that the Ophelia painting might be very good, and that Millais would then possess a part of Lizzie's beauty that Rossetti would never be able to regain, even if he were to possess her in other ways.

It had been a mistake to allow Lizzie to sit for Millais, but he had felt that he owed too many of his commissions to Millais's influence to refuse him the favor. And he hadn't been able to object on the grounds of propriety, since they weren't married. He ought just to marry her, he thought, and be done with it.

And why hadn't he married her? The question seemed always to be hanging between them these days. He could sense her expectations, like the drag of a current beneath the water's brilliant surface. But even when he gave himself over to the ecstasy of painting her, he always pulled back at the last moment, stubbornly resisting the tide that should have borne him along to the moment where he declared his love, plucked it down from the heavens and presented it to her like a gift in a silver box. And yet—why should he rob the heavens of that star?

He told himself that his love for Lizzie had nothing to do with the things of this earth; it was neither the feverish satisfaction of desire that he found in other models, nor the steady companionship of husband and wife. It was as pure as poetry and as delicate as a gossamer web; it could only be marred by human touch. How could he take such a love and lay it out in his mother's drawing room, to be handled and picked over by those who knew nothing of its secrets? To the outside world it would look cheap and tawdry, he an artist and she a model from the lower classes, and their judgment would make it so.

And so the question of marriage had remained just that: a question. But the answer could not be put off forever—he couldn't race out into the cold night like a lovesick schoolboy every time Lizzie was out of his sight. He knew he ought to give her the position that she deserved, and make sure that Millais's painting was the last one that she sat for, save for his own.

He arrived at the studio and saw that the lamps were still burning and Millais was at his easel, his brush poised over the canvas. Millais put one finger to his lips, indicating that Lizzie was not to be disturbed. "She's been in that position for hours," he whispered. "She really is quite a skilled model. I can tell what you see in her."

"Can you?" Rossetti shot Millais a wary look. Millais shook his head dismissively and turned back to the painting, and Rossetti joined him by the easel.

The painting showed Ophelia spurned by Hamlet and driven mad by his betrayal. She has raced from the castle and thrown herself into the weeping brook, but it has not yet pulled her to her muddy death. The stream is tranquil, the water smooth and dark, and field roses spill over its banks like a protective veil. In the midst of the calm water floats a girl, her face and hands just breaking the surface and her lovely features pale and still. It was a dream tinged with horror; the sublime beauty of youth and love preserved for one moment on the cusp of death.

Lizzie made a perfect model for Ophelia; her translucent skin and heavy eyes suggested a girl on the threshold of the next world. But most importantly, she was willing to indulge Millais in a rather unorthodox scheme, submerging herself in a tub of water every day for hours on end so that he could capture the exact look of a drowned girl and make his painting as true to nature as possible.

It was one of the guiding principles of the Brotherhood: A painting must reflect the truth of nature. In keeping with this principle, Millais had painted the background entirely in the open air, on the banks of a river in Surrey. But it was not practical, particularly at this time of year, to paint Lizzie floating in a real creek. He'd mentioned the possibility, but it presented far too many difficulties, not the least of which was the chance of his model drowning, just as Ophelia had. Instead, he'd painted her as she lay floating in an old tin bath filled with warm water. The studio could be cold, but he heated the water with oil lamps placed below the tub, and the lamps made the water just warm enough to keep Lizzie comfortable. It was awkward, to be sure, and the lamps had to be refilled with oil several times a day, but Millais was not one to sacrifice his artistic principles over a matter of mere comfort.

Each morning, Lizzie donned an antique wedding dress that had cost Millais a small fortune. Then she climbed into the tub, fully clothed, and lay back, letting her face and hands float just above the water. Her red hair fanned out, undulating like sea grass, and her gown, all silver embroidery and tiny seed pearls, floated around her like a shroud.

Rossetti needed to see the painting only once to know that it was a masterpiece. It was at once hauntingly dark and full of a radiant beauty. His first acute pang of jealousy was quickly overcome by admiration. "It's wonderfully like her. It gives me chills just to look at it. You've captured the sad, sweet moment of transcendence perfectly. Is Ophelia still among the living or not? The canvas doesn't tell. It's like a secret taken to the grave."

"Thank you. It's coming along, but slowly, and I'm afraid that poor Miss Siddal must be soaked right through. I'll just be a few more minutes, and then I promise to release her to you."

Rossetti looked at Lizzie lying silently in the tub, as still as a wax figure. Her face was tilted toward Millais, with her lips slightly parted and her eyes staring off into the distance, as if she were seeing her final vision. In her upturned palm she held a wreath of flowers, and he saw that it contained a single poppy, the bright scarlet flower of death and dreams.

Outside the studio, a high wind whipped down Gower Place. It tugged at the shutters, and one flew open with a bang, letting in a cold gust of air. The shutter beat against the wall and the lamps danced, casting their flickering lights over Lizzie's face. Rossetti watched in horror as the play of the light transformed her delicate features into a grotesque mask. Her cheekbones stood out in stark contrast to the dark sockets of her eyes, and the shadows ate away her flesh, revealing her skull. He shuddered and stumbled back, convinced that he saw some grim omen in her face.

The shutter banged once more and then the wind stopped, just as suddenly as it began. The lamps calmed and the shadows retreated to their corners, restoring Lizzie's youth and beauty. The studio was quiet for a moment, but it was like the eerie silence before a storm. Rossetti waited, his body tense, and when a terrible sob broke the silence, he jumped more out of reflex than real surprise. Lizzie sat straight up in the tub, her chest heaving and the water swelling violently around her.

He ran the few steps to her and tried to pull her from the tub. Her body was limp and heavy in his arms. "My God, man! This water is freezing! How long has she been in here?"

"I-I don't know." Millais came over to help him. "I don't remember when I last filled the lamps. They may have gone out some time ago." Together they lifted her, in her soaking gown, out of the bath and onto a nearby sofa. Rossetti held her cold hands in his warm ones, and pulled a shawl around her shoulders.

"Miss Siddal, why didn't you say something?" Millais demanded, clearly distraught. "It was madness to sit in that cold bath! You may have done yourself harm!"

Lizzie cupped her fingers together and blew on them. "I'm so sorry. I tried to keep still for as long as I could. You were so intent on your work, and I didn't want to disturb you. But I couldn't stand it any longer." She looked at Millais with eyes filled with tears. "I must get into some dry things. I'm really very sorry if I've failed you."

"Please, don't apologize; you haven't failed me in the least. Rather, I've failed you. Go change into something warm at once."

Lizzie walked behind the oriental screen in the corner of the studio, her wet finery dragging behind her. Shivering, she started to undo the tiny satin buttons of the dress. Her fingers were numb, and she struggled to get them loose. On the other side of the screen, she heard Rossetti laying into Millais for neglecting the lamps.

At last she freed herself from the soaking gown. She threw it over a rack to dry and slipped into a dressing gown. Now that she was warmer, she felt tired. It would do little harm, she thought, to sit by the fire in her robe while she combed out her hair.

She stepped from behind the screen and Rossetti and Millais fell silent. She knew that they were looking at her, but exhaustion made her unmindful of her modesty. She walked unsteadily toward the sofa, and each step seemed to take a tremendous effort, as if she were walking through water. She felt hot, and she wanted to ask if they could open a window to let in some of the cool night air, but she couldn't form the words. She stood in the center of the room, staring blankly around her, not knowing, suddenly, where she was, or where she was going.

Rossetti watched as Lizzie emerged from behind the screen in a silk dressing gown that swirled around her ankles as she walked. Her skin was still pale and her eyelids were lowered drowsily, but the effect was mesmerizing. When she stopped before the fire, the light from the embers caused her copper hair to blaze like a flame.

He had the disorienting sensation of having seen this all before. The vision of white skin and red hair was intensely familiar, and yet it was not an image of Lizzie that tugged at his memory. He closed his eyes, and he saw the girl on the bridge, the red-haired beauty who had raced past him in the night, fleeing the unhappy scene.

It was Lizzie—she was the girl whom he saw that night last year, he was sure. And it was fate, he thought, that had led him back to her. Entranced, he walked toward her, his hand extended. But before he could reach her, she let out a soft sigh, looked around with unseeing eyes, and collapsed into a dead faint.

CHAPTER II

❧

Ophelia wandered through the woods, her shrill laugh ringing out in the quiet forest. She carried a bouquet of wildflowers, and she threw them one by one onto the path, like a bridesmaid. She followed the path to a brook, singing a melancholy song:

> To-morrow is Saint Valentine's day,
> All in the morning betime,
> And I a maid at your window,
> To be your Valentine.
> Then up he rose, and donn'd his clothes,
> And dupp'd the chamber-door;
> Let in the maid, that out a maid
> Never departed more.

The brook was high and the water rushed by, catching fallen flowers in its eddies. Tall reeds rose up along the banks, and a weeping willow let down its branches to skim the water's surface.

The water was cool and inviting. Ophelia stepped onto the low branch of a willow tree and inched out along its length. The branch formed a gentle curve over the water, and she lay down in its cradle.

She heard the snap before she felt the branch give way. In an instant she was in the water, its icy fingers pushing beneath her dress and combing *through her hair. The shock of the cold seized up her breath, freezing the scream in her throat. Her gown wrapped around her like an anchor, and she began to sink, pulled down by its weight.*

She searched desperately for a hold in the banks, but she couldn't get her footing in the soft silt. Her head went under, water filling her mouth and stinging her eyes. Above her, the surface shimmered and she stretched her fingers up to it. With the last of her strength, she gave a mighty push, fighting her way toward the light. Her face broke the surface of the water, and she took a grateful, gulping breath of air.

Lizzie bolted upright in bed, eyes wide, gasping for breath.

"What is it?" cried Lydia.

Lizzie stared at her sister, who stood above her, holding her by the shoulders, her face fearful. Still half dreaming, Lizzie looked around wildly. For a moment she didn't know where she was, but then she realized that she was at home, in her own room.

"You're very ill," she heard Lydia say. "You must lie back down." Lydia eased her back against the pillows and drew the blanket over her.

Lizzie could hear voices in the kitchen below. First her father's, tense and angry, and then her mother's calm tones. Her eyelids felt heavy and she let them drop. She remembered Millais's drafty studio, the cold bath, and then nothing. "Have I been ill?" Her voice was hoarse, and her lips felt dry and cracked.

"Yes, with a terrible fever. These are the first sensible words that you've uttered in two days. You hardly knew me when they first brought you home! The doctor's been several times. He said it's an infection of the lungs, on account of the bad chill that you received."

Lizzie tried to think, but her mind was a confused procession of dreams and memory: the drafty studio and the cold forest path, the icy swell of the water and the memory of a lilting song. Or was it the sound of voices, calling to her? She shivered and pulled the quilt tighter, as if the memories were a cold wind.

"Mother will want to know that your fever has broken."

"Wait." Lizzie put up a hand to stop her sister. "Who brought me home?"

"Two gentlemen carried you in. You could hardly walk yourself." Lydia paused for a moment, remembering. "One was Mr. Millais, who introduced himself to Father, and the other man I recognized as Mr. Rossetti, from your stories. He seemed quite frantic, but I didn't speak with him. Father sent us straight out of the room when they arrived."

"Yes, that would have been Mr. Rossetti. Father must have been livid—did he make a terrible fuss, Lyddie? Oh, if he did, I'll be too ashamed to see them again!" For a moment, she forgot her illness and thought only of her mortification. "And I suppose they saw our poor little house, with the shop downstairs. It must have looked very shabby to them, and Father very coarse."

"That's a terrible thing to say, Lizzie! Father has been beside himself while you were ill. Anyway, I hardly know what sort of gentlemen they could be to bring you home in such a state. Of course Father was angry! He threw them both straight out of the house. He had no idea that they were artists; he couldn't think what you were doing with them. He thought . . . well, I'm sure that you know what he thought! Mother had to tell him the whole story, so he wouldn't assume something worse."

Lizzie's face went paler, and Lydia grew alarmed. "I'm sorry, Lizzie. Please don't upset yourself. The important thing is that you're making a recovery." She laid a gentle hand on her sister's brow. "Much cooler. Now, I mustn't delay another moment, Mother and Father will be so relieved." She rose and left the room before Lizzie could object.

Lizzie sighed and turned to face the wall. Her shame at the imagined scene burned as hot as any fever, and she suspected that its effects would be just as harmful. She'd never intended to introduce Rossetti to her family until an engagement was firmly in place. He may not, after all, have turned out to be quite as wealthy as she had supposed, but the genteel Charlotte Street of his upbringing was miles away from the shabbiness of Kent Place. She wasn't so foolish as to think that such things wouldn't matter to him, despite his professions to the contrary.

Mrs. Siddal appeared at the door, and Lizzie watched her face, lined from many years of nursing sick children, soften. She came over to the bed and smoothed Lizzie's hair back from her brow. "We were very worried for you. Thank God the fever has passed."

"I'm so sorry, Mama. I never intended this to happen."

"But what were you thinking? It was madness to sit in a cold tub, in the middle of winter, no less. If I'd known, I never would have allowed it. I've told you before that these notions that you get are going to lead you to no good. Your father . . ." She stopped as Lizzie began to cough, unable to chastise her daughter while she was so ill.

"I *am* very sorry, Mama. I'm sure that Mr. Millais never meant to cause me any harm. He had no idea that the water was cold. Is Father angry? Will he forbid me from sitting for paintings?"

Mrs. Siddal sighed. "I have only myself to blame, I suppose. I agreed to let you sit for that painter in the hope that you might make some good connections. But it's been nearly a year now, and nothing has come of it. Perhaps it would have been better if I'd forbidden it."

"How can you say that nothing has come of it? I've met Mr. Rossetti!"

"Yes, but where has that left you, other than ill in bed? No, Lizzie, I'll not hear any arguments. You know that I dreamed of a good marriage for you, but at the moment I can see no hope for it. You're ill, and people are starting to talk. The neighbors know that you aren't working for Mrs. Tozer any longer. If Mr. Rossetti doesn't marry you, what decent man of our acquaintance will have you? It was a mistake to ever let you take up with those people."

"You don't understand. They do things differently in his circle."

"You're right, I don't understand. But I do know that you need rest. There will be no question of your modeling at the moment."

Lizzie's disappointment was blunted by exhaustion. She lay back in bed, the pillows swallowing her thin frame. "Then I'm to give up hope?"

"Oh, Lizzie, you've always been dramatic! When you're well, I'll see what I can do. Naturally, your father is angry, but he may come around. But I'll hear no more talk of it now."

Lydia returned to the room with the tea tray and a bowl of broth. Mrs. Siddal kissed Lizzie on the forehead and rose, leaving the sisters alone. Lydia waited for their mother to close the door, and then nearly upset the tray in her eagerness to retrieve an envelope that she had secreted beneath the cloth. "Look, a letter, from Mr. Rossetti. It was mixed up in some notes from our cousins; I don't think that Father even noticed it."

Lizzie tore it open and began to read:

Chatham Place, February 1, 1851

My Dear Miss Siddal,

You've made everyone quite frantic over your health, and you should know that not so much as a single flower has been painted by any of us in our concern for your well-being. Millais is beside himself, and of course I gave him quite a lecture on your behalf. Please write immediately to set us at our ease on your account or Art itself may be in danger of extinction, lacking its muse.

Do take good care of yourself—I must have my little dove back, as my work goes nowhere without you. Deverell sends his regards. He's laid up as well, some problem of the kidneys, but I've just been round to see him and he seems to be on the mend. He insisted that I not worry you on his account.

I think that I caught sight of a charming sister or two when we brought you home. Perhaps one of them would be so kind as to post a letter for you, assuring me that you're no longer in danger?

Your affectionate,
D. G. Rossetti

She read the letter twice over. Lydia looked on expectantly, but Lizzie didn't hand it to her to read, as was their usual practice. It was hardly a love letter, but it was too intimate to share. Lizzie flushed with pleasure, and hope once again filled her heart. Perhaps he had not found her family too far beneath him after all.

"Well," said Lydia. "I can see that you're pleased. But come, have some tea and something to eat. You've got to get your strength back."

"I can't eat now, I haven't a bit of appetite. Be a dear and fetch me my notepaper and a pen. I must write him back."

Lydia gave her an exasperated look, but she fetched the paper and Lizzie composed her note to Rossetti. She assured him that she wished nothing more than to return to his studio, but that the doctor, judging her condition serious, could not allow any thought of it at the moment. She would allow him to worry a little longer on her account; such fears, she knew, had a way of working on the heart.

Satisfied, she signed the letter and gave it to Lydia to post. Then she settled back into her pillow, exhausted by the effort. She let her eyes close. It would not be so long, she thought, until she was back in Rossetti's studio, lounging on his sofa as he painted her, or read his poetry to her. As she drifted off to sleep, her thoughts lingered on Rossetti, and her dreams played across the lush landscape of a medieval painting.

CHAPTER 12

Lizzie was young and healthy, but her recovery proved much slower than everyone had hoped. For several weeks she hardly moved from her bed, stirring only when she heard the sounds of the post delivery.

Just as she began to regain her strength, the fever returned with a viciousness that had the family on near constant vigil for her life. The doctor was called to her side almost daily, and the bills began to accumulate. The lines on Mrs. Siddal's face deepened each time she passed the sideboard where they sat, unpaid.

At first, Rossetti's notes came regularly. Lydia read them to her as she lay in bed, half delirious with fever. Lizzie was often too ill to reply, but she thought of little else. Of course there was no question of his coming to see her, but as the fever raged, he visited her dreams. He came to her as the poet Dante to his beloved Beatrice, eyes wild with love as she held his burning heart in her hands. She imagined them embracing, and then woke with a start, the sheets soaked with sweat.

At last the fever passed, and the household settled into a wary sort of relief, tested often by Lizzie's lingering cough. Her skin, always fair, turned a more troubling shade of white, and when she was at last able to rise from bed, her clothes hung from her thin frame. If not for her hair, still bright, she might have been mistaken for a ghost haunting her old rooms.

She lay sick for most of the winter, but at last a mild spring day presented a good opportunity for her to venture outside, and Lydia brought her shawl and boots, along with a few letters from the last post. Lizzie sorted through the letters, scanning each for a familiar hand. She hadn't received a note from Rossetti in over a week, and she was anxious for news.

When she saw that there was nothing from him, her heart dropped. His letters had once been filled with lamentations over her health and prayers for her quick return. But lately, if he wrote at all, he spoke more of his own comings and goings, and his plans for new paintings. She could see that he was increasingly caught up in the world outside, while she was left pathetic and dull in her little room in Kent Place.

She was about to toss the pile of letters aside when a note at the bottom of the stack caught her eye. She was pleased to see that Walter Deverell had written, but as she read, what little color she had drained from her face.

Kew Green, April 10, 1851

Dear Miss Siddal,

I hope that this letter finds you in better health, and that your strength is indeed returning, as I have been told. My mother and sister also send their regards and sympathy.

I'm afraid that I am not writing under the happiest of circumstances. As I'm sure you know, your father has threatened a lawsuit against John Millais for his carelessness in your regard. Please know that Millais is beside himself on your account, and that he intended you no harm, and blames himself entirely for your illness.

In the hopes of avoiding the notoriety of a lawsuit, he has charged me with trying to settle with your father, as your father refuses to speak with Millais, save through his lawyers.

I have written to your father, offering on Millais's behalf to cover whatever expenses may have been incurred. I write to you because I didn't like to do such a thing without your knowledge.

It's my great hope that we will be able to settle all this quickly, and that we may then concentrate solely on getting you back to health, which is, of course, of the utmost concern to all of us.

Regards,
Walter Deverell

Lizzie finished the letter and thrust it at her sister. "Did you know?"

Lydia glanced down at the letter and blushed, avoiding Lizzie's gaze. "I didn't want to upset you. You haven't been well, and you know that Father can't be reasoned with—Mother tried, but there was nothing she could do."

Lizzie's face was tense with anger. "Father has humiliated me! How can I ever show my face again among Rossetti's friends? Doesn't he know that these men are gentlemen? They don't take each other to court over such petty matters as doctor's bills!"

"Please try to be calm, you'll make yourself ill again!"

"I don't care!" Lizzie threw herself on the bed. "What do I have to live for now? This is why there's been no letter from Rossetti. No doubt he believes that Father will bring some suit against him, and is ashamed of our acquaintance!"

"What a thing to say! At any rate, I'm sure that's not why." Lydia stopped short, her hand flying to her mouth.

Lizzie looked at her with narrowed eyes. "And what does that mean?"

"Perhaps it's better that you be done with all of them. They never seem to behave so much like gentlemen as you would make them out to be."

"Lydia, what do you know?"

Lydia bit her lip and sat down in the chair. "I suppose that I've never been any good at keeping secrets from you. Emma Brown came to visit last week, but you were too ill to see her. I sat with her in the parlor for a moment, and something that she said led me to believe that Mr. Rossetti may be . . . well, it seems that he is very much involved with a new painting. Perhaps that's why he hasn't written to you."

"A new painting? But why shouldn't he be? He may have sworn to me that he couldn't paint without me, but of course that's just lovers' talk." Lizzie colored at the daring of her words, but then went on. "He's an artist by trade, after all; he has to paint to make his living." She turned her back to Lydia and began to arrange the combs on their dresser, feigning indifference.

"It was my impression, Lizzie, that he was involved not only with his new painting, but also with his new model."

Lizzie turned, and her lip trembled, though whether it was from sorrow or anger it was hard to say. "His new model? Who is it?"

"Please don't ask me. I really know nothing of it; I shouldn't have mentioned it. Lizzie, you've lost all your color; you ought to sit down."

"Who is it?" Lizzie asked, ignoring Lydia's protests. "Who is his new model?"

"I told you, I really know nothing of it. Please sit down, I'm afraid you'll faint again!"

"Lydia! I'm sick to death of having things hidden from me. I may have been ill, but I'm not simple. Whom has Dante been painting?"

Lydia didn't reply, and the two girls stared at each other in stony silence until a knock sounded at the door.

"Well, there's an answer to it," Lydia said. "I'm sure that will be Emma now; she said that she would come by again today. You can ask her yourself about your gentlemen artists."

The door opened and Mrs. Siddal entered with Emma Brown at her side. Emma bustled into the room, looking lovely in a gown of lavender satin that complemented her dark hair perfectly. She untied her bonnet of woven straw and pale pink primroses, and threw it onto the bed. Her eyes danced as she kept up a stream of greetings, embracing Lydia and congratulating Lizzie on her return to health.

"Emma, dear," Mrs. Siddal said. "It does us good to have you here. You're a breath of fresh air, and I expect that there is hardly a house in Southwark that is more in need of one. I'll leave you girls to your talk, but Emma, please convince Lizzie to get out and take some of this nice spring air. If anyone can get her back to herself, it's you!"

"Leave it to me, Mrs. Siddal. We'll have Lizzie dancing till midnight before long."

Emma settled into a chair and removed her gloves, which were done in the same pale lavender as her gown.

Lydia looked at them enviously. "You look very fine this morning."

Emma laughed. "Yes. Ford has had a good run of sales, including an excellent price for an oil painting of me. And when my darling Ford is doing well, I'm in satin and kid gloves. Of course, when he can't get a commission, I'm in last season's muslin and an apron. That, I'm afraid, is the life of an artist's wife. You never know where your next gown, or your next meal, is coming from."

"But at least you know that you are his wife, and that his fortunes are your fortunes, for better or for worse," Lizzie said, unable to hide her unhappiness.

"That's true." She gave Lizzie a sympathetic smile. "Has Dante not been writing as often as he might? Everyone knows that he's a terrible correspondent."

"No doubt my father's suit against John Millais has scared him off. Or is it something else? Lydia tells me that he's busy with a new picture."

Emma sighed. "We're good friends, so I won't pretend that all is well when I know that it isn't."

"Thank you. I only wish to know where I stand."

"I must ask you a question. I don't mean to pry, only to understand. There's talk, of course, but there's always talk, and trying to sort out the grain of truth from the chaff of gossip is difficult at best. I must know: Is there an engagement between you and Dante Rossetti?"

Lizzie sat silent for a moment before replying. "No, there's no definite engagement between us. He's promised that there will be, as soon as he has his work in order, and I had thought—had hoped—that it was only a matter of time. . . ."

Lydia watched her sister with a pained face. "But if you had no understanding with him, why did you allow yourself to be paraded around on his arm?"

Lizzie shook her head. She knew how it must look to Lydia. The strictest rules of propriety could be bent, but only so long as a marriage was sure, at some point, to take place. It was as if the sacrament of marriage could wash away the sins of that which came before it. She only needed to look as far as Emma Brown, who was now a respectable wife and mother, to know that it was true. But if Lizzie was seen to be acting as a married woman, and no marriage followed, well, that was another thing entirely.

"Don't despair, Lizzie," Emma said, suddenly businesslike. "No harm has been done, and perhaps it is all for the best. You've had a brilliant career so far as a model, and everyone speaks quite highly of your sketches, and of your poetry. I suppose that the news of your latest victory hasn't reached your sickroom? Millais's painting of Ophelia is an absolute success. They're saying that it's his masterpiece, and that his model must be part nymph to possess such otherworldly beauty. You're famous, my dear! Every painter in London will want you to sit now. And no doubt your affair with Dante can be used to your advantage. You're known as part of their circle, and if you wished to publish some of your own work, you might depend upon those connections."

"My affair with Dante? Emma, you can't think that I've done anything of which I should be ashamed!" Lizzie faltered for a moment. "Of course, I know that the appearance of things is against me, but I swear to you that I've done nothing with Dante that can't be undone. If we've been conspicuous, it is only because of the demands of his art—he hates to have anyone else in the studio with us while he paints. And if nothing else, I've never, until this moment, doubted that he loved me, and would one day make me his wife! Oh, Emma, if there's some reason why I should doubt it, please tell me!"

Emma sighed again. "You're very much in love with him, aren't you? Well, perhaps there's nothing to worry over. But I'm sure that you remember Annie Miller?"

"Holman Hunt's fiancée?" Lizzie asked, a sinking feeling beginning to form in her stomach. She could picture Annie, with her generous curves and easy smile. "Is she sitting for Dante? But I thought that Hunt forbid her from modeling for other painters? They're to be married!"

"They're engaged, but Hunt has left for his painting expedition in Palestine. While he's away, he's got up some ridiculous scheme to have his friends educate her. His idea, as I understand it, is that they'll scrub the gin-shop smell off of her and replace it with expensive perfume and lofty ideas on art and music. Then she'll be able to greet him at the altar as a lady."

Despite her dawning worries, Lizzie couldn't help but laugh. She'd seen enough of Annie Miller to know that it would take much more than some friendly tutelage to turn the former barmaid into a gentle maiden.

"Yes, I know," said Emma. "It's the height of arrogance on Hunt's part. I really can't say what he sees in her—other than what's obvious. But apparently he's not alone in his regard. I'm afraid that in Hunt's absence, Rossetti has . . . taken up her case. He's painting her by day and taking her around to the restaurants and theaters at night. They've been seen together at the pleasure gardens at Cremorne many times. So there it is, Lizzie. Of course, it could be nothing—a passing fancy, perhaps. But why should you let your reputation get caught up in such a thing? It's better, I think, that you know his heart now, rather than later. I am sorry, my dear."

Lizzie barely heard her. The buzzing in her ears drowned out all other sound. She could see them now: Rossetti and Annie, their arms around each other, laughing as they made their way through Cremorne Gardens. She pictured the crowds under the soft glow of the Chinese lanterns. The band's music wafted across the lawn to a pier over the river, where Rossetti took Annie in his arms, and she let him, not caring who saw them.

Lizzie shook her head in disgust. She'd always declined Rossetti's invitations to the revelries at Cremorne. Despite the popularity of its cafés and fireworks, the gardens had a reputation as no place for ladies after nightfall. But Annie wouldn't care about such things, and perhaps that was what Rossetti had wanted all along.

Lydia handed her a kerchief, and she put a hand to her face, surprised to find her cheek wet. She hadn't realized that she was weeping. "How could he? Annie Miller is as common as a kitchen maid. How can he be seen with her? What will I do?"

Lydia placed a consoling hand on her arm. "I'm sorry. I know that you admired him very much."

Emma looked at Lizzie with sympathy, but she quickly returned to her natural cheerfulness. "I'll tell you what you won't do. You won't waste away in this room, when you're in the prime of your youth and beauty. You must hold your head high, my dear, and carry on. Perhaps Dante will come to his senses, and perhaps not. In the meantime, you must do nothing to admit of your heartbreak to the world. This is only the first of many adventures. It may be bitter-sweet, but you have so much to look forward to."

Lizzie tried to compose herself. She knew that she shouldn't show the true extent of her grief in front of Emma, who meant so well, but was sure to repeat everything to Ford. "Of course you're right. I blame my illness for my poor nerves."

"We must get you well. Occupation and exercise are the best cure for any illness of the body or the heart, and you will need your strength, my dear. There's a new circular being published by some friends of Ford, and I've told them that you will submit a poem for the first issue. I've seen some of your verses, and they're lovely, but too sad! Rest today, and tomorrow you must write me some beau-tiful little thing that I can submit on your behalf."

"You're a dear to think of me," Lizzie murmured. Then, anxious to speak of anything other than herself, she changed the subject. "And how is little Catherine? I haven't seen her, I'm afraid, since she was no bigger than a kitten and wrapped in swaddling. She must be nearly ten months by now. How does the dear baby get on?"

Emma was only too happy to talk of her little girl, and the con-versation continued along those more pleasant lines. Emma regaled the sisters with stories of how Catherine was just beginning to crawl and had gotten into Ford's paints and brushes, resulting in some very rudimentary paintings in which her doting papa saw great promise. When Emma finally left, it was clear that she thought she left Lizzie in a better state than she had found her.

But when the door closed behind her, Lizzie collapsed under the effort that keeping up appearances had cost her. She went to the bed and sat, staring out of the window with unseeing eyes. Was it just this morning that she had wondered if she might soon be permitted to sit for him again? The promise of seeing him had sustained her through her illness. But now she knew that he wasn't waiting and longing for her return, as she had imagined. He had forgotten her.

The splendid days spent in his studio began to take on shadows. She had spent so many years daydreaming of such an adventure—had she fabricated a dream of love from nothing more than her own desire? Outside the door of her room she heard the familiar rhythms of the household: dishes clinking in the scullery, children playing in the parlor, and the door of the shop downstairs closing with a bang. The sounds that she had heard as a child, and the sounds that would fill all her days to come.

She finally roused herself to look at her sister, who was hovering over her nervously. "Leave me, please. I need to rest."

When Lydia shut the door, Lizzie went to her desk and pulled a sheet of paper from the drawer. Emma thought her poems too sad. But what happy event should serve as her inspiration? Just as she had found happiness, it had been ripped from her, and shown to be as cheap as anything from Southwark's streets.

Nonetheless, she took up her pen and tried to conjure a few verses. But no words would come, and the dull ache in her chest only seemed to intensify in the empty room. Mute and raging, she paced the room, until at last a crack appeared in the brittle surface of her anger. She remembered the tender compliments that Rossetti had often whispered into her hair, and the thought of his deceit pierced her like a blade. Her anguish spilled out as from a new wound, and she wrote with an angry scrawl. The words formed quickly, and her hand raced to follow her heart:

> *O God, forgive me that I merged*
> *My life into a dream of love!*
> *Will tears of anguish never wash*
> *The poison from my blood?*

Love kept my heart in a song of joy,
My pulses quivered to the tune;
The coldest blasts of winter blew
Upon me like sweet airs in June.

Love floated on the mists of morn,
And rested on the sunset's rays;
He calmed the thunder of the storm,
And lighted all my ways.

Love held me joyful through the day,
And dreaming through the night:
No evil thing could come to me,
My spirit was so light.

Oh heaven help my foolish heart
Which heeded not the passing time
That dragged my idol from its place
And shattered all its shrine!

Putting the words to paper calmed her, as it had in days past. She finished and leaned back in her chair, spent. Exhaustion fell over her like night, and she hardly made it from the desk to her bed before she collapsed into a deep, dreamless sleep.

CHAPTER 13

Rossetti never would have guessed, when pulling Lizzie from the cold bath, that she had suffered such a grave injury. She'd been pale, of course, and badly chilled, but her very pallor had made her all the more beautiful, and it had seemed at the time that nothing more than a hot fire and a glass of whiskey were in order. And then she had collapsed, and all was chaos.

Millais called for a doctor and a carriage, and Emma Brown was called for as well, when it was discovered that neither man knew Lizzie's address. Their arrival at the Siddal home was just as confused. Lizzie fainted again on the doorstep, and her father screamed like a teakettle and boiled over with threats and insults as the ladies hurried about, preparing the sickbed.

It was, in the end, with equal measures of worry and relief that Rossetti was chased from the house, and he didn't need Mr. Siddal's shouts echoing down the street to tell him that he was a scoundrel. He felt his lack of care for Lizzie quite keenly on his own, and he cursed the day that he had permitted her to go sit for Millais. He worshipped her; why had he let another man paint her?

At first, Rossetti couldn't work without her. For many months she had been his near constant companion: sitting for his drawings and reading poetry aloud to him, walking with him for hours through the city. And then, suddenly, she was gone.

He wrote to her daily, anxious for news of her health. He rejoiced in the receipt of her rare answers, and then fretted that they were often no more than a few weakly scrawled lines. He was restless, unable to concentrate on his work. Now that her life was in peril, he castigated himself for not marrying her and giving her a proper position, as he knew he should have. He made such thoughts the basis of many anguished rants to his friends, saying that if he were to lose her now, he would go mad with grief. His friends consoled him the best that they could, while privately shaking their heads over what they had come to refer to as Dante's obsession. Only Walter Deverell had rebuked him, saying bluntly that if Rossetti had acted as more of a gentleman, and treated Lizzie as a lady, and not some common model, none of this would have happened. Rossetti shot back that Deverell had had his chance with Lizzie and had failed to take it, and that he was only jealous. The two parted that day on cold terms, and neither raised the subject again.

As the days turned into weeks, the Lizzie of Rossetti's memory became more ethereal and more beautiful than the real Lizzie had ever been. In his memories, she was always just striking a statuesque pose, her eyes bright and a smile forming on her lips, as if she were whispering a secret. She spoke only in murmured lines of poetry, and moved about the studio as lightly as if she were carried by the same breeze that rustled the sketches pinned to the walls.

He longed for her, but he found that he could translate his longing into exquisitely executed works of art, just as Dante Alighieri had wrought his best verses from the pain of losing the lady Beatrice. Soon he was painting with more fervor than ever before. His paintings of Lizzie had always been beautiful: lush portraits of burning eyes in a pale face, crowned by the golden-red halo of her hair. But now his paintings described not only her physical beauty, but also its counterpart, the elevation of his spirit through beauty and love, longing and despair. They had a depth and resonance that he had not thought possible, and he often worked all night. He may have longed for her return, but her absence was also precious.

The more he painted, the more he wanted to paint. He wrote, asking her if she might soon return, but there was no reply. It could be months, he finally realized, until she was able to sit for him again.

In the meantime, he had an ambitious new painting in mind, and he cast about for another model to use while Lizzie was recovering. He finally decided on Annie Miller, whom he'd thought of often since they met at Lord Lamberton's party. He remembered her warmth and her wide, easy smile. She seemed to bloom from the earth like a tiger lily, vibrant and inviting.

He sent her a note, inviting her to sit. But the reply came back written in Holman Hunt's bold hand and declining on Miss Miller's behalf. No doubt Hunt suspected that Rossetti might have more than a painting in mind. But Rossetti would not be dissuaded. When Hunt's ship sailed for Palestine in February, Rossetti appealed to Miss Miller again. This time a note came back, unexpectedly, from Ford. It seemed that Hunt was no fool. In his absence, he had left Annie's care to friends who would make sure that she sat for only a few select and respectable painters, so that she could make a living while Hunt was away. To no one's surprise, Rossetti's name had not made the list.

Rossetti wasted little time in stewing over Hunt's slight. He was enjoying the chase—it worked to sharpen the image in his mind of the subject he wanted Annie to sit for, Helen of Troy.

He took care with his next note. He wrote to Annie that he wished to paint her as the face that had launched a thousand ships. It was a vision of her, he said, that he saw when he thought of Helen, the most beautiful woman in the world. He sealed the letter and paid a boy to deliver it by hand, telling him to give it over to no one but Miss Miller herself.

What woman made of flesh could resist such a note? Not Miss Miller, who arrived at his studio with a great rustle of new silk and happy laughter. She came right up and embraced him as an old friend, though they had met only once. Her smile was open and she seemed immediately at home.

"Miss Miller," he said, bowing. "Thank you for agreeing to sit for me at last."

"Think nothing of it! And call me Annie. I can't understand all of this formality, no matter how many lessons my dear Hunt gives me on manners and such. It seems an awful lot of fuss, if you ask me." She laughed and colored a bit. "But I expect he's used to having things a certain way, and I've promised to keep at my lessons while he's away."

Rossetti laughed as well. "Well, you needn't be formal with me. It will be our little secret."

Annie giggled. Then she turned and walked over to the chaise that Rossetti had come to think of as Lizzie's chair. Rossetti glanced at the sketches of Lizzie that lined the far wall. Was it his imagination, or did she look back disapprovingly? She would never have allowed him to talk like that to her, no matter what else she had let him do. For a moment he wished that it was Lizzie, and not Annie, who would be sitting for the painting. But Lizzie would have made a strange Helen of Troy—her beauty spoke of heavenly worship, not earthly lust. He turned to watch Annie cross the room, her hips swaying beneath her dress.

She sat down by the window and began to unbraid her hair. It came loose in a cascade of golden curls, like a watch spring uncoiling. Without a word from him, she undid a few buttons of her gown, so that the sleeves slipped down and he could see her white neck and shoulders. She sat still, waiting like a siren on a rock.

He cleared his throat, but his words still came out hoarse. "We'll start with a sketch, just to capture the feel of the thing. When I'm ready to start painting, we'll have to see about a costume, but for now you can wear what you like."

"How shall I sit?" She began to turn in the chair, throwing her hair back over her shoulders and widening her eyes. She pursed her lips, almost into a kiss. Rossetti laughed. He didn't care that she wasn't being serious; her levity was contagious.

"You needn't try so hard. You are Helen of Troy. The entire world has gone to war for the right to possess you, and every hero in Greece falls to his knees before your slightest glance. You've never been denied a thing that you want, and your very presence is a pleasure to others. It shouldn't be difficult for a woman like you to imagine these things."

Annie laughed, but she seemed to understand what he wanted. She turned her body slightly away from him and looked back over her shoulder, without reservation or modesty. She let her lips drop into a hint of a pout.

"Yes. That's just it." He began to draw, and the shape of her image already felt familiar to his hand. He worked without stopping, and several hours passed before the fading light forced him to put aside his charcoal. He thought that the sketches looked good, and he could already envision the warm colors he would use to paint her pink cheeks and yellow hair. The painting would be different from anything he'd done before: It would show only Helen, in all her beauty, without background or unnecessary adornment. The entire story of the fall of Troy would be written in the beauty of her features.

The sun dropped low in the sky, and the room filled with a golden light. Rossetti stood and stretched, then motioned to Annie that she could do the same. For a moment they just stood smiling at each other. "Would you like anything? Tea? A glass of water?"

Annie stretched like a cat. "I'll take a taste of something stronger than tea, if you have it."

He pulled a bottle of whiskey from the cabinet and poured out two generous glasses. "To the new picture, and to my new model," he toasted, raising his glass in cheers. They clinked glasses and tipped them back, emptying their cups, and Rossetti poured two more. The liquor burned warm and cheerful in his stomach. "Has Hunt's absence been very hard on you? A beautiful woman like you must not be used to spending all her nights at home."

Annie didn't blush; she had no false modesty. "It's not my intention to spend all my nights at home alone. Hunt will be gone for a very long time. He could be gone for two years."

"You must be very lonely," Rossetti muttered. In one quick movement he pulled her toward him and felt her body, warm and generous, press back. She tilted her head up, eager for his kisses.

For an instant, an image of Lizzie standing before that same window troubled him. But the many months of tension and waiting overcame him, and he felt powerless against his own desire. The girl in his arms, pliant and tender, was all that he could think of.

"You must be lonely as well," she murmured as he kissed her neck. "I heard that Miss Siddal isn't well. You must miss her very much."

"I do," he said, annoyed. He didn't want to discuss Lizzie with Annie Miller.

Annie laughed again. She wasn't given to jealousy. "Perhaps we can help each other. Come by my rooms tonight. If the weather is mild enough, we can go to the café at Cremorne together and hear the music. And then who knows what else the night might bring?"

"You may expect me," he said, thinking that he had a fairly good idea.

In the weeks following Emma's visit, Lizzie settled into a melancholy pattern, moving about the house as mutely as a figure in a painting. She helped her mother with the chores, but otherwise kept to her room. The coldness of her once affectionate father, and the pitying looks of her mother and sister, were more than she could bear. If Rossetti's paintings of her had helped her to discover her true self, to gain gravity and confidence, then his absence worked an opposite spell, and away from his adoration Lizzie felt herself once again fading into the background, becoming as dull as the routines that now made up her days.

Alone in her room, she found some solace in writing, and in sketching little scenes from her favorite poems. True to her word, she sent a few of her poems to Emma, but they were returned by the editor with compliments and regrets. Apparently Emma was right—her poems were too sad to be sent round in a circular. A few more letters arrived from Rossetti, but she threw them away without opening them. She didn't want his pity, and she didn't care to hear how his new painting was getting on. Eventually the notes stopped coming. It had been many months since the terrible day in Millais's studio, and Lizzie began to retreat into her old way of life, living through books and daydreams, trying not to think of Rossetti.

Mrs. Siddal tried her best to draw Lizzie back into the world, but Lizzie resisted all of her efforts, and would not be persuaded to leave the house. Eventually even Mrs. Siddal threw up her hands and decided to let Lizzie heal in her own time. But when she saw an advertisement for the Great Exhibition, she wouldn't let the chance pass, and she insisted that Lizzie must go.

On the first of May, with much fanfare, Queen Victoria opened the Great Exhibition in the extraordinary Crystal Palace in Hyde

Park. All the papers said that Prince Albert had outdone himself, and that the world had never seen such a gathering of its many achievements of art and industry under one roof. The building itself was a miracle of engineering, with massive glass walls, and soaring halls filled with the newest machinery, finest textiles, and the most beautiful works of art from all four corners of the world. Prince Albert promised that the exhibition would cement England's place at the forefront of modern technology and design.

When the Exhibition first opened, admission cost a pound, but by the end of June the cost was lowered to five shillings, so that the industrial classes could attend. Mrs. Siddal somehow found the money in her small reserves and sent Lizzie and Lydia off to Hyde Park on a bright June morning. The brisk walk did Lizzie as much good as the promise of entertainment, and by the time the girls reached the park they were in good spirits. They stared at the throngs of oddly dressed foreigners who had flooded into the city for the Exhibition, and then joined the crowd making its way into the park.

As they came down the path they were greeted by the sudden vista of the Crystal Palace, rising up from the dusty walk like a glittering mirage. Lizzie drew in her breath. It was a marvel—like a conservatory, but a thousand times larger, with a high vaulted ceiling and wings that stretched out like arms flung open to welcome the crowds.

All of London seemed to have turned out for the display. Families dressed in their Sunday best picnicked on the lawn in front of the palace, and hawkers lined the paths, selling commemorative pictures, flags, and flower boutonnieres. The tourists approached the palace like pilgrims journeying to a holy site, some even crossing themselves as it came into view. The better-heeled visitors arrived in carriages with paired horses and footmen, and did their best to appear worldly and jaded in the face of the new wonder.

A sea of pastel parasols bobbed before the gates of the palace, and the girls pushed their way through, waving away the pamphlets and religious tracts that were pressed into their hands. Lizzie glanced longingly at a vendor selling lemonade, but she only had enough money for the admission. Lydia pulled her toward the queue and they paid their fare and received their tickets and a plan of the exhibits.

They entered a soaring space large enough to house full-grown elm trees, left intact while the palace was constructed around them. Their branches rose to the highest reaches of the dome. Potted palms and beds of flowers thrived in the warmth of the glass palace. In the center of the hall, a stunning fountain of pink cut glass threw arcs of water nearly thirty feet into the air. A great mass of people filled the hall, but it was an orderly crowd, with adults and children alike on their best behavior.

Lizzie glanced at her plan, but found it of no help: There were thousands of exhibits that they might visit, and she could hardly decide where to begin. Before she could pick a direction, Lydia led her to a crowded display of modern cold-storage devices where they had a free taste of ice cream, deliciously cold and scented with vanilla, stored in an American freezing machine. They were tempted to wait for a second taste, but instead they made their way down the main hall.

The breadth of the exhibits was astounding: marble sculptures and gleaming steam engines, trays of medical devices and displays of the finest Sevres porcelain plates and figurines. Lizzie was invited to peer through a microscope at the eye of a dragonfly, which looked to her like a beehive. At another booth they watched cotton being made on a massive machine, which performed all the steps from the combing of the raw cotton to the finishing of the cloth.

Tiring of the scientific displays, the girls moved on to the hall of foreign lands. It seemed that every country in the world had sent an envoy to the Exhibition. Stall after stall showed both the new and traditional wares of Europe, Asia, Africa, and the Americas. Lizzie gazed in wonder as they passed colossal Egyptian statues, and longed to touch the display of luxurious Russian furs.

They stopped in front of an exhibit showing the riches of the Indian court, a magnificent display of wealth. Every shawl, sword, and instrument was decorated in iridescent jewels and minute gold work. A heavily secured cage at one end of the exhibit housed the Koh-i-Noor diamond. A card proclaimed it to be the largest in the world, and said that it carried a curse of misfortune for the unlucky owner. A stuffed elephant stood nearby, topped by a tiny gold carriage where a person could ride. Lizzie murmured to Lydia that the trappings of the conquered nation were exquisite, but what a shame it was that their beauty had proved no defense against their subjugation.

Lydia shook her head at Lizzie's sad observation. "Why don't we go see the medieval court? It's supposed to be the most beautiful of all of the exhibits." Lizzie nodded, content to follow Lydia, and they joined the crowd flowing to the European hall.

Although the exhibition was devoted to modern innovation, it also nodded to England's past. In the medieval court, the walls were hung with finely embroidered tapestries of knights and ladies, and stained glass windows caught the light streaming in through the glass walls. Gilt swords and scepters glinted in their cases, and brass chandeliers hung from the ceiling.

"This is every bit as beautiful as the Indian court," Lizzie said, leaning over a case of jewels. "Lydia, look at this." She pointed to a richly embroidered tapestry of a unicorn. "It's just the sort of thing that Deverell and Rossetti would love." She stopped short, embarrassed, and Lydia squeezed her arm.

"Come, let's go see the portrait of Queen Victoria and Prince Albert." Lydia steered Lizzie toward the far wall, where a small crowd was gathered around an oil painting.

The portrait showed the royal couple dressed as a medieval damsel and knight in armor, attired for a famous costume ball. Although richer in materials, the queen's gown was not so different from the style of Lizzie's dress. Lizzie had found that, particularly since her illness, the looser cut of the medieval dresses that she had sewn to sit for Rossetti's drawings did more to flatter her thin frame, and she had kept wearing them, despite the fact that she was no longer modeling.

As the girls waited to get nearer to the painting, a few of the ladies around them began to shift their admiring stares from the painting to Lizzie. "Are you part of the exhibit?" a little girl asked, fingering the dark velvet of Lizzie's gown.

"No, dear," Lizzie laughed, patting the girl's head. Many of the ladies were now staring at her, curious where she'd found such a gown. Both pleased and embarrassed, Lizzie turned away from the group. There was a time, not so long ago, when she had reveled in such attention. But now she only wished to be left alone.

She pushed back through the crowd, and then stopped. There, among the thousands of people who filled the hall, was the one person in London she both longed and dreaded to see: Dante Rossetti.

She stood completely still. Rossetti said nothing, but his face told her everything she needed to know. Surprise and relief were written across his brow, and his eyes shone with joy. "Are you a mirage?" he asked. "One of these medieval paintings sprung to life? Or are you my Lizzie, returned to me at last?"

He didn't wait for a reply. Without a word he drew her into his arms, burying his face into her hair and inhaling deeply before releasing her. She didn't resist; she didn't care who saw them, what people might think. Despite all that had occurred, she was only grateful to be near him once more. The idea that anything could separate them now seemed a farce.

"Lizzie, Lizzie," he said, shaking his head. "Why didn't you send word? I've been so worried."

"Dante," she murmured, forgetting in the joy of their reunion that his worry hadn't prevented him from enjoying himself with others. "I'm so sorry. I thought that perhaps . . . that perhaps you would be ashamed, that you were occupied with others. . . ." She let the silence hang, no longer sure why she had feared that he'd forgotten her. Neither could she reproach him for his betrayal, if he had indeed betrayed her. His eyes told her that he loved her. It could be nothing more than a vicious rumor, she thought, that he had turned his attention to Annie Miller.

Dispelling any lingering doubts that she may have had, he said simply: "You are mine, and you must return to me."

CHAPTER 14

"Here, my dove." Rossetti placed a pillow behind Lizzie's back as she lounged in an armchair in his studio. She was half asleep, dozing in the sun that streamed in through the studio windows. The balcony doors were open, and a warm breeze rustled the sketches pinned to the walls. When she stretched, her hair, loose and simply parted, tumbled over her shoulders.

Since her return, Rossetti had tended her like an exotic orchid, fretting over her care and comfort. She was too weak to go out much, and he was happy to stay with her all day in his studio. He sketched her and read poetry to her, much as he had before her illness. They had few visitors, and the studio was once again their private world, full of pet names and secret meanings, references decipherable only by themselves.

Her weakness may have cooled another man's regard, but Rossetti was more drawn to her than ever. The more ethereal she became, the closer he wanted to hold her, as if he could keep her from floating away, like the last fading memory of a dream.

Lizzie's eyes fluttered open and she peered up at him. "Have I been asleep long? I dreamed that we were in a little cottage together, somewhere in the country, with a thatched roof and chickens in the front yard. You were painting in the garden while I tended the roses."

"Even your dreams are lovely. Would you like to go to the country?"

"I'd be happy to leave London—especially for the summer." She glanced out the window at the Thames. Now that the August heat was upon them, it would soon begin to stink and they would have to shut the windows against its stench.

"I'd like to paint you crowned in roses," Rossetti said. "And perhaps I can—I've been offered the use of a cottage just outside the city. Should we go set up house there? I could do some painting out in the fields. I've been away from nature for too long; I'm afraid that my work suffers for it."

"Would it be just the two of us?" Lizzie glanced at a half-finished painting in the corner of the studio. The alluring eyes of Annie Miller stared back at her, an unwelcome intrusion in a room that was otherwise a shrine to Lizzie's image.

"Just the two of us, as we're meant to be. Though we'll have friends come to visit—we can make picnics and go out on great rambles to paint by the streams and the woods."

Lizzie looked away from the portrait of Annie, but not before she noticed that Rossetti had been working on it since her last visit to the studio. She tried not to worry. After all, it was she, and not Annie, whom Rossetti wished to take to the country.

"I'd love to go away with you. But what will I tell my mother and father? The only reason that I'm able to sit for you is that my father is still so angry with me that he's decided that I'm below his notice. He's content to pretend that I'm working at the shop when I come here during the day, especially since he needs the money that you send home. But if he thinks that we've gone away somewhere together . . . I hate to think what he might do."

"Tell them anything you like. Tell them that you'll take a room at an inn. Why should they care so long as you're handing over your wages to them?"

It was just like him, Lizzie thought, not to concern himself with the details. How could he profess his love to her and then turn a blind eye to the difficulties of her situation? It would be so much easier if he would finally declare an engagement between them. Then she might travel with him wherever he liked, with less worry as to propriety. For a moment her frustration boiled over into anger. "Should I go with you as your lover, then?"

Rossetti looked shocked—Lizzie did not usually speak so coarsely. "Of course not, Lizzie. You will come with me as my beloved." He turned, red-faced, back to his easel. Lizzie was quiet, and he could see that she was cross. "Come, my dove," he said, taking her hands. "You know that I want to marry you, and we shall marry, as soon as it is practical. The moment just isn't right. I'm just beginning to make my name, and I must put all of my effort into my painting right now. Please be patient."

"Of course. I understand." She didn't want to ruin her chance to get away from the city, and away from Annie Miller, with a pointless row. She went over and put her arms around him, laying her head on his shoulder. "Let's go to the country. There will be no one around to bother us, and you can work hard at your painting. I'll think of something to tell my parents. I can tell them I'm staying with a married friend from the shop."

"Then I'll make the arrangements. Now please, lie back down. You're going to tire yourself out." She did as he asked, and he began once again to sketch her. The afternoon faded into dusk, and Lizzie dozed off again.

When she woke, Rossetti was at the other end of the studio, working on the painting of Annie by lamplight. She sat up. "What are you doing?"

He glanced up from his work. "Just working on the background. I've got to get the canvas prepped before Miss Miller comes to sit this evening."

Lizzie rose from the chair, angry. He'd never had Annie Miller in the studio while she was there before. But of course, it was getting late. Perhaps Annie always came in the evenings after Lizzie left? She began to collect her things. "It's late. I must go."

She began to cough, and the force of her cough brought her back down into the chair. Rossetti was at her side in an instant, pouring out a glass of water. He put his arms around her and held her as the cough racked her frail frame. When she finally caught her breath, she lay back, exhausted.

Her skin was so white that Rossetti felt a chill of fear looking at her. "You're not well. You mustn't go anywhere. I'll send a note to Miss Miller—I can work on the painting another night."

Lizzie tried to rise from her seat. "No, I really must go. I'm supposed to finish a few bonnets for Mrs. Tozer in the morning."

"I didn't think that you were still working at the shop."

"It's just for the day. They're short on help." Lizzie began to cough again, and the deep rasping sounds were painful to Rossetti's ears. "I must stay in her good graces in case I need my position back. I know that you don't want me to sit for your friends' paintings anymore, and I must make my living somehow."

"No. Your health is too delicate. Besides, if you're going to be my wife, it's no more appropriate for you to work in a shop than it is for you to sit for other artists' paintings. I've had a few good commissions lately. I can cover any expenses that you have."

Winded, Lizzie said nothing, but she smiled as she leaned back to rest. "I'll send Mrs. Tozer my apologies."

"Good. I'll write my excuses to Miss Miller. You'll rest here until you're strong enough to go home."

Lizzie reclined, content. How easily Rossetti's mind had been turned from his painting of Annie. His concern for her trumped even his desire to paint. It was a small victory, but a victory nonetheless.

They travelled to the country cottage in late August, and it proved just as charming as Lizzie had imagined. It wasn't far from the city, but the air was better, the heat held at bay by a gentle breeze. There was a garden, enclosed by a stone wall, and a studio at the back of the yard where Rossetti could paint. The garden was still in full bloom, and fat honeybees floated between the heavy blossoms of hydrangea.

The borrowed cottage was like a place out of time, far from prying eyes and pressing bills. They had few guests and didn't bother to keep regular meals, eating when they were hungry and enjoying the solitude. Rossetti painted during the day and Lizzie sat for him as a model for his watercolor of *Dante's Vision of Rachel and Leah*, from the *Purgatorio*. In the painting, Rachel stares into the water of a stone fountain, symbolizing the contemplative life, while Leah makes a wreath, an allegory of the active life. Rossetti modeled both figures after Lizzie, telling her that she was the rare woman who possessed a perfect harmony of the two. The resulting picture was gorgeous, with Rachel and Leah in rich purple and emerald gowns, and the fountain glimmering with iridescent blue water.

They'd been at the cottage for a week when Rossetti emerged from his studio, tired from his work, and dropped onto the grass beside Lizzie's garden chair. He pulled an apple from his pocket and bit into it hungrily.

"Are you finished for the day?" Lizzie asked. "I thought that we might take a walk into the village."

Rossetti stretched out on the grass. "I'm through with the watercolor. When it's dry I'll send it to Ruskin. With any luck he'll want it and send round a check. We won't have to go back to London for another week. Though I may have to pay a visit to my sister, Christina."

"Christina?" Lizzie was always interested in any bit of news about Rossetti's family. Though she had known him for nearly a year and a half, he hadn't yet introduced her, and she longed to meet them. It wasn't idle curiosity; it seemed impossible that he would propose before he introduced her to his family.

"I've just had a letter from my mother. It seems Christina has surprised everyone by agreeing to marry James Collinson, the painter. You haven't met him, have you? He's a member of the Brotherhood—very talented, but poor as can be, and until he met Christina, a Catholic. It seems she's gotten him to convert."

"So she'll marry for love and nothing else, then?" Lizzie hardly dared to breathe. If Christina was permitted such freedom in her choice of husband, surely Rossetti's family could have no objection to his marrying for love as well?

"It appears so. Though it's not so much her choice in a husband that surprises me, as that she wants to marry at all. I would have placed a wager on it that she would choose her poetry over the comforts of a husband and home."

"And can't she have both? I can't see why her being a wife would prevent her from carrying on with her writing?"

"I can't imagine that it would prevent her, exactly. But naturally she'll want to concern herself more with the children and the household after she's married."

This more conventional side surprised Lizzie; she wouldn't have guessed that he harbored such traditional views. "And when we marry? Will I have to give up my writing and drawing as well? I've hardly just begun!"

"Of course not. I'd never expect my wife to do anything that didn't suit her. If that means that the house is filled with paintings and poetry and there is never anything to eat and the curtains are dusty, so be it."

Lizzie laughed, and Rossetti reached up a hand to her. "Come lie with me in the grass."

"It's wet. My dress will get damp."

"Then I'll hang it in the sun to dry." He propped himself up on one elbow and considered her. He bit into his apple, but he looked as if he would rather devour her.

She could guess what he was thinking and blushed. Since her illness he had been very gentle with her, never pressing for more than a few kisses, though they sometimes slept side by side. But in the last few days his glances had become more frank and his kisses rougher and more insistent. And she'd felt herself giving in to them, unable to resist the pull of his desire. She hated to deny him anything. She could see that for Rossetti, his passions were entwined inextricably with his art. She wanted to inspire him fully, to be everything to him, in art and in life, but she couldn't give him what she knew he wanted most, not yet.

Rossetti sat up fully. "I want to draw you."

Lizzie laughed with relief. "You may draw me whenever you like. Shall I come into the studio, or should we sit in the garden where it's cooler?"

"No. I want to draw you . . . as God made you."

Lizzie blushed again, but she wasn't shocked. Emma had told her that Ford often sketched her in the nude.

"Dante," she murmured, "I can't. There are other girls for such things. . . ."

"I don't want to draw other women." He stood and took her

hand. "Yours is the only figure that interests me. I'll draw you from the back, so your modesty won't be offended."

"I'm afraid that I lost my modesty when I agreed to come away with you to this cottage." But she felt oddly flattered by the request. She suspected that Annie Miller had posed in the nude for him, though she had no proof.

"Come," he said, pulling her up from her seat. He led her through the garden and into the studio. She stood with her back to him, and he unpinned her hair, letting it fall down her back in loose ringlets. He removed her dress, fumbling over the tiny buttons and slipping it over her shoulders and onto the floor. She sat on a stool with her back to the easel, her head turned to the side and her eyes cast toward the floor.

Her bare skin felt alive to every gust of air, and she shivered as her hair brushed against the small of her back. She wasn't embarrassed by her nudity, as she'd expected. Instead she felt beautiful and natural, just as Rossetti had promised. She had crossed this boundary, and if it had been scary to contemplate, in practice it was exhilarating, just as each new experience with Rossetti had been. She couldn't see him, but she could hear the quick whisper of his pencil as he sketched.

She sat perfectly still. The heavy scent of roses drifted in through the open window. The sun began to set, and the drone in the garden grew louder, a chorus of crickets and toads heralding the day's end. Lizzie felt deeply content. She suddenly didn't care that they weren't married or what people would think if they knew what she was doing. She was just happy to be here, with Rossetti, living a life so filled with romance and art that she never could have imagined it, even in her wildest daydreams. Nothing else mattered.

What would happen next? Would he walk over to her, run his fingers across her bare skin, kiss her neck? And what would she do? Would she let him draw her up from her seat, wrap her arms around him, give in to his touch?

But he didn't come to her. Instead, he spoke. "Do you remember the first time that we saw each other?"

"Of course." She remembered the day well—how he'd bounded

into Deverell's studio with an impish grin. "You read to me from *Twelfth Night*, and we spoke of love. I should have known then that I would fall in love with you."

"No. That wasn't the first time. Do you really not remember?"

"I don't know what you're talking about. Are you finished with your sketches? I'm beginning to feel chilly."

"I knew that I'd seen you before, and I had. On Blackfriars Bridge." He paused and Lizzie waited, an image forming from the fog and sharpening into unwelcome recollection. "It was late, and there was a heavy mist. But I'm sure that it was you. You were with an older man, and he was holding you. I called out, and you ran away. But you stopped for a moment, and I saw your eyes. I couldn't forget them."

Lizzie said nothing, and she didn't turn to look at him. She remembered that night well. She'd never told anyone about what had happened—he must have been the man who had happened upon them. Why hadn't he spoken of it before?

"What were you doing there?" he asked. "With that man?"

Lizzie felt faint. She knew, as Rossetti did, that many of the shopgirls supplemented their meager wages by obliging the occasional customer. Is that what he thought of her, after all this time? "I was walking home from work." Her voice was flat. "He accosted me. He insulted me, and wouldn't let me go. If you hadn't come along, I don't know what would have happened."

Her contentment was gone—she now felt exposed and ashamed by her nudity. She grabbed a draping cloth from the table and wrapped it around herself, then turned to face him. "I'm very grateful that you came along when you did. I can't believe that it was you."

Rossetti nodded, accepting her words. He walked over to her, but she put up her hand. "I hope that you have what you need for your sketches. I'm afraid that I'm not feeling well. I'm going to lie down."

She gathered up her clothes and left the studio, hurrying back to the cottage. She was unsettled, as if the ground were no longer firm beneath her feet. She ought to be grateful that it was Rossetti who had saved her that night. But the idea that he had kept this knowledge secret from her, as if it were something not to be spoken of, colored her own memory of the night, making her wonder if she were, somehow, to blame.

All the time that Rossetti had painted her and tended to her lovingly, he had been harboring these suspicions, wondering if she was not what she seemed. It was impossible to reconcile these two sides of him. But what did she really know of him, besides what he told her? She had never met his family, and the only friends whom she met were fellow artists, men like him who took pleasure in the company of their models, but who did not necessarily take them anywhere respectable. The idea that he was toying with her seemed so ludicrous that she dismissed it immediately. And yet, how else to explain why he painted her and courted her, but insisted on delaying any formal announcement of their love?

She reached the cottage and began to pack her things. Whatever the case may be, she must return to London immediately. For a moment she had thought that she could be satisfied with living with Rossetti and taking part in his art, with being his muse and nothing more. But now she realized that she could no longer play at being his wife, with no guarantee to her place or happiness. His changeability, which she had once admired as artistic temperament, now scared her. It was all well and good for him to indulge in such games, but she had her reputation to consider, or what was left of it.

Lizzie insisted that Rossetti take her back to London, and they left that night. He did his best to repair things between them, knowing that he had offended her. He wrote to her daily, swearing that he couldn't work without her, and promising that he loved her, and wanted to marry her as soon as he could. He sent poems that he wrote for her and gifts of drawing supplies that Lizzie knew he could barely afford for himself. She was angry, but her anger faded in his absence. How could she be angry with him for not marrying her, when she refused even to see him? He had always been truthful with her, telling her that they had to wait until his future was secured to marry. If the wait was longer than she had hoped, it was only because it took time for an artist to build his reputation. She told herself that if she loved him, she would do everything within her power to help him.

And so, as the months passed, they reached a delicate truce. He continued to paint her, and the beauty of the paintings built a bridge between them, and gave them a shared purpose in the creation of his art.

As a peace offering, he read her Tennyson's poem about Sir Galahad's quest for the Holy Grail, and suggested that they work on an illustration from the poem together. He wanted to draw the scene where Galahad forsakes the adoration of the court ladies so that he might remain chaste and pure of heart in preparation for his quest, saying, "I never felt the kiss of love, Nor maiden's hand in mine. More bounteous aspects on me beam, Me mightier transports move and thrill; So keep I fair thro' faith and prayer A virgin heart in work and will."

Lizzie, however, was more interested in drawing the angels who bear the Holy Grail and reveal its vision to Galahad: "Wings flutter, voices hover clear: 'O just and faithful knight of God! Ride on! the prize is near.' " Each felt that their choice best represented the romance of the poem, but Rossetti at last relented, wanting to please her.

All through the winter they took turns working on the illustration. Lizzie did a study of Rossetti for the figure of Galahad, and he drew her as one of the angels. Her talent for figure drawing had grown more adept under Rossetti's guidance, and Sir Galahad's hunched shoulders and outstretched hands captured the knight's humble acceptance of his task. She made quick and competent studies of the angels' draped garments, and Rossetti worked on the faces, which were not yet her strength. When he turned to other commissions, Lizzie spent hours on the details, determined that the swoop of an angel's wing and the fall of light from the shrine's windows be perfect.

The result was beautiful, evoking the mystery of the secret shrine where Galahad has his vision of the Grail. Rossetti was pleased with Lizzie's work, and the light touch that she brought to the picture.

He suggested that they might do an entire series together, and Lizzie sprang from her chair and gave him a kiss. For the first time, she felt that all of her work was paying off, and that her drawings were finally showing promise.

But as winter turned into spring, the studio began to feel stuffy rather than cozy, and Rossetti grew restless. He found more and more excuses to be away, eagerly taking any invitation to draw or visit in the countryside, and leaving Lizzie to draw alone in his studio. Her health suffered in his absence, and as she became weaker it was harder to sit at the easel for any length of time. She ate very little, and once again grew thin. Rossetti was convinced that it would be best for her to leave the city. Lizzie's mother was equally concerned for her health, and so Lizzie told him that he might ask around for recommendations for seaside resorts where she might convalesce.

John Millais was eager to help, as he still felt responsible for Lizzie's ill health, and he suggested the seaside town of Hastings, where the weather was mild and many doctors and specialists could be found. He arranged for a commission for Rossetti, and Rossetti used the funds to pay for rail tickets and lodging for Lizzie and Lydia.

Lizzie was grateful for his attentions, but she didn't want to leave the city, particularly since Annie Miller remained in town. She put off her departure, preferring ill health in Rossetti's company to a holiday by the sea without him. But eventually her symptoms overcame her, and Rossetti insisted that she go. "It's for the best. I'll devote myself to my work here, while you rest and regain your health. As soon as I've finished a few pictures, and am sure of funds, I'll join you at Hastings."

Lizzie glanced at the pile of sketches on Rossetti's desk. She'd looked them over while he was out, and she knew that he was planning a new painting with Annie Miller. "Wouldn't you prefer me to stay, so that I can sit for you? I want to be of use to you."

"My little dove," he said, patting her hair. "You're selfless, as always. But I insist that you take care of yourself. In your state, you can hardly sit for me for more than an hour, and that really is of no use to me. Hastings will be just the thing. When you're well enough, I'll plan a beautiful painting of you—perhaps something tragic and romantic from the *Inferno*."

Lizzie was not comforted by his words, but she couldn't deny that her health was only getting worse. She had no choice but to pack her little case, and hope that the city would not prove too distracting to him in her absence.

CHAPTER 15

The town of Hastings was a small collection of inns and houses perched between the sea and the white cliffs, popular with invalids and the doctors and charlatans who attended them. They came for the sea air and mild climate, though the most desperate drank the seawater, believing it had the power to restore health.

Lizzie and Lydia arrived in March, by rail, and went straight from the station to a hotel in the center of town. The inn was respectable but dull, occupied by elderly ladies who spent their days roaming the halls, fading in and out of the dreary wallpaper as they shuffled by. The sisters were given two small rooms on the second floor, from which they could just glimpse the sea between the surrounding rooftops.

Once they were unpacked, Lydia wasted no time in taking Lizzie to see a series of doctors. Dr. Wilkinson, recommended by the innkeeper, took a special interest in her case. He saw her in a cluttered office that reeked of chloroform and soap. He gave her a thorough examination, listened to her lungs and heart, and noted each of her symptoms: lingering cough, loss of appetite and weight, frequent spells of dizziness and weakness. At last he announced that Lizzie was not, as she had feared, consumptive.

"She suffers from exhaustion, with a slight infection of the lungs," he declared, speaking to Lydia as if Lizzie were not there. "She's clearly been overtaxed by her attempts at painting—it's not a natural occupation for a woman in her state of health. She must be kept quiet, and she must abstain from all activities that could cause excitement."

Lizzie flushed with anger. "I'm not to paint? But what else is there to do in this dull little town? I'll go mad if I can't at least work on my drawings!"

Dr. Wilkinson chuckled indulgently. "I'm sure that our town *does* seem very quaint after the excitement of London. But you'll soon find that a short walk in the morning and quiet rest in the afternoon will agree with you much more than the irregular habits that you kept in London. The serious pursuit of art is better left to the gentlemen, I'm afraid. A lady's delicate constitution isn't up to the strain. No, my dear, I think that you'll find that a simpler style of living will suit you better. You're very weak, and if you continue on this way, the next attack may place you beyond my care."

Lizzie's eyes flashed, but before she could argue, Lydia placed a calming hand on her arm. "Of course, Dr. Wilkinson," Lydia said. "We intend to live quietly here, and devote ourselves to my sister's convalescence. I couldn't agree with you more that her recent excitement is at least partly to blame for her ill health."

"Just so." The doctor reached into his bag and produced a small glass vial, which he handed to Lizzie. "Laudanum; a tincture of opium. It should ease any coughing or aches, and allow you the rest that you need. It's also useful for calming the stomach—you must take a little more food. Three drops at a time, and no more. Many ladies find it useful to calm the nerves as well. I'll write you out an order for the chemist's. But mind that you watch the doses carefully— a few drops too many and the effect has been known to be deadly."

Lizzie left the examination room without another word, and Lydia stayed to wait for the chemist's order. When Lizzie was out of earshot, Lydia turned to Dr. Wilkinson with a question. "Then, she will recover? It's not as grave as we've feared?"

"Her case is certainly serious, but not at all hopeless. It's imperative that she be kept calm and comfortable, and that she take some food and fresh air. If she doesn't regain some strength, any new development could prove very serious."

"Of course," Lydia murmured, and then said, almost to herself, "but it will take a stronger will than mine to keep Lizzie from following her flights of fancy, or from painting."

But Lydia needn't have worried about keeping Lizzie quiet. As the weeks passed and Rossetti put off his arrival, Lizzie's condition began to worsen, rather than improve. She soon lost all interest in drawing or exploring the coast, preferring to lie in bed, staring at the same page of a book and falling into fitful spells of sleep. Though Lydia occasionally managed to coax her out for short walks in the sea air, her appetite didn't improve, and she could hardly be persuaded to take tea or broth. The laudanum eased Lizzie's cough, but it also seemed to increase her indolence, and the little bottle was emptying more quickly than it ought to.

Lizzie wrote to Rossetti daily, but only a few notes came back. At first she made excuses for him, but eventually she admitted that she was afraid that Rossetti had abandoned her down here, and that he was happy to be left alone in the city, free to see Annie Miller and his other models as much as he liked.

"You ought not to write to him," Lydia said. "I don't see why you go on with him, when he treats you in such a shabby way."

Lizzie shook her head in despair. "I love him, Lyddie, can't you see? And he loves me, too, I'm sure of it. If only he would come down to see me! When he gets caught up in painting he isn't quite himself—it's hard for him to think of other things. And that Annie Miller is trouble. He's promised me that she's nothing to him but a model, but what man can resist such easy prey? If only he were here, things would be different."

When a letter arrived from John Millais, Lizzie tore it open, eager for any news of her friends in London.

It read:

London, May 15, 1852

Dear Miss Siddal,

I hope that this letter finds you feeling much restored. I'm more sorry than I can say that my neglect has caused you so much lasting suffering. If there's anything you need, you are only to ask, and I am at your service.

I hope that you will find some solace when I tell you that my portrait of you as Ophelia has been a great success wherever it is shown, and now is sold to an eager buyer. I owe so much of the praise to you, and I'm grateful for your great patience with my methods. As to your beauty, if I should describe it, I would only be adding my poor voice to a great chorus.

As I go on, I've begun to feel that each painting, if it is truly good, takes a little something from me—something that I can never recover from the canvas. But if the painting is fine, then I feel that it is worth it, to sacrifice a bit of myself for the sake of my art. I can only hope that you feel the same.

Gratefully yours,
J. E. Millais

Lizzie read the letter through and then tossed it aside. "It's from John Millais. He writes to say that his *Ophelia* has met with success."

"I am glad to hear it. Emma Brown seemed to think that if the painting did well it could only be good for you."

"She only said that to make me feel better," Lizzie snapped, surprising Lydia with her anger. "She said that when she thought that Dante would throw me over for Annie Miller. She knows full well that the more fame I have as a model, the less likely it is that any decent fellow will have me for a wife—Dante included, though he would never say so."

She paused, her anger dissipating as quickly as it had come on. "Of course, I *am* glad that the painting is beautiful, but look what I have sacrificed for it." She looked around the dingy room. "If anyone still looks upon the painting a hundred years from now, Millais will be remembered as its brilliant author, but my name will be forgotten, and I will meet the same obscure fate as poor Ophelia."

"I can't stand to hear you speak so!"

"I only speak the truth. I begin to fear that I am lost. Things with him have gone so far—I have to trust that he will do right by me. If he doesn't, what will I do? What man would have me now, sick, and with a reputation as an artists' model. And how could I ever love another man—Rossetti will always have my heart. Could I even go back to Mrs. Tozer's? What will become of me?" Lizzie knew that she shouldn't speak so in front of her sister. But waiting for Rossetti, day after day, was wearing on her. When she was with him, it was easy to get caught up in his enthusiasm, to feel that what they were doing, making art, was more important than anything else. But here at this sad little hotel she had only her own thoughts for company, and it was impossible not to worry. She wondered all day where he was, what he was doing, whom he was with. And what if he didn't come after all? She shook her head, trying to shake the thought. "I'm sorry, Lydia, I don't know why I say such things. It must be my illness."

Lydia was silent, unable to offer any comfort. What girl in Lizzie's position would not be half sick? She didn't object when Lizzie reached for the laudanum bottle and took a generous dose. When Lizzie drifted off into a fitful sleep, Lydia wrapped herself in a shawl and went out to walk along the sea wall. The sea was rough, whipped into a frenzy by the wind, and the spray stung her cheeks as it crashed against the rocks. But it was a long time before she returned to the airless room, with its stale scent of illness and waiting.

Spring turned into summer, and still Rossetti remained in London, deaf or indifferent to Lizzie's increasingly frantic entreaties for him to visit. Lydia was on the verge of taking Lizzie back to London, where she could at least convalesce in the bosom of her family, when Lizzie's health took a turn for the worse.

A knock at the door in the middle of the night brought Lydia flying from her bed, as if she had been waiting for such a sound. The innkeeper stood at the door, a lamp in her hand.

"What's happened?" Lydia demanded.

"It's Miss Elizabeth. She's not well."

Lydia followed the innkeeper to Lizzie's room, where a maid was bending over Lizzie's bed, putting a cool cloth to her head. "What's happened?" she asked again.

"I was bringing in the coal for the morning fires, miss, when I heard a cry. I came rushing in and poor Miss Elizabeth had fallen to the floor. She must have been trying to get up from her bed."

Lydia knelt at Lizzie's side. Her skin was damp and her cheek-bones protruded sharply from her face. Lydia grabbed her hand and felt nothing but skin and bones. Lizzie muttered wildly, her eyes opening and closing. Lydia glanced over at the table beside the bed and saw that the bottle of laudanum was nearly empty.

"Call for the doctor!" she cried.

Lydia tended to her sister, trying to coax her to drink a little water and keeping her brow cool with wet cloths. At first Lizzie was insensible to her presence, but then her eyes locked on Lydia, and she grabbed her hands. "Is Dante coming? Is he coming to me? I must see him!"

"Hush, Lizzie, please be calm!"

"Is he coming?" Lizzie repeated, her voice pleading. "Is he coming to me?"

"Lizzie, please! Yes, he's coming," Lydia fibbed. "But please, dear, have some water, just a sip."

Lydia's answer satisfied Lizzie, and she became calm and compliant. She took a long sip of water and laid her head back on the pillow. Lydia sat by her side and waited for the doctor. After a few minutes, Lizzie seemed to fall into a deep sleep, and when Lydia felt her brow again, it was cool.

Dr. Wilkinson arrived, looking concerned despite Lizzie's return to calm. He questioned Lydia, who admitted that Lizzie had taken little food in the last days, and had relied heavily on the laudanum for rest.

"The danger has passed for now, but it's of the utmost importance that she avoid these attacks in the future—any excitement could overwhelm her. She must be compelled to take some food. She seems to have lost what little weight she had. And she must not be upset at all."

Lydia looked over at the bottle of laudanum. "I didn't expect that she would need quite so much."

The doctor didn't look concerned. "She's an ill woman. The laudanum may be particularly useful in helping her to keep some food down. I'll write out another order. But the most important thing for your sister is quiet rest. Make sure that she's not upset or excited."

Lydia thanked the doctor and then sat down at the small desk next to Lizzie's bed. The light of dawn was just beginning to show beyond the lace curtains. She pulled Lizzie's writing paper and pen from the desk. The pen hovered over the paper for a moment, as if she were reconsidering, but she glanced over at Lizzie and at last began to compose her letter.

Hastings, June 22, 1852

Mr. Rossetti,

I am sorry to write to you that Lizzie's condition has deteriorated since our arrival in Hastings, and tonight she suffered an attack that left her very weak. She asks for you, and, as I am afraid for her life, I must beg you to come to Hastings as soon as you possibly can get away.

Please reply by soonest post that you are coming,

Miss Lydia Siddal

Lydia's missive hit its target. Rossetti read the letter the way it was intended—as a rebuke for his callousness. He'd meant to follow Lizzie to Hastings, but his days had been filled with painting and visits and meetings with the Brotherhood, and it never seemed to be the right time to leave. It was difficult to admit, but with Lizzie in Hastings he was able to get on with his work much more quickly. He didn't need to worry about her comfort, or whether she would mind if he brought another model home. And the image of her in his mind was often enough to inspire him to paint—whenever he missed her he painted her, and he was satisfied.

He finally finished the painting of Helen of Troy, which had taken him nearly a year to get just right, and he started another picture with Annie Miller as his model. This was an intimate portrait, not unlike the studies that he made of Lizzie. It showed Annie wearing a fine yellow satin dress, in the same honeyed hue as her hair. Flush with money from a recent sale, he bought the gown for her as a gift. Annie had been free with her gratitude, and he was in no rush to leave her. She was easy to be with, and asked nothing from him other than amusement and friendship.

But Lydia's letter reminded him of his duty, and of his failings. He knew he'd acted badly, and the feeling was disorienting, like looking at a painting where the perspective is off. He had always prized chivalry and devotion, following the example of Dante Alighieri. But his own behavior, he knew, fell far short of that ideal. He now admitted that he had sinned—a sin for the sake of his art, but a sin nonetheless. Filled with remorse, he planned a drawing that would buy his ticket to Hastings.

There was no mistaking the tone of Lydia's letter. Lizzie had taken a turn for the worse, and she was suffering, perhaps even dying, without him there to give her comfort. He worked for three days in a state of high agitation, and the resulting picture—Saint Cecilia, imprisoned for her faith and gratefully receiving the kiss of death from a guardian angel—was grim but compelling. He sent the picture off to Ruskin and prayed that he was not too late. He had heard nothing from either of the sisters since Lydia's last letter.

Rossetti took the train to Hastings and went immediately to the inn. At the desk, he was told that Miss Siddal was in her room, and he ran up the stairs, not waiting for the clerk to notify her, and causing a stir at the front desk. He had no time for proprieties; his heart was in his throat, and he tried to prepare himself for a much weaker and ailing Lizzie.

He knocked on the door and Lydia answered. "Mr. Rossetti," she said, not meeting his eye. "You've come. At last."

Rossetti took her coldness as his due and followed her into the room. There he saw Lizzie, looking small and delicate, curled up in an armchair. A heavy shawl covered her shoulders, and the teacup in her hand trembled slightly. She was pale, and certainly thinner. But it was clear that she was not dying, and he uttered a quick prayer of thanks. He dropped to his knees and laid his head on her lap. "My dove. I was so scared. I thought that I might lose you."

Lizzie put down her tea and stroked his hair. "It was the thought of you that sustained me. You're here now, and that's what matters."

Rossetti lifted his head and looked into Lizzie's large gray eyes. "Yes, I'm here, and I won't leave your side again. If anything should have happened, I would never have been able to forgive myself."

Before Lizzie could reply she began to cough, softly at first and then deeper, raspier. Her face was white and Rossetti saw that her eyes were red-rimmed and bloodshot. He turned to Lydia in alarm and Lydia grabbed the laudanum from the table and gave Lizzie a small dose. In a few minutes the coughing fit calmed and Lizzie lay back in her chair, exhausted.

She managed a smile for Rossetti, however. "I know that I'll improve now that you're here."

"Let's hope so," Lydia said. "Now, Lizzie, you need your rest. I'll take Mr. Rossetti down to the desk and see about his rooms, and then perhaps later we can have dinner sent up to us here."

Rossetti kissed Lizzie on the top of her head. "Your sister is right. Rest, my dove, and I'll come back to see you very soon."

Lizzie nodded and Rossetti followed Lydia out of the room. On the landing Lydia paused and put a hand on his arm. "I'm sorry if my letter came as a shock to you. Lizzie has been quite ill, and I was afraid . . . I was afraid that if you didn't come soon, it might be too late. She was very anxious for your company."

"I'm grateful that you wrote to me. I am more relieved than I can say to see that the danger has passed."

"The danger has passed for the moment. But she's in a very weak condition—a very *precarious* position—and I must beg you not to do anything that might upset or excite her. With her health in such a state, she really can't have any other uncertainties weighing on her."

The adrenaline that had driven him through the past days began to ebb. He suddenly wanted very much for Lydia, a girl he barely knew, to understand, and to forgive him. "You're right to chastise me. I've been selfish, and given everything to my art, and nothing to your dear sister. I don't mean to wrap myself up in my work, you know. The paintings envelop me, and I must submit to them; I have no choice. Lizzie understands, I think. She's an artist at heart, and she knows what it's like to live in the service of art and beauty. If I have to be away from her, it's only because I am like one of those poor knights in old stories, who must part from their ladies to fulfill their duty. I do it with a heavy heart, but a true one. My art is my quest; I can no more deny it than I can stop myself from breathing."

Rossetti's grand speech seemed to have little effect on Lydia. "I wouldn't know about such things," she sniffed. She looked at him through narrowed eyes. "I see only Lizzie, and her suffering. You say that you have no choice, but neither has she; she is at your mercy. If your heart is true, as you say, then you would not toy with hers." With that, Lydia turned on her heel and walked down the stairs, leaving Rossetti to follow, red-faced, in her wake.

That evening they ate dinner in Lizzie's room, and the conversation was light and cheerful, despite the gloomy room. Lydia mentioned nothing of their conversation in the hallway, and Rossetti went out of his way to compliment Lizzie and make himself useful.

After the dishes were cleared, he used a pair of sewing scissors to clip a single auburn curl from Lizzie's hair. He pulled a brass locket from his waistcoat, tucked the curl inside, and pinned it to his watch chain. Then he clipped one of his own brown curls and placed it in a matching locket, which he strung onto a piece of ribbon and hung around Lizzie's neck.

Lizzie's face lit up with pleasure at the gift, and even Lydia seemed to approve this obvious sign of devotion. For the first time since their arrival in Hastings, Lizzie spoke of going to see the local sights, and by the end of the evening, a hint of color had returned to her cheeks. Affection warmed them, and the dreary inn room was made bright by their laughter. The little flame of hope, so nearly extinguished, was once again fanned back into existence.

Rossetti's company proved to be the most effective treatment that Lizzie had yet tried, and her health and spirits improved in his company. He was as attentive as any new lover, and he was constantly at her side, amusing her with stories from London, and fetching endless cups of tea. He urged her to draw, and they passed the days in her room, sketching and speaking in low tones, their heads bent together. Lydia sat nearby, looking up from her sewing to watch the pair with wary eyes.

In July, when Lizzie was strong enough, she and Rossetti linked arms and took off for a walk in the hills above Hastings. They passed through town, taking a shady lane that led up into the hills. Chestnuts towered overhead, and delicate branches of dogwood formed a canopy of blossoms. The road climbed quickly, and the trees grew fewer and farther between, before finally giving way to great rolling fields of green and gray grass. A bend in the road revealed the unexpected vista of the town below, a clutch of peaked roofs and white steeples against the vast blue sea.

Lizzie took a deep breath, relishing the sea air and the baked scent of the warm earth. The distant roar of waves breaking against the cliffs mingled with the drone of crickets and bees in the hedges. The heat had discouraged other walkers, and Lydia was at home with a headache. They were alone, at last.

"My dove, have you ever seen more beautiful countryside?"

"Is it the hills that please you?" Lizzie asked, teasing. "Or those who walk among them?" She took a few steps forward and then turned back toward him, posing against the canvas of the view.

Rossetti laughed, happy that Lizzie once again seemed to be herself. "Why, of course, the landscape is lovely only so far as it makes a fitting setting for your beauty, my love." He took her hands in his and spun her around. She threw her head back and laughed, and her hair streamed out behind her. The months of illness were erased from her face, and Rossetti glimpsed the naïve beauty that he had first seen in Deverell's studio. He felt an artistic stirring, a sudden and intense desire to paint.

"Tomorrow I'll bring my things to sketch you along the cliffs." He was sorry that he hadn't thought to bring even a small tablet along with him. "Or perhaps we can look for the waterfall that's supposed to be up here somewhere, and I'll draw you as a nymph on the rocks."

Lizzie became serious. "Will you always want to draw me as you do now? Or will you tire of me?"

"Lizzie, you are my muse. Without you there is no art in me." Here in the pristine hills above Hastings, with Lizzie by his side,

London and its inhabitants seemed a long way off. It was Lizzie whom he loved; his paintings of other women could not change that.

Lizzie watched him, trying to see how far she could trust him. "Without you, there is nothing in me. We must not be apart again, Dante."

"Come, you have nothing to worry about. I love you, and I'll always take care of you. Let's not think of anything sad for the rest of the day. We're here together, and that's enough for me."

Lizzie was satisfied, and she let him wrap his arm around her waist as they continued up the road. Rossetti spotted a path leading off into the meadow beside the road. He grabbed Lizzie's hand and pulled her, laughing, down the path.

A lone apple tree stood in the center of the meadow, its branches spreading out wide and low, offering shade. They walked toward it through grasses as high as their knees. He helped her over a rock, and she stepped ahead of him. He stopped for a moment and watched her as she went: Her white linen dress whispered invitingly around her ankles, and the parasol that rested on her shoulder bobbed as she walked, giving glimpses of her bright red hair. A warm breeze blew across the field with a hushing sound, and the grass rippled and swayed. She turned to smile at him, and he saw her framed for a moment by the hillside and the blue sky. She was more beautiful than any painting, the fields around her made more glorious by her presence.

He felt a sense of awe, as if he had beheld a miracle, and he knew that he would never paint anything so fine. But he was grateful to witness it, to feel the warm sun on his shoulders and the breeze in his hair. He wanted the afternoon to last forever.

When they reached the shade of the tree, he plucked an apple blossom from a low branch. He slipped the flower between Lizzie's fingers and tied it so that the stem became a ring and the blossom its jewel. She gazed down at it, her skin as white and perfect as the flower's petals. When she looked up, Rossetti was kneeling before her. "I almost lost you once. I will not make that mistake again. Lizzie Siddal, will you be my wife?"

Lizzie's face filled with joy, but her voice was solemn. "Nothing would make me happier. I feel that I am your wife already."

"Then I'll always be as happy as I am at this moment, beneath these flowering branches." He stood and kissed her, brushing his lips softly across hers. He lingered there for a moment, and then began to kiss her earlobe, her cheek, and the delicate skin of her neck.

Lizzie turned her head to the side and looked down at the apple blossom encircling her finger. She didn't protest as his fingers drew a delicate path over her collarbone and then drifted down to search beneath the light cloth of her dress.

She had resisted for so long, and she felt that to deny this moment would be an act almost of heresy. To turn away was impossible, unnatural. The sun continued to shine in a cloudless sky, but the air between them was as heavy and alive as if a storm approached.

She closed her eyes, and the sun that shone through the branches played across her eyelids in a shifting kaleidoscope of light and shadow. He kissed her on the forehead and then laid her down in the soft green grass, as tenderly as if she were a sleeping child being laid to bed.

He stood over her and his shadow fell across her. Then he lay down next to her and continued his gentle but insistent explorations. He slid her linen dress up to her thigh and ran his fingers along the bare skin of her leg. She turned her head to the side and stretched her arms out into the grass, drawing in her breath and digging her fingers deep into the warm dirt.

The sound of the birds in the leaves above her drowned out all other thoughts. He began to breathe more quickly, and he buried his face into her hair as he moved above her. She tried to hold herself as still as if she were sitting for a painting, but she soon moved to embrace him as well. She thought of nothing but his closeness; the scent of his skin and the roughness of his face against her shoulder. Time stretched out indefinitely, and then his cry brought her back to her senses. He kissed her once more and then rolled off of her and lay beside her in the grass.

She pulled her skirt back down, but did not otherwise stir. She was not fully sensible of her surroundings, and the half-dreamed words of a poem drifted through her mind: *Slow days have passed that make a year, slow hours that make a day, since I could take my first dear love, and kiss him the old way.* She was comforted by a sense of inevitability, as if they had always been heading toward this time and this place. Then she shivered, feeling for a moment the shock of what she had done.

Rossetti was quiet beside her. Soon she heard his breathing become slow and shallow. She sat up, reached into the pocket of her skirt, and withdrew the tiny glass bottle of laudanum. She let three small drops of the mixture fall onto her tongue. Then she too lay back under the tree.

There was no blame, really, in what she had done. She would soon be his wife, and her position at his side would be secure. She drifted off to sleep, and the tall blades of grass seemed to bend over her, lovingly folding her into their bed.

When she woke, Rossetti was propped up on one elbow, looking down at her. He traced a pattern across her brow and then recited slowly: "You have been mine before, how long ago I may not know. But just when at that swallow's soar, your neck turned so, some veil did fall, I knew it all of yore."

"Beautiful."

"I wrote it for you." He lay back and gazed up into the branches above. "Is this not Eden?"

She could also feel the perfection of the place, the refuge of the tree's spreading branches. "I suppose it is Eden." But, she thought to herself with a chill, if this is Eden, then we are Adam and Eve, and our happiness is not to last. She sat up and brushed the grass from her skirt in an attempt to hide the slight tremble in her hands.

"No, don't move. You look perfect lying in the grass like that. I want to remember you exactly like this. Perhaps I can paint it from memory." He searched around in the grass for wildflowers, unconscious of any change.

She lay back and Rossetti made a frame of poppies and buttercups in the grass around her hair. She smiled, relieved that nothing seemed changed between them, despite her foreboding.

Rossetti brushed the flowers aside. "No, you don't need a wreath of flowers to improve your beauty. I like you as you are."

Lizzie gathered together the flowers that Rossetti had tossed aside and wove them into a chain, making a thick braid and fashioning a crown of blossoms, which she placed on her head. "I'll wear a crown like this for our wedding, made from wildflowers. And we should fill the church with orange blossoms and lilies. It will be lovely."

"There's plenty of time for all that," he said. He stretched, restless, and reached out a hand to her. "Come, my dove. Let's walk some more."

They rose and set off as if they had stopped for no more than a picnic in the grass. The path was steep, and the hills gave way abruptly to white cliffs that dropped into the sea below. They picked their way along the bluffs, climbing small hills and following the path as it dipped down to meet with the cliff's edge, walking in companionable silence and taking in the vast view of the sea.

As they came over a small rise, Rossetti spotted a pile of stones farther up the hillside. "A ruin, I think. Shall we go explore?"

"It looks like an old chapel," Lizzie said, and the romance of stumbling upon such a setting was not lost on her.

They quickened their steps, anticipating the discovery of some mystery. But as they drew closer, the ruined chapel revealed itself to be only a crumbling stone wall and a blocked-up door set into the hillside.

"It's nothing but an old cellar." It was silly, but Lizzie felt that coming upon an old church, after what they had done, would have been a good omen.

"No matter," Rossetti said, sensing her disappointment. If he had painted the scene, they would have come upon a medieval chapel, covered in rose brambles, with a single window of stained glass still intact. But life was not a painting, and even its most perfect moments lacked the symmetry and detail that he could create on the canvas. But he was determined to salvage the moment. He picked up a sharp piece of rock and set to work carving letters into a stone at the base of the wall. It took a few passes, but the letters soon stood out white against the gray stone.

"DGR and ES," he read, looking over his handiwork. "Now this will always be our place, and that will make it special."

Lizzie looked at their linked initials, set in stone, and smiled. Exhaustion overcame her. It was the best kind of weariness, earned by exercise in the fresh air and good company. She put her arms around Rossetti and leaned her head on his shoulder. "If only we never had to leave Hastings. I should be happy right here forever."

It was late by the time they returned from their ramble in the hills. Lizzie had hoped to slip in unobserved, and she was annoyed to find that Lydia was waiting for them in the salon of the hotel. Lydia was pacing back and forth in front of the empty grate, her eyes darting between the front door and the desk, and there was no way to avoid her. Lizzie sighed and went in to greet her, but she was brought up short by the sight of Lydia's face, white and strained.

"Lydia, what is it?" she asked, with the confused thought that her sister knew what had happened in the meadow. Then she saw the black-edged envelope clasped in her sister's hand.

Lydia held out the letter, saying, "It's from Emma Brown. I haven't opened it." Lizzie tore it open and read:

London, July 20, 1852

Dearest Lizzie,

I hope very much that Hastings agrees with your health, and that you will be much better when I see you next.

I'm afraid that I write with sad news. Our dear Walter Deverell passed away last night, his condition of the kidneys having suddenly worsened. He was, at the last, peaceful, and my dear Ford was with him yesterday to give him comfort.

Ford wanted to write immediately to Dante, but I told him that I would write to you instead, so that you might break the news to him yourself. I know that he will take this very hard, as they were friends of such long standing, and they were all convinced that the prognosis was not so dire as it has turned out to be.

I know that Deverell admired you very much as well, Lizzie, and that he thought his painting of Twelfth Night the finest he ever did. Before he died, he begged Ford to pass along to you a very fine sketch of his, which he called The Pet, *and which I have enclosed with this letter.*

My condolences to you all, and may God keep you well.

Emma Brown

Lizzie read the letter twice before she understood what it said. She stood for a moment with her back to the room and tried to compose herself. She thought of the last time that she had seen Deverell. It was in his studio, and if he had been paler than usual, he had also seemed so full of life and enthusiasm, for himself and for her. It didn't seem possible.

Rossetti had followed her into the salon, and she turned to face him. He hadn't heard Lydia, and no doubt he thought that the letter was some matter of the Siddal family. His face was full of polite concern, ready to express his sympathy.

"I'm so sorry," she said, her voice breaking. "It's from Emma. She writes to tell you that . . ." She found that she could not continue. Rossetti stared at her for a moment, his frown deepening. He took the letter from her hands, and she watched as his face mirrored her own: first confusion and disbelief, and then the taut whiteness of grief.

"I'm so sorry," she said again, feeling the lameness of her words. It seemed impossible to comfort him when she could hardly believe the news herself. He leaned against the mantel, holding on to it as if it were the only thing keeping him up. He made no attempt to hide his grief.

"My God," he said, his voice stunned. "He was only twenty-six. We have lost a great talent, and a great friend." They were silent for a moment, absorbing the unwelcome news. "I'll return to the city at once. I've lingered too long in Hastings." The thought seemed to bring with it a surge of energy. "I must see what assistance I can give to his family. This will be a terrible blow to his father."

Lizzie rose from the sofa and went to him, catching his arm. "Dante, you can't leave like this. You're in shock. Please, come sit."

Rossetti shook her off. "I must join my friends. I can't delay."

She stepped back as if she'd been slapped. "Am I not your friend? Was I not also a friend of Deverell? His loss grieves me as it does you!"

Rossetti rounded on her, his face ugly with suspicion. "And why should it? Why should it grieve you so?" He glanced down at the letter in his hand. "And why did Deverell make a special gift to you?"

He slipped the enclosed sketch out of the envelope and they both looked at it. It was the last sketch that she had sat for, when Deverell had posed her in the doorway with the little birds. The drawing was indeed fine. Deverell had kept his word, altering the hair just enough so that it was not quite possible to say who had been the model. Looking closer, she could see that there was an inscription at the bottom. Rossetti saw it as well, and read it aloud: " 'But after all, it is only questionable kindness to make a pet of a creature so essentially volatile.' Does this have any special meaning to you, Lizzie?"

"No, of course not," she lied. "It was surely only meant as a kind gift. Dante, what's gotten into you? I'm sure that you've made many gifts to your models with no thought of any special meaning being attached."

Rossetti didn't reply, and they stood there for a moment, staring at each other with faces full of hurt and grief, letting the unspoken accusations hang in the air.

It was Lizzie who looked away first. The strain overcame her and she began to cough, hardly able to catch her breath. The harsh sounds of her struggle to breathe seemed to bring Rossetti back to his senses. He held her as she coughed.

"I'm so sorry," he muttered. "I've lost my head." He led her to a sofa and sat her down gently. Deverell's death was a warning. He could lose her as well. "Lizzie, my love, you will join me in London as soon as you have your strength back. We can't risk your health, especially after this shock. You must stay here and take the sea air and continue to get well. But my friends will expect me, and I must return today."

"Yes, of course." Lizzie was determined not to argue any more in front of her sister. The morning spent beneath the apple tree seemed to fade a little in her memory, like paint laid upon an improper ground. She looked down at her ring finger, but the blossom must have fallen off hours ago. She sighed. "I'll have your things packed and sent after you. You're a kind friend to go to his family in their time of need."

Rossetti was visibly relieved. He threw his arms around her and kissed her several times on the brow and cheeks. Lydia raised her eyebrows, but said nothing.

"Thank you, my dove." He ran his hands over Lizzie's hair and looked into her eyes. "I will write to you daily." Then, without a second look, he dashed off to make his train arrangements.

Lydia took Lizzie's arm and led her up to her room. "I'm so sorry," Lydia said. "I know that you liked Mr. Deverell very much. And to have Mr. Rossetti run off like this—it's very unfeeling."

"Nonsense, Lydia. Of course he must go back to the city, and help the Deverells in any way that he can. I shouldn't have questioned him."

Lydia nodded and then spoke to Lizzie without quite looking at her. "You were out for a long time. I had begun to wonder what had become of you."

"Were we? It was much farther to the cliffs than we supposed."

But Lydia would not be brushed off. "You must take care now that he makes you his wife."

Lizzie stared at her sister, wondering how she knew. But she supposed that it was the sort of thing that a sister could guess, and she decided to confess. "Well, there won't be an issue with that." She allowed herself a tentative smile of happiness. "Lyddie, he's asked me to marry him! He tied an apple blossom round my finger, took my hand, and asked me to be his wife. It was the most romantic thing you can imagine. I'm so very happy. Kiss me, Lyddie, and tell me that you're happy as well."

Lydia came forward and kissed Lizzie on the cheek. "I am glad for you."

"Of course, we will have to wait to announce the engagement, given the news about poor Deverell. And please don't write anything to Mother until Dante can make them a proper visit."

"It's only right that you wouldn't want to announce the engagement now, and have your joy overshadowed by sadness. But please, Lizzie, don't wait too long. It's better that everyone share your happy news, and know that you'll soon be married."

"Of course it will be better to have things settled. But I do feel that we are already married, at least in spirit."

Lydia pursed her lips. "It's only the indifference of the landlady at this hotel that makes you feel so, and not the approval of God and the church."

"Oh, Lyddie. It will all be settled as soon as it can be done properly. Now, I'm afraid that I'm exhausted, and more than anything I need peace and quiet. I'm going to lie down. Will you see that no one disturbs me?"

Lizzie pulled the door of her room shut behind her. She thought of Deverell, and her eyes filled with tears. She had lost a true friend and an ally. He would have been the first to heartily congratulate her and Dante. But now he was gone. She picked up his sketch and reread the inscription: *But after all, it is only questionable kindness to make a pet of a creature so essentially volatile.*

She bit her lip, thinking of the pleasant day that they had spent together in his studio. Then she looked back down at the drawing and felt a flash of irritation. It was so like a man, she thought, to concern himself over the creature's loss of freedom, and think nothing of what it gained: the security and comfort of a soft place to rest. Deverell had expected so much from her, from what he called her budding talent. He had no understanding of what it cost her just to maintain decent appearances.

But she shouldn't think of such things, she knew, now that he was gone. She sought instinctively for the little bottle of laudanum. She measured out a few drops and felt an almost immediate relief. The light in the room softened and faded, and her anguish, so acute just a moment ago, was now tolerable.

In the soft hold of the laudanum, she felt a need to put words to the heaving tide of her emotion. She sat at the window and began to write. The tune of a ballad played in her head, and the words spilled quickly across the page, forming a song of love and loss, relief and fear.

Many a mile over land and sea
Unsummoned my love returned to me;
I remember not the words he said
But only the trees moaning overhead.

And he came ready to take and bear
The cross I had carried for many a year,
But words came slowly one by one
From frozen lips shut still and dumb.

How sounded my words so still and slow
To the great strong heart that loved me so,
Who came to save me from pain and wrong
And to comfort me with his love so strong?

I felt the wind strike chill and cold
And vapours rise from the red-brown mould;
I felt the spell that held my breath
Bending me down to a living death.

CHAPTER 16

Lizzie waited for weeks for Rossetti's summons back to London, but when word finally came in early October, it was not the letter she had hoped for. She'd imagined returning to the city in a flurry of wedding preparations—introductions to the Rossetti family, congratulations from their friends, and fittings for a new gown and veil—but it was not yet to be.

Instead, he wrote to say that he regretted that the moment was not yet right to announce their engagement. He assured her that it pained him greatly, but his finances were stretched to breaking, and he could not in good conscience make their engagement public when he didn't know when he would have the means to marry her. Wouldn't it be for the best, he asked, if she were to return to her father's house until things were more settled? If he could just concentrate on his work for several months, he would soon be able to rent a house and make her his bride. Lizzie and Lydia therefore returned to London unaccompanied, lugging their suitcases home from the station behind them to save the cab fare.

Mrs. Siddal greeted them at the door. She embraced both girls, but there was something restrained in her affection. "I'm relieved that you're well, Lizzie," she said in a resigned voice. "But I had hoped that you would be returning to us on a wedding visit, and not to take up your old room."

Lizzie colored. Had Lydia written to their mother, despite her promise of secrecy?

Lizzie was silent, and Mrs. Siddal sighed, any remaining hope that Lizzie had come with good news apparently extinguished. "Your father is waiting for you in the parlor. You'd best go in right away."

Lizzie frowned. Her father so rarely took any interest in her affairs; she couldn't think what he might want. With a shrug, she passed into the parlor to greet him.

Mr. Siddal was sitting in front of the hearth with hunched shoulders, glowering at the fire. "Elizabeth. You've returned in good health?"

"Yes, Father. Are you not happy to see me?"

"And your gentleman? Where is he?"

Lizzie was surprised into silence, but only for a moment. "If you refer to Mr. Rossetti, I presume that he is at his studio."

At the mention of Rossetti's name, Mr. Siddal's eyes flashed. "Then I see that he is content to accompany you to your rooms in Hastings, but not to your father's house in London? He can't be parted from your side when he thinks no one can see, but he won't claim you as his own in front of your kin, and his?"

Lizzie turned to look at Lydia, who had followed her into the parlor. But Lydia gave a slight shake of her head, looking as confused as Lizzie.

"So, it's true, is it?" Mr. Siddal said, watching the silent exchange between the sisters. "No, it wasn't Lydia who told, though she should have written to us at once, so that we could have put a stop to it. It was Mrs. Crane, the grocer's wife. She was in Hastings, with her ailing sister. She said that the whole town was abuzz with nothing but the news of the famous painter from London and his pretty young model. She couldn't wait to come see your mother and offer her congratulations on your engagement! Her congratulations! The old busybody, I'm sure that she knew that no congratulations were in order. Just think how your poor mother must have felt! And what about your sister? I'd be very surprised if Mrs. Crane let her son marry Lydia, now, with the family's reputation what it is."

Mr. Siddal's voice had steadily risen, but now he became quiet again. "I blame myself. I should never have let you keep running with that lot. It was the good wages that blinded me, and that will be your downfall, I'm afraid. Now, tell me plainly, Lizzie, what's between you and this artist?"

Lizzie turned to look at Lydia, who was staring at the floor, her face red. Lizzie's heart ached for her. Lydia had loved Robert Crane since the day she saw him. If Lizzie had ruined Lydia's chances at marriage, she would never forgive herself. If only, she thought, she could tell her father of her engagement. Then he could announce her marriage into a genteel family, and perhaps the family's reputation would be repaired. But Rossetti had asked her to wait, and she was afraid of angering him, and ruining everything.

"Please, Father. You must trust me. Mrs. Crane is nothing but a terrible old gossip. It was very wrong of me not to write to Mother that Mr. Rossetti was in Hastings. But I swear to you that he behaved honorably, and treated us only with kindness and affection."

"Affection? You are a green and foolish girl! What you see as honorable affection, the world sees quite differently. You've brought shame on us, Lizzie, and I have a mind to tell you to go to him then, and test his honorable behavior! I've been lax with you too long, and I have your sisters' reputations and prospects to look out for, such as they are."

Mrs. Siddal stood by the door, her face as white and pained as Lizzie's. She lowered her head and avoided Lizzie's gaze, and in that one gesture, Lizzie read her disappointment. Even her mother believed that she was beyond hope.

"You're wrong. Mr. Rossetti has made me vows of his love, and I've done nothing of which I'm ashamed."

"Then go to him, if you believe his vows. But if you want to stay in this house, you will swear that you will never see him again. I will not have these goings-on under my roof!"

"You can't ask me that!"

"I can, and I must. You *will* stay away from that man, or I will not have you here!"

Lizzie drew herself up and turned from her father. "Then I'll go," she said, her voice breaking. "I have no other choice. I can't be parted from him."

Her mother reached out a hand to hold her back, but Lizzie brushed past her. If she lingered a moment more, she would lose her courage, and she could not be separated from Rossetti, not now.

She ran through the streets, hardly seeing where she was going. Her thoughts circled around each other: She loved him, she must go to him; he loved her, he would do right by her. She'd given up everything—her position at the shop, her good reputation, even her family—but she had his proposal, and his promise. Still, the fear that she would be no more welcome at his studio than she was at her father's house plagued her all the way to Chatham Place. She stopped to take a steadying draught of her laudanum, but its effect was not as strong as it had been at first, and by the time she arrived at Rossetti's door her hands shook with nerves.

But she was wrong to worry, for he greeted her tenderly. He was moved by her distress, and blamed himself for being the cause of her trouble. Faced with the trembling girl before him, it was easy to assure her that the studio was as much her home as his. "Don't worry," he said. "You will stay here as my pupil. Until, of course, we can have the great happiness of announcing our engagement."

"You've made the forearms too long," Rossetti said, looking over Lizzie's shoulder at a half-finished oil painting. He made a few quick marks, correcting her proportions. "But the head looks better, and the draping of the clothing is excellent."

The picture was giving her trouble. Drawing in pencil was one thing, but painting in oil was quite another. It was easy to get lost in the problems of color, and forget something else, like proper perspective. Still, even she could see that her work had made a marked improvement since Rossetti began to teach her in earnest.

He watched as she reworked the figure. "Much better. You'll be submitting to the exhibitions before long if you keep it up."

Lizzie shook her head dismissively. His enthusiasm was out of proportion to the slow progress that she made on the canvas. It was so frustrating—she had so much to express, but her hands lacked the skill to bring her thoughts to life. It would take years of training to accomplish anything of merit. And she had wasted so much time sewing bonnets while Rossetti and the rest were hard at work learning their craft.

Rossetti sensed her agitation. "Are you tired? Perhaps you're working too hard. Why don't we get some fresh air? I need to go round to the shop for new brushes. Come with me."

"You're sweet to worry, but I'd rather keep working." Lizzie tried not to look at Rossetti's nearly blank canvas on the easel by the window. He was sensitive enough about it to see even a curious glance as a reproach. In the months since she had come to live with him, he hadn't finished a single picture in oil, and now that spring was nearly upon them again, he would have to rush if he wanted to submit to the exhibitions. He had been particularly touchy about his lack of progress since Holman Hunt had started shipping home stacks of finished paintings from Jerusalem.

"I won't be long. When I get back, we'll have tea."

Rossetti was gone for only a few moments when Lizzie heard someone on the landing. She thought that he must have forgotten something, and she went to the door to see what he needed.

But instead of Rossetti, she was greeted by a tall man lounging against the bannister. "Mr. Ruskin!" Lizzie said, recognizing Rossetti's patron. "I didn't know that Dante was expecting you! I'm afraid that he's just gone out, but I expect him back very soon. Won't you come in?"

"Thank you," Ruskin said, following her into the studio. He looked at her with the eye of a practiced appraiser of beauty. "It's been too long since we last met. And I always see you in a crowd, surrounded by admirers. I'm glad to find you here alone."

"I'm afraid that I am rarely in a crowd these days. My health keeps me from going out very much, and my work keeps me here, toiling away over my poor sketches."

"I was sorry to hear of your ill health. But surely you have Dante for company? I should hate to think of someone so lovely being lonely."

"Yes, of course, I have Dante." She colored slightly. "Though he cannot be expected to always be at my side." Then, feeling that there was a plaintive quality to her voice that she didn't like, she added, "He has, however, been very attentive to my painting lessons."

"He told me you were making progress. I believe that the word genius may have been bandied about." Ruskin smiled as he said this, and Lizzie couldn't tell whether he was serious or joking. He picked up a pile of her sketches that lay on the table. "May I?"

"Oh, no. I'm afraid that Dante was kidding with you. I'm hardly a genius, though I do believe that I study under one."

"Dante is a genius, I'm certain of it," Ruskin agreed. "Now, if only I could convince the British public of what you and I see so clearly. But they are coming around, bit by bit. I'm no longer the only critic standing behind this Brotherhood of his. I really must be careful, or I'll no longer be able to get his paintings at such a good price!"

"Dante is not a man who would forget his friends," Lizzie said quickly. She didn't want Ruskin to know that he still had little competition for Rossetti's works, or at least those that were not commissioned. Though his paintings had lately had more interest, Ruskin was still by far the wealthiest and most enthusiastic patron that Rossetti had found.

"But enough about Dante." Ruskin turned to Lizzie's easel. "He's spoken to me about you at length, and I'm afraid that I won't be put off of seeing your work."

Lizzie hesitated only briefly. She was intimidated, but Ruskin's kindness put her at ease. There was something about him that was so sad and serious; she instantly felt that she could trust him.

Ruskin studied the oil painting on the easel, and then began to page through her sketches, idly at first, and then with more interest. He was fully absorbed in looking at them when Rossetti banged into the studio. He swept Lizzie up into a kiss before he realized that Ruskin was in the room. Lizzie pulled back, embarrassed, but Rossetti only laughed.

"John!" he said, walking over to shake hands. "I'm glad you came. I've got a few new watercolors that I think you'll like. Has my Lizzie kept you entertained?"

"Indeed she has. It was a lovely surprise to find her here, and to finally see her drawings. You weren't wrong—they show real talent. Technically, they are sufficient. But the genius is in the style of them. They're so emotional, almost primitive. A talented paintress is a rare bird, Dante. You were lucky to catch her."

Rossetti slipped his arm around her waist and beamed. "She's beginning to work in both watercolors and oils. I have a little plan for her to do some illustrations for my sister Christina's new poems."

This was the first that Lizzie had heard of this plan, and she was thrilled. If he hoped that she might work with his sister, he must at last be thinking of introducing her to his family.

"Is that right?" Ruskin asked, looking more intently at Lizzie's drawings.

"Lizzie," Rossetti said. "Be a dear and fetch us some tea, will you? I want to show John the new watercolors."

Ruskin looked up from the drawings, amused. "You would send the Princess Ida for the tea tray?"

"The Princess Ida?"

"Is your Miss Siddal not the very image of Tennyson's Ida? 'Such eyes were in her head, and so much grace and power, breathing down, from over her arched brows.' "

"By God, she is. But I've never come across a lady of poetry who was not the image of my dear Lizzie."

"You flatter me too much," Lizzie said, laughing. "I'll go for the tea tray before there's a duel on my account."

When she returned with the tea things Rossetti and Ruskin were deep in conversation over his watercolors. Rossetti looked content and she thought that Ruskin must have agreed to take them at a good price. She brewed the tea and they sat down as best they could in the irregular surroundings of the studio, drawing up chairs to one of the worktables and pushing the painting tools aside to make room for cups and saucers.

The three talked as if they were old friends, and Ruskin was particularly solicitous of Lizzie's opinions. But he made no more mention of her drawings, and she began to think that he had complimented them only out of kindness. He could hardly have said otherwise, after all, with her standing right there. She felt foolish for thinking that a great critic such as John Ruskin could be interested in her own poor work. She was surely nothing more to him than Rossetti's lover, to be petted and treated kindly out of deference to his friend.

She consoled herself, however, with the news that she would soon meet Rossetti's sister. Even if his plans for her illustrations should come to nothing, it would at least give her a chance to be introduced to his family, as she should have been long ago. No understanding between them, no matter how many times it was sworn to in private, could be depended upon until she had been welcomed by his family.

Rossetti was as good as his word. The first week of May they swept the studio clean of its dust, bought fancy tea and biscuits, and displayed Lizzie's sketches on the walls to their best advantage. Lizzie donned a demure blue dress, tied her hair back, and waited nervously for the arrival of Christina Rossetti.

Lizzie was determined to make a good impression. She was anxious to move forward with their marriage, but whenever she pressed Rossetti to set a date, he always had some excuse as to why the time was not quite right. Soon, he said, soon. But she was tired of waiting, and she hoped that a successful introduction to his sister would reassure Rossetti that she would be welcomed by his family. He would never say it aloud to her, but she knew that he worried that she wasn't refined enough for his mother. Lizzie hoped that if Christina liked her, Rossetti would take her to meet his mother next.

Christina entered the studio on Rossetti's arm, her back as straight as an arrow and her dark eyes inscrutable. Her face was already familiar to Lizzie—Christina's high cheekbones and strong brow peered out from many of Rossetti's early paintings. She had modeled for his painting of the Virgin Mary, and Lizzie thought that Christina carried herself with an air of calm superiority that would have befitted that sainted lady herself.

Lizzie stepped forward and embraced Christina with affection. "Welcome, Miss Rossetti. I am so glad to meet you at last. I hope that we will be great friends. I admire your poetry very much."

Christina leaned into Lizzie's embrace stiffly and made a small smile that did not extend to her eyes. "I'm pleased to meet you, as well," she said, not sounding at all pleased. "Dante has told us so much about you, and about your interesting history."

Lizzie colored, thinking that Christina was not at all what she had expected of a poetess. She seemed instead like a very cross abbess, with none of the flairs of dress or manners that Lizzie associated with artists. She swallowed hard and kept her smile pasted on her face. She was determined to win Christina's approval, and she would not be put off by a few icy words. "Will you have some tea? I've prepared everything myself."

Rossetti joined them at the table and they sat down to eat. Lizzie poured out the cups of tea and passed around the cakes, very conscious that she was being watched, and judged.

"You manage everything so well," Christina said. "Considering that you have so little to work with."

Both women were now staring at each other with frozen smiles, that feminine armor for the battlefield of the tea table. Lizzie could see that Christina was not prepared to give her an inch. She turned to Rossetti for help, but he was oblivious to the silence that had settled over the table.

Lizzie groped around for a neutral topic. "You're engaged, I believe, to the painter James Collinson? I know that Dante admires his work very much."

Christina blushed and Rossetti cleared his throat. "I'm afraid that the engagement has been broken off. Terrible of course, but probably for the best."

Lizzie was mortified. She couldn't believe that Rossetti hadn't shared this news with her. She felt keenly how cut off she was from his family, how little she really knew about them.

When Lizzie said nothing, Christina took pity on her. "My work has been a great consolation to me, of course."

"Of course," Lizzie murmured, thinking that her own work had lately been a consolation as well—something to keep her mind from dwelling constantly on what Rossetti was really thinking, or whether his attentions were engaged elsewhere.

Christina seemed to follow Lizzie's thoughts, and for a moment the hard lines of her face softened. She looked around the studio, at the many sketches of Lizzie that lined the walls, and then down at Lizzie's hands, and her bare finger. She let just the hint of a sympathetic smile pull at the corner of her lips.

Lizzie smiled back, but as soon as it had begun, the moment was over. The sympathy passed from Christina's face, and coldness once again dropped over her features like a mask. They sat in silence for another moment before Rossetti finally noticed that the conversation was lagging.

"Christina, why don't I show you some of Lizzie's work? She's a very apt student, and she's done some excellent illustrations from Wordsworth and Tennyson. You'll see, I think, that she has a real gift for capturing the nature of a poem on the canvas. As I mentioned in my note, I think she might be just the person to illustrate your new poems. And I know that Lizzie would devote herself to the project—her dedication can be much greater than my own, I'm afraid."

"Dante, we do so hate to see you waste so much of your time with trifles when you should be painting." She glanced over at Lizzie, who remained at the table, silently fuming.

Rossetti didn't seem to notice the slight. He was used to being worried over by his sister and mother, and he hardly heard their admonishments anymore. He gave Christina his arm as he showed her around the studio.

Christina glanced over at the wall where Rossetti's sketches were pinned up. A hundred drawings of Lizzie stared back. She raised her eyebrows and sighed, then moved on to look over Lizzie's drawings. Lizzie heard her turn to her brother and say, "She has real talent, but the style is crude," as if Lizzie weren't standing right there. But Lizzie seized on it as an opening.

"It would be an honor to illustrate for you. Would it be possible for me to see your new poems, to get a feel for the work?"

Christina turned to Lizzie as if she had, in fact, forgotten that Lizzie was present. "They aren't yet ready to be seen." Then she looked back at Rossetti, and her tone warmed as she addressed her brother. "I've been doing a little painting of my own, you know. I have a mind to do the illustrations myself. Miss Siddal is not the only woman, after all, who can be taught to paint."

"Is that so?" Rossetti asked. "Well, that's grand, but you must be careful not to rival dear Lizzie, but to keep within respectful limits! No, Christina, I think that you'd better stick to poetry, and awe us with your words alone." He laughed, thinking it a joke, but both women were now looking stonily at their feet.

"Perhaps you should come home for a visit, and you can judge my work for yourself. And of course Mother would love to see you. She longs for your company." Christina gathered her shawl up and wrapped it around her shoulders. "As for myself, I must be on my way." She turned to Lizzie. "It was so lovely to meet you." She did not, Lizzie noticed, extend the invitation to visit to Lizzie, and Lizzie thought longingly of her own sister, Lydia, whom she hadn't seen in months. She wondered how her mother was managing, and whether Lydia had ever been able to repair things with Robert Crane after Lizzie's scandalous departure. The thought filled her eyes with tears, but she held them back, not wanting Christina to think that it was her coldness that had upset Lizzie.

"How does Tuesday sound?" Rossetti was saying to Christina. "You can expect me for lunch," Rossetti promised, kissing his sister on the cheek and showing her to the door. He made no mention of Lizzie joining them, either.

When Christina had gone, he turned to Lizzie and said, "Well, I think that went well."

Lizzie paused and turned to look at him, to assure herself that he did not jest. "Did you?" Lizzie knew that there was nothing to be gained in picking a fight with Rossetti, but she couldn't hide her disappointment. "Dante, your sister barely said a civil word to me! It's obvious that she thinks you're wasting your time, and that I'm a detriment to your work. And how could you have failed to tell me that her engagement was broken off? It was humiliating."

Rossetti laughed uncomfortably. "I'm sorry you felt that way. But you shouldn't be so sensitive. Christina is no different from the other artists we know—she's very serious, and not given to pleasantries and small talk. I'm sure that she meant nothing by it."

"And why," Lizzie asked, finally posing the question that really bothered her, "didn't you introduce me to her as your betrothed?

Why must there be this secrecy about our engagement? It's been almost a year since you asked me, Dante, and we haven't told a soul."

"Lizzie," Rossetti sighed, exasperated. "I've told you, the time just isn't right. I couldn't very well tell my sister without telling my mother. And once we announce our intentions to our families, they will want us wed as soon as possible. You know how mothers are."

"And what's wrong with that? Why shouldn't we marry as soon as possible?"

"I just need more time, Lizzie. I have so much more that I want to accomplish with my painting before I settle down into married life. Why should we spoil this idyll? We have everything we need right here—a place to work, each other, a few willing buyers to keep us in canvases and paint. We can do what we like and go where we please. And you are just beginning your own career. Why should you wish to take on the duties and obligations of a household when you can instead paint and create and be free? Let's not leave this Eden just yet, Lizzie. There is time for all that later."

Lizzie stared at him for a moment, struck by his allusion to Eden. Hadn't he said the same thing to her that day under the apple tree in Hastings? How quickly his definition of perfection could shift to suit his whims. How could she have pinned her hopes on a man who seemed to create his reality to meet his needs as easily, and as often, as he created new worlds in his paintings? She would never be sure where she stood with him, what version of her he wanted at any moment—whether he wanted the woman or the muse; the collaborator in his art or merely the silent beauty in his paintings.

And what of what she wanted? Of course she wanted to paint, to have the satisfaction of doing good work and maybe one day earning a living by her painting. But she couldn't see why this should prevent her from marrying, and securing her place in society as well. Not for the first time, Lizzie felt the vast difference between her and Rossetti's upbringings. The idea that a respectably married woman might still work was not so odd to her. But to Rossetti and his sort, it would be strange for a married woman to enjoy the freedoms that Lizzie now took for granted. For all of his talk of artistic freedom and bohemian ideals, it seemed that Rossetti was still very much a product of his conventional upbringing, and all of the expectations that entailed.

"Dante," she said carefully. "Of course I want what you want. Your work, and my own, are of the utmost importance to me. But you know the difficulty of my position. You gave me your promise. I'm willing to wait, but I need to know: Is there is any reason why I shouldn't rely on your word? I can trust you, can't I?"

"Of course you can trust me," he replied, his voice sounding tired.

Lizzie nodded and let the matter drop, seeing no point in pursuing it further tonight. She cleared the table and took down her sketches. She thought longingly of the laudanum bottle in the bedroom, and the easy oblivion it offered, the chance to forget her humiliations, if only for a few hours. But instead she returned to her easel and took up her brush. If the studio had once been her refuge, she now found comfort more readily in the landscape of her imagination, and the careful, detailed work that rendered it onto the canvas. Perhaps, like Rossetti, she could learn to paint herself into her own Eden.

If there was a coolness between Lizzie and Rossetti after Christina's visit, there was no sign of it a few days later when Rossetti burst into the studio with a smile and a shout, pulling Lizzie from her seat and spinning her around.

"What's this?" she asked. "Good news?"

"The best—a sale!"

"Was it the painting of Lancelot and Guinevere? It was so beautiful, I knew that it was bound to sell quickly, but I'm sad to see it go."

"You've got it quite wrong. It's you who's made a sale."

Lizzie laughed, thinking it some sort of joke, but Rossetti held a letter out to her. "It's Ruskin. I knew that he would be interested in your drawings. He wrote to me, asking me to name a price for all the works that he saw. I told him that twenty five pounds would take the lot—I hope that you don't mind—but he's just written back to say that he wouldn't take them for less than thirty. Thirty pounds, Lizzie! Can you believe it?"

She could not. She sat down on the sofa while Rossetti danced a little jig before her. Thirty pounds was more than she had made in a year at Mrs. Tozer's. And all for a pile of sketches. It seemed too good to be true. "It's too great a sum. What can he mean by it?"

Rossetti stopped dancing and looked at her with disbelief. "It's a fine sum. But not a penny more than those sketches are worth. I gave him a low figure in the hope that he would take your work and show it around, stir up some interest in your painting." He knelt before her. "I'm not jesting with you when I tell you that you have talent. John Ruskin can see that as plainly as I can."

Lizzie was flattered, but not convinced. She couldn't look at Ruskin's offer as a plain business deal. "Dante, I can't possibly accept that money. How would it look? People already say that I'm kept by you, and if I were to accept money from John Ruskin, Lord knows what they would call me."

To her surprise, he laughed. "You've no need of worrying about that. Haven't you heard about his troubles? It's all that London society is talking about at the moment."

She blushed. His words reminded her of her days at Mrs. Tozer's, when the other girls would make fun of her for not sharing in their gossip. It was a sore point between them that, since they were not in fact married, Rossetti could only take her to the more informal gatherings of friends that he attended. "You might remember that I have little to do with London society."

Rossetti ignored the jab. "It's been in the papers, as well. Ruskin's wife, Effie, has just sued for annulment of the marriage, on the grounds of non-consummation. It's quite a scandal. Everyone is saying that Ruskin has no eye for women. Doesn't bother me a bit, of course, what they say about his romantic tastes. The public would never question his eye for art, and that's all that matters to me. The scandal seems not to have touched his reputation as a critic."

Lizzie remembered Ruskin's sad eyes, and she suddenly understood. She knew how terrible it was to have one's most personal business on everyone's lips.

"How horrible," she said. "Can it be true?"

"He's chosen not to fight it. To my eye Effie Ruskin is as pretty as they come, but Ruskin's attorney submitted a statement to the court saying that Effie's person was not formed to excite passion, but rather to check it, whatever the devil that means. It's always difficult to imagine what goes on in another man's bedroom, though all of London seems to be trying in the case of John and Effie. I wouldn't have guessed that anything was wrong between them, but then they came back from a painting trip in Scotland with John Millais and all of the sudden they were separated. John refuses to say what happened, if he even knows.

"But you're right to pity him—the poor man can hardly walk down the street without some bawdy comment being hurled after him. But he seems to be weathering it, turning to his work and all that. And at any rate, I don't believe I need to worry about him in your regard. It's truly your art that he seeks to buy, and nothing else. He loves to sniff out talent before the rest of the city gets wind of it. And as for my not taking you among London's society, you have nothing to complain of in that regard, either. Ruskin has invited us to a lunch at the home of his parents, and one couldn't find nicer society than the Ruskins, scandal or no."

Lizzie couldn't brush off her misgivings so easily, but Rossetti seemed so eager for her to be happy, and she hated to deny him anything. "In that case," she said, finally breaking into a smile, "I'm happy to accept his invitation, and his offer to buy the drawings."

The Ruskins' home was very grand, and the ride up the sweeping driveway gave Lizzie plenty of time to worry. When she first met Rossetti and his friends she had felt shy, but their admiration had won her over and made her feel that she belonged with them. Her education, meager though it was, was enough to carry her through, and she was able to join in their conversations about art and poetry. Lately, however, she'd begun to suspect that she was tolerated as Rossetti's mistress, but nothing more. The failure of her meeting with Christina had made her position clear. If Rossetti's own family did not accept her, how could she expect anyone else from their circle, especially the very refined Ruskins, to take her seriously?

But she needn't have worried. Though Mr. and Mrs. Ruskin were well regarded in society, they weren't conceited, and they had a fondness for their darling John's artistic causes. Lizzie's way had been paved by John's glowing review of her talent, and the Ruskins were curious to meet the young beauty who had turned her hand to painting with great success.

Lizzie and Rossetti descended from their cab and the Ruskins greeted them at the door. Mr. Ruskin senior was tall, like his son, but rounder, with cheeks that were red and jolly from his years working as a respected wine importer. Mrs. Ruskin stood next to him, a thin woman with an indulgent smile. Though they must have been suffering under the notoriety brought by their son's divorce, they showed no sign of the strain and presented a united front to the world.

Mrs. Ruskin took Lizzie's hands as she walked up the steps. "Welcome, my dear. We're so pleased that you could come. John has told us so much about you, and about your work."

"Father," Ruskin said. "May I present Miss Elizabeth Siddal, or as I like to call her, the Princess Ida."

Ruskin senior gave her a little bow and then turned to his son. "I don't know about this Princess Ida business, John, but by the look of her, she could be a countess! Come, my dear, I've heard you're not well. Let's get you inside and find you a seat somewhere comfortable."

The kindness of the Ruskins was such a marked change from Christina's coldness that Lizzie was instantly at ease. They ate lunch in an airy dining room with a long row of French doors that opened onto the terrace. The walls of the room were hung with many paintings by artists familiar to Lizzie, and the table was set with fresh flowers and fine china. The footmen glided silently between the guests and served a parade of delicacies, starting with consommé and ending with éclairs and coffee.

Lizzie was in her element. The least bit of admiration acted upon her as the sun upon a morning glory, and during lunch she displayed the full blossom of her charm and wit. After the meal the men went into the study to smoke cigars, and Mrs. Ruskin and Lizzie took a turn together on the terrace. John Ruskin had given his mother a full account of Lizzie's poor health, and Mrs. Ruskin fretted over her and advised her on a number of remedies. She was convinced that Lizzie's ailments could be helped by a jelly of ivory dust, and she insisted that Lizzie take a generous amount of the rare and expensive remedy from her own stores. She also advised Lizzie to reduce her laudanum use. "A dangerous medicine, dear; one that is as like to kill you as to cure you."

When the ladies came back in, they found John waiting for them by the stairs. He offered to show Lizzie around the house's extensive gardens. "I have a few matters to talk over with you. Would a walk in the fresh air agree with you?"

"Very much," she said, taking Ruskin's arm and letting him lead her out onto the terrace.

"Miss Siddal, I asked you here today because I have a proposal to make to you."

"I know. Dante told me that you offered to buy my drawings. The terms are very generous."

"No. I mean, yes, I did offer to buy the sketches, and I hope you'll let me have them. They showed a lot of promise. But I have another proposal in mind, one that I hope will be acceptable to you as well."

Lizzie felt herself blush. Perhaps Rossetti had been wrong, and the purchase did come with strings attached. Lizzie wondered, for a moment, if Ruskin hoped to use the appearance of an affair with her to quell the nastier bits of gossip about his marriage.

"I propose to settle an annual sum on you, Lizzie, in the amount of one hundred and fifty pounds per year, in return for which I'll take any works that you produce. I'll keep the best ones for myself, and in regard to the others I will act as agent and sell them for you. Of course I'll give any amount that I receive over your settlement directly to you. I believe the terms are quite fair."

Lizzie stopped and stared at Ruskin in disbelief. She couldn't quite make sense of his proposal. Could he really want to settle a very large sum of money on her for works that she hadn't yet produced? It was absurd. "Mr. Ruskin," she said, her voice strained. "That's a very generous offer, but I cannot possibly accept. I do indeed hope to become a painter, but I've hardly begun my training!

I couldn't make a fair exchange with you. I really must ask you not to press the matter."

But Ruskin wouldn't be put off so easily. "You would argue with the judgment of one of Britain's leading critics?"

"No, no, of course not," she stammered, afraid that she had offended him. Then she saw the twinkle in his eye. "But surely such an arrangement would be highly irregular?"

"Nothing irregular about it. It is no more than I would do for any young artist who was struggling to make his start." He surprised Lizzie by taking both of her hands and looking her straight in the eye. "You're very talented. I would not say that lightly. In your work I already see the stirrings of something new, something different than anything I've seen before. See it from my perspective: You, a woman, and with no formal training, are producing drawings on a level with many students at the Academy. Your work may not yet reach the level of its graduates, but why should it? Yours is a talent still in its bud. I pride myself on finding hidden gifts, and I'm sure that I see in you the makings of an artist."

Ruskin sounded so kind, and so sincere, that Lizzie regretted her suspicions about his motives. "I hope that you're right. It's my greatest wish that my painting show potential. Sometimes I feel that I have more hope of making a success of myself as an artist than I have of anything else. But I can see that I have a long road ahead of me, and I'm afraid that my health prevents me from applying myself as I would like to."

At the mention of her illness Ruskin frowned. "But don't you see? That's precisely why you must accept my offer. We can't have you tiring yourself out with purely mercenary work. You must be free to paint only what you love. I wish only to preserve your genius, Miss Siddal, as one would a beautiful tree from being cut down, or a bit of a Gothic cathedral whose strength was failing."

His voice was sincere, but Lizzie sensed in his tone something more tender than pure respect for her skill as an artist. "But it's not only my painting that you admire," she said, not as a rebuke, but just as a statement of fact.

Ruskin sighed and released her hands. He offered his arm to her and they walked farther down the path. "No. There's much else about you that I admire."

She took this in silently, and Ruskin went on. "But you would never have to worry—I know only too well what it is like to have someone courted out from beneath my nose. My wife, Effie . . . well, I'm sure that you've heard the gossip—all of it vicious and quite untrue, of course. All it comes down to is that her affections are now engaged elsewhere. Perhaps I neglected her, but it's too late now. . . . At any rate, I would never think to visit that kind of pain upon a friend, especially one as dear to me as Rossetti." He hesitated, and then added: "Though I can't help but think that Rossetti has not acted as well as he might."

Lizzie nodded. "There's no point in pretending—you know Dante too well not to see how things are between us. You must know that I have been living with him these many months, and my family is ashamed, and won't see me. May I confide in you? He's given me assurances that we will marry, but it's been such a very long time, and there is always some excuse, some delay. I'm afraid that we shall go on this way forever."

"And yet you stay by his side?"

"Yes. I love him. Despite everything, I suppose that I'd rather be his lover than some dull man's wife. From the first moment I met him, I felt that I'd stepped into another world, one more beautiful and magical than I ever could have imagined. It's as if he can create vast scenes of romance not only on the canvas, but also in life. And I am a part of both."

Ruskin nodded. "It speaks to the fineness of your artistic sensibilities, that you would choose the world of art and the imagination over the comforts of an ordinary life. It's no small thing to serve as inspiration to such a great artist. But you must look after yourself as well."

"Sometimes I think I must be mad to stay with him. But then I remember that while some women must settle for clichéd love letters cribbed from bad poetry, Dante's love letters to me are his paintings and his verses. When he paints me as the noble Beatrice, I am that woman. In some ways, I believe that's worth everything that I have given up in return."

"But Beatrice died very young," Ruskin murmured, almost to himself. "Perhaps she could not bear the weight of so many virtues heaped upon her."

"Perhaps. But I'm sure that Dante sees my failings quite clearly. If he did not, he would have made me his wife long ago."

Ruskin looked pained. "Or perhaps you are too perfect, and he feels that he can love you only from afar. I cannot admit of any failings in my Princess Ida."

"I wonder why it is that I should always be seen as a figure in a poem, and never as myself?"

"I should like to see you as a painter. Say that you'll accept my allowance. I've already talked it over with Rossetti, and he has no objection. Please accept it as you would a glass of water when you are thirsty."

Lizzie suspected that Rossetti might not be so eager for her to take Ruskin's money if he knew Ruskin's real feelings. But perhaps he didn't care. Perhaps he was grateful to Ruskin for taking her care off of his hands and his conscience. She decided that she would accept Ruskin's proposal. She must start to look after her own interests if Rossetti was not to bother himself in her regard.

"I accept. And I'll do my best to be worthy of your patronage."

"Then it's settled. Now let's return to the house. I don't want to tire you out."

They found Rossetti in the drawing room with the elder Ruskins, amusing them with greatly embellished stories of his days at the Academy. When Lizzie entered the room he shot her a questioning glance and she nodded to indicate that she had accepted Ruskin's allowance.

"Sit down, you two," he cried gaily. "Let's call for more Madeira."

"I'm afraid that Miss Siddal is quite worn out," Ruskin said, his voice full of kind concern. "Perhaps it would be best for her to return home to rest after all this excitement."

Rossetti looked disappointed, but he looked at Lizzie's pale face and nodded his agreement. The group made their goodbyes, and Ruskin took Lizzie's hand. "Please come back whenever you like. You have the run of the house, and you must come walk in our gardens, or make use of our library, whenever it would please you."

"Thank you. You've been very kind." She walked down the steps on Rossetti's arm, and then turned to look back at Ruskin. He stood smiling and waving from the brick path, and for a brief moment she thought of Deverell, waving in just the same way after her last time sitting for him. She hadn't realized until that moment how un-moored she'd felt since his death. The quiet afternoon passed at the Ruskin house reminded her what a sanctuary Deverell's hospi-tality had been, and she thought that she might impose on Ruskin's kindness, and make use of his library. But now she joined Rossetti in the waiting cab, and they began to bump and lurch through the London streets, like sailors on a storm-tossed sea.

A few weeks later, Rossetti was once again hurrying toward Gower Place, late for a meeting of the Brotherhood at John Millais's studio. They hadn't held a formal meeting in many months, and he was looking forward to seeing his friends, and to the fortitude that he usually drew from their gatherings. He needed inspiration, and he worried that his work was foundering.

The domesticity that Lizzie brought to the Chatham Place stu-dio, in which he first took such joy, was at the moment proving a li-ability. Her frequent illnesses were taxing, and not just on her—Rossetti had little patience for nursing her. She couldn't pose for him for the long stretches that he required, but she sulked if he had other models in the studio. When she did have energy, she often preferred to work at her own paintings. And when he went out in the evenings with friends, he could always expect to see the silent accusations in her eyes the next morning. He loved her, of course. But he was beginning to see why his married acquaintances kept both a home and a studio.

Adding to his anxiety was a letter that he had received from Christina:

Charlotte Street, June 17, 1853

Dear Dante,

I'm sorry that you couldn't make it home for lunch after all—we missed having you. I enjoyed my visit to your studio, as I always do. I sometimes think that if I had a studio of my own, somewhere quiet with a nice view, I might write twice as much as I do in a day here, working in the parlor and listening to the cook and the maid bicker in the kitchen.

I told Mother all about your new paintings, and about your kind tutelage of Miss Siddal. She's very anxious to meet Miss Siddal, and insists that you bring her to dinner as soon as you are free. I'm sure that she'll write to you herself. I spoke of nothing but your work, of course, but she's heard whispers, and begins to dream of the patter of little feet. She has despaired of me, I'm afraid, and so she looks to you to put a pink-cheeked grandchild on her knee. If I should disabuse her of this notion, do tell me at once.

Your loving,
Christina

He knew that he should have taken Lizzie home to meet his mother months ago, but there was always a reason to put it off. He wasn't sure what worried him more: that his mother would take to Lizzie immediately, or that she would find her common and not worthy of their family. It hardly mattered. In either case, the last thing that he needed was more voices in his head, reminding him of his duties and obligations. The important thing right now was his painting. He must find a way forward in his work.

The meeting of the Brotherhood was already underway when he arrived. Holman Hunt was still in Jerusalem, but he was due home soon, and he had sent home more paintings. The men were passing them around, exclaiming over the stark and beautiful desert scenes. Rossetti stared at a small watercolor study painted at the edge of the Dead Sea, a barren expanse that met a ridge of dusky mountains under a yellow sky. He held the paper up to his nose and imagined that he could smell the salt-caked banks and a hint of incense. He imagined an unshaven Hunt bent over his painting under a makeshift tent. The image stirred his desire for adventure.

Hunt was not the only member of the Brotherhood who had been hard at work. Millais seemed to have completed more canvases since the last meeting than Rossetti had finished all year. And they were solid work, sure to be accepted at the next Exhibition. "You must have been painting day and night," Rossetti said to him.

"I can't afford to waste my time." Millais paused, and blushed unexpectedly. "I'll soon have a wife to support."

"A wife? My dear John, I had no idea that you were engaged. And to whom should I offer my congratulations?"

"Effie Ruskin." Millais looked at Rossetti with a challenge in his eyes. "Her divorce from John just came through and we'll be married as soon as possible. It will be a quiet ceremony, for obvious reasons."

Rossetti laughed. "Effie Ruskin? My God, I wouldn't have pegged you for a man to involve himself in a scandal."

Millais tightened his jaw. "I know that you're close with Ruskin. But he treated dear Effie terribly. She's the injured party—no word can be said against her, and I don't see why any scandal should attach to her name in the matter."

"I heard rumors that there was another man, but I wouldn't have guessed it was you."

"I've only acted as any gentleman would have under the circumstances. She wants a warm home and children, Rossetti, like any natural woman would. Ruskin married her in the way one might purchase a statue. He praised her, put her on a pedestal, and then hardly looked her way again. He didn't understand that she was a real woman, not another piece for his collection. He was never a real husband to her."

"So they say. But must you marry her? Is there no other girl who has caught your fancy? Why risk the gossip?"

"I'm not a man to pursue every fancy that crosses my path. Speaking of which, you would do well to abandon your attentions to Annie Miller. Hunt writes that he'll soon be back from Palestine, and he won't be pleased to find Miss Miller occupied with anything other than her lessons. And besides, you're hardly fit to rebuke me for courting gossip. You've been living openly with Miss Siddal for nearly a year. That's hardly free from scandal."

"Yes, but I haven't married her, have I?" Rossetti stopped short, immediately regretting his cavalier tone. Of course he meant to marry her.

Millais gave him a meaningful look. "No. You haven't."

"We are engaged, you know," Rossetti muttered. "We've kept it private so that I might have a chance to make my name, and some money for a house and such, before we set a date. I've not been as lucky as you in my sales."

"Does Love need a house to live in? Isn't the house of life sufficient for poets such as yourselves?"

Millais was teasing, but Rossetti was in no mood for jokes. "And will you install Effie in your studio, then?" he snapped. He rubbed his eyes, suddenly tired. "I'm sorry, I don't know what's gotten in to me. Do you feel how quickly the time is passing? I've squandered so many days, when there is so much work to be done; so many paintings that go unpainted, poems that fade from my mind as if they never were."

"Time is passing for all of us. Why not let Miss Siddal be a consolation to you? Time passes for her as well."

Rossetti shook his head impatiently. "There will be time for all of that later. The work is the important thing now. Nothing must stand in the way of the work."

CHAPTER 17

Emma Brown stood at the door of her house, waving to Lizzie and Rossetti as they opened her front gate. Her daughter, Catherine, was on her hip, her thumb tucked neatly in her mouth.

"Hello, Aunt Lizzie," Catherine said in a childish lisp.

Rossetti rumpled the child's hair. "Why, she's already speaking in sentences!"

"She's no longer a baby, Dante! She just turned three in August. And she's looking very forward to a visit from her dear Lizzie and Dante. She thinks you've brought her a treat!"

"Then she won't be disappointed." Rossetti handed the little girl a piece of taffy, and she reached out to take it, glancing at her mother to be sure that she should accept.

Lizzie could hardly believe that Catherine was already a little girl—it didn't seem possible that it had been so long since the party when she first saw Emma, who was just expecting at the time. Emma embraced them and together they went into the house.

"Ford is just finishing up with his painting in the garden. Dante, why don't you go out and hurry him along? Lizzie can help me set the table."

Rossetti went around to the garden and the ladies went into the sitting room. Ford Maddox Brown made a steady living with his painting, but his work had never caught the popular eye in the way that Millais's had. His small income, combined with his propensity for generosity to those in need, meant that his family often lived hand to mouth, just scraping by on his commissions.

The house was small, but what it lacked in luxuries it more than made up for in charm: little Catherine's rocking horse in the corner, Ford's chair and pipe by the fire, and a lovely portrait of Emma above the mantel.

While Emma fetched a doll for Catherine, Lizzie wandered around the room, taking in the touches that made it a home. She ran her fingers longingly over a neat stack of china in a blue willow pattern on the sideboard, and then settled down on the sofa by Emma's cast-aside knitting. She felt a pang, thinking of her own family home, from which she was now barred, and the sparse comforts of Rossetti's studio.

She thought of the parlor of the Siddal house in Kent Place, and now it wasn't the shabbiness that she remembered, but the warmth of the fire and the laughter as she or Lydia read silly stories aloud to their younger sisters and brothers. Would they ever welcome her back? She had given them all up for Dante. And what had he given her in return, that he hadn't given to all of the other models who seemed to sit for him more and more often? She knew that he needed her, relied on her to inspire his work, but she needed more from him than the images that he painted of her. She needed the comfort of a home and the security of marriage. She needed to see her family again.

Then something caught her eye and she looked more closely at Emma's knitting. She saw with surprise that it was a small pair of booties, far too small for even Catherine's tiny feet.

Emma walked back into the room and caught Lizzie looking at the socks. She smiled. "Yes. Catherine will have a little brother or sister to help look after come spring."

"Oh, Emma," Lizzie said, and then paused, unable to go on. Tears sprung to her eyes, too many to be blamed only on happiness for her friend.

Emma wrapped her arms around Lizzie and petted her as if she were a child. She'd spent too many hours listening to Lizzie's worries not to know the cause of her tears. "Please don't cry. Everything will turn out all right in the end, you'll see. Dante does love you, I know that. You'll soon have a little one of your own."

Lizzie wiped at the tears with the back of her hand and turned away from Emma.

"Things can't go on like this forever," Emma said. Then, seeing the doubtful look on her friend's face, she burst out: "But surely you will marry? He can't possibly do otherwise after all the talk that he has exposed you to!"

Lizzie let out a short, bitter laugh. "Is it that bad, then? What is said about us?"

Emma sighed. "No, of course not. It's only that it has been such a long time, and everyone supposes that you intend to marry, but people are bound to talk."

"And I suppose they say that Dante will leave me for Annie Miller? That he has tired of me, and finds her more amusing?"

Emma looked strained. "I've heard that they're often seen together. But who's to say what that means? Perhaps nothing. And Hunt will be back from Palestine very soon, and that should put an end to it. They say that he still means to marry her, though I doubt he has any idea of what's been going on since he left. Her name has been linked with several others." She paused. "I'm sorry, Lizzie, I don't mean to upset you, but I don't want to keep anything from you."

"I'd rather know where I stand. I'm so far outside of respectable society now, I wonder if any of it even matters."

"But can't you speak to Dante? Surely he can be made to see the difficult position that he's putting you in?"

"No, he's not like your dear Ford, who's always so concerned with everyone's well-being. Whenever I bother Dante about the delay in our marriage he gets very defensive, or else brushes it off as a joke. He thinks that, as an artist, he's above such worries, and that his art is the only thing that matters. Sometimes I think he loves only himself. But he's given me his word that we will marry. That seems to be good enough for him, and so it must be good enough for me, whether I like it or not. He introduces me now as his pupil, though. Not as his intended."

Emma pursed her lips. "You have to be firm with him. Your

health is so delicate; it would be better for you to have things settled. The strain can't be good for you. Oh, Lizzie, I only wish to see you happy."

Lizzie took Emma's hand. "I'm sorry to bother you with my troubles. This is hardly the time or place. . . . At any rate, sometimes I think that with my poor health it would be better if Dante didn't marry me, lest he find himself a widower no sooner than he is a husband."

Emma looked shocked, and Lizzie regretted her words. She tried to smile. "Don't listen to me, Emma, I don't know why I say such things. Besides, everything is not so bad as it seems. With John Ruskin's allowance I've been able to concentrate on my painting, and that's made me happy. And I really do mean to make a success of myself. Why should the men have all the laurels?"

"If John Ruskin believes in your work, then I have no doubt that you have talent. It is quite an accomplishment, Lizzie, to have caught his notice." Emma's words were kind, but her voice was forced. "I only wish that Ford could attract the notice of a patron like Ruskin. With another baby on the way, a regular allowance would give me so much peace of mind. But Ford hasn't been lucky enough to gain Ruskin's patronage. How on earth did you manage it?"

Lizzie blushed. "Ruskin has been very generous with me in his terms, but I assure you that I've done nothing out of the ordinary to gain his support. I only hope that my work lives up to his very high standards."

"I didn't mean to imply . . ." Emma started, and then stopped. She tried again: "I know that you take your painting very seriously. And I wish you only the best." She put a conciliatory hand on Lizzie's shoulder. "I'm sorry if I've been as guilty as everyone else in thinking of you only as a beauty, and as nothing else. Why shouldn't you be a great painter? Dante speaks highly of your talent."

"Sometimes I feel that art is the only thing that still gives me hope. Even when I'm so tired that I can hardly stir, I can still coax myself from the bed with the promise of painting. It's different from anything I've ever done. To create something from so little, from nothing but pure emotion and imagination and raw paint—it's a wondrous thing."

"You sound just like Ford when he talks of painting."

"Do I? I suppose that I can thank Dante for that, even if I can never thank him for anything else."

"Don't say such things. You'll tire yourself out with such distressing thoughts. You must save your strength for your painting. Come sit with Catherine by the fire while I finish laying out the table."

Lizzie was only too happy to comply. She gathered Catherine into her arms and tickled her, eliciting screams of delight. Then she set the girl down on her knee in front of the fire and held her close. Together they began to braid her doll's hair.

Emma looked at the pair, sitting together so sweetly. "Just please do be careful, Lizzie," she said. "Dante is no different from other men, and you must take care that he doesn't feel that your affections are engaged elsewhere. While you tend to your painting, don't forget to care for Dante as well."

"I'll do my best." Lizzie brushed her cheek against Catherine's silky baby hair. The little girl smelled of fresh washing and sweet taffy. "I'm not yet beyond caring. One day he must remember his promise to me, and make me his wife. Look at you and Ford—your happiness gives me hope."

"What did you say, Auntie Lizzie?" Catherine asked.

"Nothing important, darling. Nothing but a fairy tale."

"Oh, tell me!" cried Catherine.

"I will," she said, and she began to spin a story for little Catherine, while Emma set the table. "Once upon a time, there was a princess, the most beautiful girl in the country. But she was under a curse, and she was forced to live as a pauper, working all day and all night for nothing more than her bread and a place to sleep. No one recognized that she was a true princess; they could see only the rags that she wore for clothes. The only way for her to return to her castle was for a prince to find her and kiss her, which would break the curse.

"One day, a prince came to town in search of the hand of a

princess. The wicked fairy who had put the curse on the princess was afraid that he would recognize her as a true princess, and so she gave her a potion that made her fall asleep, so that the prince wouldn't find her. . . ."

Lizzie trailed off, staring into the fire. The laudanum that she had come to rely on made it hard for her to concentrate.

"Well," Catherine demanded, "did the prince find her?"

Lizzie looked around, roused from her daze. "Did the prince find her? Oh, Catherine, I certainly hope so. And then they could be married and live happily ever after." Before Catherine could press for more details, the men came in from the garden and Emma announced that dinner was served.

Emma and Ford were indulgent parents, and instead of sending Catherine up to bed they let her play under the table while the adults ate. When it was time for dessert, Ford handed down bits of the pudding to Catherine, who amused herself by untying one of Lizzie's boots.

The dinner was, on its face, a success. The wine was poured freely and their laughter floated out through the open windows into the cool night air until well after midnight. Rossetti and Ford spoke of their work, and for once Lizzie felt that she was included as a fellow artist, and not just as Rossetti's model and lover. Ford congratulated her on her allowance from Ruskin, and offered to take her out shopping for some painting supplies of her own, to Lizzie's delight. When they said good night at the door, it was with glowing faces and heartfelt affection.

But for all of her good cheer, Lizzie couldn't stop thinking of the small booties sitting by the fire, and the scent of Catherine's hair as she held the little girl in her arms. Were things different, she thought, she too could have had a little babe of her own, asleep in her cradle, waiting for her mama to return home.

The thought was too sad to bear, and for the thousandth time, she repeated to herself her catechism of despair: He loves me, he will marry me, I must be patient. What else could she do, and where else could she go? She was banished from her home, too ill to go back to the bonnet shop, and too far outside of decent society to hope that another man might have her. She had her painting, but she had so much work ahead of her. Rossetti's promise was her only chance.

When they returned home that night, her instinct was to sulk, to lapse into one of her fits of illness that seemed to rise and fall with the tide of her emotions. It was so easy to punish Rossetti for his failures and his affairs by giving him reason to fear for her life. And it was little more, she thought churlishly, than he deserved. But she remembered Emma's advice, and dipped deep into the well of tenderness and love that she still felt for him. She went to him and wrapped her arms around him. She let her head rest on his shoulder for a moment, and felt him warm to her touch.

He looked at her with surprise. It had been a long time since she had invited him into her arms, and he rarely insisted. But of course he had longed for her, even as he found pleasure in other women.

He led her to the bed and began to undress her carefully. He loosened her hair and let it fall onto her shoulders, tracing his finger from the base of her neck down to the small of her back. He didn't immediately lay her down on the bed, as he had when she first came to live with him at the studio. Instead he sat before her and studied her as if he were going to draw her. It was humbling to see her like this, with nothing but her glorious hair for ornament. No painting would ever match her living, breathing beauty, or the depth of spirit that showed in her eyes.

He pretended to paint her, using her body as the canvas. He touched his finger to the tip of hers and then ran his hand lightly up on her arm, over her shoulder, and across her collarbone. He moved to her face, tracing the outline of her lips, her eyes, and the curve of her ear. He used his palms to follow the slight curve of her waist, her hips, the soft skin of her calves. At last he was kneeling before her, and she bent down toward him, as Guinevere bent over Lancelot to knight him. She bestowed upon him a kiss, offered her hand, and led him to bed.

The night of their visit to the Browns marked the beginning of a long period of peace between them. Rossetti ceased his nighttime wanderings, preferring to stay home with Lizzie in the evening and entertain a few friends for impromptu dinners or cards. During the day they worked on their paintings side by side. He was writing poetry again, and Lizzie provided some illustrations for his work. For once, money was not an issue; Rossetti's commissions and Ruskin's allowance were more than sufficient for their needs.

Rossetti never mentioned their delayed marriage, but they lived together much like man and wife, and Lizzie did not press. She missed her family, Lydia especially, but otherwise she felt happy. Her work absorbed her, and when she wasn't painting, she read voraciously, searching through old books of poetry and myth for suitable subjects for her illustrations. Her health didn't improve, but neither did it deteriorate. She took the laudanum for her aches, but it was just as effective at easing her worries, and she visited the chemist often to refill her bottle.

Their door was always open to friends, and John Ruskin was a frequent guest at Chatham Place. He was always kind to Lizzie, almost to the point of tenderness, but Rossetti didn't mind. Ruskin was a friend as well as his patron, and it seemed only natural to Rossetti that Lizzie's health and development as an artist should be of interest to him. Ruskin treated her almost as a favorite daughter, a girl who, through his patronage, he could care for, instruct, and take pride in. But the peace at Chatham Place was not to last.

Ruskin managed, through his recommendation, to secure Rossetti a new commission from a wealthy Irish merchant. The merchant admired Rossetti's style, but he was a man of modern tastes and cared little for myth or antiquity, preferring subjects of current fashion. Ruskin expected Rossetti to balk at the request, but Rossetti surprised him by agreeing. He wanted to try something new, perhaps a comment on the perils of the city, and the commission gave him the opportunity. Despite his best efforts, however, his subject proved challenging, and Rossetti found that months had slipped by, and by the summer of 1854 the painting was still only half finished.

The scene was the Thames embankment at dawn, the gaslights still bright against the lingering dark. A farmer from the countryside drives a calf into town to sell at the market. A girl hurries past him in the road, and despite the dim light, he recognizes her immediately: She is his sweetheart, a simple country girl, who left for London to make her living. He abandons his cart and steps toward her. But when he sees her cheap dress and her sallow face, his joy of recognition quickly turns to horror. There can be no doubt—his beloved has fallen into despair and prostitution.

Rossetti could see it in his mind's eye: the dawning dismay of the young man and the burning shame of the woman as she tries to hide her face. Touched by her plight, he runs to her, grasping her hands just as she falls into a faint under the weight of her disgrace. Behind them, the calf struggles vainly to free itself from its bindings.

The longer that he worked on the painting, the more he came to consider it as one of his most important works. But he couldn't seem to finish it. He was both drawn to and repelled by the painting. At times he worked at it all night, and then abandoned it for weeks while he busied himself with other projects.

Today he was getting nowhere. He cursed and threw aside his brush. He looked over at Lizzie, hard at work on her painting, single-minded in her attention to her craft. Usually he found the sight charming: her lower lip caught between her teeth and her white hand brushing her hair back from her eyes as she dabbed at the canvas. But today he found it irritating.

Ruskin had told him in confidence that he was trying to arrange a showing for Lizzie's work. At the moment Rossetti had clapped his friend on the back and thanked him for his support of Lizzie's art. But on further reflection, he'd felt less pleased. The thought was ugly and distressing: What if she surpassed him in her art? After all, Ruskin had said nothing of arranging a show for him. It was a terrible thought, but he wondered if he would have done better to keep her as his model, and not tried to make her into his pupil after all.

Lizzie felt Rossetti's eyes on her and turned. She smiled and put down her brush to join him at his canvas. But when she saw that he was working on his picture of the fallen woman, her face tightened and she stepped back. She hated this painting. She'd many times wished it finished and shipped up to Ireland.

"The Prostitute and the Virtuous Sheep Herder. Is it giving you trouble again?"

"I'm calling it *Found*. You know that." Rossetti hated Lizzie's invented name for his painting.

"She certainly has been found," Lizzie observed. "But to what end? Will the young man take her home to the country and make her his wife now? What good is it to her to have been found at all? It only puts her shame on display. And her young sweetheart—why didn't he marry her when he had the chance, so that she might have escaped her sad fate?"

"Perhaps he couldn't afford to do so. You know very well, Lizzie, that this is meant to be a commentary on the perils and corrupting forces of the city. It's not a fairy tale." They'd argued over this many times before.

"So you say. But I can't help but think that this is much more than a commentary on the plight of the fallen woman. Is the setting not suggestive to you?"

Rossetti couldn't think what she was getting at. The problem, he thought, was that he had used another woman as a model. She always disliked the paintings that he made of other women, and it was becoming tiresome to constantly fight over his models. It wasn't possible that he only ever paint Lizzie, no matter how much he loved her, but she didn't seem to understand.

"The embankment of the Thames, under the gaslights from the bridge? Does that setting mean nothing to you?" she asked.

He shook his head, tired of feeling that Lizzie was always looking over his shoulder.

"Dante," Lizzie insisted. "Isn't it Blackfriars Bridge? Where you first saw me, on that terrible night? You can't pretend to me that the setting is a coincidence. Is the fallen woman meant to be me?"

He flushed. She was right, of course. How could he have failed to see it? Was it possible that he had been thinking of that night? He walked over to the cupboard and poured himself a generous glass of brandy. He could feel her disapproval, but he looked straight at her as he took a long drink from the glass. "But if that's true—if the painting really *is* of you," he said, choosing his words carefully, "then that would make you the whore."

Lizzie looked as if she'd been slapped; her face went white and her lips parted in surprise. She'd thought it many times, but to have it said out loud was too cruel. "No. It means that you think me the whore. But you know perfectly well why I was down there that night. I was doing nothing more than walking home from work— and let me remind you that although I may have had a humble position, it was, at least, respectable. Not like the position that you've given me. If I am a whore, Dante," she said, beginning to cry, "it's only because you've made me one. You've imagined me into the role of the whore just as you once imagined that I was your Beatrice. You like to think of yourself as my savior, like the young man in the painting. But you are really no different from the old drunk who accosted me."

Rossetti slammed his glass down on the table. "Are we going to argue about this again?"

"No. But I'll remind you of your promise to me when I became your lover. Surely you haven't forgotten? You're a gentleman; you wouldn't place me in the same predicament as that poor girl." She gestured toward the painting without looking at it.

Rossetti sighed and sat down. There was no argument to be made with her. She was right. He'd made a promise to her, and he owed her that much and more. "Please don't press me. We will marry, I promise you."

"But why not now? I can't understand the delay. We already live together as if we were married."

"It's not the right moment. I'm just starting to make my name, and now you have your allowance from Ruskin. You'll have to give it up when we marry—it wouldn't be proper. I'd hate to see you lose his patronage. As soon as I'm making enough from my work to support you in the way that you deserve, we will marry."

"I don't care about the money, Dante. I care only about you. I'm happy with the way we live now, here in the studio. I don't need anything else."

"If you're happy, then why should we change anything? Do you want to be an artist, Lizzie, or do you want to be a wife? You have a chance at greatness, especially with John Ruskin as your benefactor. This is not the time to give all that up. We must put everything into our art right now. Later, when we've established ourselves, it will be the right time for marriage. I promise you, Lizzie."

Rossetti could see that his assurances had lost their effect on Lizzie. She didn't look satisfied as she turned and walked back to her easel. He wondered if he had given her his promise too soon. He had been only twenty-two when he met her, after all, a mere boy. He had been entranced by her beauty, and he still was now, four years later. But he had come to see that there were many pleasures in life, and he wasn't ready to forsake them just yet. The looming necessity of a proposal was beginning to feel like another debt that he had accrued but could not make good on.

"I'm afraid that I have to be away from London for a bit this fall," he said suddenly. "There's a group going to Kent on a painting trip. Holman Hunt will be back from Jerusalem, and a few others will join us. I've been longing to paint real girls under real trees. A return to nature." He paused. "Of course, you're welcome to come along."

She was quiet for a moment. She had pushed too hard, she realized, and now Rossetti would run off with his friends to be free of her. "You're going to Kent to paint? Will Annie Miller be going?"

"Most likely. No doubt Hunt will want to bring her along after his long absence."

"No doubt," Lizzie agreed, her clipped tone matching Rossetti's.

"And of course, I'll be working on my painting of her, so we really must have her there."

Lizzie could see that she was not wanted, and she knew that to chase Rossetti would only drive him further away. But she couldn't resist one jab. "And whose bed will Annie be sharing? Yours or Hunt's?"

Rossetti flushed scarlet, and Lizzie surprised herself by laughing, though it was a mirthless laugh. The fact of Rossetti's affair was always unspoken between them, though its evidence, in the beauty of Annie's half-finished portrait, stood in the corner of the studio. It was a relief to Lizzie to speak, and she went on, the torrent of anger unleashed. "If Hunt doesn't know already, he'll figure it out before long. He's not stupid." She gestured to the painting of Annie. "He'll see the same thing in that picture that I do. You may have told yourself that it's all for art's sake, that it means nothing, but I don't suppose that Hunt will see it that way. No, I don't think I want to be there when he realizes that you've been bedding his intended while he's been trudging through the desert. I'd prefer to stay here and see to my own work."

Rossetti had no answer to this, and so Lizzie turned back to her easel. But she couldn't paint. Despite what she'd said, she wasn't sure that Hunt would put the pieces together. How smart could he be, to expect a woman like Annie Miller to spend two years sitting by a lonely fireside, waiting for his return?

She sat rigidly, imagining Rossetti and Annie Miller on long rambles together through the woods in Kent. It seemed so long since she and Rossetti had enjoyed their walks in the countryside at Hastings. She thought of the day beneath the apple tree, when Rossetti had asked her to be his wife. They would never, she thought sadly, return to their Eden.

Fall came quickly, ushering in cool evenings that relieved the oppressive swelter of the city. Rossetti's mood improved with the weather. He looked forward to the trip to Kent, and knowing that he would soon be free of Lizzie's care made him more solicitous of her health and comfort. On the day that he left, he even brought her a bouquet of forget-me-nots and lilies. He kissed her and told her that he would miss her terribly, and would write every day. But he didn't renew his offer for her to join them. She watched him pack his things through a hazy veil of laudanum, grateful for its comfort.

When at last the door closed behind him, she collapsed on the bed, raging at his abandonment. Her anger was like a hot beast clawing its way up from the pit of her stomach, and her sobs, muffled into the bedsheets so as not to alarm the landlady, provided no relief. She took drop after drop of laudanum, and though the medicine did not sate the jealous beast, it mollified him, and he curled up, content to take his hourly dose.

Several days must have passed this way. Her waking hours seemed no different from her dreams, and life was reduced to a simple series of rituals: Uncork the green glass bottle and measure out the drops, lie on the bed to wait for the shivers and sweat to melt away in the drug's balmy caress, then wake, stumble into the studio to make tea, stare out the window, and wonder at her own lack of wonder about the world outside. Then back to the bed, back to the green bottle.

On the third day she woke from her opium dream, slippery and sly, and reached for the bottle. But it was empty, and she was forced to sit up, her head pounding. The shutters were open and the sun was pouring in through the windows, blinding her. Her dress was damp with sweat, and her hair hadn't been combed and was knotty. She couldn't go out to the chemist's like this.

She stood slowly and walked into the studio. The landlady had set a pitcher of water and a loaf of bread on the table in the hall. Rossetti must have told her that Lizzie was staying in the studio. At least he'd done that, she thought. She couldn't stomach the thought of the bread, but she used the water to make tea. She combed out her hair and braided it. She thought that she might vomit, but she didn't.

She wrapped a shawl around her shoulders and checked her purse, but as she readied herself to leave, one of the unfinished drawings on her easel caught her eye. It was her illustration of the Robert Browning poem *Pippa Passes*. It showed the virginal Pippa, her spine straight and her head high, passing a group of loose women who lounge on some steps, staring at her curiously. When Lizzie started the drawing, she had thought of herself as Pippa, poor but virtuous, holding her head high in the face of adversity. Now she was sickened to think that she looked more like the loose women: sloppy and lazy, watching life pass them by in the street.

She decided at once: She wouldn't go to the chemist. She was ashamed. Ashamed that she had wasted so much time when she might have been working; ashamed that she'd given in to the easy comfort of the laudanum. What if Rossetti had returned to find her like this? Even she wouldn't have blamed him for running back into the arms of Annie Miller. She took her shawl off, put her purse away, and went back to the bedroom. She needed to paint, but first, she needed to sleep.

When at last she rose, drained but clearheaded, she tried to take up her painting again. Each morning she sat before her easel, but the work did not come easily, and by afternoon she would throw down her brush, gather up her shawl, and head outside to roam through the city in the hope that fresh air was all she needed to forget the painting party in Kent, and the lure of the green bottle.

The walks improved her appetite, and the small meals that she took gave her the fortitude to sit longer at her easel. As the days passed, she started to enjoy the solitude of the studio. She finished the drawing of Pippa, and was pleased with it.

Before she started on her next piece, she sent a note to Ford Madox Brown, asking if he might still be willing to take her to buy some painting supplies. He replied that he was eager to assist her in any way that he could, and on a windy October morning they set out together for Winsor & Newton's, London's finest color men.

The shop was bright and cheerful, and the bells at the door jangled at Lizzie's entrance. She was as excited as she might have been at entering a fashionable dressmaker's. Her purse was heavy with Ruskin's allowance, and she decided that she wouldn't deny herself anything that might be of use in making her name as a real painter.

The shop was filled from floor to ceiling with everything an artist might want: cases full of brushes, palettes, knives, and chalk; canvases ranging in size from the palm of a hand to outstretched arms; easels of solid oak, and lighter ones that were meant to be folded and carried into a field. And then there were the paints. Lizzie had never seen so many colors. There were oils and watercolors in shiny metal tubes, their names printed beneath a dab of the color: French Ultramarine, Cadmium Yellow, and Cobalt. The shop chemists mixed custom orders, and the air smelled of turpentine and linseed oil.

Ford motioned for one of the clerks, and a young man scurried over and bowed to them. "How may I assist you?"

"We're going to need everything, and only the best," Ford said with a smile, and Lizzie laughed. "But we'll start with the basics—a dozen brushes, half in sable and half in hog's hair, please. As for paints, I'll let the lady choose, but we'll take one of these fine wooden boxes with the palette built in. You can use that to store them, Lizzie, or to take them with you to the park or the countryside. A palette knife, of course, and a box of charcoals. And we'll need several canvases. I'll choose the sizes while Miss Siddal looks over your colors." He turned to Lizzie. "You'll find the expense worth it, I think. A real painter should have her own materials. They become a part of you, you know. You'll quickly find which are your favorite."

Lizzie ran her finger over the cool tubes of paint on the counter. "Thank you for helping me, Ford. I'm so anxious to really begin. I've done a few things, of course, but I want to paint something worthy of Ruskin's patronage. I think I might try my hand at a self-portrait."

"An excellent idea. A painter must know himself, after all, if he wants to paint others truly."

Lizzie spent the next hour choosing colors, shaking her head yes and no as the clerk took them from the display case. She finally settled on a handful of shades in both oil and watercolor, along with a tube of Chinese white, which the clerk assured her was the best that could be obtained. He wrapped her purchases in brown paper, and Ford helped her carry them back to Chatham Place. She thanked him again, sending her love to Emma, and then bid him good-bye, anxious to start on her painting.

She sat down in her corner of the studio, secured a fresh canvas to her easel, and placed a looking glass on the table in front of her. She stared intently into the glass. In the dim light, a softly lit angel out of one of Rossetti's paintings stared back at her, beatific and beautiful.

She began to draw what she saw, but then stopped, shaking her head. She knew that she was drawing a dream, not a portrait. She stood and dragged her easel and the mirror directly in front of the window. When she looked back into the mirror, the harsh morning sun shone on her face.

What she saw there was not a saint or a myth, but a real woman. She stared at herself for a long time. She found things to admire: large eyes, white skin, and hair that still shone as brightly as when she was a girl. But illness had taken its toll. Her face was thin and her features stood out sharply. The skin around her eyes was tired, and the lids were heavy and swollen. Was it her imagination, or had her lips become a bit pinched, and had two faint lines appeared between her brows?

She took this all in calmly, and then began to draw exactly what she saw, no more and no less. She glanced around the studio at Rossetti's many paintings and sketches. In some cases, even she couldn't tell if he had been drawing her, or some other girl—they all seemed to merge together into one ideal, unreal woman. It suddenly seemed very important to Lizzie that she paint the truth; that there be some record of her as a living, breathing woman.

She worked intently for several hours, and then sat back to survey the results. The woman who was taking form on her canvas was beautiful, but she was also thoughtful and sad. Lizzie was satisfied.

She spent the next week working on the portrait. She chose her palette carefully: red and gold for the hair, emerald green for the background. At the last moment she added a touch of white, a flash of light. The woman in the portrait was still and silent, watching and waiting, but a glint of expectation shone in her eyes. Lizzie thought it very much like her.

Absorbed in her work, she enjoyed her time alone in the studio. She was able to work intently, without the bother of tidying up or worrying about her dress. There was no one to please, and no one's likes or needs to consider, save her own. This must be, she thought, what it's like to be a man.

No one came to visit, and she realized that almost all of the people that she now considered her friends were, in fact, friends of Rossetti's. She had Emma Brown, of course, but Emma was going to have her second child soon, and was busy with the preparations.

It came as a surprise, therefore, when a rapping at the door broke the silence of the studio. Lizzie jumped, startled, and smeared paint across her canvas. She cursed, then quickly rubbed it out and went to get the door. It would, no doubt, be some creditor of Rossetti's. He was behind on his bills, spending his money as quickly as he earned it, and there wasn't an art supplier in the city at whose shop he could show his face.

She opened the door, ready to send whoever it was on their way. She stopped short, however, when she saw John Ruskin.

"Hello! Have I disturbed the genius at work? You look as cross as can be."

Lizzie laughed, pleased to see Ruskin. "Hello, John. Don't mind me, I didn't expect you. I thought it was someone come round to collect on a bill. I've been locked away in here for days, and I'm hardly fit for company. I jumped like a hare when you knocked."

Ruskin's face darkened. "Is it that bad? If you're in need of anything, you know that you only need ask . . ."

Lizzie waved him into the studio. "No, no, I'm fine, but you know how Dante is. The minute he has some money, he spends it, and then some. Besides, you've been too generous already, you really mustn't let me take advantage of you."

"And where is Dante today?"

"Didn't he write to you? No, I suppose that he didn't, he never writes. He's in Kent with Holman Hunt and a small party. They've gone out there to paint real girls under real trees or some such thing."

"Will you join them?"

"No. I thought it best to stay here and work. You know how they can be when they're together—they have the best of intentions, but picnicking and drinking often prevail over painting."

Ruskin nodded with a dawning understanding. "And I suppose that they took some models along?"

"Annie Miller went with them."

"How can you . . ." Ruskin began, and then stopped, perhaps remembering his promise to Lizzie that he wouldn't intrude on her relationship with Dante. "You were no doubt right to stay here. I can see that you've been hard at work."

He walked over to her easel and looked at the self-portrait. Lizzie couldn't tell if he liked it or not, and she tapped her foot nervously as he surveyed the painting. He looked at it for a long time without saying anything, and she felt exposed, as if he were examining her very soul, and not her mere portrait. At last she felt that she must say something to break the silence. "It's hardly a portrait of the Princess Ida. But I think it might be the first real portrait of Lizzie Siddal that's ever been painted."

"It's a beautiful painting. Its beauty lies in its truth. But it's not the only truth." Ruskin looked around the studio at Rossetti's many studies of Lizzie. "All of these are just as much portraits of you as the one that you've painted."

Lizzie followed Ruskin's eye. "These are Dante's dreams. They're beautiful, but they're not me."

Ruskin turned back to her. "Surely you see that physical truth is not the only truth? These saints, these queens, they are paintings not only of your face, but also of your soul, of the beauty and imagination that you inspire in Dante. His paintings of you are an expression of his desire . . . of his love."

Lizzie blushed deeply. "I think that you see more in our art than we see ourselves."

"I have the advantage of seeing it with fresh eyes." He turned back to the self-portrait. "And what I see here I like very much. It should have the place of pride at your show."

"My show? Am I really to show my work?" She rushed up to him and gave him a friendly embrace, kissing his cheek before releasing him. Ruskin turned bright red and stepped back, and Lizzie remembered the gossip, that he hadn't touched his wife. She wondered how a man with such warmth of personality and kindness could feel distaste for the more physical side of love and affection. "I'm sorry," she murmured.

"Think nothing of it," Ruskin said, clearing his throat. "Your happiness is all the thanks I need. I only wish to watch you in your success, and know that I've played some small part in it. That's why I've arranged for a small showing of your work at a gallery in Charlotte Street. You'll have several months to finish up that self-portrait and anything else that you want to show. I've been in contact with a few buyers, including some Americans. I thought that it was high time that we get you into the public eye."

Lizzie was already bustling around the studio, taking stock of what she would need to work on. She felt an energy that she hadn't known in a long time. She stopped and looked at Ruskin. "This means the world to me. If I can keep working as I have been, I should have several new things ready by then. And of course you have the drawings that I sent to you last month—will they be included? And Dante has a few things that are nearing completion; they should be ready. Have you told him about the show yet? You must write at once, he'll be so pleased."

"The show will be of your work only. A small, private show is just the place for an artist's debut. Dante already has plenty of interest in his work, and he'll want to save his best work for the exhibitions next spring."

A show of her own. The thought was nearly overwhelming. "Your kindness to me, it's been my one constant."

"It's not kindness—it's business. You're a talented painter, and I want the world to value your art as I do. You see, I have my own interests at heart, as an early investor in your work. Now I suppose that I'd better leave you to your painting. I'll come by again next week so that we can discuss which pieces you'd like to show. In the meantime, just write to me if you need anything at all—supplies or anything else."

"I'll look forward to your visit." After Ruskin left she leaned against the closed door, overcome with happiness and as giddy as a child. She began to build castles in the air: She might get a notice in the paper; perhaps she would make a few good sales. Would Lydia be allowed to come see her work? By this time next year, Lizzie thought, she might be painting something larger, something good enough to submit to the big exhibitions. Her lingering doubts about Ruskin's motives were gone. She wasn't his charitable case. She was a real painter, a painter with a show of her own. She laughed in wonder. A few years ago she would never have believed herself capable of such a victory.

$\mathscr{C}$HAPTER 18

On the whole, Rossetti's painting trip to Kent was not a success. The idea had been to immerse himself in nature, but nature had proved as fickle and ungovernable as a woman—at first promising a clear sky and a hint of sun, and then turning rainy and cold the moment he walked a mile from the house and set up his easel and paints.

The first day out he was soaked to the bone and had to run back to the house with his jacket draped over his canvas. The next days were no better, and though he persevered, even the beautiful Annie Miller looked like a drowned rat after a few minutes in the rain—hardly an inspiring sight. Unable to paint outdoors, the group was stuck inside the small house all day, getting in each other's way and on each other's nerves.

Rossetti was forced to admit that perhaps Lizzie had been right: It was awful sharing close quarters with Holman Hunt and Annie Miller. Rossetti hadn't slept with Annie in months—it was too difficult with Lizzie living in his studio and Annie wishing to keep up appearances at her own lodgings—but he was still painting her, against Hunt's explicit wishes. When Hunt returned from his trip and discovered this fact, he wasn't happy. But, on the grounds of brotherly goodwill, he had grudgingly allowed Rossetti to finish his painting.

Still, every time Rossetti and Annie set out into the countryside to paint, Hunt looked after them suspiciously, and he didn't bother to hide his joy when the rain kept driving them back to the cottage. Annie wasn't in a very good mood, either. The liberty that she had enjoyed in Hunt's absence was suddenly at an end, and she chafed at the new limits on her freedom. She snapped at Rossetti and glared at Hunt, and claimed that the rain caused her aches that prevented her from sitting for either of them.

The painting party had not, therefore, produced much painting, or even much camaraderie. Rossetti was anxious to return to London. Annie was a joy to take to the pleasure gardens or the theater, but sharing a house with her was somewhat less agreeable. Her loud voice grated on his ears, and her perfume made him half sick.

When a letter arrived from Ruskin, he hoped that it might offer a new commission, and an excuse to return to town. The letter contained no commission, but it did offer a reason to return to London.

London, October 20, 1854

Dear Rossetti,

I hope that you're getting on well in Kent, and that you'll bring me back lots of good canvases. I went by your studio this afternoon and was surprised to find Miss Siddal alone. She's busy painting, and doing some very fine work.

I wonder if you thought it right to take me entirely into your confidence, and to tell me whether you have any plans or wishes respecting Miss Siddal which you are prevented from carrying out by want of a certain income, and if so, what income would enable you to carry them out. My feeling is that it would be best for you to marry, for the sake of giving Miss Siddal complete protection and care, and putting an end to the peculiar sadness, and want of I hardly know what that I see in both of you.

Please take this letter in the spirit that it is written—I do only want what is best for both of you.

Yours,
J. Ruskin

At first Rossetti was annoyed. He could accept Ruskin's advice on his paintings, which Ruskin doled out with a fatherly expectation of obedience. There weren't many men, after all, who would pay for a painting and keep their mouths shut when they weren't happy with it. And there were none at all who would pay what Rossetti was asking and not feel entitled to an occasional quibble. At least Ruskin had a real sense for painting, and an eye for color and form. And though Rossetti may have hollered and protested at some of Ruskin's demands, he knew in the end that his advice was valuable.

Ruskin's interference in Rossetti's personal affairs, however, was much less welcome. Why was it that everyone felt that Lizzie was in need of their aid? Not for the first time, he wished that he had been able to keep Lizzie separate from the rest of his life; not a secret exactly, but a thing apart from the daily business of his work and family obligations. He was tired of having to defend himself in her regard.

He thought of the day that he met her at Deverell's studio, and how her very existence had seemed a revelation. When he saw his friends later that day, he'd known instinctually that to tell them about Lizzie would have diminished the truth of his vision, and made the divine more ordinary by dressing it in the common language of models and bonnet shops. Now he wished that his love for Lizzie didn't require banal explanations and dutiful actions to make it right.

He wondered if he did, as Ruskin asked, have plans regarding Lizzie, and if there was, indeed, a certain sum that would enable him to carry them out. Of course a regular income would make things easier. If he could install Lizzie in a good house in, say, Chelsea, her health might improve, and his studio would once again be his private sanctuary. He could paint all day, whichever models he wanted, and then at night he could return to the loving arms of his wife, who could have her own studio at the back of the house.

No doubt Ruskin hoped that the steadiness of married life might improve Rossetti's own work, and, though he resented Ruskin's intrusion, Rossetti wondered if he might be right. Certainly the shared house in Kent and the looming brawl over Annie Miller's affections wasn't helping him get any painting done. For a moment he was tempted to dash off a note to Ruskin, naming a sum for his marriage as he might name a sum for a painting. But of course he didn't write. It was one thing for Lizzie, a woman with great talent but no training and no resources, to take Ruskin's allowance. For Rossetti to do so would be degrading.

Still, he began to long for Lizzie's company. He may not have wanted Ruskin's voice in his head, but he heard it anyway, and he wondered what sorts of paintings Lizzie was working on, and whether she was looking after herself properly. He forgot that they had bickered over his painting of the fallen woman, and he was relieved when Hunt said that the weather showed no signs of improving, and that they had better return to town.

Rossetti returned from Kent and begged for Lizzie's forgiveness, giving her a paisley shawl in the softest wool as a token of his contrition. But Lizzie was too caught up in her work, and too excited for her upcoming show, to bear any real grudge against him. She welcomed him home eagerly and showed him her new paintings, asking for his opinion on which pieces she ought to send to Ruskin.

Rossetti praised her paintings, but he worried, as always, over her health. Was it possible that in his absence she had grown even thinner? He wasn't at all convinced that she'd eaten regularly while he was away, and he blamed the laudanum, which seemed to have become the mainstay of her diet. But her excitement was infectious, and he put his worries aside, convincing himself that if the laudanum made her well enough to paint, then it was, after all, a good remedy.

Ruskin leased a small gallery in Charlotte Street for Lizzie's show, not far from the Rossetti family home, and he oversaw the hanging of her work himself. The subjects were mostly from poetry, and by the time of the show she had a nice collection of illustrations and watercolors, including scenes from the work of Robert Browning, Sir Walter Scott, and her beloved Tennyson.

The two most striking pieces in the collection, however, were her self-portrait, which Rossetti had exclaimed over to no end upon his return, and her illustration from the old English ballad *Clerk Saunders*. It showed Margaret, a maid who is persuaded to go to bed with her lover before their marriage. Later, his ghost visits her in her room after her brothers kill him. Lizzie had rendered the figures in rich colors, which shone out brightly from the shadows of the dawn light. Margaret wishes to kiss her lover, but he must refuse; his kiss would kill her. Instead, her face taut with grief, Margaret kisses a branch to lay upon his grave. It was a touching painting, and Ruskin hung it in a place of honor in the gallery.

On the first day of the show, Lizzie stayed in Rossetti's studio, waiting for word of her success or failure. She was far too nervous to attend the show herself, and Ruskin would be there to promote her work.

Rossetti, trying to patch over the hard feelings between them, invited Holman Hunt to go to the show with him. Ruskin greeted them at the door of the gallery, and Rossetti saw that it had been very well put on, and that Ruskin had secured a good attendance for the private view.

"Look at this one," Rossetti said to Hunt, pointing to an illustration that Lizzie had done from a Browning poem. "She's captured the form of the women perfectly. They're so natural. She really is becoming quite a genius."

"Very natural," said Hunt. But under his breath he muttered, "Though I'm not sure I would say genius."

"And here," Rossetti went on, leading Hunt over to the watercolor of *Clerk Saunders*. "This is her best work. She has such depth of feeling, and such a natural understanding of color and shade."

Hunt looked at the picture closely. "This one really is quite good! If I hadn't known that it was Lizzie's, I would have thought that perhaps it was yours, or maybe the work of poor Deverell. The style and the colors are so similar, don't you think?"

Rossetti looked angry. "I wouldn't say that at all. Deverell was a man of great talent, but Lizzie has real genius. Her work is completely original. It's an insult, Hunt, to even suggest that she was influenced by him."

Hunt was taken aback. "You misunderstand me!" he cried. "I meant it as a compliment. After all, she's been studying with you for only such a short time. I didn't mean to insult her talent, or her originality. And besides, weren't they friends? I always find inspiration in the work of my friends, you included, Rossetti."

Rossetti frowned, then turned on his heel and stalked away, leaving Hunt bewildered. Rossetti hated to be reminded of the old rumors: that Deverell had been in love with Lizzie, and that he had painted her in secret, behind his back.

Hunt shrugged, used to such outbursts from Rossetti, and walked after him. He found him speaking with John Ruskin and another man who was exclaiming over the paintings in a brassy American accent. Hunt laid a hand on Rossetti's arm and said, in a conciliatory tone: "You're right. *Clerk Saunders* is surely Miss Siddal's finest work. It shows not only skill, but also perception. The true artist's eye."

"Well, I'm glad to hear you say so!" cried the American. "I've just agreed to purchase it!"

Rossetti and Ruskin were beaming; they'd made Lizzie's first real sale.

"You'll have to excuse me," Rossetti said, his quarrel with Hunt forgotten in light of the good news. "I want to be the first to congratulate the artist in person."

He turned to the American. "You must have Ruskin bring you around to our studio. I'm sure that Miss Siddal would like to show you some of her work in person."

He shook hands all around, and then dashed off into the street. He couldn't wait to share the good news with Lizzie.

Rossetti didn't have to go far to find her. He was barely at the corner of the street when he ran right into her, hurrying in the other direction.

"Lizzie! What are you doing here?"

"I was going mad just sitting and waiting. I had to see what sort of impression my work was making."

Rossetti swept her into his arms and spun her around, surprising the other people in the street. "You've made your first sale to the public, Lizzie, and a good one at that. An American purchased *Clerk Saunders*."

Lizzie broke out into a wide smile. "Then, I am an artist."

"Let's celebrate. What would make you happy? The theater? Oysters and champagne? Tonight you must have whatever you want."

Lizzie glanced around her. The news of her success made her feel bold. "Whatever I want? I don't want champagne. Dante, I want to meet your mother. Doesn't she live in Charlotte Street? Why don't we pay her a visit. It's high time, I think, that we met."

"You want to celebrate in my mother's drawing room?" Rossetti laughed, but he could see that Lizzie was serious. It was obvious that she intended to have her way. He shrugged. "As you wish. Today, I'm at your service."

He led Lizzie a few blocks down the street to the door of a small but respectable house. Any remaining illusions that Lizzie might have had of Rossetti's wealth were finally laid to rest. When she first met him, she thought that anyone who didn't work at a trade must live a life of leisure. But she'd since learned a great deal about London society, and the artist's place in that world. It was fitting that she first glimpsed Rossetti as the court jester in Deverell's painting. Painters, she now saw, were admitted to society, but only so far as they were pleasing and amusing.

Rossetti paused on the doorstep. "You're right, Lizzie. It's time that you met my mother." He'd put off this moment for far too long, and now that it had arrived, he couldn't quite say why. It was a relief, after all this time, to finally be settling the question of their marriage. Once he introduced Lizzie to his mother as his intended, his future with her would feel more real, like a painting long in planning and finally marked out in pencil on the canvas. He knocked on the door.

The maid let them in, and Lizzie and Rossetti entered the drawing room and found Christina at her desk and Mrs. Rossetti reading a volume by the fireplace.

"Dante!" Christina cried. "You're a welcome sight!"

Lizzie was standing slightly behind Rossetti, but now she stepped forward. She was prepared for a cold reception, so she was surprised when Christina's smile did not dim at the sight of her.

"And Miss Siddal, as well! It's been entirely too long. Please, come in and meet my mother. Here, this is the most comfortable chair. I know that you've not been well. This is my mother, Mrs. Rossetti. She's heard so much about you, and she's anxious to make your acquaintance."

Lizzie swallowed her surprise. She followed Christina and sat in a chair by the fire, and Rossetti stood by her shoulder.

"Mother, this is Miss Elizabeth Siddal. Miss Siddal is a talented poet and painter, and she's done me the honor of agreeing to marry me. I hope that you'll give us your blessing."

Mrs. Rossetti embraced them both, tears in her eyes. "Welcome to our family, Elizabeth." She turned to Rossetti. "You've picked a pretty one, dear, and made me a happy old woman. Now come and sit with me by the fire. I want to know everything."

Rossetti told his mother about Lizzie's painting, and about the success of her first show, but his mother and sister, as predicted, only wanted to talk about the wedding.

"Have you set a date?" Mrs. Rossetti asked.

"Not yet," Rossetti laughed. "But I think you'll agree that it would be best to wait for the nice weather in the spring."

"Why not a Christmas wedding?" Mrs. Rossetti asked.

"That would be lovely," Lizzie agreed, smiling at Rossetti.

"But we'll want to travel after the wedding, so a spring wedding makes the most sense."

Lizzie frowned, and Mrs. Rossetti watched the exchange with a keen eye. "There's no reason to decide tonight," she said, smoothing over the disagreement. "But these decisions are best left to the women, dear. I'll write to Father Healy and see when he might be available." Then she turned to Lizzie and asked after her family and her work. Lizzie obliged her, giving vague answers about her family that painted them as a poor but respectable and literary clan. Christina ordered the tea and pulled up a chair to join them, and Lizzie felt that Rossetti's family had welcomed her with affection. She couldn't help but wonder if Christina's own romantic disappointments had made her more sympathetic, but whatever the change was, Lizzie welcomed it.

Rossetti watched his mother and sister, and saw that the Rossetti women had, as women will, quietly rallied around Lizzie. No matter what they may have thought of her background, it was their nature to feel indignant on behalf of a woman in distress. He knew that they disapproved of what they heard of his living arrangements, and that now that he had brought Lizzie home, they would do everything in their power to see that he did right by her. And of course, Mrs. Rossetti could forgive a lot for the promise of a grand-child.

Rossetti did what any man in his situation would do: He ignored the tea completely and poured himself a generous glass of port from the side table. The drink steadied his nerves, and after a second glass, he began to enjoy the sight of his dear, talented Lizzie sitting between his mother and Christina. Domesticity may have its con-straints, but surely it also had its advantages? Perhaps Ruskin was right and a steadier way of life would allow him to concentrate more on his work.

When Rossetti and Lizzie rose to take their leave, the Rossetti ladies both embraced Lizzie, and offered her their compliments on her success. As she walked Lizzie to the door, Christina leaned close to her and whispered: "I'm sorry that I haven't been a better friend to you. I hope that you'll depend upon my friendship in the future."

Lizzie nodded, feeling for the first time since her father had cast her out that she was safe and welcome in a real home. She won-dered if now that Rossetti had announced their engagement to his family, she would finally be able to return to her house with her head held high. Sitting by the fire with Mrs. Rossetti had made her long for such moments with her own mother. Surely her family would welcome her again once she was a respectably married woman?

As they made their way out into the street, Rossetti took special care with her, making sure that her cloak was tied tightly around her shoulders and grasping her arm as they stepped over the curb. Lizzie was giddy with her accomplishments; she had sold a paint-ing and she would soon be married to the man whom she loved. Everything would work out in the end, after all—she had been wrong ever to doubt Rossetti, or her own talent. She felt no need to resort to her bottle of laudanum. No anxiety plagued her, and the dulling effects of the laudanum would only have robbed the joy from the day, while offering an empty comfort. For the first time in as long as she could remember, the world was clear and bright, and she walked by Rossetti's side with the feeling that all was just as it should be.

CHAPTER 19

Fall turned into winter, and it became clear that there would be no Christmas wedding. January of 1855 was cold; the coldest, some said, in the forty years since the last time the Thames froze over, when there was skating and sledding, and an elephant led across the ice under Blackfriars Bridge. The Thames did not freeze, but the sleet was constant, pooling in the streets in a cold black stew and coating everything from lampposts to ladies' hems in a thick layer of ice and grime. Rossetti fed the fire at Chatham Place, but the hearth did little to drive away the damp that settled in the beams of the building, and soon invaded Lizzie's delicate constitution as well. Her thin frame was no protection against the chill, and she coughed through much of the winter. A fire was lit in the bedroom, and some days she stayed there from morning till night, taking laudanum and hot tea, and leaving Rossetti to his own devices.

Spring came as if it had always been there, like a guest who arrives at a sleeping house and greets the family at the breakfast table. One night they went to bed to the howl of a hard wind blowing in off the Thames, and the next morning they woke to warm pale sunlight and the sound of gulls flying over the river. But the fine weather boded no better for Lizzie's hopes of marriage than the paralyzing freeze of winter. It was a pattern as familiar to her as the changing of the seasons: Rossetti's devoted attention persisted for several months before other concerns clamored for his attention, and Lizzie was once again forgotten, relegated to the corner of the studio to work on her own drawings.

She knew that he didn't mean to be cruel; it was just that there were paintings to be finished and dinners to attend, poems to be written and sold off to magazines, and outings to the pleasure gardens at Cremorne now that the evenings were warm. John Ruskin was no longer the only man championing Rossetti's work, and with the new interest in his painting came a flood of commissions and invitations. The winter left Lizzie weak, and Rossetti was not willing to give up his newfound celebrity to sit at home by her side.

The waiting—waiting for Rossetti to set the date, waiting for him to return home in the evenings—wore on her, and she once again turned from the demanding solace of her painting to the easy comfort of the laudanum. Rossetti grew concerned whenever he saw her taking it, but he accepted without argument her claim that it was the only thing that eased her aches. Emma Brown, on her frequent visits, was more skeptical. "Lizzie," she said, "you're poisoning yourself. If you took as much food as you take of that nasty potion, you might put a little meat on your bones. Why don't you come stay with Ford and me for a few weeks? The children would love to see you, and chasing them about would give anyone an appetite." But Lizzie demurred. "My work keeps me here," she said, and Emma raised her eyebrows, looking at the small pile of sketches that Lizzie had completed, but held her tongue.

Rossetti traveled frequently that spring, spending weeks at a time in Oxford while he worked on a mural in the old debating hall at the Union Society. It was a group project that he'd undertaken with a few other painters, including his new friends Ned Burne-Jones and William Morris.

The mural would encompass ten panels that stretched from the tops of the bookcases that lined the room to the vaulted ceiling. The theme was Malory's *Morte d'Arthur*, and Rossetti's panel showed Lancelot prevented from entering the chapel of the Holy Grail by the sin of his adultery with Queen Guinevere. Lancelot has fallen asleep before the shrine, and he dreams that Guinevere is gazing at him with her arms spread out against the backdrop of an apple tree. She is at once Eve in the garden, the cause of Lancelot's fall, and Christ at the crucifixion, savior of his soul. As Rossetti painted Guinevere's outstretched arms, he imagined her holding scales: measuring the weight of their passion against the code of chivalry to which Lancelot is sworn.

If the size of the murals was grand, the painting party that set up camp at Oxford was even grander. Painters, poets, and friends from the city came and went, and Rossetti spent as much time making up silly verses and pursuing the local girls to sit for him as models as he did working on the mural. He became fast friends with Ned Burne-Jones, a young painter who had not only heard of the Brotherhood, but also admired them, and treated Rossetti as a mentor.

They began to refer to the undertaking as the Jovial Campaign, and when the six weeks allotted for the project came and went without much progress being made, the committee overseeing the work was at a loss and wrote to John Ruskin for advice. But Ruskin was of little help, writing back that painters were all a bit mad, and difficult to manage, and that the best thing to do was to let them have their way and hope for the best.

The mural was still far from finished when a letter came from London that broke up the painting party. Lizzie was ill again, and Christina wrote to Rossetti to urge him to return to the city. He was enjoying his new friends and new surroundings, but Christina's words reminded him of his duty. He returned to Lizzie, chastened and bearing gifts, and swearing that he had thought of no one but her while he was away. Lizzie rallied, but she was still weak, and Rossetti found himself wondering, not for the first time, how long he would have to sit by her sickbed.

In June, Ford and Emma Brown proposed an outing to Hampton Court Palace, and Rossetti jumped at the chance to get out of the house. The city was already hot, and everyone longed for the fresh air of the countryside. A party was put together and two carriages were hired to take them west of the city to the palace grounds, which had been opened to the public by the Queen. At first, Lizzie demurred. But for once Rossetti insisted that she come with him, and she gave in, convinced that the change of scenery would do her good.

Hampton Court was famous for its hedge maze and its excellent picnicking grounds. Baskets were packed with a glorious spread: cold hams and wheels of cheese, fresh strawberries, a salad of peas and mint, and bottles of wine and beer.

Lizzie and Rossetti rode in the first carriage with Ford and Emma. Holman Hunt and Annie Miller, on precarious terms since Hunt's return from the East, rode in the second carriage with John Ruskin. Ned Burne-Jones, who came down to the city from Oxford for the outing, rounded out the group.

The ride was difficult for Lizzie. The jolting and rocking of the carriage upset her stomach and made her head ache. But Rossetti tended to her lovingly, and, as always, Lizzie improved under his care, gaining strength from his attention. He measured out a generous portion of her laudanum, and had the carriages stop so that beer could be fetched from the other carriage to settle her stomach. By the time the party reached Hampton Court, Lizzie was sleeping peacefully, her head resting on Rossetti's shoulder.

When they arrived at the gates, Rossetti shook her awake. She peered out of the window as the carriage rolled down a broad avenue toward the palace. White paths crisscrossed the manicured lawns, and iris, foxglove, and lilies bordered the lane. The sun reflected off of the water of the curving canal that bordered the garden. The carriage rolled down an allée of trees trimmed into perfectly matching cones. The palace, visible ahead, was massive, built of pale pink brick, with hundreds of chimneys rising up from the roof against the bright blue sky. It couldn't have been a more perfect setting, or a more glorious day, for a picnic.

The carriages pulled up short of the palace and the party began to unload. Ruskin helped Lizzie down from the carriage. Rossetti offered her his arm and Ruskin held a parasol over her head as they escorted her through a small garden, dotted with stone sculptures and bounded by hedges. They picked a spot in the field beyond the garden and settled Lizzie in the shade of a great plane tree. The rest of the party followed behind, carrying the blankets and baskets of food.

Annie Miller watched as Rossetti and Ruskin fussed over Lizzie. Lizzie overhead her say to Hunt, "Well, ain't she the Queen of Sheba?" But Lizzie ignored the slight, shaking her head at the crassness of the woman that so fascinated Rossetti.

They shook out the blankets and Lizzie lay down with her head in Rossetti's lap. The sun shone down through the branches of the tree and played upon his face, and she was reminded of their one perfect day together in Hastings. She smiled at him, feeling the easy intimacy of their early days, before illness and the bothers of money and marriage and everything else had crowded out the thing that she had almost forgotten—that she loved Rossetti from deep within her soul; that she had only risen from her waking slumber when he had looked upon her and seen saints and angels, noblewomen and goddesses.

He smiled back, and she saw him clearly, as if they were alone. Then her focus shifted and became hazier, and the faces of her friends seemed to glide by slowly and indistinctly. Her heartbeat, slow and regular from the laudanum, sped up, and her hands began to tremble. The dose was wearing off.

She reached for the bottle and Rossetti noticed her movement. His face registered his surprise that she needed more so soon. Then he shrugged and reached out his own hand. He had started to take it a bit himself, just a touch here and there, saying that the opium encouraged his artistic vision.

The picnic baskets were unpacked and they ate their meal on the grass, washing down the food with generous glasses of sweet wine. When they finished, they lay back on the blankets, full and happy. The talk was slow and idle, and Rossetti drifted off to sleep under the shade of the tree. Ned Burne-Jones had brought a small portable easel with him, and he set it up to make studies of the ladies, capturing their whispers and laughter in a series of quick sketches.

Lizzie had almost fallen asleep herself when Emma's cheerful voice roused the group. "I'm tired of sitting. Let's play a game!"

"Charades?" Ford suggested.

"No, we always play charades. Besides, Hunt and Ruskin will pick the most obscure books. It leaves me quite out of the game."

"If you read more, my dear, you wouldn't mind so much," Ford said with a smile.

Emma ignored him. "Let's go into the maze! There should be enough light left to see our way back out, unless we get hopelessly lost."

"I suppose we should see it while we're here." Ford rolled over on the blanket. "But I'd much rather lie here and have Ned tell us what he's working on."

Ned blushed and smiled, delighted to have the notice of a painter he admired. He'd said little during the afternoon, but now he rose to his feet. "Perhaps I can please both the ladies and the gentlemen. I propose a game in the nature of my new painting. It's only in designs at the moment, but when it's finished it will show the fall of Troy, starting with the golden apple of discord, tossed among the goddesses. I hope you don't mind—I've taken a few quick studies of the ladies today for my goddesses, as I'm not often in the company of three women so clearly on loan to us from the gods."

"How interesting," Emma said. "Do go on."

"It all began with a trick played by Eris, the goddess of discord. Eris wasn't invited to the wedding feast of Peleus. Her feelings were hurt, and she decided to go anyway. She arrived at the celebration with a golden apple, on which she inscribed, *To the Fairest One*.

"There were many beautiful goddesses at the wedding, and Hera, Athena, and Aphrodite all claimed the apple as theirs. The goddesses asked Zeus to judge which of them was the fairest, but Zeus was far too clever to be drawn into such an argument, and to show favor to any one goddess. Instead, he declared that Paris, the Trojan prince, would be the judge. And that's how Paris found himself tasked with judging among the beauty of three lovely goddesses, who each offered him bribes of earthly glories to gain his choice."

"It's a wonderful tale," Emma broke in. "But I don't see how we should make a game out of it."

"Don't you see? Here, today, we have three of the most beautiful ladies that I've ever laid eyes upon. It would not go too far, I think, to call you goddesses, and certainly you've been painted as such."

He reached into the picnic basket and found an apple, which he began to carve with a pocketknife. When he held it up for them to see, it had Eris's inscription upon it: *To the Fairest One.* "Shall we have a competition," he asked, "for the golden apple?"

Emma and Annie Miller clapped their hands in pleasure, and even Lizzie was intrigued.

"I'll name each of you as a goddess, and you yourselves shall choose the gifts that you will bestow on our judge, should he choose you as the fairest."

He turned first to Lizzie. "You will be Hera, the queen of the gods, since it's said that you have the bearing of a queen. Hera offered to make Paris the king of all Europe and Asia, and he was sorely tempted."

"I accept," Lizzie said, with a gracious smile.

"And you, Emma, shall be our Athena, goddess of wisdom and war, since you've organized our outing today with the skill and forethought of a general. Athena offered to share her knowledge of war with Paris, and the glory that would come with such skill."

Emma laughed. "I'm honored, though I'm afraid that Ford will protest my being named the goddess of wisdom."

"Nonsense, my dear," Ford said. "You manage me quite well, and I'm a happy man!"

"And finally, there is Aphrodite, goddess of love, who offered Paris the love of the most beautiful woman in the world."

"Oh!" Annie Miller cried out. "That was Helen of Troy, wasn't it? Dante painted me as Helen, I remember the story!" She turned and looked triumphantly at Hunt, as if to say, see, I am not so simple as you think. But Hunt looked more pained than pleased.

"Indeed it was Helen," Ned said. "Although at that time, she was Helen of Sparta, for Paris had not yet stolen her from her husband and carried her back to Troy. Annie, you've been Helen of Troy, and now you must play Aphrodite."

"Annie as the goddess of love," Ford chuckled. "Now that's appropriate." Both Hunt and Rossetti shot him nasty looks, and Ford quickly changed the subject. "But who will judge?"

"Ruskin should be our judge," Ned said. "He is, after all, known for his good judgment in art."

"Oh, no," cried Ruskin. "Like Zeus, I'm far too clever to choose among three such lovely women. I'm confident in my judgments on the beauty of art, but that is a far easier thing than the judgment of real beauty, which is in the eye of the beholder."

"Why don't we make a sport of it?" proposed Emma, standing up and smoothing her dress. "Go into the labyrinth ahead of us and hide the apple in the maze. Whichever of us finds it first will be judged not only the fairest, but also the cleverest."

"A fine idea!" agreed Rossetti. "I want to see the maze before we lose the light. The rest of us can be mythical creatures, and act as snares and traps. We can try to turn the ladies around and distract them from their purpose."

"I'll play the minotaur," said Ford. He searched around in the grass and came back with two small branches, which Emma helped him to attach to his head as his bull's horns with a ribbon from her hair.

"Ned should play our honorary Eris, since he will hide the golden apple," Rossetti said. "And I will be Pan, and lure the ladies away from their task with the playing of my flute." He whistled a short tune and laughed.

"Are you sure that your flute is the only thing that you use to lure the ladies?" Ford asked. He began to laugh, but stopped when Emma shot him a withering look.

"And I'll play Ares, god of war," Hunt declared, looking irritably at Rossetti, "and make battle with anyone who crosses my path."

"And Ruskin?" Lizzie asked. "What role shall he play?"

"Why, none other than Zeus!" said Ruskin. "I'll roam the maze and make sure that the game is played in accordance with my law."

"Then we're set," Ned said. "Let the game begin."

The party gathered at the entrance to the maze, which was formed by dark green yew hedges that stood ten feet high, planted in a winding series of paths. It had stood on the palace grounds for more than a hundred years, but it seemed to breathe an even more ancient history, recalling the labyrinths of ancient Greece.

Ned went into the maze to hide the apple of discord, and Ruskin,

Hunt, and Ford went with him to take up their positions. Rossetti stayed with the ladies to ensure a fair start.

Lizzie leaned heavily on Rossetti's arm. The wine and the laudanum made her unsteady, but she didn't want to miss out on the game. She was determined to find the apple before Annie could get her plump pink hands upon it. They would never hear the end of it if Annie were to win.

After a few minutes Ned's voice rose up over the tops of the hedges: "The apple has been thrown!"

Emma and Annie laughed and entered the maze. Rossetti whispered in Lizzie's ear: "The key to the maze is to always keep your hand on the hedge to your right, and follow where that leads you. No doubt Ned has hidden it at the center." Then he surprised Lizzie by dropping her arm and racing off into the maze without another word. He ran down a long corridor of hedges, turned at the first corner, and disappeared. Lizzie wasn't sure if he'd gone in the same direction as Emma and Annie or not.

She stared after him, dismayed, and then entered the maze herself. The walls of greenery rose up steeply and engulfed her. All was silent; the hedges muffled any sound from outside. Lizzie felt unsure of herself without Rossetti's arm to lean on, but she pressed ahead, not wanting Annie to get too far of a lead on her.

At the first fork, she followed Rossetti's advice and held to her right. The path ahead of her was empty, and seemed darker and more foreboding than it had at the entrance. She thought of going back and taking the other path, but when she glanced behind her she was confused over which way she had come. She looked up and saw that the sun must be very low in the sky; it was no longer visible above her, and the light in the maze was a hazy violet.

She heard the sound of two sets of running feet very near her, as if someone was being chased. She peered up and down the path and then realized that it must have come from the other side of the hedge. She listened closely, and thought that she heard the sound of low whistling, but she could not be sure.

"Emma? Dante?" she called out, but no one replied, and she decided to go on. She ran as quickly as she could down the paths, always trying to turn to the right, though she found that it wasn't always possible. Or perhaps she was just confused; in the low light, and the fog of her own mind, she began to see false turns and shadowy figures lurking everywhere.

She was turning yet another corner, beginning to despair of ever finding the apple, when a real figure leapt out from the shadows. Lizzie gasped and stepped backward. Then she realized that it was only Ford, with his Minotaur horns. "Oh, thank God it's you, Ford. I thought I'd seen a ghost."

"Halt!" he said in a booming voice, trying not to smile. "None shall pass through my maze without doing battle. I propose a game of wits."

"Have you seen any of the others?" Lizzie asked, feeling too tired and confused for games. "I feel that I'm running in circles."

But Ford kept to his role. "You shall not pass to the prize without answering my question. I am the mighty Minotaur of the maze!"

Lizzie sighed. "Go on then."

"If you answer correctly, you may pass in peace. Here is your riddle: Without you, I am nothing, and with you, we are one and the same. If you look closely you can see my face, but I haven't got a name. What am I?"

Lizzie laughed. A face without a name was how she often felt, looking at herself in Rossetti's paintings. But it wasn't a painting that Ford was after—she had heard this riddle before. "Are you a mirror?" she asked.

Ford raised his eyebrows, impressed. "Correct. You may pass."

Lizzie begged him once again to point her toward the others, but he stayed in his role, and merely moved aside to let her pass.

Lizzie ran on, thinking that she must be close. No cries of triumph had rung through the hedges. She was sure that the apple must still be unclaimed.

Now the light in the maze had grown so dim that Lizzie could barely see a dozen feet in front of her. Had the hedges grown closer together? She felt tired and short of breath. She reached for her laudanum bottle, and then remembered that she had left it with their picnic baskets.

She'd lost interest in finding the apple. Now all she wanted was to find her way out of the maze and into a comfortable seat in the carriage. She was about to cry out for help when she saw what looked like a familiar turning up ahead.

She hurried around the corner, but she was greeted by another empty corridor that seemed to lead nowhere. Tears of frustration sprung to her eyes, and through their blur, she saw a moving figure at the end of the path. Could it be Ned, with the apple of discord?

She ran forward, and was halfway down the path when she heard a low whistle and a high, girlish laugh. She saw that it was not one figure, but two: a man and woman entwined, half pressed into the wall of hedges. She heard the whistle again and as she walked toward them she saw that it was Rossetti, and he was with Annie Miller.

It's a mistake, she thought desperately, a trick of the light.

The hedges seemed to grow taller and close in over her head, and the path felt as if it were falling away before her. Almost against her will, she took a few more steps forward, feeling that she was stepping into an abyss.

Rossetti's face was buried in Annie's neck, and he didn't see her approach. But Annie must have sensed her presence, and looked up. She stared straight at Lizzie with no trace of shame, and a wide, scornful smile spread across her face. Then she tilted her head back, closed her eyes, and sighed with pleasure.

She murmured something into Rossetti's ear, and he turned, startled, and faced Lizzie. She was rooted to the spot, unable to run or to speak. He spoke her name, entreating her understanding, but he was too late. The abyss had opened, and Lizzie tumbled into the oblivion, collapsing into a dead faint on the path.

The moments that followed passed in a blur. Ruskin heard Rossetti's cries and came running down the path. He stopped short when he saw Lizzie's body on the ground, with Rossetti and Annie standing over her, understanding at once what must have happened. Their eyes met, and Rossetti's face twisted with guilt.

Ruskin knelt at Lizzie's side. "Will you not be happy until you've killed her?" he muttered. Rossetti kneeled down beside Ruskin, Annie Miller forgotten for the moment. "I didn't know that she was there." Annie, realizing when she wasn't wanted, shrugged and went off to find the others, to tell them that Lizzie had spoiled their game.

The two men worked to revive Lizzie, but she didn't stir. Her skin was white and waxy, and her breath was shallow. She made a pathetic sight, and Ruskin at last gathered her up in his arms and said that they had better take her back to the carriages, to see if there were any smelling salts. When he lifted her, he was shocked at how light she was, as if she were no more than bones beneath her gown.

"Her laudanum," Rossetti said, still in shock and trailing behind Ruskin. "It's with the picnic baskets. That ought to revive her."

Ruskin turned around with a frown. "And has she taken any regular sustenance besides her laudanum? She feels as if she could float away at any moment."

"I . . . I don't know. Not much, I don't think. She hasn't been well."

Ruskin let his temper flare. "You've let this madness with Lizzie go on for far too long, Dante. It's obscene for you to be living with her without marrying her, and at the same time bedding every model you bring into your studio. No wonder the poor woman is ill! Who wouldn't be sickened by such a display? She deserves better than this. Is she your muse, or your whore?"

Rossetti looked at the ground as they walked. "I'm not sure I know. I'm afraid that if I marry her, she'll no longer inspire me, and if I don't marry her, it will kill her." His voice was sad, almost childish, as he made his confession. But then he added, churlishly, "I wouldn't expect a man like you to understand."

"No, I don't understand. And I'm afraid that I've had some part in this unfortunate business. I've supported her in her work, and perhaps made it possible for you to delay doing right by Lizzie. Don't you see what a rare thing you have in her? She's a woman almost beyond this earth, a woman of artistic ideals and otherworldly beauty. She deserves protection from this world. You must not destroy her."

Rossetti merely bowed his head, taking Ruskin's reproach as his due. When they reached the picnic spot, Ruskin laid Lizzie down on the blanket. Even before they put the dropper of laudanum to her lips, her eyes began to flutter. At last she was able to sit up, and she drank from a flask of water and asked, "Have I been dreaming?"

"You've been ill," Ruskin said, leaving out any mention of the scene in the maze, in case she might have forgotten it. "Don't stir."

Ruskin turned to Rossetti and spoke quietly. "Things cannot go on like this. Lizzie is very ill, and you seem to be neither fit, nor inclined, to look after her properly." He sighed, as if he had been too hard on Rossetti. "And you must, after all, be able to paint. I know that Lizzie's illness must take a toll on your work."

Rossetti nodded, and Ruskin turned to Lizzie. "Miss Siddal, I'm going to insist that you see another doctor, a personal friend of mine from university, Dr. Acland, at Oxford. Now, don't protest." He held up his hand as Lizzie started to murmur something. "I really must insist, and I'll take care of all the expenses, so you can't object on that account. I know that Dr. Acland and his wife will be very glad to receive you, and I don't doubt that you'll find the society, and the country air, a pleasant change."

"If you insist," Lizzie finally agreed. "I don't mean to seem ungrateful for all of your kind help."

"It will be for the best," Rossetti said, relieved to have Ruskin take things in hand. "The air in Oxford will be better this time of year, and seeing as how busy I am with my work, it would be a relief to know that you're well cared for. And I'll be up in Oxford often, to work on the murals."

Lizzie ignored him. "I'll go to see this Dr. Acland," she said, addressing only Ruskin. "But I must ask something of you as well."

"Anything."

"The arrangement between us—your generosity in purchasing my work—must come to an end. I've been too ill to paint very much this spring, and nothing of quality. I can't hope to give you a good return for your generosity, and so I can no longer accept it."

"Lizzie!" Rossetti said, before Ruskin could reply. "Don't be a fool!"

"I'm not a fool." She finally turned and looked at Rossetti. "I'm only being truthful. The arrangement was purely one of business, as you said yourself, and I can't hold up my end of the bargain. I'm sure that Mr. Ruskin understands."

Ruskin was nodding. "It saddens me for our arrangement to come to an end. But I do hope that when you're ready to take up the brush, you will look to me as a patron. I'll always be happy to purchase any of your fine works."

"Thank you. I think that I hear the others returning, and just in time. It's very dark." She turned to Rossetti. "Dante, will you walk me back to the carriage? I'm afraid that I still feel faint, and I want to settle down beneath a throw."

Rossetti glanced in the direction of the cheerful sounds of the approaching group, but he dutifully took Lizzie's arm and began to steer her toward the carriages. As soon as they were out of earshot of Ruskin, he leaned in close and began to whisper to her. "I'm afraid that you *have* been foolish, Lizzie. Don't you realize that without Ruskin's stipend you'll be entirely dependent upon me?"

"Isn't that how it should be?" She paused. "I've been foolish. But not in my dealings with Ruskin."

Rossetti colored. "I'm sorry," he said. Then he stopped. There didn't seem to be anything else to say.

Lizzie made no further accusations. There were no recriminations and no entreaties that she had not already made. She'd made her choice, and there was no going back. But there didn't seem to be any going forward, either. She sighed and took his arm, clinging to him like a shipwrecked sailor, surprised by how flimsy the wrecked splinters of a once great vessel could feel.

CHAPTER 20

London, June 20, 1855

Dear Dr. Acland,

I'm sending you a talented young artist by the name of Elizabeth Siddal. Her health, sadly, has been in a state of decline over the last months. As an admirer of her work, I'm very concerned for her well-being. She's the finest sort of person, and a great favorite of Dante Rossetti, John Everett Millais, and the other artists of their group, of whom I know news and praise have reached you at Oxford. Perhaps you've heard of her as the model for Millais's much-celebrated picture of Ophelia?

She has previously been diagnosed with an infection of the lungs, and she shows very little appetite. I have great faith in your skill, and I know that I can rely on you to look into her illness with all of your expertise.

Would Mrs. Acland be so kind as to see to arrangements for Miss Siddal at a proper lodging house, and to make sure that she is well looked after? All expenses should be forwarded on to me.

Your grateful friend,
John Ruskin

Oxford, June 23, 1855

Dear John,

I'm happy to do you any favor, and in particular to look into Miss Siddal's case, which sounds from your description to be quite acute.

Mrs. Acland has arranged rooms for Miss Siddal at Mrs. Johnson's Lodging House, and will make sure that she is well looked after, and does not want for company during her stay at Oxford.

Your friend,
Henry Acland

Chatham Place, June 26, 1855

Dear Dr. Acland,

I am writing to tell you that Lizzie Siddal will arrive at Oxford on Tuesday, by the two o'clock train. Our mutual friend, John Ruskin, has told me of your great skill, and I write to beg you to send word to London as soon as you have made a diagnosis. I hope that you might shed some light on what has so far seemed an almost hopeless case.

D. G. Rossetti

Chatham Place, July 5, 1855

Dearest Lizzie,

It's been nearly a week since you left London, and I've not had a single word, either from you or from Dr. Acland. I don't know what to fear most—that you are too ill to write, or that you are angry with me. If you are angry, I know in my heart that I deserve it, and I won't attempt to excuse myself. I only ask you to take pity on me, and to not leave me in the agony of not knowing whether you are well or not.

I know that you will forgive me for fearing the worst, for in your absence I have no little dove to distract me from my worries. Holman Hunt and Annie Miller have left town for the country, and

Ford and Emma are busy nursing of their little boy, who is ill with fever. John Millais, as usual, is busy turning out painting after painting and being celebrated in every drawing room in the city. I myself am preparing to travel north so that I might meet with several friends of John Ruskin. I fear that your letters might not reach me immediately, so please direct your letter to Charlotte Street, and my Christina can forward them on to me.

Please, Lizzie, forgive me for not looking after you more carefully. I should have tended to my little dove with a gentler hand, and put aside all of my work until you were fully well again. I've been selfish, I know. But I pray that you will forgive me, and that I hardly need tell you that all of my work has been for you, so that I might build a reputation, and a fortune, upon which our hopes for the future can be laid.

I'll keep this letter brief, so that I won't strain you with the reading of it, and in the hope that you will have some little energy to write to me that you are improving.

Your devoted,
D. G. Rossetti

Oxford, July 12, 1855

Dear Dante,

Forgive me for not writing sooner.

I arrived in Oxford without incident. I can't imagine what John Ruskin has told them, but the Aclands greeted me with all the attentions that I imagine are given to arriving royalty.

As usual, you and John were quite correct. The weather here is much more pleasant than in London, and that alone is a great relief. Mrs. Acland took me directly from the train station to my lodgings, and then waited while I unpacked, in case I should want to go home with her for tea. She fussed over me a great deal, and I admit that I found her tiresome, so I claimed a slight headache from the travel and declined. I had glimpsed the town from the carriage, and wished immediately to explore it further. As soon as Mrs. Acland departed, I put on my bonnet, and although I was tired from the journey, I went out for a short walk.

*The town is very sleepy, and everything here looks very old, and
puts me in mind of one of your medieval scenes. The streets, if
possible, are often narrower and more prone to unexpected twists
and turns than the streets of London. They are cleaner, however, and
it's a pleasure to lose one's self among them, and to look up and see
nothing but spires, chimneys, and domes above one's head. As soon
as I'm well enough, I intend to walk out with the little easel that
Ford lent to me, and to set it up to make sketches of the lovely little
courtyards and gardens and (don't think me too morbid, as I know
you will) the graveyards, which are possibly the most lovely and
peaceful that I have ever seen.*

*But of course you will see all of this when you come to visit, which
I hope will be soon, and you will, of course, describe it in much more
charming words than I could ever manage. As for your letter, if
there is something to forgive, I should prefer to forgive you in
person, as I am always able to summon my happiest spirits when
you are with me.*

*I'll write to you again tomorrow, after I have consulted with Dr.
Acland.*

Your loving,
Lizzie

Oxford, July 14, 1855

Dear Dante,

*I've met Dr. Acland, and had a thorough examination. He's very
odd, which doesn't surprise me at all as he is a friend of John
Ruskin, who seems to collect rare species of friends, ourselves
included. Dr. Acland was not at all like the doctors that I've seen
before, and I really can't say whether I liked him or not, only that he
did ask very many odd questions.*

*He's older and very thin, with white tufts of hair that protrude
behind his ears. He wears a thick pair of eyeglasses, which rest on his
long nose like a bird perching upon a finger, and he has an
exasperating tendency to purse his lips and tap his finger against his
chin when listening to me speak.*

He made the usual examinations, and then questioned me quite closely about how I occupied my days, whether I felt that I suffered melancholy at certain times, and other things of a personal nature that I can't imagine had any bearing on his examination. I'm not sure that I altogether liked his questions, nor he my replies.

As for Mrs. Acland, she's very much what you would expect of a doctor's wife: matronly, officious, and entirely confident in her own abilities. She has been very kind to me, however, and offered to escort me to several parties, if I feel strong enough, so that I might meet the local celebrities, of which it seems that there are a few. She also arranged a dinner at their home to introduce me to their friends, next week. I hope that I didn't presume when I told her that you would likely be dining with us—I can't imagine it will be many days until you join me at Oxford, although you didn't say in your letter when you are coming.

> *Yours,*
> *Lizzie*

Oxford, July 15, 1855

Dear Mr. Rossetti,

I'm writing to you regarding my diagnosis of Miss Elizabeth Siddal, for which I understand you are quite anxious for news. It is my opinion, after a thorough examination, that her symptoms are entirely due to an overtaxing of mental powers. I have prescribed a change of scenery and rest from work, until she has regained her appetite and strength. I see no reason that she should not make a full recovery, given the proper time and care.

> *Dr. Henry Acland*

Chatham Place, July 20, 1855

Dear Dr. Acland,

I received your letter with surprise, as Lizzie has been ill so often these last years, but also with the greatest relief. Nothing gives me more joy than to hear that my dear Lizzie suffers from nothing so dire as we might have supposed, and will require only rest and fresh air to aid her recovery.

Your letter reaches me at the most opportune of times, as I am obliged to travel for my work, and I hesitated to pass too far from reach, in case there was any turn for the worse. Now I may go forth without worry or reservation, in the secure knowledge that Lizzie is in your care, and will recover presently.

D. G. Rossetti

Oxford, July 15, 1855

Dear John,

I promised to write to you as soon as I made a diagnosis regarding Miss Siddal, and I received similar entreaties from Mr. Rossetti, to whom I have already written. I have now made a thorough examination of Miss Siddal's case, and I must admit that it is a very curious one.

The fact is that I find no real physical signs of ill health in Miss Siddal, excepting the obvious fact that she is quite thin. This, however, and many of her other symptoms, such as loss of appetite and strength, can be explained by her reliance on laudanum. It's a treatment of the highest efficacy, but when taken over time I've found that it can decrease the vital force. It has even, I am afraid, resulted in death of the patient where the use has been too heavy and protracted. I have therefore advised Miss Siddal to resort to its use only when strictly necessary.

My final diagnosis is that Miss Siddal's illness is due to mental power that has long been pent up and lately overtasked. That is, exhaustion due to mental strain, possibly from her painting and the excitements of the city. I suggest that she might benefit from some travel abroad, for a change of scenery, and an abstention from work, until she regains her strength.

I should like to keep Miss Siddal here for a few months to observe her progress, and so that she can benefit from the quieter society found in Oxford. If this is agreeable to you, I will see to all of the arrangements.

Your friend,
Henry Acland

London, July 20, 1855

Dear Dr. Acland,

I received your last letter with great consternation. Of course I submit to your professional judgment, of which I have the highest opinion, but after having watched Miss Siddal's decline over the last several years, I must insist that you examine her once again. She has previously been diagnosed with infection of the lungs, in particular after an unfortunate incident in which she sat too long in cold water while sitting for John Millais. In the interest of thoroughness, perhaps an examination of her lungs might be of use?

You will forgive me, I know, for insisting. I hate to see a talent such as Miss Siddal's go to waste, and to see her prevented from painting, which I believe is the one thing that does give her comfort, when she is able to work.

Your grateful friend,
John Ruskin

Oxford, July 25, 1855

Dear John,

Regarding Miss Siddal's case, if she suffers from infection of the lungs, then it is due mainly to weakness and the lack of a good diet.

I know that I write to you in the strictest confidence, and as an intimate friend of your family, so I will not hesitate to give you my personal opinion of Miss Siddal's condition, which I hold separate from my medical opinion, as it is based only upon the observations of Mrs. Acland and myself, and is, after all, only conjecture.

It appears to me that many of Miss Siddal's symptoms are caused by the worry and strain particular to the weaker sex. That is, to put it plainly, worry over affairs of the heart. Miss Siddal has confided nothing in me, but my wife tells me that she has been involved in a very long engagement with Mr. Rossetti, and that the uncertainty caused by the length of the engagement has been particularly trying to her.

Although there is no particular medical diagnosis for the effects of such strain, it has been my experience that it can manifest itself in physical symptoms such as Miss Siddal complains of: exhaustion, poor appetite, and a general decrease in overall health. It is interesting to note that the promise of distraction or amusement, or the return of one's affection, often have the effect of alleviating many of the symptoms in these patients.

Of course you can claim a much closer knowledge of Miss Siddal than I, and I leave it up to you whether to give my observations any credence. I share them with you only to illuminate my own thinking in the matter.

Yours sincerely,
Henry Acland

Chatham Place, July 30, 1855

My dear Christina,

I'm sorry that I haven't written more regularly, but I think you would hardly recognize your brother lately, as I've been much in demand, and have been travelling the countryside from London to Birmingham and back again, bringing home with me a string of commissions that I carry with as much pride as a hunter carries his quarry. If only I could stuff them and hang them upon the wall, I would have quite a collection. Instead, I must now apply myself as never before, and finish the paintings with as much haste as possible. I've no doubt, however, of my inspiration, as I've found a fascinating new model, a Miss Fanny Cornforth, a person of the utmost vitality, with hair of a golden hue that is meant to be painted (though I am sure that she would not be the sort of person that you would go in for, being, as she is, very common in her speech and manners). But she will do quite nicely for one or two paintings that I have in mind.

I know that you and Mama must be anxious for news of Lizzie's health, which was so poor when she left London for Oxford, and I'm happy to report that I had a letter from Dr. Acland. He assures me that she's rather better than otherwise, and at any rate is not worse. He is convinced that, with the proper rest, she will make a full recovery, and John Ruskin has had reports that she's been much in society in Oxford, and has been strong enough to go walking. I'll get down to Oxford to see her as soon as my work allows, and I'll write you a fuller report when I see her, although I fear that I will not be able to get away from London for some time.

In answer to your question (put very much like a sister would) about the date of our impending marriage, I'm afraid that I can hardly set a date when Lizzie is obliged, by order of the doctor, to maintain rest and calm away from the city, and when I myself am hardly free to set foot from my studio, with the great heap of work that has been commissioned and paid for, but which still has to be done. It is my hope, however, that with proper time for Lizzie to regain her health and for me to finally make my reputation, our wedding cannot possibly be delayed beyond next spring.

Your most affectionate brother,
D. G. Rossetti

Oxford, August 15, 1855
Dear Dante,

I haven't heard from you for several weeks, and though I know that you're busy with your work, I worry that perhaps you yourself are ill. Please write as soon as possible, and tell me that all is well with you.

I'm so lonely for you here. Oxford, which at first seemed so lovely, has grown very tedious, and filled with people just as dull and odd as the Aclands. As for Dr. Acland, I have decided that I don't like him at all. He's quite unsympathetic for a man of medicine, and his wife is shocked by nearly everything I say, even when I try to limit myself to her own favorite topics: the laziness of the kitchen maids, the brilliance of Dr. Acland, and the prospects of her children.

All of the promised amusements have turned out to be quite singular, and are probably more in your line, or perhaps in John Ruskin's. This week I was escorted to the Bodleian Library, which was impressive, though drafty, and filled with more volumes than I ever imagined existed. My guide was one of the ancient fellows of the university; a small man, with bright eyes beneath the folds of his heavy eyebrows and hands that were spotted with age but flitted about like newly hatched chicks whenever he was excited by some old manuscript or other, which was very often. I did my best to share his enthusiasm, but I must admit that nothing made so much of an impression on me as the dust, which was everywhere. There was one item of great interest to me, however, and I wished very much that you had been there to see it. I was shown an original engraving by Albrecht Dürer—a study of a black beetle, executed with great skill. I believe that there was much in its work that you would have found interesting. I had to demur, however, when my old fellow offered to fetch me a live beetle from the cellar, so that I might compare the two. Really, it was too much!

So, you see, I'm getting along in Oxford, but I long for your company, and for your cozy little studio. I'm always stronger when you are by my side.

Please do write that you will arrive soon,

Lizzie

Chatham Place, August 20, 1855

Dear Lizzie,

I deeply regret that I cannot immediately join you in Oxford. I've just received several profitable commissions, and I must remain in the city to begin the paintings. Ned Burne-Jones will be coming up to Oxford soon, to finish work on the murals. I'll write to him that you are there.

I've had a report from Dr. Acland, and I feel entirely secure knowing that you are in his care. I'm also heartened to learn that you have been well enough to enjoy the sights in Oxford, and as soon as I'm able, I'll write to you with a few more suggestions of places that you might enjoy. I will keep this letter brief, however, as I am feeling very inspired to paint at the moment, and as you know, it is imperative that I paint when I am able, and that I not lose a moment in securing my reputation, and our future.

Yours,
D. G. Rossetti

Oxford, August 24, 1855

My dear sister Lydia,

I don't know whether this letter will reach you, or whether Father will throw it into the fire, but I write to you in utter desolation. I've been staying at Oxford to convalesce for two months, and I've hardly had word from Mr. Rossetti. I can no longer willfully ignore what has, I am sure, seemed plain to everyone else for quite some time: He does not intend to marry me. I've been a fool, and ruined myself and shamed our family, just as Father said. Even as my health fails, he finds his other occupations too consuming to come to my side. In my darker moments, I believe that he would greet my death with relief, and after so long a struggle, perhaps so would I. Oh, Lydia, tell me what to do. I love him, but I'm afraid that I am nothing more than a shadow to him now, which is what I shall soon be to myself.

I have no one else to turn to, and I await your advice, which I should have asked for long ago.

Lizzie

London, August 28, 1855

Dearest Lizzie,

My heart breaks for you.

Here is my counsel: You must go to him, without delay. Put aside your pride, and lay before him your case. He has badly misused you, and whether from artistic temperament or something worse, he has failed to fulfill his promise, which is shocking behavior from any man, and in particular from a gentleman. He lived with you as a married woman, and now he must marry you in fact. Go to him. He cannot be such a monster that he will not, if pressed, do what is right and just.

Your sister, always,
Lydia

Oxford, September 1, 1855

Dearest Dante,

If you are feeling inspired, then don't you wish me by your side to sit for you, or to aid you in any way that I can? I've benefitted as much as I will from my visit to Oxford and to Dr. Acland, and I feel quite strong enough to travel. I return to London tomorrow by the last train, and will come directly to your studio.

With love,
Lizzie

Chatham Place, September 2, 1855

Dear Lizzie,

Received your letter by the last post yesterday evening and am sending this one by the first post this morning, so that it might reach you before you depart.

You are a dear little dove to offer to join me here, but I must insist that you do not. The heat has not yet broken in London, and I fear that any progress that you've made in the cooler air of Oxford will be lost if you make too hasty a return to the city. Besides, I'm very occupied with my painting at the moment, and want for absolutely no one—I am in one of those states where the artistic soul requires nothing but solitude and application to work.

I'll come down to Oxford to see you as soon as possible, but do not, dear, come up to London until Dr. Acland deems it absolutely safe.

Yours,
D. G. Rossetti

Oxford, September 3, 1855

Dear Mr. Ruskin,

I write to you as I'm quite at a loss—your Miss Siddal, without any warning or goodbyes other than a scribbled note, took off on the last train for London yesterday evening. She gave no explanation to the landlady, and when a letter from Mr. Rossetti came for her just after her departure, marked urgent, the landlady did not know what to do, other than to bring it to Dr. Acland. I enclose that note with this letter, in the hopes that you may be better able to find her than we are.

I know that in your work as a critic of the arts you must, by necessity, associate with all sorts of persons. But Miss Siddal was truly a person quite outside my experience. I must say that we found her rather more melancholy and willful than the ordinary invalid, and on occasion I found her behavior quite shocking!

All I can say is that I hope that we have been of service to Miss Siddal, and have not given her any offense that would cause her to flee in such a manner. She left a few things here—a shawl, a book of poems—that I will forward to you or to her, when I receive your instructions.

Regards,
Mrs. Acland

CHAPTER 21

Rossetti posted his letter to Lizzie, advising her to stay in Oxford for the time being, and sighed with relief, a great weight off of his mind. Then he hurried back to Chatham Place, where his newest model, Fanny Cornforth, was waiting for him.

Fanny Cornforth; what could be said about her that was not immediately obvious to the eye? Everything about her was large: her great head of rippling blond hair, her generous flesh, her full lips and wide yellow eyes. There was nothing hidden about her, no pretense or hint of secret longings or tragedies. She was simply beautiful, and her whole body radiated the promise of warmth and comfort.

Rossetti found her plump and cheery bearing refreshing. He was tired of painting wan women whose faces, though beautiful, projected nothing so much as their suffering. His studio was filled with scenes from Dante, images of the courtly love of restraint and suffering. He wanted to paint something new—images of love that did not deny sensuality, portraits that celebrated pleasure as a virtue.

When Rossetti returned to the studio, Fanny was waiting for him, still in costume. He sat at his easel and studied her, taking in every detail. Then he began to paint, filling the entire canvas with her face, her hair, her hands. Her golden hair was decorated with marigolds and jeweled pins. A black velvet robe was draped over her shoulders, and an intricate gold necklace encircled her white throat. He painted each detail, but he lingered over the execution of her lips, which were full and slightly parted. He called the painting *Bocca Baciata*, or the Mouth That Has Been Kissed.

The painting was based on a princess from the *Decameron*, who takes eight lovers before marrying her ninth, and who is hailed, rather than condemned, for her passion. Unlike his previous work, this painting didn't tell its story through symbols and sideways glances, and it didn't trade on hints of coded meaning. Instead, he had painted one pure idea: sensuality in the absence of shame.

Fanny couldn't have been a more perfect model; there was no better history of love than her look of frank and unconcerned desire. Rossetti was enthralled. And his passion wasn't limited to his painting. When he finished painting Fanny, he drew her up from her seat and let his lips reach for hers, kissing her deeply. The movement felt as natural as his new style of painting, and he led her to his bedroom at the back of the studio. He slipped the velvet robe from around her shoulders and let it drop on the floor. She stood before him without shame, smiled invitingly, and pulled him onto the bed.

Lizzie was exhausted by the time she reached Paddington Station, but she went straight from the station to Chatham Place. She was determined to follow Lydia's advice, and to put her case to Rossetti once and for all. She had waited quietly for far too long.

It was dark when she arrived, and there was no light at the top of the stairs to greet her. She lit a lamp and carried it into the empty studio.

There was a fresh canvas sitting on the easel in the center of the room. It was turned away from her, but she could see an inscription scrawled across the back. She held the lamp closer and read: *The mouth that has been kissed loses not its freshness; still it renews itself even as does the moon.*

Lizzie hesitated for a moment before turning the canvas around. A silent prayer formed on her lips: Please, God, let me find my own image on that canvas. She touched her lips gently with her fingers. They were dry and cracked, and felt as thin as the rest of her. She shuddered, sensing that she wouldn't see her reflection on the canvas. She had grown frail. How could she hope to inspire a great artist?

But still, the flame of hope, the voice that refused to be silenced by the long years of waiting, made its well-worn plea: He does love you, you are his muse, do not give up hope. She turned the canvas around.

With that simple gesture, the little flame was at last extinguished. She saw the blond hair, the full cheeks, the rosy lips. Rossetti had forsaken her.

She turned away from the painting, unable to look any longer. She staggered over to the sofa and collapsed, nearly choking on all the words of love and entreaty that she had planned to put to Rossetti, words now trapped behind mute lips. Her chest was tight and her breath painful.

She reached in her pocket for her bottle of laudanum and cast the stopper aside. With the mouth of the bottle pressed to her lips, she drank hungrily, not bothering to measure out her dose in drops or teaspoons. Dr. Acland's warnings were a dim memory. She had only one goal: to ease the panic that pounded through her body, radiating from her heart and marching along her veins, an invading army on undefended roads.

It was only a moment before her breathing slowed and became less labored. The medicine washed over her like a warm sea, and for a moment she was confused: What was she doing here? Then she remembered, and the warm sea turned rougher and more treacherous. She felt as if she were sinking.

She gathered what strength she had and stood. She walked toward the bedroom and paused at the door, holding up the lamp. She drew in her breath sharply, and the two figures on the bed stirred. Rossetti sat up, and his face was white, as if he'd seen a ghost. He rubbed his eyes. "Lizzie? What are you doing here? I wrote to you to stay at Oxford."

The woman beside him was awake now, too, and she wrapped the sheet around herself and walked out of the room, passing Lizzie. As she went by, she looked at Lizzie with what seemed like pity.

Lizzie stared after her for a moment and then turned back to

Rossetti. "And who are you to tell me whether to stay or to go? My betrothed? No! You're nothing to me!"

Rossetti looked tired. "Lizzie, please calm down. I love you, you know that. Nothing else matters, does it?"

"You love only yourself, Dante, and your work. You've used me up in its service, and now you'll discard me, like one of your failed sketches. You're a monster."

Lizzie began to sob, and to flail her arms about uselessly, as if she were fighting off some unseen adversary. Rossetti rose from the bed and grabbed her wrists, trying to calm her. "Lizzie! Calm down. You're not yourself."

"No! At last I remember myself! At last I can see clearly. I've been blind, very blind, but you've been blind as well. You can't even see what you've done to me. You've never really been able to see me."

Rossetti looked at Lizzie, at her wild eyes, and shivered. He pushed her onto the bed. "It's that damned medicine. You've taken too much. You don't know what you're saying."

"I know exactly what I'm saying." She knew that she was ranting, but the words poured out unbidden, and as she heard them, she knew that they were true. "You've never seen me as I really am. You never even tried. I'm not just the girl in your paintings, Dante. I'm not a reflection that requires nothing more than hope to feed upon. I've been making a meal of such scanty offerings for too long. I've forsaken everything for you, and you've given me nothing but false promises in return."

Rossetti turned on her. "I've given you nothing? Have I not given you immortality? Have I not painted you as the most beautiful and sainted women who have ever lived? Is that nothing?"

All of the rage that had driven Lizzie up to this moment suddenly left her. "It's not nothing, but it's not enough. It's no more than you will give to that whore who waits for you in the studio, and no more than you've given other women in the past. I always wanted more."

Rossetti was quiet for a moment. "I don't know what more I can give you, Lizzie. I must be allowed to paint, and to explore the things that give my painting meaning. I need love, passion, adventure. I thought that we wanted the same things, but I was wrong. I never should have given you my promise. It's a promise I can't keep. I'm sorry."

Lizzie nodded and rose from the bed. Her legs were weak beneath her and she struggled to stand. Rossetti went to her side. "You aren't well. Don't try to stand."

"No. I must go." She stared at Rossetti, taking in every feature of the face of the man whom she had loved, and longed for. She saw that she wasn't the only one who had grown older. The years had also left their mark on him, and his face was already beginning to thicken, helped along by drink. His eyes, which had once danced with such mischievous joy and kindness, now seemed more guarded. But the life in them was still strong, and Lizzie could see that even as they looked at her, they looked beyond her, to the promise of tomorrow and the days beyond.

She turned away and with her last strength she pushed past him. When she glanced back, she saw that he stood several paces behind her, his hand stretched toward her irresolutely, in a gesture that was as familiar as his kiss. She turned and slipped through the door, down the stairs, and out into the street.

Chatham Place was nearly empty, and Lizzie stumbled down the street, hardly aware of where she was going. Nearby she heard the lapping of the Thames against its banks, and the water called out to her, offering its soothing, silent embrace. She paused at the foot of Blackfriars Bridge, listening to the water rush by the pilings and feeling its unceasing pull.

Blurry images tugged at her memory, but her thoughts were confused and her recollection indistinct. She tried to sort through them: the painful grip of a man's heavy hand around her arm, the heavy drag of a soaking gown as cold water swirled around her, the shock of recognizing her own image in the ghastly painting of a prostitute.

Lizzie shuddered, her whole body convulsing. She leaned over the edge of the embankment, testing the feeling of vertigo, and then, with a wrenching motion, she turned away from the river and fled into the twisting alleys of Southwark, which welcomed her back into their dark and obscure fold.

She remembered nothing until she arrived at the door of the

house in Kent Place. Her feet must have carried her along her old route by instinct, her cloak of unhappiness shielding her from the reaching hands and hungry eyes that trailed after her. She knew that she was not welcome here, in her father's house, but she had nowhere else to go. Like a dying animal, she sought out a soft and familiar place to lay her head.

When she reached the door, the desperate strength that had led her there abandoned her. She knocked weakly, despairing that any-one would hear her in the slumbering house.

But the door opened, and Lizzie collapsed at the feet of her father. He stood in his nightshirt, a flickering candle in his hand.

"Good Lord!" he cried. "Lydia, come quickly! It's your sister, and she looks to be at death's door!"

CHAPTER 22

The lodging house room was unbearably stuffy, and Lydia threw open the shutters to coax in the fresh sea air. The smells of the sickroom were stifling: the sharp scent of smelling salts, the untouched broth, and the one that Lydia hated the most, the sickly sweet smell of laudanum.

Their second trip to Hastings was not proving as successful as their first. Lizzie languished in the cheap lodgings. She didn't have the strength to leave her room for fortifying walks by the sea, or even to join the other invalids for tea in the sunroom. She lay night and day in her bed, too weak and indifferent even to speak.

Lydia was afraid to leave her, and so she spent the days pacing back and forth across the worn rug. She tried to get Lizzie to take some broth, and provided her with what cheer she could, reading letters and books aloud to her. But Lizzie was beyond such easy cures, and hardly seemed to care whether she lived or died.

The doctor came daily to take Lizzie's pulse and frown over Lydia's reports. At last the doctor drew Lydia into the hallway and delivered the news that she was expecting, and dreading. It was his opinion that Miss Siddal was failing, and that, as she wasn't able to eat without vomiting, and took very little water, she didn't have long to live. He advised writing at once to her mother and father, so that they might have time to make the journey.

Lydia left Lizzie in the doctor's care and went next door to her own room. She shut the door behind her and then sat down on her bed to sob, pushing her handkerchief against her mouth to dampen the sound of her cries, lest she do anything to disturb poor Lizzie.

When her sobs subsided, she rose and once again paced the room, which was far too small to contain her grief. The doctor seemed so sure that Lizzie was beyond hope, and Lydia could hardly argue with him. But she couldn't let Lizzie go so easily. She must do everything in her power, even if that meant calling upon the one man whom she loathed with all of her soul. She had written to him once before in a time of need, and he had come.

She sat down at her desk and pulled out a clean sheet of paper. But try as she might, she couldn't bring herself to write his name. After a struggle, she finally settled on writing to Lizzie's old friend, John Ruskin, instead. If John Ruskin thought that Rossetti might be of comfort to Lizzie, then surely he would be able to convince him to come better than Lydia herself could.

She wrote:

Hastings, January 2, 1856

Dear Mr. Ruskin,

It is with a very heavy heart that I write to you. I know that you have, in the past, been a great friend to my sister, Lizzie, and I write to you in the hope that I can call on that friendship for your aid and advice.

Lizzie has, these past months, lain ill at Hastings, and her doctor has just told me that he does not believe that she has long to live. It seems that there is nothing that can be done, and I wonder if, in these last moments, she might find some comfort in the company of Mr. Rossetti. She hasn't asked for him, but then so few words have passed her lips that I can only guess at what may be in her heart. They have been long apart, and so I write to you as their mutual friend. If you believe, as I do, that he might be of comfort to her, then I entreat you to write to him, and to beg him to make haste.

Your grateful friend,
Lydia Siddal

John Ruskin received Lydia's letter with shock and regret. He cursed himself for becoming so engrossed in his writing that he had neglected to enquire after Lizzie in the last months, and he cursed Rossetti, that monster of a genius, for allowing her to languish for years and then to discard her in her time of greatest need.

He called for a boy from the stable to take a letter by hand, and then dashed off a note to Rossetti while the boy stood waiting.

Rossetti, you damned fool—

Lizzie lies dying at Hastings, while you cavort with that great elephant, Fanny Cornforth. Have you no shame? The woman was your intended, and you have let her pass into obscurity. Forgive my tone, but I've had word from her family that this is truly the end, and I would hate to be the man with that dear angel's death upon my shoulders. Listen to your friend: Go to her at once, and do what you should have done long ago. Do not delay, in case you should arrive too late.

Ruskin

The train ride to Hastings was the longest of Rossetti's life. Nothing felt solid; the perspectives were wrong. His stomach lurched inside him and his hands felt fit for nothing but prayer and grasping, as if he were crossing a vast sea, rather than the gently rolling hills of Sussex.

He sat in silence, with no companion other than Ruskin's note of reproach. He read it over and over, staring at it as if it were the bottom of a teacup, trying to read some hint of his fortune in its leaves. Was it possible that he would be too late?

The thought acted as a bitter tonic, and Rossetti's vision cleared and focused, as if he were coming out of a fever. He saw everything in minute detail, so real that it felt like a hallucination: each glossy leaf of the trees that rushed past his window, the starched lace collars of the elderly women in his car brushing against their feathery necks, the speckles of orange and blue paint that he hadn't bothered to wash from his hands before rushing from his studio to the station.

He realized with a start that he hadn't seen so clearly since the first moment he glimpsed Lizzie, sitting in her page's shift in Walter Deverell's studio. He'd felt so sure of himself at that moment; sure of what he desired, and what he must do. He'd wanted nothing more than to be near her, to paint her and read poetry to her, to hear her laugh and touch her white skin, and her red hair.

Somehow he had lost sight of that truth, its simplicity obscured by a thousand trifling concerns. But he found that it was still there, like a half-finished canvas cast aside in favor of a new design. It still waited for him, ready to have its lines filled in with rich color, its promise fulfilled.

How foolish, how utterly foolish he had been. Why hadn't he married her when he had the chance?

He looked down again at Ruskin's note: *I would hate to be the man with that dear angel's death upon my shoulders.* He shuddered. If he were to lose her now, he couldn't account for the effect that it might have upon his mind. Could he even paint without his muse, his Beatrice? Or would her spirit haunt him, casting its shadow across his paintings and driving him mad? He'd been so callous. At this last moment, it seemed clear to him that she was what was important, not his work. But he couldn't think of Lizzie without thinking of his work; the two had never been separate. The artist and the muse, the poetry and the painted images: He saw them suspended like heavenly bodies, each dependent upon the others for its delicate balance. If one were to be extinguished, the rest might tumble from the sky, or spin off wildly into the unknown. He must get to Lizzie in time; everything depended on it. Ruskin was right: If he had to bear the weight of Lizzie's death, it would crush him. He willed the train on, praying for haste.

When they at last pulled into the station, Rossetti was the first to grab his case and leap from the carriage. He ran along the platform, past the station, and into the quiet streets of Hastings.

The streets were nearly empty. The invalids had retreated into the courtyards of their hotels. The sun beat brightly upon the town, and Rossetti looked scornfully at the cheerful façades of the hotels, behind whose whitewashed walls lay fear and illness and common tragedy.

Every fiber of his being called him to Lizzie's side, but he couldn't go to her empty-handed. He knew how little his promises and words of comfort were worth. He walked quickly along the high street and ducked into the first church that he saw. He was in luck. The clergyman was in, and in a shaky voice, Rossetti made his application for a marriage license.

He paced the church impatiently while the papers were drawn up, and the clergyman smiled at him knowingly. "The girl must be very pretty, and you must be very much in love, to be in such a hurry!"

At last the license was signed, and Rossetti had the paper in hand. He paid his fee and dashed back out into the street. With a burning face, he thought of all the times that he had told Lizzie that he was setting aside this or that sum for their marriage license, and then, finding some other more tempting use for the money, how he had told himself that the matter was not pressing, and could wait.

The address of the lodging house that Ruskin had given him was in a less fashionable quarter of the town than the hotel where they had stayed in their happier days, when Lizzie's illness seemed to be on the mend and they had spent long days wandering along the beaches and bluffs. When Rossetti arrived at the door, he saw that the flower boxes in front of each window were empty, and that the parlor was dark, but not quite dark enough to hide its shabbiness. The landlady barely looked up from her book when he inquired after Lizzie, and waved him up the stairs without a word.

Rossetti took the stairs two at a time, but when he reached the door to Lizzie's room he paused. The terrible memory of Lizzie, lying cold and white in the tub in John Millais's studio, came unbidden into his mind, and he felt himself go cold with fear. He whispered a quick prayer—please, God, do not desert me—and pushed open the door.

The sight that greeted him was sadder than he could have imagined: Lizzie lay upon the bed, completely still. Even under a pile of quilts, Rossetti could see that she was terribly wasted. Her eyes were closed, and her face was without color, except for her large eyelids, which were as purple as fresh bruises. Lydia knelt at her side, holding her sister's thin hand to her cheek.

"Am I?" Rossetti choked, unable to get the words out at first. "Am I too late?"

Lydia looked up at him, startled, and dropped Lizzie's hand. Rossetti saw Lizzie stir—a faint movement, but a sign of life nonetheless. In two steps he was at her side, kneeling beside Lydia and taking Lizzie's hand in his own.

"My dove," he murmured softly. "My little dove. I've come back to you, and I'll never leave your side again. Only, you must come back to me as well. Come, my little dove, and say a word to me, so that I know that you hear me."

Lizzie's eyes fluttered open, and for a moment they seemed to fix on Rossetti's face before they dropped closed again. Rossetti once again feared that he had come too late. "Lizzie!" he cried. "Open your eyes!" He pulled the marriage license from his pocket. He knew that the gesture was desperate, but he couldn't help himself. He felt as sure as he had ever felt of anything that if he could only get Lizzie to the church, if he could only marry her as he should have done long ago, that he would somehow be absolved.

"Look, my love!" He waved the license before her half-closed eyes. "We will be married. Open your eyes and we will be married!"

Lizzie sighed and turned her face toward the wall, silent. She was, Rossetti saw, past caring. Her indifference stirred him. She was a stone saint upon her tomb, well beyond the earthly pleasures of love and desire, and at that moment, Rossetti perversely decided that there was no woman on earth more deserving of his love.

Lydia took pity on the hunched man by the bed, and pulled him to his feet. "Let her rest. You're not too late, but I'm afraid that there is nothing else to be done. If you could only talk to her, and give her some comfort, it might make it easier for her. . . ." Lydia could not finish the thought. "It might give her some final peace."

Rossetti frowned and looked at Lydia, not understanding. "The only comfort that I intend to give her is the comfort that I should have given her long ago: that of marriage, and a home."

Lydia shook her head. "Mr. Rossetti, I know that this is a great shock. But you must understand—Lizzie hasn't stirred from her bed for days. She can keep nothing on her stomach for five minutes altogether. Like you, I want nothing more in the world than for her to be as she was. Indeed, that's why I wrote to John Ruskin—in the hope that if you were to come, she might rally. . . . But I fear that it's too late. I'm afraid that I've called you here in vain."

"Nonsense." Rossetti surprised her by rising and beginning to bustle about the room, straightening the cups and cloths on the bedside table and throwing open the window. "I will nurse her myself. And mark my words: I do intend to marry her. I will not lose her again."

Rossetti set about nursing Lizzie with all of the dedication that he usually reserved for his paintings. He saw at once that Lydia had not exaggerated; Lizzie's health was failing, and quickly. At first she hardly seemed to recognize him. Her state varied between a listlessness that left her too tired even to speak, and terrifying fits, which caused her face to enliven horribly as she screamed for aid. At such moments Rossetti would rush to her side, desperate to help her. He held the laudanum to her lips, feeding it to her like a child. It was the only thing that seemed to calm her and ease her pain.

He tended to her with a single-minded devotion. He was a pilgrim, trudging toward the holy land, borne along by faith and fear, love and guilt, long after the exhilaration of the journey has worn thin. He spoke to her constantly: reminding her of happier times, weaving plans for their wedding and honeymoon, praising her talent and speaking of the great works of poetry and art that they would create together as man and wife. He made little sketches to amuse her: caricatures of their friends and drawings of curious animals at play. Spoonful by spoonful, he fed her by his own hand: first water, then tea, and finally broth. And at last, ever so slowly, Lizzie began to improve.

When Lydia was at last called back to London to help with the nursing of one of the younger children, she was able to leave Hastings with an easier mind. Lizzie was now regularly sitting in a chair by the window, while Rossetti sketched her or read to her. There had even been some talk of her being taken in a chair down to the seaside. Rossetti was set on marrying Lizzie the moment that she could make the walk to the church, and Lydia was inclined to believe him. But Lizzie's progress was slow, and it was May before Rossetti was able to write to his mother with the happy news:

> *Dearest Mother,*
>
> *I write with the greatest joy to say that Lizzie and I are going to be married at last, in as few days as possible.*
>
> *I know that you should have liked to see us married at your church in London, with you and dear Christina in attendance, but I'm afraid that I must disappoint you, as we shall be married here in Hastings, at St. Clements. Like all the important things I ever meant to do—to fulfill duty or secure happiness—this one has been deferred almost beyond possibility. I would not now delay it any longer than necessary. I have hardly deserved that Lizzie should still consent to it, but she has done so, and I trust that I may still have time to prove my thankfulness to her.*
>
> *As soon as Lizzie is well enough to travel, we will return to London, and our first stop shall be at your doorstep.*
>
> *Your son,*
> *D. G. Rossetti*

On the morning of the appointed day, Lizzie rose alone and made her small toilet at the washstand in her room. She fixed her hair the best she could, brushing it out and letting it fall loosely over her shoulders, rather than in the more traditional chignon. Her face in the mirror looked pale and thin, but her hair was still her crowning glory, bright and thick despite her long illness. There was a knock at the door, and the maid, a local girl of seventeen, came in with a small sewing basket. The landlady of the lodging house, upon hearing that Lizzie would have no attendants, had taken pity on her, and offered her the use of the maid for her dressing and to act as witness.

"Miss Siddal! Isn't it nice to see you up and about, and with your hair so pretty! You will make Mr. Rossetti a proud husband, I should say! Well, let's have a look at the dress, shall we?" the maid asked, walking over to the wardrobe. "I'm sure that we can have it fixed up for you in a moment."

Lizzie pulled her gray silk gown from the wardrobe. The fashion, since the wedding of the Queen, had been for a white wedding dress, and Lizzie had imagined herself standing at the altar in a cloud of white organdy and lace. But there had been neither time nor money for a new gown; and besides, she didn't have the strength for the many fittings that a new gown would require. Instead she settled on the old gray silk, which brought out the clear gray of her eyes. Mrs. Rossetti, upon receipt of her son's letter, had sent down a new collar and a matching veil of the sheerest lace.

Lizzie handed the gown to the maid, who quickly set about attaching the new collar. When she finished, Lizzie slipped the dress on and frowned. She had always been thin, but the dress now hung sadly. The maid hurried over with her kit. "Not to worry. I'll take it in here in the back, and no one will notice."

No, Lizzie thought, no one *will* notice, since no one will be there. Now that the day had finally come, she could not help but think that it was a woeful victory. While the maid worked on her dress, Lizzie slipped a well-worn letter from an envelope on her desk. It was from Lydia, who had written to say that Robert Crane, the grocer's son, had taken over his father's business and come to the Siddals to ask for Lydia's hand in marriage. Lydia had presented all of this in a kind, straightforward manner—she was too conscious of Lizzie's feelings to speak much of her own joy. But Lizzie could imagine the scene well enough: her father proud and serious as he pretended to think it over, her mother embracing the happy couple, Lydia blushing and smiling. The wedding would be held at their local church, with a breakfast afterward—well provisioned, too, since Lydia would now be a grocer's wife. Meanwhile, Lizzie's wedding ceremony would take place among strangers, far from her home.

The maid finished altering the dress, and Lizzie did have to admit that it did look rather well. She chastised herself for her gloomy thoughts, and tried to remember that in an hour's time, she would be Rossetti's wife. And now that they would be married, he would be her family, and her home would be where he was. The thought alone cheered her. She peered into the mirror, and pinched her cheeks and bit her lips, as she used to do before she entered

Rossetti's studio. Then she strode from the room, the maid scurrying behind her, and shut the door.

Rossetti was waiting for her at the bottom of the steps. The moment that she saw him, all melancholy and misgivings vanished, and she smiled at him as shyly as she had on the first day that they met. Rossetti glimpsed her shining eyes and gentle smile, and then Lizzie let the veil drop demurely over her face. She floated down the steps, and her gown, fussed over by the maid behind her, looked to Rossetti as if it were held aloft by fairies.

When she reached him, he whispered, as he had many times before, "You are a vision." Then he handed her a bouquet of the most exquisite orange blossoms and lilies of the valley. "Lizzie," he said, taking her hands. "If this happy day has been too long in coming, then it's only because I have always felt in my heart that you were my wife, the companion of my body and the savior of my soul. Whether we stand together before an altar or under an apple tree, my heart knows no difference. But come to the church with me, my love, and let us be married before God and man."

Lizzie smiled at him from behind her veil, and they stood for a moment, their fingers interlaced. Then the maid let out a little sob and blew her nose in her kerchief, breaking the spell. "Oh, Miss Siddal!" she exclaimed, her simple nature overcome by the scene. "Isn't it too romantic!"

Lizzie laughed, and Rossetti took her arm and led her down a narrow street of old Tudor houses to the ancient church of St. Clements. When they arrived, Rossetti went to look for the vicar, and Lizzie and the maid waited in the vestibule. Lizzie peered down the aisle and decided at once that she couldn't think of a more perfect place to be married. The church had a high arching ceiling and a floor of cool stone, and woodwork that gleamed in the sun pouring through the windows. A stained glass window of opaque white plates and glittering rubies filled the space with a soft prism of light. The only other person in the church was a stout older woman, dressed entirely in black, who was sweeping out the pews. She hunched over her work, paying no attention to the visitors.

Rossetti returned with the vicar and the curate, who would act as the second witness. The little party walked down the aisle to the altar. As Lizzie passed the old woman, she stared at Lizzie's veil and bouquet, then she reached out a gnarled hand and caught Lizzie by the sleeve, pulling her close.

"Foolish girl!" she whispered, her voice hoarse. "Don't you know? Marry in May and rue the day! No happy wives have been made in this month!"

Lizzie gasped and pulled her hand back, her face white. Rossetti was ahead, speaking with the vicar, and didn't notice, but the maid heard the warning. "Hush, you silly old woman!" she scolded. "That's nothing but an old wives' tale." She turned to Lizzie. "Don't mind her. I can just tell by looking at you and Mr. Rossetti that your wedding is blessed."

Rossetti held out his hand and drew Lizzie to his side. The vicar began the ceremony with a prayer, and Lizzie closed her eyes and prayed as ardently as she had ever prayed in her life. Dear God, she whispered, please grant us the peace and happiness for which I have longed. Make me a good wife to Dante, and let him find with me the inspiration he requires. Then she turned to Rossetti with a clear heart and looked into his eyes as he repeated the wedding vows:

"I, Dante, take thee, Elizabeth, to be my wedded wife. To have and to hold from this day forward; for better, for worse, for richer, for poorer, in sickness and in health, to love and to cherish, till death us do part, according to God's holy law."

Rossetti slipped a plain gold band onto Lizzie's finger, lifted her veil, and chastely kissed her hand. Then they joined hands and walked down the aisle and out into the brightness of the afternoon. The little maid followed after them, wiping away tears and throwing rice from her pocket over their heads.

On the steps of the church, Rossetti kissed her. "And now," he said, "my happiness is complete."

Lizzie looked at him adoringly. "And mine," she said, "has just begun."

Rossetti was eager to please his new bride, and he gathered all the funds that he could and took her on a short honeymoon to Paris. They stayed in a small hotel in the rue de Rivoli, and when Lizzie felt up to it, they set out on long walks through the city. In the

Jardin de Tuileries, they sat on wrought iron chairs, and Rossetti sketched Lizzie among the fashionable crowds that came to parade down the neat paths. Rossetti visited the Louvre to make studies of the old masters, and Lizzie read poetry, and wrote some of her own. Together they visited the exquisite shops in the little streets and arcades near the Place Vendôme, and Rossetti bought Lizzie trinkets that he could hardly afford: a sterling dragonfly pin set with a sapphire, an ivory pendant, and two splendid tortoiseshell hair combs, each set with a tiny diamond.

They returned to London triumphantly happy and bursting with ideas and images for their work, inspired by their travels. Their hearts were full, but their purse was empty, and so they set up house for the time being in Rossetti's studio at Chatham Place. It had served them well enough in the past, and they saw no reason why they should take on the extra expense of a proper house now. Rossetti had many commissions, but the commissions had been paid and the money spent, and now the paintings must be done before he could hope to take on any more.

He set to work with a renewed vigor, and Lizzie didn't complain when Fanny Cornforth came to sit. She was too aware of the great price that Rossetti's portraits of Fanny could fetch, and too enamored of her own image in the glass, the diamond combs glinting in her hair, to make a fuss over Rossetti's choice of models. She worked on her own pictures, including an ambitious and original design that she called *Lovers Listening to Music*. It showed a couple, the man with his arm around the woman's waist. Their heads are bent close together, and the woman's eyes are closed in a gesture of trust and happiness. A child, representing love, stands nearby.

Lizzie also kept house, after a fashion, planning dinners in the studio for their friends and the many painters and poets that Rossetti brought home. Soon after they came back to London they threw a party in celebration of their marriage, and invited their closest friends: Emma and Ford, John Millais, and Ned Burne-Jones, with his new wife, Georgie. Rossetti selected good wines, and Lizzie arranged a generous platter of oysters on ice, and another of the delicate éclairs and tartes aux pommes that she had loved in the Paris patisseries. Emma and Lizzie hadn't seen each other in many months, and they reunited joyfully, and Ned and Georgie brought Lizzie a gift of a lovely serving plate in the blue-and-white willow pattern that she adored.

The calm of married life agreed with Lizzie. Her illness may have left its mark on her, but it was hard to discern it behind the brilliance of her smile. She resumed her long walks through the city with Rossetti, and she took her laudanum only sparingly. Soon, her appetite returned, and she began to add a little flesh. At first it was only ounce by ounce, but it was not long before she had gained a softness at her bosom and hips. Rossetti was enchanted, and began to paint her more often, and with renewed passion.

As the months passed, her curves became even more noticeable and, once she was sure, she found that she had good news to share with Rossetti: they were going to have a baby. If she felt any trepidation over the toll that carrying a child would take on her already delicate health, she didn't share it with him. She knew as well as any woman the dangers of childbirth, but she had come so close to death before that she no longer feared it. Her only fear was losing Rossetti again, and now that they had the promise of a child to bind them, she felt safe and happy.

Rossetti heard the news as a man should: with a combination of joy and trepidation that left him ricocheting about the studio, sweeping Lizzie across the room in a waltz at one moment, and then carefully settling her down on the sofa the next, as if she might break. Lizzie was serene, accepting the miracle of the child, despite her long illness, as a sign from God that her marriage was, after all, blessed.

Emma laughed with joy when Lizzie told her the happy news, and insisted that Ford dash home immediately to fetch their little wooden cradle, which she wanted Lizzie to use for the new baby. Lydia, too, was elated at the prospect of being an aunt, and began at once to sew a tiny christening gown and bonnet. Even Mr. Siddal, who had grudgingly begun to receive Lizzie since her marriage, sent his congratulations and promised to engrave a tiny spoon with the baby's name. Mrs. Rossetti, fretting over Lizzie's health, took it upon herself to engage an obstetrician and a nurse for Lizzie, despite the cost. Rossetti watched the preparations with pride, finding that the responsibilities of a wife and a household, which he had for so long feared and avoided, were a boon, rather than a burden, to his work.

Lizzie resumed her old place, in the sunny chair by the balcony doors. She let her hands rest on her growing belly, and her daydreams were as sweet and rosy as the cheek of a newborn babe.

CHAPTER 23

For what seemed like the thousandth time, Rossetti stood and stalked the perimeter of the studio. He sat back down in his chair, and then rose again and retraced his steps. He could hear Lizzie's screams from behind the bedroom door. The raw chords of suffering echoed through the studio, and his veins pulsed with the animal instincts of fear and flight.

Her labor had begun in the night, and the obstetrician, Dr. Hutchinson, had arrived with the nurse and set about preparing the room for the birth. Rossetti sent a note to Lydia, who came in the early hours of the morning to help.

Rossetti was not permitted to enter the bedroom, but the doctor appeared at the door periodically to answer his questions with a furrowed brow and one-syllable replies. Ford Madox Brown had tried, without success, to persuade Rossetti to go with him to a pub on the corner and wait there for the news. Ford had been through this before. He knew that there was nothing for the father to do but wait, and that this uselessness could be as hard to bear as the terrible cries. But Rossetti refused to leave. He felt that something wasn't right, and he was rooted to the spot by an awful conviction that he had nursed Lizzie back to health, only to now have her die in childbirth.

It was nearly nightfall again before Lizzie's cries, closer now to whimpers than screams, stopped abruptly. The sudden silence was jarring, and Rossetti snapped to attention in the chair where he was dozing. His eyes fixed on the closed door. He strained to hear a sound, any sound, but he couldn't hear anything. Finally the door opened and the doctor, his face lined with exhaustion, stepped into the studio. He looked at Rossetti with professional pity and sighed. "I'm sorry. The child is stillborn. It was a girl."

Rossetti stared at him. He hadn't been thinking of the child, and the news came as its own shock. "And my wife? My wife, is she . . . ?"

"Mrs. Rossetti is resting. It's too early to say for sure, but I believe she will make a full recovery."

Relief flooded through him, leaving him lightheaded. She was alive. "And the child? What happened?"

"It's impossible to say. It's not uncommon. There's no reason why Mrs. Rossetti shouldn't go on to give you healthy children."

Rossetti nodded and went into the bedroom. He kneeled beside the bed. Lydia was sitting white-faced in a chair with a bundle of linens in her arms. He stared at her for a moment, then realized with a start what the bundle must be. He turned back to Lizzie, aghast. She was pale and clammy, but she was breathing, the soft rhythm of her breath visible in the rise and fall of the sheets that covered her. He took her hand. "My dove," he whispered. "My little dove."

She rolled her head to look at him, and the dull, unseeing gleam of her eyes sent a shiver down his spine. "Where is my baby?" Her voice was flat. "Where is my little daughter?"

"Oh, Lizzie." He didn't know what to say. He looked to Lydia, who met his eyes with a troubled frown and mouthed the words, "She's been told."

He turned back to Lizzie. "My love, you mustn't tire yourself, or wear yourself out with worry. After all, the most important thing is that you are well. I feel nothing but thankfulness that I haven't lost you as well."

Lizzie continued to stare at him, either not hearing him or not understanding, he wasn't sure which. Then her eyes fluttered closed, and she seemed to pass into a peaceful sleep.

Rossetti stood up and left Lydia and the nurse to do their sad work. Back in the studio, he found that its familiar lines were already altered, slightly but indelibly, by the events of the night. They had lost the child, and his grief for the unknown life felt like a hard knot, whose contours and weight he would examine and learn by heart in the coming days. But for the moment, he could think of nothing but his relief that Lizzie had survived.

He stumbled over to the sofa and lay down. The studio was warm, but he was shivering from shock and exhaustion, and he pulled a throw over his shoulders. Tragedy, whose cold shadow had loomed over him all through the night, tapping his fingers on the windowpanes and breathing his dark fortune under the door, had somehow been averted. So why was it, he wondered, that he still felt its chill, as if the wind had only shifted for a moment, ushering in the false calm of the eye of the storm?

People came in, and then went out again. Rossetti was with her, and her sister, and others—the nurse perhaps? She was urged to drink, and to eat; to get dressed and to take the fresh air; to make some efforts at a sketch, or a little watercolor. Their words passed over her and passed through her. She heard them as if from a distance, and nodded vaguely, agreeably consenting to nothing.

If Lizzie had ever before paused to consider the nature of time, she would have thought of it only as constant and unremarkable: the tapping of her mother's knitting needles or the rising and setting of the sun outside the studio windows. Out in the street, men checked their pocket watches and the massive new bell in the Westminster clock tower kept the hour with startling accuracy, ordering and measuring the little lives that scurried below according to its steady rhythm.

It came as a surprise, therefore, to find that time was not so dependable as she had thought. Instead of an orderly march of seconds and minutes, time now seemed to proceed in fits and starts, stretching out and then warping, while whole hours and days disappeared into the ether. She was often surprised to notice the last dying rays of the sunset, when she would have, not a moment before, set the hour at no later than one o'clock.

In her moments of clarity, Lizzie repeated to herself what the

doctor and Rossetti had told her: The baby had been born dead;
there had been no question of saving her; it was not uncommon.
She was buried in the cemetery, but there was no funeral service,
since she hadn't been baptized. It was important for Lizzie to repeat
these facts, because she often forgot them, and would wake from
dozing thinking that she was still pregnant, or dreaming that she
heard a child crying. Rossetti had seen to the burial alone, and
Lizzie didn't know if he had named her, or if there was a stone to
mark the grave. She couldn't ask him, couldn't form the words to
make it real. There were things she knew he couldn't say, either:
He never blamed her, never mentioned the laudanum, never said
they would go on to have more children. She knew, somehow, that
she would never have another baby. The stillbirth seemed both an
omen and a punishment, and she would not tempt fate further.
Marry in May and rue the day. She gave her daughter a name, which
she kept secret and whispered to herself as she stared out of the
window. This was her story. And then time would warp again and
Lizzie would be back at the beginning, feeling as if for the first time
the pain of each of these facts.

Rossetti, she noted with interest, appeared untouched by this
new accounting of time. He mourned alongside her, and then,
slowly and steadily, he returned to his old life. He rose each morning and painted, often at Ford's studio, so as not to disturb her. In
the afternoons he returned home to work at his translations and
verses, or to catch up with his correspondence. And then, as evening
fell, he would sit with Lizzie, reading poetry to her and trying to
draw her out, or else he went out to dine with friends, or to the theater. People came to visit: potential patrons and buyers, members of
the Brotherhood, and the plump and beautiful models who sat for
Rossetti's paintings and giggled at his whispered observations and
compliments.

Rossetti tried to be patient. He watched Lizzie carefully, willing
her to come to her senses. He gave her a little laudanum when her
hands shook, and he pretended not to notice when she helped herself to more from the green bottle that rested always by her side.
With a heavy heart, he packed the collection of tiny clothes that

had accumulated over the past months into a chest under the bed, and pushed the cradle, delivered with such enthusiasm by Emma and Ford, to a corner of the studio. He covered it with a drop cloth, and tried to forget it.

Even if Lizzie could not feel its steady pulse, time did go on, and its progress was marked in strokes both large and small. Rossetti's reputation as both a poet and a painter was growing, and his painting of Fanny Cornforth, *Bocca Baciata,* had been particularly well received. The picture's frank sensuality and Fanny's beauty made it an object of desire to all who saw it. Gentlemen whose decency prevented them from inviting women like Fanny into their drawing rooms had no compunction about commissioning Rossetti to create images of her to hang above the mantelpiece. As Lizzie had once predicted, Rossetti couldn't paint fast enough to satisfy his admirers, and he felt at last that he was making a real start of things.

Each day the mail was full of invitations. He always extended these invitations to Lizzie, telling her how Emma Brown longed for her company, and how he missed having her on his arm. If she wouldn't come out, he said, then she should at least take up her work again. It was unfair, a crime against Art, to let her genius go to waste. But Lizzie was deaf to his entreaties. She claimed exhaustion or an upset stomach, or simply turned her head away from him and stared out of the window.

For the first time since his marriage, Rossetti chafed at his domestic duties. He hesitated to bring models home, and upset Lizzie, lest he lose time to nursing her when he should have been painting. When he was able to work in the studio, he could feel Lizzie's eyes following him, as focused and intent as a sailor watching for the first signs of shore. He sensed that he was her anchor, and he felt unbearably heavy: the anchor's chain running through his core, its weight rooting him to the studio, and to her.

He tried to draw her, to find inspiration in her as he once had. He painted a portrait of them as young lovers walking in a wood. But it was a gloomy scene, with the lovers meeting their own eerie doubles at twilight, a terrible portent of death. He drew her as Ophelia, spurned by a cruel and dismissive Hamlet. Each scene he imagined was darker than the last, but he found himself compelled to draw them, and later to hide them from her.

Frightened by the awful omens that he was creating with his own hands, he painted her as Regina Cordium, the Queen of Hearts. The painting showed her in a three-quarter profile, her thick hair falling simply over her bare shoulders, a bloodred strand of beads circling her neck and a pansy clasped in her fingers. The portrait was striking, but the girl in it was pale and listless. She was beautiful in an ethereal way, but hardly a symbol of desire, like Rossetti's lusty and inviting portraits of Annie Miller and Fanny Cornforth. Lizzie simply lacked the appetite for life that was so great in his other models that it seemed to burn through his canvases, threatening to devour those who looked too long.

Perhaps if Lizzie had regained a little of her health, she might have found some comfort in taking up her art again, and she and Rossetti would have worked side by side, in the artistic partnership that each had once imagined. Or perhaps, if the child had lived, the demands and pleasures of attending to that little, shared life might have inspired in Rossetti some of the domestic habits for which he had not yet acquired a taste. But Lizzie and the child remained ghosts of one sort or another, and Rossetti, chilled by their haunting presence, fled toward life.

"Oh, come on! Just one more dance!" Fanny cried, pulling Rossetti back toward the swirling mass of merrymakers who twirled across the dancing platform at Cremorne Gardens.

The dancers, in dinner jackets and silk gowns, glided and dipped around a pagoda that held the orchestra beneath its eaves. The walls of the pagoda glowed with thousands of emerald-cut crystals and mirrors, and cast a shimmering light over the dancers. Fanny's eyes glittered, and Rossetti followed her willingly onto the carousel of dancers.

"Just one more dance, and then I really must be off," he murmured, taking her hand and pulling her close. Fanny smiled and shrugged, happy to have him there for the moment at least. They glided and turned across the platform, and when the orchestra started up a new tune with a quicker tempo, Rossetti stayed for a second dance. Everyone was drinking champagne, and the dance floor was a barely controlled chaos, with dancers changing partners and then finding each other again, laughing and smiling beneath the lights.

Rossetti and Fanny paused for a drink, and then returned to the fray. He knew that he was being reckless, that he ought to go home and see Lizzie before the evening was through, as he always did. But he couldn't bring himself to abandon the boisterous crowd for the lonely studio.

Fanny seemed to read his mind. "Don't worry. It's just a bit of fun."

When the closing bell rang at five till midnight, Rossetti was still among the crush of people—young and old, of all stations of life and all shades of virtue—who let out a collective sigh at the ending of an amusing evening. Cremorne, with its colorful lights and lively cafés, offered up a feast to anyone hungry for beauty and life, and Rossetti didn't care if the colors, or the women, were sometimes too bold, or the fireworks too loud. He was drawn to its festivities as a cold man is drawn to a warm fire.

The bell rang once more and Rossetti led Fanny from the dance floor. Just as they reached the gate, he spotted a familiar profile in the crowd. It was John Ruskin, and Rossetti pushed forward to catch up with him.

"Hello!" Ruskin cried when he spotted Rossetti. "I thought that you might be here."

"An easy guess. Is there any place more inviting on a warm evening?"

"No, I suppose not." Ruskin glanced at Fanny and shook his head ever so slightly at Rossetti. Rossetti knew that Ruskin had never really approved of his dalliance with Fanny Cornforth. But Ruskin couldn't deny that Rossetti was painting great pictures of her, and he knew that Ruskin was willing to ignore his whims in women as long as the paintings were good.

"Anyway, I'm glad that I've run into you," Ruskin said. "I have excellent news. My publishers, Smith and Elder, have agreed to undertake a printing of your translations of Dante's early poems. They've consented to a run of six hundred copies, which is quite good, I think, for a work of its sort."

Rossetti grinned and clapped Ruskin on the back. "Excellent news, indeed! I'd begun to despair of ever having them published. And I suppose that I have your backing to thank for this? How can I ever thank you for all of your help?"

"You can thank me by agreeing to come to dinner at the Sablonière tomorrow evening. We'll celebrate in style."

"By all means."

"Then I'll see you there at eight o'clock." Ruskin paused and then added, for Fanny's benefit: "It will be an *intimate* dinner. Just a few old friends."

Rossetti was too pleased with the news to be annoyed by Ruskin's disapproval. When Ruskin sauntered off to find his friends, Rossetti turned to Fanny. "Why don't we start the celebration tonight? If I remember right, there's a little restaurant where drinks can be had in the small hours just around the corner. Will you join me?"

"I thought that you had to be getting home!"

"Don't tease," Rossetti laughed. "This is no night for going home. This is a night for taking a beautiful woman out to drink champagne. And I can think of no more beautiful woman than you."

Fanny let Rossetti slip his arm around her waist, and with no thought of tomorrow, they went forth into the promise of the London night.

The sun had already been up for an hour by the time Rossetti stumbled home the next morning. He climbed the stairs slowly, his head pounding from drink. He had hoped to slip into the studio quietly and wash up before Lizzie woke, but she was already up and sitting in a chair, staring at the door as he entered. He couldn't tell whether she had been there all night or not.

"Lizzie," he said tiredly. "Are you well?"

"As well as can be expected after I spent the night worrying. Where were you? Why didn't you send a note?"

"I'm sorry." Rossetti sighed. "I was working late at Hunt's studio.

By the time I realized the hour, it was too late to send word, and I didn't want to wake you, so I just slept there."

Lizzie stared at him, taking in his rumpled clothes and his swollen eyes. He didn't look like a man who had spent the evening working.

"You were painting? Whom were you painting? Which girl?"

Now Rossetti frowned. "Really, Lizzie, can't this wait? I'm tired and I want to lie down in my own bed for a few hours."

But Lizzie pressed on. "Isn't it enough that you're gone all day? Must you spend your nights away from me as well?"

"Damn it, Lizzie!" Rossetti slapped his hand on the table in frustration. "You're not happy if I bring my models here to paint, and you're not happy if I paint elsewhere, at a lot of inconvenience to myself. It's impossible! Tell me, what can I do to make you happy? Should I become a cutler, like your father, and keep a shop downstairs? Is that what you want? I must pay the bills somehow, and God knows that you're too ill to work, or even to sit for me for very long."

Lizzie stepped back from him. "I'm sorry if my illness has inconvenienced you."

"No, no, Lizzie, forgive me." He put a hand on her shoulder, and when she didn't respond, he turned her firmly around and pulled her into his arms. "I'm tired. I don't know what I'm saying."

Lizzie stood rigidly in his arms, letting him hold her, but not returning his embrace. He hated the coldness between them, and longed for the days when they would lounge for hours in the studio, limbs entwined, reading poetry to each other and talking nonsense.

"Come out with me tonight," he found himself whispering into Lizzie's hair. "To the Hotel Sablonière. Ruskin is giving a little party to celebrate the publication of my translations of Dante. You're my wife. I want you by my side."

"Your translations are going to be published?" Lizzie asked, momentarily surprised out of her anger. "Why, that's marvelous!"

Rossetti smiled, and Lizzie returned his smile. The high current of their anger was replaced, as it sometimes is, by an equal measure of giddy affection.

"Yes, at long last. It wasn't until I met you, you know, that I understood Dante's love for Beatrice, and it wasn't until I looked upon your beauty that I knew how a man could be consumed by love. I'm going to dedicate the volume to you."

Appeased, as she always was, by Rossetti's compliments, Lizzie at last relaxed into his embrace. "Then you'll come with me tonight?" he asked.

"Yes. We've been apart for too long. Even when we're here together, we've been alone. I know that I haven't been a good wife to you. I've barely been able to see beyond my own grief. But tonight I want to come with you."

Lizzie dressed, selecting an old velvet gown from the back of the wardrobe. It was one that she had cut in the medieval style, in the early days of her courtship, when Rossetti had painted her as the beloved Beatrice. She hadn't worn it in a long time, and the pile of the velvet was still thick and luxurious between her fingers. She slipped it on and found that it still fit, if a bit loosely. She brushed her hair out until it glowed, and wrapped the strand of seed pearls around her neck. She sensed that everything depended upon this evening being a success, and she wanted to remind Rossetti of the girl that he had fallen in love with.

She gave her hair a final brushing and then took a long, steadying draught of laudanum to calm her nerves and give her the strength that she needed. It had been a long time since she'd gone out with friends. She took one last sip for good measure, and they went down to the street to hail a cab. Rossetti settled Lizzie into the facing seat, and she smiled at him with bright, unfocused eyes.

"Are you well?" he asked, thinking that there was something not entirely natural in her demeanor. He wondered if it was a good idea, after all, for Lizzie to go out. She still wasn't fully recovered.

"Quite well! I can't think when I've felt better," she cried, her voice strange and her words ever so slightly slurred. The laudanum had begun to work almost immediately, and Lizzie was relieved to find that it had wrapped her up in its warm spell, padding her against the bumping of the cab and rendering everything rosy, as if the gaslights were wrapped in pink satin. The carriage wheel struck a loose stone, and the jolt made Lizzie fall sideways in the seat. Unable to right herself without his help, she laughed, and Rossetti looked at her with real concern.

"Lizzie, please, I don't think that you're well. I'm going to tell the driver to take us home. I'll send a note to Ruskin. He'll understand."

Lizzie sat up straight and frowned. "Don't you want me to come with you? You're always saying that it would do me good to go out."

"Yes, of course I want you to come. I'm only worried about your health." He was already regretting his spur-of-the-moment invitation. "You're looking awfully pale, and you know how these things are—it's bound to drag on very late. I'd hate for you to tire yourself."

Lizzie frowned, and it looked as if she were about to put up a fight, but then her face softened instead. "Dante, dear, I'm perfectly fine, and I'm very much looking forward to our evening. Let's please go on as we planned."

Rossetti leaned back into his seat, unsure of what to do. Finally he shrugged. "If you're well enough, then by all means let's go on."

The cab pulled up at the hotel, and Rossetti paid the driver and helped Lizzie down. The dinner crowd at the Sablonière was just beginning to arrive: a mix of university students in elegant evening wear, artists and writers in somewhat more eccentric dress, and ladies in a variety of pretty silks and social positions.

Ruskin and Ford were already sitting at the table when Lizzie and Rossetti entered. Ruskin rose with a broad smile when he saw Lizzie.

"My dear Mrs. Rossetti!" Lizzie noted that he used her married name, and not his pet name for her, the Princess Ida. How funny men were. In private they loved nothing more than to play at the bohemian—the lover or the poet—but in public they thought only of respectability and the following of conventions.

"I'm so happy to finally see you up and about," Ruskin said, helping Lizzie into a chair and filling her glass with champagne. "To what do we owe this wonderful surprise?"

"I grew lonely for my old friends, and for my dear Dante, who is so often away in their company." She smiled as she said this, but her voice was not entirely light.

"Well, we're very glad of your return." Ruskin stole a quick glance at Rossetti, and Rossetti knew that Ruskin suspected that he had never made it home last night.

"Hunt will join us after dinner for cognac," Ruskin said as they all sat down. "But before we dine, I propose a toast. To Dante Rossetti, whose new volume of poetry will teach the English how to love like the Italians, and to England, who shall be the better for it!"

They all laughed, and raised a glass. But before they drank, Rossetti proposed his own toast. "And to my dear Lizzie, who has inspired me as Beatrice inspired Dante, and who taught me what true love is. It is to her that I shall dedicate my translations."

Ruskin cried, "Cheers to that!" and they clinked glasses all around.

Despite Rossetti's worries, the evening started out well. If Lizzie's spirits seemed unnaturally high, they were not out of place at the Sablonière, where one had to shout to be heard above the clamor. She seemed genuinely happy to be out in company, and Rossetti wondered if their long winter might be over at last.

He was just turning to Lizzie to pour her more champagne when he saw her smile freeze and her eyes grow cold and opaque. She was staring at something just past his shoulder.

"Lizzie?" he asked, and then the question died on his lips. The scent of jasmine and the weight of a plump hand on his shoulder told him that Fanny Cornforth was standing behind him. For one moment he sat frozen, his eyes focused on Lizzie, willing Fanny with all of his heart to just go away. But it wasn't to be. He felt her lean down and rest her face next to his. Ruskin and Ford were watching them, their faces wary.

"Hello, sweets," Fanny said, laughing. Rossetti could smell the gin on her breath. Usually it was a sign of good times to come, but tonight it was a scent of warning.

"Miss Cornforth." He pushed his chair to the side and slid out from under her hand. "I didn't expect to see you here."

"Miss Cornforth!" Fanny mimicked Rossetti, laughing again and leering at Ruskin and Ford. "Well, isn't he formal tonight? Have I interrupted some important gentlemen's business, perhaps? But, then, I thought that *I* was your business, or is it perhaps that you are mine?" She laughed again at her own nonsense. "But of course! How could I have forgotten? You're celebrating! Last night's celebrations weren't sufficient, I suppose!" She glanced around, but Ruskin and Ford were both looking down at their plates.

Rossetti stared at Lizzie, unable to look away from her stricken face. In the silence that followed, Fanny finally seemed to recognize Lizzie. When their eyes met, Lizzie's eyes narrowed and her cheeks flushed a dark scarlet. Fanny tilted her head back and considered Lizzie, a small smile curling the corner of her lip. "Oh, I see. There are *ladies* present."

Rossetti instinctively reached out a hand to grab Lizzie's wrist, but he was a second too late; she had already sprung to her feet. She glanced at Fanny imperiously and then turned, seeming to dismiss her from her consideration. She focused instead on Rossetti. Her eyes were wild now, and Rossetti felt rooted to his chair.

"You've been consorting," she said, her voice loud and even, "with whores."

Behind her, Fanny made an angry sound and moved toward Lizzie, but Ford had risen from the table and held her back. He took Fanny by the arm and dragged her away from the table. Lizzie paid them no attention at all. She had eyes only for Rossetti, and those eyes were filled with rage.

"I am your wife. Your wife! Does that mean nothing to you?"

"Lizzie!" Rossetti implored in a harsh whisper. "Control yourself! Please, not here!"

"Why not here?" Lizzie stared around defiantly at the other tables near them, which had all, by now, stopped their conversations to watch. "Here is where you've brought me to dine among your whores. Excuse me, your models. I should know better, after all. I was one of them. One of many."

Rossetti grabbed Lizzie's arm. Her face had lost all of its color, and she was trembling. She wasn't in her right mind, he decided. The laudanum made her agitated. "You aren't well," he said loudly, for the benefit of their onlookers. "I'm taking you home." He tried to lead her by the arm from the table, but she wrenched herself free.

"You'd like that, wouldn't you? You'd like me to go home so you can be left in peace with your friends, and your drink, and your whores. I'm nothing but a bother to you, a nuisance to be over-come."

He began to argue, but she cut him off. "Very well. I'll take my-self home. Don't bother about me; I'm not worth bothering over." Without giving him a chance to reply, she pulled her shawl around her shoulders and darted off into the crowd, which watched her go with silent amusement before returning to its roar of conversation.

Rossetti watched her walk away, Ruskin at his side.

"She's obviously not well," Ruskin said. "You can't let her go off by herself in that state."

"Can't I?" Rossetti snapped. "She's never well, is she? What am I supposed to do about it?"

Ruskin looked at him reprovingly and Rossetti sighed. "Oh, I know that it's my fault. I never should have brought her here. She can't leave the damned laudanum alone and it makes her odd. I can never predict how she might behave." He paused, and then went on. "And, of course, I haven't treated her as well as I might. But I must make my art—you know that. And without models, without inspiration, I can't work. She knows that. Anyway, it's best that we leave her alone. She'll go home and calm herself down and we'll talk it out in the morning."

"If you think that's best." Ruskin frowned. "Or I could go look in on her."

"No." Rossetti stiffened. "That won't be necessary."

"Perhaps you're right," Ruskin said, avoiding Rossetti's eye. "Your work, of course, is of the utmost importance."

"Oh, my work be damned," Rossetti cursed. He had no wish for more of Lizzie's hysterics, but neither could he allow her to go off like this, on her own. "I'll be back in an hour," he said to Ruskin, and then rushed off through the crowds to find his wife.

Lizzie stood on the sidewalk outside of the Sablonière and waited with her back turned against the brightly lit windows. She expected that Rossetti would be after her at any moment, and she watched the door out of the corner of her eye. When the doorman asked her if he could hail her a cab, she demurred. But at last the delay grew too long to ignore, and she had to admit that he wasn't coming.

Anger had carried her from the table, but standing alone on the sidewalk she felt deflated, and she seemed to grow smaller and more frail beneath her large shawl. Whatever the truth was about his betrayals, she had expected that he would, at the very least, make an attempt to mollify her, to pretend that it was all in her head, so that she could pretend the same. A few moments ago she'd been furious enough to shout in a public restaurant, but now she was mute. What could be said when there was no one to say it to?

The doorman asked her again if he could be of some assistance, and Lizzie nodded dumbly and pointed toward the row of cabs at the corner. He whistled for one and gave the driver her address. Before she climbed in, she looked once more at the door, but there was no sign of Rossetti, or even of Ford or Ruskin. They had all stayed, preferring the company of Fanny and her sort, women who would smile with them and drink with them, and then lie in their beds and in the morning ask for nothing, because they were too accustomed to nothing to know that they should want more.

She had just turned away when she felt Rossetti's hand on her waist. In earlier days she might have protested, brushed him away, and drawn the scene out. But tonight she was simply grateful that he had followed her, and keenly aware that he might just as easily have not.

In the carriage Lizzie was calm. She lay back in her seat, looking at Rossetti through half-closed eyes. Rossetti was disconcerted by the change. "Are you feeling better?" he asked. And then, more peevishly, for the scene in the restaurant was still fresh in his mind: "If you had only listened to me, Lizzie, and gone home when you weren't well, we could have avoided all this trouble, and not made ourselves ridiculous, and an object for gossip. You know that I can't help who comes up to our table at a place like the Sablonière. You used to enjoy it for just that reason, you know."

Lizzie shifted her gaze out of the carriage window, only half listening to his words. "But you *were* with Fanny last night, weren't you? Is she your muse now?"

"I paint, Lizzie, what I am paid to paint. Or have you forgotten that we must have something to live on? Dr. Hutchinson's fees alone . . ." He trailed off. It was unfair, he knew, to blame her for being ill, or for losing the child.

But she could read the accusation in his eyes. Counterarguments and accusations welled up in her, springing from the rawness of her hurt with clear and undeniable certainty. If he had said one word, made one accusation or rebuke of his own, perhaps her hurt and anger would have poured out in all of its ugliness, leaving her weak but purged of its poison. He would have taken her in his arms and whispered all the words she needed so desperately to hear: that he loved her alone, that he needed her, that the other women were nothing to him but pretty faces. But that scene had played out many times before, and neither of them had the energy for its hackneyed revival. And so instead they rode on in silence.

By the time they reached Chatham Place, Lizzie's anger had subsided. She knew how useless words were to mend the break between them. Her entreaties died on her lips, just as the child, the one thing that might have given some meaning to their union, had died in her womb. She had nothing left to give, and nothing left to ask, and so she let herself be guided up the stairs of the studio, with blank, unseeing eyes.

Rossetti led her to the bed, and she lay down, fully dressed. He sat next to her, not quite looking at her. "You need to rest," he said mechanically. "You're not well."

"I would rest better if you lay down beside me."

Rossetti hesitated for a moment.

"You're not going back there, are you?" she asked, hysteria once more creeping into her voice.

"No, of course not." Rossetti reached for the laudanum bottle and poured a few drops onto her lips. "To help you sleep. Lie back, my dove, and if you don't want me to go, I won't. I'll stay right here by your side."

Lizzie placed one limp hand on Rossetti's arm and then, satisfied that he would stay with her, she let sleep overtake her, as the laudanum drew its strange and troubled dreams across her eyelids.

When she woke again the studio was still dark, and she felt that not very much time had passed. She reached for Rossetti, but she was alone in the bed. She called out for him, but there was no answer, and no need to call again. She could feel the emptiness of the studio. He had gone back to the restaurant, after all.

It was more than she could endure. She'd fought for so long to make this her home, and now she had the distinct feeling that she didn't belong here, that she had driven Rossetti from his studio just as the summer heat and the stink of the Thames had once driven them to the countryside.

But no, he would come; he would not abandon her here.

Her head ached and her stomach was wracked with cramps. Despite the heavy dose that she had taken, the laudanum seemed to have worn off, leaving her weak and shaking. She sat on the side of the bed and loosened her gown. She looked over to the table and saw that the little bottle was half full. It was enough, far more than enough, to get her through the night. She removed the stopper and put it aside; now was no time for carefully administered drops. She poured a generous dose into a glass and drank it down in one long sip.

The effects were immediate and unexpected. She had thought she might lie down and wait for Rossetti to return, but she suddenly felt a great welling of energy, and she was compelled to rise and move about.

She walked back and forth through the rooms of the studio, unwittingly tracing Rossetti's path on the night of the stillbirth. She stopped at the window often, looking down into the street and listening for the sound of footsteps that would signal his return. He would come back to her, she was sure. He would not abandon her for the cheap pleasures of Fanny Cornforth.

As she paced, her hands fluttered nervously, running lightly and insensibly over the familiar objects of the studio: the panels of rich cloth that Rossetti had hung along the walls, the canvases and sketches that covered every surface with their wealth of stories and history, and the blue-and-white willow dish, a wedding gift, which sat in a place of honor above the mantel.

At last she came to the easel. She hadn't paid much attention to Rossetti's work lately, but now she turned the easel around and drew in her breath.

It wasn't a portrait of Fanny, as she had feared. But the drawing filled her with an ominous fear. It was a portrait of her, unmistakably, but one for which she could not remember sitting. He must have been drawing it, she thought with a chill, while she posed for *The Queen of Hearts.*

The drawing was small, done only in pen and ink, but the detailed work showed that Rossetti had taken great pains with it. The two figures were done after her and Rossetti. The woman sat, half-fainting, in a chair, with her face turned away from the man as if he had assaulted her. The man stood over her, his face twisted with some strong emotion, sorrow or anger. But the most telling detail was his hand, which was open to the viewer in a gesture of frustration and assaulted innocence, an attitude that Lizzie well recognized. It was the very gesture that Rossetti often made during their arguments, as if to say, "I'm sorry that I've hurt you, but it was never my intention; in fact, you were the furthest thing from my mind."

Lizzie read the monogram in the corner of the drawing: "I did love you once." The words were as familiar to her as one of her own poems.

I did love you once.

Indeed, my lord, you made me believe so.

*You should not have believed me; for virtue cannot
so inoculate our old stock but we shall relish of it: I loved you not.*

"I did love you once," Lizzie repeated. "I loved you not."

He had drawn her as Ophelia, and himself as Hamlet. *I was the more deceived,* she mouthed silently. *O, woe is me, to see what I have seen, see what I see!*

She stared at the drawing, and her eyes filled with tears. Once, she thought, he wished me to be his Beatrice, and he painted me in all her glory. But now he draws me as the doomed Ophelia. She remembered the icy grip of the cold bath in Millais's studio and shivered. *Be thou as chaste as ice, as pure as snow, thou shalt not escape calumny.*

In a burst of anger she knocked the drawing from the easel. Then she turned to his table and dug through the piles of sketches, tossing them to the floor until she found what she was looking for. There were dozens and dozens of them. Gorgeous drawings of Fanny, of Annie Miller, and of other girls that Lizzie didn't recognize. Many of them looked new.

What a fool, what a stupid fool she had been. She gathered up a great heap of the sketches and carried them to the window. She stepped out onto the small balcony that overlooked the river, and, with a heave, she sent the whole lot of them, months and months of work, over the ledge. They were caught by the wind, and a rising current sent them up, high over the water, before letting them float gently down toward the dark and swirling body of the Thames. Hundreds of Rossetti's stunners, her own image mixed with those of the others, landed on the surface of the water, where they shone for a second in the moonlight, like a flock of swans, before sinking.

As Lizzie watched them disappear she felt the cold water on her skin. First the icy shock, and then a creeping, unnatural warmth. It felt too real; everything looked too real, as if the whole of the London night were drawn in precise and awful detail. She longed for the soft fold of oblivion, the warm nothingness of sleep.

She stumbled back into the studio. The bottle of laudanum waited for her, calling to her. She put it to her lips and drank, the medicine sliding hot and welcome down her throat. Already she could feel its relief, the promise of a deep sleep.

And if, she wondered, she did not wake tomorrow? What would it matter? Why should she wake to the bitter recriminations and lies that such a morning promised? Or worse, she thought, the absence of those lies, the silence that would mean that those lies were not worth the telling. Better a true silence, one that didn't ring with such sad echoes.

The bottle drained, she sat on the bed, and the room around her faded in and out of focus, the shadows dark and foreboding one moment, welcoming the next. She felt the beating of her heart slow and she smiled, stretching her hands out upon the bed.

She longed to lie upon it, as if it were soft spring grass under a spreading shade tree. But something tugged at her memory, something small and indistinct, yet terribly insistent. "Hush," she said, flinging an arm over her eyes. But the thought grew louder, and then became a wailing and could not be ignored.

She sat up straight in bed. It was a baby crying. My baby, she thought; she's crying and there's no one to comfort her! She rose unsteadily from the bed and stumbled into the studio.

The cradle that Rossetti had stowed in the corner was visible beneath its drop cloth. Lizzie threw the cloth aside and dragged it into the pool of moonlight that shone in through the open doors of the balcony. The baby's cries were growing louder, and she wished to quiet it, but she was so very tired. She sat down at Rossetti's desk and pulled a sheet of paper from the drawer. She began to scrawl a note to Rossetti. Her hand was unsteady and she thought it odd how hard it was to write, when the thing she had to say was so simple. Finally she managed a short note:

> *Dearest Dante, Please take care of the child. She will go on crying, and I'm so very tired, too tired by far to look after such a little thing. It's late, too late for me, I'm afraid, but I know that you shall look after her the best that you can. If only you would come back to me. Your loving, Lizzie.*

Then, afraid that he might not see the note, and thinking it of the utmost importance, she pinned it to her dress. Feeling that she'd done her best, she lay down on the floor next to the cradle. She rocked it with one hand, softly singing an old lullaby. She couldn't remember why she'd been so upset. Here, with the child by her side, she was peaceful and content. The motion was soothing, and the crying, which had begun to sound more like sobbing than the sharp wails of an infant, eventually ceased.

To her surprise, she found that after a time she was floating on a gently rocking sea, and she relaxed into the pull of the currents, content to let the tides take her where they may. The water calmed her, and cleaned her, and sweetly welcomed her into its fold.

> *She floated on the water, and the forest formed a canopy of silvery willow and wild roses above her. She was in a brook, so narrow that she could have reached out and touched the reeds and nettles along the banks.*

She'd been here before. She could remember the snap of a branch, and the struggle for footing as the water rushed over slippery stones. But now she didn't struggle. The tide pulled her toward some unknown goal, and she let her hands drift down to drag beneath the surface like watery weeds.

She sang a song that was little more than a whisper, and she was so pale and still that it was impossible to say at what moment the song ended on her parted lips and the light died in her half-closed eyes. Her fine gown, which had borne her along like a mermaid, became heavy with its drink, and pulled her down, gently and silently, to the muddy banks below. Drowned, drowned.

CHAPTER 24

It was nearly morning when Rossetti made his way home, but the dawning light did nothing to illuminate the foyer at Chatham Place. He felt his way up the stairs, the night's champagne still warming his veins and fueling a spirit of love and forgiveness. He'd left the studio filled with resentment, but a night of dancing and laughing in Fanny Cornforth's generous embrace had exorcised his demons, and now he was eager to slide into bed beside his wife, to be lulled to sleep by her gentle breathing.

He opened the door, trying not to wake her, and slipped across the studio in the dark. His foot caught on something heavy and out of place, and he tripped. He dropped to his knees and felt around in the dark. First he felt the carved wood of the cradle, which he thought he had packed away in a corner. Then he felt something softer: Lizzie's sleeping form.

"Lizzie?" He gently shook her shoulder, but she didn't reply. Her body was oddly pliant to his touch. He felt the first prickling traces of fear, and his mouth was suddenly too dry to call her name again.

He stood and backed away, knocking over his easel, which clattered loudly to the floor. He felt for an oil lamp, and then burned himself trying to light it with shaking hands. Cursing, he finally got it lit, and in its blaze he saw Lizzie's limp body curled around the empty cradle.

She has had some accident, he thought; she tripped in the dark, as I did. He hurried back to her side and lifted her up in one quick movement. Her skin was cool and damp, and her eyes were half-closed, with a slight glimmer just visible beneath her heavy lids. He couldn't tell if she was breathing or not.

"Lizzie!" he cried, shouting. He shook her, hard, but there was no reply. He carried her to the bed, and it was then that he saw the note, pinned to her dress.

He stared at it. He wanted to run, but he couldn't. He thought, or hoped, that if he remained completely still, he could prevent the terrible scene from playing out.

But he had to know. He reached out and tore the note from her dress. As he did so, he saw her eyelids flutter, ever so slightly.

Was it his imagination? He put his ear to her chest. At first he heard nothing but the frantic beating of his own heart, his pulse throbbing with fear. He took several deep breaths and listened again. He thought that he could hear her heart beating. It was faint, but it was there. She was still alive. He was saved.

He shook her again, willing her to consciousness. He screamed her name, but she was insensible to his cries. He was reaching for a glass of water when he saw the empty laudanum bottle lying on the table. He was sure that it was half full when he left. It was then that he noticed the strong scent of laudanum on the air. Lizzie had taken it all.

He ran out onto the landing and called loudly for help. His cries woke the landlady, and she came running up the stairs in her night-dress.

"It's my wife," he said, his fear nearly choking him. "She's dying! Please, I need a doctor immediately."

The landlady took one look at Rossetti and rushed back down-stairs to send a boy out for the nearest doctor. Rossetti went back to the bedroom and lay down next to Lizzie. He held her tightly, as if he could prevent her soul from slipping away with the strength of his arms.

"I'm sorry," he whispered over and over, burying his face in her hair. He could form no other words, and Lizzie's silence was its own reproach. His mind shied away from the enormity of his trespass. How could he have left her?

He played the night over and over in his head, feeling that if he could just understand what had happened, he could somehow change it. It was impossible that she could die. She must live. What if he could no longer paint without her?

The doctor arrived and examined Lizzie, taking her pulse and listening to her heart. Rossetti hovered at his shoulder, watching for any sign of recovery. At length the doctor looked at Rossetti and shook his head. The room stank with the smell of laudanum, and he had seen enough cases to know that the patient did not have many hours to live.

He put his hand on Rossetti's shoulder and tried to prepare him for the worst. "It appears to be a very large dose, and there's little I can do other than trying to flush the system. She's in God's hands now."

"Please," Rossetti begged. "You must save her."

The doctor sent the landlady for buckets of water and propped up Lizzie's still form on a pile of pillows. As he loosened her dress, he saw the pin with a scrap of paper still stuck to it. He looked at Rossetti. "Was the lady distraught?"

The guilt sickened him more than the smell of the laudanum. She had been distraught, and there was only one person to blame. "She, she," he stuttered, unable to form the words. He sighed. "She was very ill. She just lost a child."

The doctor's expression softened. "Then she was normally in the habit of taking laudanum?" Suicide was a very serious accusation, and doctors always hesitated to suggest it in the case of a lady, if there were any other possible explanation.

"Yes. She often took it. She could neither sleep, nor take food, without it."

The doctor nodded. "Her regular doctor should be called. In the meantime, I'll try to pump her stomach. I'll just step out of the room while I prepare my instruments."

He gave Rossetti a meaningful look and went out into the studio.

Rossetti unfastened the pin from Lizzie's dress and slipped it into his pocket. He realized with a start that he hadn't yet read the note. He pulled it from his pocket and read it through twice. The hand was shaky and the words made little sense, but he didn't need Lizzie's accusation against him to be spelled out clearly. He knew it too well in his own heart.

The doctor returned with the landlady, and together they attended to Lizzie. Rossetti could hardly watch as the doctor pumped Lizzie's stomach, passing a tube into her throat and administering quarts of water to try to cleanse the laudanum from her body. Lizzie choked and shuddered, but showed no other signs of life. The pumping went on for over an hour, as the landlady held Lizzie and leaned her over each time she vomited.

The violence of the remedy unnerved Rossetti, and he begged them to stop. The doctor took pity on him. "You would make yourself most useful," he said, "by going out to fetch Mrs. Rossetti's regular doctor."

Rossetti was terrified to leave, but neither could he stay. He raced down the stairs and out onto the street, which blinded him with its light and bustle. He went first to Dr. Hutchinson's house, where he left word with Mrs. Hutchinson that the doctor should come with utmost speed. Then, almost without thinking, he made his way across town to Ford Madox Brown's house.

He banged loudly upon the door, crying out, "Ford! Ford! For God's sake, open up!" He leaned heavily against the door, and almost fell into Emma's arms as she opened it.

"Dante!" she cried, helping him into a chair. "What's wrong?"

He opened his mouth, but he could not confess to Emma. His shame silenced him. It crowded out all other thoughts, and weighed on his chest, making it difficult to breathe. He couldn't tolerate the blame that he knew he would find in her eyes. "Get Ford," he said, and Emma, frightened, ran to find her husband.

Ford came and Rossetti told Emma to leave them. He stared at Ford for a moment and then reached into his pocket and handed him the note. "I think I've killed her."

Ford read the note and looked up at Rossetti with a white face. "What's happened? What have you done?"

"I've killed her," Rossetti repeated, relishing the sting of his own words. "Last night, I never should have left her. She wasn't well. She took too much." Then, seeing Ford's horror, he added, "The doctor is with her now, but I'm afraid she's past all help. I'll have her death upon my conscience, and I don't know what will become of me."

Ford shook his head, and Rossetti remembered how surprised Ford was when he returned to the restaurant last night. Rossetti hoped that Ford could put his disgust aside. He needed his help.

"Steady, man," Ford said, standing up and pulling Rossetti to his feet. "The doctor is with her? Then there's still hope." He paused and glanced down at the note. "Did he—did he see this note?"

"No. But he suspects. Oh, God, if she dies, I won't even be able to bury her properly. Her spirit will never let me rest. And I deserve it. I deserve it."

Ford turned to the fire and threw the note into the flames.

"What have you done?" Rossetti asked, aghast.

"Don't be a fool," Ford said in a harsh whisper. "That note was obviously written by a very ill woman. It's a private matter, and if, God forbid, anything happens, it's imperative that it not be put up for public scrutiny." He paused as Rossetti cringed at his words, and then said, more gently, "You must do what is best for Lizzie now, and for yourself. Mention it to no one, and nor shall I. Now come, we mustn't waste any more time. Emma! I'm afraid Lizzie is very ill. I'll go back to Chatham Place with Dante. Stay with the children, and I'll send word when I can."

Ford led the dazed Rossetti to the door, and Emma helped Ford into his coat. Her eyes were red-rimmed; she'd been listening. She stared at Rossetti with a strange mixture of sympathy and loathing.

"I'm sorry," Rossetti whispered lamely. "I'm so sorry."

Dr. Hutchinson was already at Chatham Place when Rossetti and Ford arrived. Rossetti expected to find him still pumping Lizzie's stomach, but he was just sitting by the bed, his hands in his lap. The landlady had cleaned Lizzie up the best that she could, and a blanket was tucked over her still form.

"How is she?" Rossetti asked. "Is she awake? Has the laudanum been flushed out?"

"I'm so sorry," Dr. Hutchinson said. "She's gone."

"No! No, she's only sleeping!" Rossetti ran to the bed and tried to pull Lizzie up to sitting. He cradled her head in his arms and stared at her, as if the intensity of his longing could bring her back. "Please, doctor, check again, I'm sure she's still alive!" Dr. Hutchinson looked at him with pity, but didn't move.

"No, no. It can't be, not like this. There must be some mistake." He repeated these words over and over, holding Lizzie to him and rocking her body in his arms. "She looks no different than when I left!"

Finally Dr. Hutchinson came forward and pulled him away. "I'll check again." The doctor glanced over at Ford, who came forward and took Rossetti's arm and led him away from the bed. The two friends stood staring at each other, waiting for the doctor's pronouncement. When Dr. Hutchinson at last said, "No, there is no heartbeat," Rossetti collapsed into Ford's arms.

"She was an angel on earth," he muttered, nearly insensible. "And now I am cursed. I have killed her, and I am cursed."

The days leading up to Lizzie's funeral were marked by a thousand heartbreaks. They endured the bureaucratic horror of the inquest, and the jury, either out of conviction or delicacy, ruled the death accidental and saved the families from scandal. Lizzie could be buried in consecrated ground. But despite the official pronouncement, doubt and rumors swirled among the friends who came to pay their respects at Chatham Place, where Lizzie was laid out. They murmured their sympathies to Rossetti, who nonetheless could sense their curiosity and condemnation, real and imagined.

Ford never left his side. It was clear that Rossetti was not in his right mind, and Ford must have feared that if he were to leave his friend for even a moment, another tragedy might occur.

Rossetti became childlike in his grief. He was convinced, more than once, that Lizzie was merely sleeping. Momentarily animated by hope, he would send for the doctor, only to suffer a crushing blow when Lizzie was once again pronounced dead. Lizzie did indeed look beautiful, but it was the beauty of a corpse: pale and peaceful. More peaceful, the mourners whispered, than she had ever looked in life.

Just before they closed the coffin, Rossetti took a small leather-bound journal from his pocket and nestled it into the red hair that had first caught his eye, and which still shone bright, even in death.

"Her Bible?" Ford asked.

"My poems. I have no need of them now. I'll never write poetry again."

"There is no other copy?" Ford asked. "Surely, in time . . ."

"No. I was often working at those poems when Lizzie was ill and suffering, and I might have been attending to her. Now they shall go."

Ford begged him to reconsider, but Rossetti was adamant. "She was my wife," he said. "And now she's gone. I am no use without her."

Ruskin overheard them arguing and put an end to it. "Well, the feeling does him honor, at least. Let him do as he likes; it's the least that he can do."

They buried her at Highgate, on a cold day that took pity on the mourners by shielding them from the sun with a dense gray fog. The Rossetti family plot was in a quiet corner of the cemetery, and the small band of friends and family shuffled down a damp path to gather at the foot of a modest grave. They laid Lizzie in the shade of an ash tree, under the benevolent eyes of a dozen stone angels, who perched atop the surrounding tombstones, handmaidens to the dead.

The vicar led them in the Lord's Prayer, and the mourners bowed their heads and said amen, and at last the coffin was lowered, slowly and finally, into the ground.

Rossetti, who had been kept on his feet mainly by Ford's and Ruskin's steadying arms, dropped to his knees as the coffin was lowered. Behind him, he heard Mrs. Siddal begin to sob, and then the rustle of skirts as she was led away by Lydia and Emma Brown. No one from Lizzie's family had spoken more than a few perfunctory words to him since her death. The service ended, and the last mourners threw dirt into the grave, muttering, "dust to dust."

Rossetti peered into the grave, overcome by the suffocating feeling that Lizzie was being buried alive. He turned to Ford and implored him, one last time: "Are you sure? Are you quite sure that she's dead?" But he didn't seem to expect an answer, and Ford just shook his head, saying, "Dante, she's at peace now."

Ford stood by his side for another moment, and then, seeing that his friend needed a few moments alone, said, "I'll wait for you by the carriages."

"And I?" Rossetti asked, once he was alone. "What peace am I to have?"

But the graves were as silent as the dead whom they marked, and not even a breeze to rustle the ivy broke the quiet. The sky grew dark, and Rossetti felt the shadows gather around his heart. He couldn't bring himself to throw dirt into the grave, and so he picked a poppy from the base of a nearby tomb and threw that instead.

"Goodbye, my dove, my life, my love." He turned and walked back to the road, each step leading him away from a grave that he carried with him just as surely as if she had been buried in the dark reaches of his own broken heart.

$\mathscr{E}$PILOGUE

The house at Cheyne Walk was particularly gloomy at dusk, and Rossetti had neglected to light any lamps in his studio. It made little difference, he told himself, for his eyesight was failing, and he could paint in only the brightest daylight. He preferred the dimness, in any case, and the shadowy visitors that haunted the corners and whispered behind the drapes. She seemed closer that way, as if he could almost reach out and touch her.

There was a knock at the door, and Fanny entered, carrying a tray. She placed it on his desk: a bottle of gin and two glasses. "Charles Howell is here."

"Send him in. And then go make yourself useful elsewhere."

Howell entered and sat down across the desk. He helped himself to a glass of gin and looked at Rossetti, who shook his head no. He'd taken a large dose of chloral to steady his nerves, and had no taste for drink.

Howell leaned back in his chair and studied Rossetti through narrow, wolflike eyes. Rossetti felt himself shrink under Howell's gaze. He shuddered, and then asked, warily, "Well, did you get it?"

Howell straightened up and cleared his throat. He smiled blandly, getting down to business. "Yes. The Home Secretary has granted all the required permissions. He agreed that it was unnecessary to secure your mother's signature, as owner of the plot, due to the very *delicate* nature of the proceedings, and the need for secrecy."

Rossetti nodded. Then they would go ahead with it, after all. "You've found men to help you?"

"You may leave everything to me. Your presence, of course, will be absolutely unnecessary. I've consulted a doctor, who assures me that, in all likelihood, the body will be perfectly preserved."

Rossetti shuddered again. "I must insist on absolute secrecy. If people were to discover what I've done, I'd be ruined."

"It will all be very discreet," Howell assured him. "We'll go tonight, after dark, so as not to attract attention."

"Tonight?" Rossetti changed his mind and poured himself a glass of gin. "Well, why not, I suppose. There's no point in putting it off. Lizzie herself would have been the first to approve, I think." He nodded his head, as if he was convinced.

He could see no other way. With his eyesight failing, he was desperate for the return of the poems that he had thrown into Lizzie's grave. He needed them to round out a very thin volume that he was preparing for publication. "Art, after all, was the only thing that she ever felt for very seriously," he went on dreamily. "I really think that if her ghost could have returned those poems to me, I would have found them on my pillow the night that she was buried."

"I've no doubt," Howell murmured, looking away. Then he stood. Before he left, he cleared his throat once more. "There is one last matter. As your agent, I am, of course, at your service for any small favor such as this. But the men must be paid, and there's a fee for the consultation with the doctor."

"Yes, of course." Rossetti snapped out of his reverie. "Pay them as you see fit. You may apply to my banker. As for yourself, if you are successful, I shall do a portrait of your wife, if you like, or any other drawing that suits your fancy."

Once again the gleam returned to Howell's eyes. He glanced at a half-finished painting in the far corner of the studio. "And that one? Is she spoken for?"

Rossetti followed his eyes and turned slightly paler.

"*Beata Beatrix*, Beautiful Beatrice," he whispered. "Lizzie." And then, louder, "No. Not that one. Any other painting, but not that one." He added, sheepishly, "I can't seem to finish it anyway. I'm afraid it's a failure."

"I see." Howell had never met Lizzie, and did not recognize her in the half-finished painting. "Well then, I'll report back to you when we're finished."

In the blaze of a great fire, four men drove their shovels into the earth, each flinty strike bringing them closer to their morbid goal. Above them, the stone angels watched in silent protest. The men, no strangers to the lowest sort of work, were quiet tonight, with none of their usual banter to break the eerie silence. When they finally struck the coffin and hauled it up onto the grass, they crossed themselves and stared at the ground, unable to meet each other's eyes.

Charles Howell, who had been sitting on a nearby gravestone, came forward with a crowbar and began to pry the coffin open. With a great grunt, he brought his foot down on the crowbar and the coffin popped open. For a moment, everything was still. Then, with a sighing sound, a cloud of dust rose from the coffin.

The men stumbled back, and even Howell felt a chill of fear. He mastered himself quickly, however, and gestured for a torch to be lit from the fire. He peered into the coffin, and then turned to the men with a smile that looked ghoulish in the flickering light. "Nothing but dust and bones. The worms had their way with her long ago."

He laughed, and the men laughed along nervously. He put on a pair of leather gloves and began to pick among the bones. Something sharp pierced his glove and he cursed and drew back. Then he saw what had stuck him, and smiled. It was a silver pin in the shape of a dragonfly, and if he wasn't mistaken, it appeared to have a very nice sapphire set as its eye. He rubbed the dust from the pin and slipped it into his pocket.

He found the book of poems and lifted it from the coffin. He held it up in the light from the fire, and began to page through it carefully. "Damn! A worm has eaten a hole right through the center. Never mind. Surely there's enough still here to jog Rossetti's memory, if the old lunatic still has half a mind left, after all the chloral he's rotted it with."

The men shuffled their feet and looked at Howell. "That's what you had us dig it up for?" one asked. "A book?"

Howell sighed. "Yes. A book." There was no point in explaining to this lot that, if Rossetti were to publish a successful volume, Howell himself would make a pretty penny off of his commission as agent. Rossetti had become less reliable in his production, and Howell was eager to get his best work from him while he still could.

"What are you waiting for?" he asked the men. "Throw her back in, and quickly. This place gives me shivers."

Rossetti was sitting in the same place that Howell had left him. The only change was in his eyes, which had grown more sunken in the intervening hours. They glowed from beneath his furrowed brow like animal eyes, with the unnatural light of madness. The chloral and the gin had him in their grip, and his words were halting and slurred.

"Is that it?"

Howell placed the book on the desk.

"And the body? Was it . . . ?" Rossetti was unable to form the words.

"Perfectly preserved, as we expected." Howell's voice was smooth. "She was as beautiful as a saint in her tomb. And her hair." He paused and looked off into the distance, as if he were remembering some wondrous sight. "Her hair had grown to fill the coffin in a crown of glorious red curls."

Rossetti sighed. "Thank God for that." He lit a candle and picked up the book. The pages were brittle in his hands. He squinted, trying to read his own writing. His face, already white, took on a grayish hue. "But the pages," he murmured. "They look as if, as if some creature had feasted upon them." The image that he had held in his mind all night of Lizzie, as perfect as she ever was in life, began to decay.

Howell frowned. "An effect, I'm afraid, of their age. The doctor warned me that paper might not fare so well in the grave. But I've inspected them, and you'll see that much is still preserved."

Rossetti couldn't reply. The weight of his crime, one of many, pressed against his chest and nearly choked the air from him. "Go," he muttered, and then, when Howell hesitated, he shouted louder: "Leave me!"

The dreams of chloral are fever dreams, and Rossetti tossed and turned in his bed, unable to wake from his nightmare. The sheets were as hot as the flames that rose high above an empty grave; they leapt and danced until the whole city was consumed by an inferno, with Rossetti himself at the center, burning and writhing in pain.

And then, in a flash, there was nothing. Nothing but blackness, and somehow this was more terrifying than the fire, for he saw nothing and felt nothing, and knew that he was nothing. He opened his mouth to scream, but there was no sound.

He was sinking into oblivion, the inky blackness of sleep, when a shining figure appeared: an exquisite angel, lighting the heavens like a second sun. The visitor hovered at the foot of his bed, held aloft by magnificent red wings. Her skin was white as porcelain and her thick auburn hair fell over her golden robes. Rossetti felt his heart beat hard in his chest. "Lizzie?"

But the figure shook her head. "I am Love," she whispered.

The angel took his hand and led him from the bed. His burning skin cooled at her touch, and he felt that he was being led forth from hell. She guided him to his studio and stopped in front of the easel. Without a word, she handed him a brush. The studio was dark, but the angel radiated her own light, and she stood silently behind Rossetti, one hand on his shoulder, illuminating the canvas.

Rossetti hesitated. The easel held the half-finished painting of Lizzie. He could no longer paint her from memory—it had been too long. He stared vainly at the brush in his hand.

He heard a whisper, breathed from the corners of the room: "Paint her. She is I. We are one." He saw Lizzie, as he had many times in his dreams, unconscious and awaiting death. Over the years, she had grown more beautiful in his memory; ever more perfect. The angel beside him nodded. He would create a final memorial to her: He would paint her one last time as Beatrice, at the very moment she was rapt from earth to heaven.

He painted all through the night, and the angel never left his side. When his hands began to shake, he drank the trance-inducing chloral. When his eyes burned, he lit candle after candle, filling the studio as if for a séance.

The picture was unlike anything he had ever painted. It was soft; the light a golden mist and the lines almost hazy. Beatrice sits with her eyes closed and her face lifted. Her lips are slightly parted, as if she were looking to heaven, awaiting a holy communion. Her hands rest open in her lap, waiting to accept a white poppy, dropped by a red dove. Behind her is the city of Florence. But it was not the Ponte Vecchio that Rossetti imagined as he painted the bridge, but Blackfriars, where he had first seen his dear, lost love.

As dawn approached, he applied a last coat to the red hair that glowed like a halo, and he pushed back from the easel, throwing his brush aside. He no longer knew if he had painted Beatrice, or Lizzie, or the shining angel who rested by his side. But it didn't matter; they were one.

He turned, and the angel was gone. He was alone. He gazed at the painting. "It's my masterpiece," he whispered. And then, to the empty studio: "It's a dream. A beautiful dream, of something that once was, and never will be again."

One face looks out from all his canvases,
One selfsame figure sits or walks or leans:
We found her hidden just behind those screens,
That mirror gave back all her loveliness.
A queen in opal or in ruby dress,
A nameless girl in freshest summer-greens,
A saint, an angel—every canvas means
The same one meaning, neither more nor less.
He feeds upon her face by day and night,
And she with true kind eyes looks back on him,
Fair as the moon and joyful as the light:
Not wan with waiting, not with sorrow dim;
Not as she is, but was when hope shone bright;
Not as she is, but as she fills his dream.

—Christina Georgina Rossetti
"In an Artist's Studio"

Acknowledgments

I want to thank my friend and agent, Jeff Ourvan, for his invaluable support, and my editor at Kensington, John Scognamiglio, for his help and guidance. I would also like to thank all of the coffee shops whose seats I hogged in Brooklyn and San Jose: Your caffeine and wifi made this all possible.

**Please turn the page for a very special
Q&A with Rita Cameron!**

What interested you about the Pre-Raphaelites?

I've always loved Pre-Raphaelite painting. I first saw Rossetti's and Millais's paintings at the Tate Britain when I was a child, and there was something in those paintings that made me want to invent stories about the gorgeous and mysterious women they portrayed. Later, when I was picking up my textbooks for my first year of law school, I stopped in the art section at the bookstore and paged through a book on the Pre-Raphaelites. It was there that I first encountered the thrilling and tragic tale of Dante Gabriel Rossetti and his first love, his model Lizzie Siddal. The story had everything—love across class lines, the mysteries of the creative process, betrayal, drug addiction, even grave robbing—it was the stuff of the best fiction! There were more than a few nights when I should have been outlining contracts law that I was actually sketching out ideas for a book based on that story. I ended up losing that laptop, but the idea stuck with me. Later, when I had some time off from work with my first child, I started doing research on Rossetti in earnest, and I felt like I had to tell their story, that it was a story that people would want to hear.

Lizzie Siddal is mostly known as a model for famous paintings— a pretty face. What did you find appealing about her as a main character?

The fact that Lizzie is known mostly through other people's interpretations and characterizations of her in their paintings and memoirs piqued my interest. A few of her paintings and poems have survived, but very few of her letters have been found, and most scholarly literature on her depends on the written opinion of the higher-class men who knew her as an artist's model. I approached her as a character with sympathy for her position as a working-class woman in Victorian England, and with respect for her attempts to transcend her humble beginnings and make a name for herself as an artist and poet in her own right, in a society that was hostile to such attempts. I wanted to give a voice to a woman who had the power not only to inspire great men, but also to work alongside them. I also felt that although her story is very much rooted in the Victorian era, it has undeniable echoes in the situation of many modern women who still find themselves choosing between marriage and career, and facing disapproval of the choices they make that wouldn't raise an eyebrow if a man made them.

The book focuses on the difficult relationship between Rossetti and his model Lizzie Siddal, which is not always a happy tale. Was it hard not to take sides in telling their story?

While writing the book I found that I had great sympathy for both Lizzie and Rossetti. It's difficult to say that they were bad for each other, because together they made great art. But on a practical level neither one could give the other what they needed from the relationship. In this day and age, they could have moved on from the relationship. But in the Victorian era, once Lizzie allowed herself to be publicly linked to Rossetti, she had no choice but to see the relationship through to marriage. Anything less would have been social suicide: She never would have been able to find a husband, and her poor health left her unable to support herself with menial work. Rossetti himself was not immune to these pressures. He knew he ought to marry Lizzie, even as he realized that he regarded her more as a muse than a wife, and sought what he felt to be necessary inspiration in other models. They were both stuck in a system, and in a relationship, that became increasingly detrimental and poisonous to their art, but neither could see a way out.

What is your favorite Pre-Raphaelite painting?

There are so many beautiful paintings from this movement. Obviously I'm partial to John Everett Millais's painting of Lizzie as Ophelia. That painting captures a very fleeting moment—the cusp of life and death, despair and release—almost perfectly. It's a painting that manages to capture a very private and lonely moment without seeming small. Similarly, I'm very fond of *Beata Beatrix*, Rossetti's painting of Lizzie as Beatrice, the muse of Dante. It's another moment that captures a woman on the verge of death, accepting into her outstretched hands a symbolic poppy from a heavenly dove. That Lizzie served as the inspiration for these two paintings raises a lot of interesting questions: What was it about her that led some of the era's best painters to both immortalize her, and to figuratively kill her?

What sort of research did you have to do to prepare to write the book?

Before I started writing, I spent about six months just reading about Rossetti, Lizzie, and the Pre-Raphaelite Brotherhood. I started with the paintings and the poetry, and then moved on to biographies, critical works, and volumes of letters. The critical works start with biography and then move on to the art, but I liked getting to know my characters through the choices they made in their creative output first. *Ophelia's Muse* takes history as its jumping-off point and then uses the poems and paintings of the era as inspiration for many of the personal scenes. I think the members of the Pre-Raphaelite Brotherhood lived as if there were few boundaries between art and life, and I wanted the book to reflect this.

What appeals to you about writing historical fiction?

For me, the research was just as much fun as the writing. I loved delving into another time and place and learning how people lived in the past. Reading about Victorian England, it was hard not to go off on tangents—the dawn of the rail system, the intricacies of women's dress, a feud between Whistler and Oscar Wilde—that weren't directly useful in writing the book. But I felt like as long as I was steeping myself in Victorian culture, it was okay to follow the occasional bit of research down a rabbit hole.

OPHELIA'S MUSE

Rita Cameron

About This Guide

The suggested questions are included
to enhance your group's reading of
Rita Cameron's *Ophelia's Muse*.

DISCUSSION QUESTIONS

1. Early in the book, Lizzie is described as being tall and thin, with "unlucky" red hair. Her looks are described as odd or striking, but never pretty in the conventional sense. The young artists who paint her, however, see her quite differently—as a great beauty. What do you think it was about Lizzie's looks that made her an attractive model to the Pre-Raphaelites? How did Lizzie's own perception of her beauty change, and how did this change affect her personality? What about later in the book, after her illness?

2. At the beginning of the book, Lizzie is accosted by a drunk man on Blackfriars Bridge, before Rossetti chases him away. How does this scene foreshadow other parts of the novel, such as her relationship with Rossetti, and her illness from sitting in a cold bath when she models for John Millais? How do Lizzie's character and social position make her vulnerable in these situations?

3. Many people point out the differences in Lizzie's and Rossetti's social standing—she is a working-class shopgirl, while he is an art student at the Royal Academy from a literary family. But in many ways their positions aren't so different: Both must work for their living, and both came from families where education is valued but money was tight. Do you think these similarities helped or hurt their chances for success as a couple?

4. In many respects, Rossetti lives a bohemian life. He rejects the conventions of the Royal Academy, lives and works out of a studio in a dingy part of London, and is happy to associate with both high and low society. But in other respects he can be much more conventional in his views. What problems does this cause in his relationship with Lizzie? What forces act upon him to bring out his more conservative tendencies?

5. When Rossetti first sees Lizzie, he thinks of Beatrice, the muse of the poet Dante Alighieri. Rossetti often paints Lizzie as Beatrice, and he comes to identify Lizzie very heavily with the saintly, silent Beatrice, who embodied virtue and died young. How does Rossetti's idolization of Lizzie as a muse threaten their romance? In what ways does Lizzie try to live up to Rossetti's ideals?

6. Although Rossetti seems to love Lizzie, he often puts his work as an artist first. How does Rossetti use his art to rationalize his mistreatment of Lizzie? Do you think that great artists are ever justified in using or mistreating the people around them in pursuit of the greater purpose of making art?

7. Why do you think Lizzie agrees to sit for Rossetti without a chaperone, and to engage in other behaviors that put her reputation at risk? How does she justify her behavior to herself, and to the people around her who are concerned?

8. Lizzie first becomes ill after sitting too long in a cold tub while modeling for John Millais's portrait of Ophelia, but as her illness drags on, her doctors begin to think that many of her symptoms could be caused by stress, by not eating, and by the use of laudanum. To what extent do you think Lizzie's ill health is caused by her relationship with Rossetti, and how does she use her illness to manipulate him?

9. Ford Madox Brown, Rossetti's friend and fellow artist, wrote in his diary about Lizzie and Rossetti: "She is a stunner and no mistake. Rossetti once told me that, when he first saw her, he felt his destiny was defined. Why does he not marry her?" Why do you think Rossetti puts off his marriage to Lizzie until it is almost too late?

10. John Ruskin is convinced that if Lizzie and Rossetti marry and settle down to a more regular life, they will be able to produce more and better art. Do you agree? If Lizzie and Rossetti's baby had lived, do you think it could have saved their marriage, and Lizzie's life?

Printed in the United States
by Baker & Taylor Publisher Services